MW00962522

The
Silent
Remainder

Bryan Norford

a novel by
Bryan Norford

Pebble Press, Lethbridge, Alberta

The Silent Remainder

Dedication

To those who gave generously of their time and care
to contribute to this book
I Thank God for you from my heart

Hanne and Manfred Fell, Elsie Morris,
Kaylen Beekman, Heather Alexander,
Sarah Sheppard, Jim Coggins,
and Ann Norford

Books by Ann and Bryan Norford

Happy Together: Daily Insight for Families from Scripture
War Kids: Growing Up in World War Two England

Books by Bryan Norford

Guess Who's Coming to Reign: Jesus Talks about His
    Return
Gone with the Spirit: Tracking the Holy Spirit through the
    Bible
Jesus: Is He Really God? Does It Really Matter?
Anointed Preaching: The Holy Spirit and the Pulpit
Getting to Know You 1: Seeking God in the Old Testament
Getting to Know You 2: Finding Christ in the New
    Testament
Prostate Cancer: My Story of Survival

.

1

The water was cold—too cold. The branch was thin—too thin. Evelyn hung on. Waterlogged clothes clung to her, then billowed out in the current. She touched bottom briefly. The undertow pulled her feet away. She screamed for help. No response. Her arms ached. A frenzied grip and freezing spray froze her hands to the branch. It was getting dark. She lost track of time.

Her mind briefly cleared of panic. She stopped screaming. What could she do? *Perhaps I can pull myself up by the branch?* Painfully peeling her lower hand from the branch, she grabbed it higher up. She started to pull, but sank back hearing a menacing crack. She looked around. The river bank was less than a meter away. She began to kick her way towards it, but the spring in the branch pulled her back. To let go of the branch was suicidal, the current would sweep her away. Panic set in again.

She shrieked, "Help me, help me. Anyone. Please help me. *Help*. HELP."

No response. The cold cramped her chest. Breathing was hard, stifling shouts for help. Scenes of her mother and deceased father and childhood memories flooded her mind. *Is life flashing before me. Am I dying?* That seemed a terrifying reality.

She tried yelling again, but the cold made her throat hoarse. She emitted a raspy cry.

"Oh my God, I'm going to die. I don't wanna die." Her voice was fading, "I don't wanna die. God, I don't . . . want . . . to . . . die."

The last words dissolved into heaving sobs streaming tears of misery and fear. In the blackness of the unknown, hope oozed away. *What is going to happen to me, how will this end?* A branch cracked somewhere. That galvanized her to a final shriek, "He-e-e-elp."

Panic subsided again. Calm for a moment. She looked at the murky water. *Giving up is too easy. Why fight this? Why fight life at all?* She recalled a suggestion that drowning was quite peaceful once the lungs filled and panic ceased. Prediction of calm underwater currents trumped her recurring turmoil. *Why not let go and let fate—whatever that is—have its way. So easy, just let go—.*

"Hey! This is no time of year to go swimming," shouted a voice above her.

She looked up to see a young man with tousled dark hair half-grinning from the bank.

"Oh! Thank God," she half yelled. "Get me outa here. Please help me." Desperation and tears choked her voice.

The young man unbuckled and lowered his jeans. Evelyn's jaw dropped; her eyes opened wide. *Is he planning to rape me—in the river?* Unformed unwelcome visions blurred her fractured mind. Her voice found a scream once again.

"What the hell are you doing? I'm *drowning* here. Get me outa here."

"Coming! My pants are all I have long enough to reach you. Believe me, I don't want to take them off, it's too bloody cold. Would you be happier if I put them on again?"

Evelyn yelled in terrified exasperation. "*Please,* For God's sake, get me outa here before I get swept away." Her voice whimpered and teeth chattered. "I don't care how you do it. Just get me out. Please, I beg you"

"I'll hang on to one pant leg, and you grab the other. Hang on tight and I'll pull you out."

The other pant leg landed in the water and floated away from her. She screamed. He threw the leg again farther up current and it floated toward her. She grabbed it with one hand, hanging onto the branch with the other.

"Let go the branch," he yelled, "so I can pull you in."

Evelyn wasn't sure of him or the branch, but the branch snapped. She screamed, but abruptly seized the pant leg with both hands. This time, the force of the current swung her to the bank. She touched bottom, but the bank was steep and her strength gone.

"Hang on, hang on," he ordered, and drew the pants in. He lay on the bank above her and grabbed her hands. *God. I hope he doesn't let me go?*

He grinned again. "Crap! With hands this cold, I sure hope you've got a warm heart."

Her eyes blazed. But fear trumped vexation, allowing him to drag her up the bank to safety. They both lay there, motionless, silent, only heaving chests betraying life. He covered her shivering body with his coat. She saw him struggle pulling on wet pants and closed her eyes.

A bright light appeared above her. *Is this heaven—or hell? Oh God no.* Beings in white moved around her. *Probably heaven.* Slowly her eyes adjusted and her mind cleared. The white beings became medical personnel.

"Where am I? What happened?" She remembered the cold rushing water and shivered.

"You're suffering from hypothermia, and you're in Vancouver General Hospital after a dip in the river," a white clad woman said. "But you're doing fine. We'll keep you in overnight for observation."

Thank God. I'm alive. But she jumped at the nurse's

next comment.

"Your boyfriend's waiting outside. Shall I send him in?"

"Boyfriend?" She raised her eyebrows. "I don't have a boyfriend."

"Well, he brought you in. Seems you owe him a thank you at least."

Evelyn stared, as memory of the wet events came into focus. She gave a slow nod. The young man with the tousled dark hair appeared above her again.

"How're you doing? You look almost presentable compared to what I remember."

There was that grin again. This time she noticed the dimples above dishevelled and damp clothing. Appearance was important to Evelyn, and his remark emphasized her messy hair and unmade look. Her brows creased. She responded to his familiarity with tight lips.

"Don't tell me how I look." But her eyes softened A rush of thankfulness invaded her soul and briefly pierced her irritation. "I suppose I do owe you a thank you for pulling me out of the river. *Thank you*."

She turned her head away from him, hands over her face, increasingly embarrassed at her appearance.

Quietly. "And for saving your life."

Fear of her watery escapade returned. Her face creased as tears threatened an appearance. In pride she wiped her face with her hands and turned slowly towards him. She let out a short sigh of agreement.

"Okay. And saving my life—even if you did have to strip off your pants to save me." She hoped a half smile would mask her distress and fear.

"Wow, you smile as well. Not just presentable, but attractive too. By the way, I'm Clark."

Evelyn's tenseness returned. *Sarcastic, intrusive bastard.*

4

"Don't take this as an opportunity to come on to me. This episode is over. Goodbye."

She saw disappointment cross his face, his arms opened in question. She turned away red-faced in misery and madness and pulled the blankets over her. She sensed Clark looking at her back for a moment, then noting her name over her bed.

"Okay Evelyn. But I'd like to meet you again, only in the dry."

Still with her back to him, she snatched the blankets tighter around her. The cozy bed lulled her to sleep.

She awoke to see Phyllis, her mother, seated beside the bed reading a magazine. Evelyn wondered what sort of reception she'd receive from Phyllis. Evelyn's father had been strict, and her mother an intervener on her behalf when he became overbearing. But since his death, Phyllis had assumed his role. This "talk" might not be pleasant. Evelyn eased herself up on the pillow, and Phyllis turned to her with a paternal smile—not the motherly kiss Evelyn would have liked.

"Oh! You're awake. How are you feeling dear?"

"I'm okay, Mother."

Evelyn was non-committal until she sensed which way the discussion would turn.

"I'm so glad. I understand you fell in the river. How on earth did that happen?"

This is going to be an interrogation, not a discussion. Evelyn folded her arms and struggled for a response and looked directly away from Phyllis.

"I wanted to take a picture of the sunset on the Frazer River. The river bank gave way and the current carried me downstream until—"

"What happened to the camera, dear?"

Evelyn had forgotten about the camera, panic erased it

from her mind.

Her hands flew to her mouth "Oh! I must've dropped it when I fell in the river."

"Did you look for it?"

Evelyn turned sharply to her mother. "Mom, I was drowning. It wasn't the first thing on my mind."

She felt inconvenient. She often did. Evelyn was an only child, and had considered herself a tiresome addition to the family for most of her life. As long as she conformed to her parents' wishes and achieved reasonable grades, they gave her scant attention, but having to deal with any bad behaviour or failure was an annoying interruption of their life. She assumed they loved her as she received most of what she wanted, but little time or commendation. *I don't know why I often feel so bitter towards them, when they have given me so much to be thankful for.* Evelyn turned away from her mother.

"Of course, dear. The camera's not really important; I'm glad you managed to get out."

Evelyn's jaw set. "Didn't you hear me? I nearly drowned. I probably would've if someone hadn't heard my screams and pulled me out."

"Oh, really? Who was that?"

Evelyn told the story, keeping it factual—no reference to her irritation with her rescuer, or those damn dimples that kept surfacing in her mind. Phyllis said she'd pick up Evelyn's car left at the scene.

She got up to leave. "Glad you're alright, dear. "I'll pick you up tomorrow." Phyllis made for the door.

It seemed Phyllis, like Evelyn, was glad the interview was over. But Evelyn would check on that camera. Phyllis hadn't pursued it, but it'd come up again. Evelyn thought of that irritating young man—with the dimples. Would he seek her out as he suggested? She wouldn't pursue that. The thought sparked discomfort from the dimness of her sub-conscious and she wondered why. As exhaustion from the day's experience drew her to a restoring sleep, her thoughts faded with it.

Evelyn woke with a start as the early fall sun warmed her face. Slowly the events of yesterday came into focus, as she lifted herself on the pillow. A cheery nurse entered the room.

"How're you feeling this morning?" She raised the bed to a reclining position.

Evelyn gave her a not feeling cheery look. "When do I get out of here?"

"The doctor has already signed you out, so you can go as soon as you like. Is someone coming to pick you up?"

"My mother should be here shortly. What's the time?"

"Nearly eight-thirty. You slept well. Must've made you feel much better."

A non-committal "Ah-ha" indicated it probably didn't.

"Well, breakfast will be here shortly. Enjoy," said the nurse and left.

Not much I can do until Mom comes. Evelyn swung out of bed, retrieved her clothes from the closet; they were still wet. She had no hair brush or make-up; her appearance in the bathroom mirror appalled her. *Matches the way I feel.* Sitting on the bed she nibbled at the meal that arrived. Her mind kept replaying the previous day's events, each time deepening an emptiness of heart. The images of her rescuer, Clark, *arrogant bastard,* only produced a scowl.

Barbara walked in the door. "Not a pretty face!"

"Hey Barb. What're you doing here?" The face improved immediately.

"I work here, remember. But I'm not working today—wish I had been yesterday to welcome you in. But your mother called and asked me to come pick you up. Hope that's okay?"

"Okay? More than okay. I don't really want to face my mother again this early in the morning."

"Oh?"

"Wasn't a good discussion last night. Just so glad to see you."

Evelyn was always glad to see Barbara. Friends since childhood, they were the same age, and lived on the same street in the British Properties of North Vancouver. Barbara had sympathized with Evelyn's distant relationship with her mother, but admitted she couldn't identify with it. Barbara's home was a typical suburban two parent home with one younger brother that, for the most part, she apparently enjoyed. Evelyn envied and admired Barbara's sense of security and stability; being with Barbara eased her own restlessness.

"Ev. That must've been a terrifying experience yesterday. How do you feel today?"

"Okay, I guess. It's over now and I'd rather forget the whole thing."

Barbara nodded. "But let me help you clean up, and I brought some fresh clothes."

Barbara pulled out her own make-up for Evelyn, and began brushing Evelyn's hair.

"Your mom also gave me keys to swing by and pick up your car."

Evelyn snorted. "Did she mention looking for the camera as well?"

"No." Barbara chuckled. "But it sounds like she spoke to you about it."

"She seemed more concerned about that bloody camera than about me."

"I doubt it," Barbara countered.

Evelyn grimaced, rose and dressed herself.

"I'm ready to go. Let's get outa here. This place gives me the creeps."

As they drove to the river, Evelyn answered Barbara's questions about the previous day's events, but fell increasingly silent as they neared the place of her plunge. Barbara moved to open the car door. Evelyn sat pensively, looking down and fingering the glove-box latch.

"Coming Ev?" Barbara spoke softly. "Anything the matter?"

Hesitantly, Evelyn spoke. "I nearly let go."

"Let go of what? What are you talking about?"

"Let go of the branch."

Barbara sat quiet for a moment, knitting her eyebrows trying to figure Evelyn's meaning.

"I'm not surprised," she finally said. "The current was pretty swift."

"It wasn't the current."

"It wasn't—you mean—"

Barbara searched Evelyn's face for meaning, but Evelyn continued to look down impassively.

"Oh Evelyn! You didn't *want* to let go—?" Barbara's arms encircled Evelyn. "What made you think—why . . .?"

Evelyn erupted into deep sobs, and for a full minute Barbara just held her; there were no meaningful words.

"Barb. Please don't tell anyone—especially Mom. I'm so ashamed, but I had to tell someone."

Barbara produced some tissues and started wiping Evelyn's face as well as her own.

"I'm glad you shared that with me. I'm so sorry. Tell me what I can do to help." Barbara replied. "But why, do you know why?"

Evelyn was silent for several moments, struggling to find a logical reason.

"Life seemed as murky as that damn river water. There are times when life seems so empty it's not worth staying alive." Silence. Then, "I just feel so worthless."

Barbara continued to hold her. Evelyn felt comforted.

Suddenly, Evelyn sat up. "Guess we'd better look for that damn camera," and she struggled free of Barbara's embrace.

They searched in vain for the camera, and decided it must be in the river somewhere. Evelyn stood on the river bank looking at the river that nearly claimed her. The water was still at that moment, the incoming tide matching the river's downward flow. For the moment, she felt a measure of peace and lucidity. She needed to know why life seemed a void so much of the time.

"I'm going to find out why I feel wretched so often," she said aloud, mostly to herself.

Barbara smiled at her. "Need a shrink?"

Evelyn smiled back. "Need something, God knows."

"Want me to come home with you Ev?"

"Nah. Better face Mother alone. Not sure what mood she'll be in. I know it's going to be my fault somehow."

Evelyn gave a desperate grin as she clung to Barbara in a long hug. Barbara caressed Evelyn's hair and kissed her lightly on the forehead.

"See ya soon," Barbara promised as they drove to their homes.

2

Phyllis wasn't home, still out on the errand that prevented her from making the promised pick-up. Evelyn put the coffee pot on and sat at the kitchen counter waiting for that interminable drip to finish. She casually began to read an open letter that lay in front of her. It was from Sophia, Mother's cousin in England. The name was vaguely familiar. She knew they had family in England, but recalled little about them. It appeared to be a catch-up airmail about family; apparently Sophia didn't use a computer.

Evelyn heard Phyllis' car in the driveway. Placing two mugs on the counter, Evelyn poured coffee in one. Phyllis came in the back door. Evelyn stiffened but tried to soften the atmosphere.

"Coffee Mom?"

"Oh! Yes please. Just ready for one. Thanks." Phyllis appeared in good spirits.

Evelyn poured it and Phyllis took a few sips. "Ah! Just what I needed."

Evelyn waited for her mother to open the conversation. When she did, it was not what Evelyn expected.

"Did you notice the letter from Sophia, Ev?" Evelyn nodded, her face in the coffee cup. "She wrote that her nephews are running a hotel in Brighton, England, since her brother Demetrius—their father—died. Did you read it?"

Evelyn nodded again, *What's all this leading up to?* She found out and five minutes later, stormed out of the kitchen, and called Barbara.

"Can we meet for coffee?

"What? Right now?"

"Yes, now."

"Guess so. What's the rush?

"Tell you when I see you. I'll pick you up."

Evelyn arrived and Barbara opened the car door and looked warily at the driver.

"Will I be safe?" she enquired, seeing Evelyn's dark expression.

"Get in and find out," Evelyn replied with a grim smile.

Evelyn's drive was both exhilarating and frightening. The tires screeched resistance at starts, corners and braking. The car fairly took flight at the crown of Lion's Gate Bridge. Evelyn said little, banging her palm against the steering wheel at irregular intervals. Barbara just held on. Evelyn parked outside their favourite Robson Street cafe with one wheel on the curb.

"Wow! That was quite a ride," said Barb as she gulped mouthfuls of coffee. "Suppose the police had stopped you on our glorious ride, how would you have responded to them?"

Evelyn grinned. "They wouldn't have stopped me. I'd have led them on a merry chase!"

"I almost believe you. But what's made you so mad?"

"I'm mad at Mom,"

"I gathered that. What happened?"

"Mom wants me to go to England."

"To England?" Barbara shot Evelyn a puzzled look. "Is she sending you to a psychiatric clinic there or something?"

"No of course not."

"What then?"

"Her cousin over there has two nephews who run a hotel, and she wants me to visit them."

Barbara remained puzzled. "What? A sort of vacation or something?"

"Huh. Vacation my ass. She said I need a break. It's her way of telling me I'm messed up and this might be good therapy for me."

"Did she say that?"

"No, of course she didn't. But it's implied. Not only that, I think she's trying to pass me off to one of these guys so she doesn't have responsibility for me anymore. I think she's tired of having me around. In some ways I don't blame her. I'm pretty hostile most of the time."

Barbara blew out a column of air and fell back in her chair. *Typical Evelyn*. Barbara sat up and grabbed her coffee mug, and held out her hand for Evelyn's mug.

"Another one?"

"Sure."

Placing the refills in front of them, Barbara's nurses' training kicked in.

"Ev. I'm concerned about your suicidal thoughts you mentioned down at the river. Have you had those thoughts before?"

"I've mused about it, but not a specific desire like that. But was it really? I was screaming for help at the same time."

"We're all born with an instinct for self-preservation. That's obviously still alive and well in you. But if suicidal thoughts become too strong they can overcome it. I'd be concerned if the impulse was getting stronger or more frequent."

Evelyn talked about her childhood, alternately looking down at her restless fingers and up at at Barbara,

"Barb, I feel as though I was born with a hole in my

heart. As far as I can recall my childhood, it was a natural part of life, but as I grew into my teens it became increasingly unnatural. Much of the time it's not significant, but I'm always conscious of it undermining any pleasure of life. Other times it blows up to a size that makes me desperate—for what, I don't know. Barb, I just don't know what's going on, but I'm fearful of how I may respond some day."

Her lips pursed, Evelyn faced Barbara with hardened eyes.

"But Barb, one way or another, I have to beat this thing—I'm going to beat it."

Barbara held her hand up for a high five, and reached across the table to hug Evelyn, knocking her coffee over in the process. They both laughed.

"Think about it Ev," said Barbara as she grabbed a handful of napkins to mop up the coffee. "A trip to England might be the best thing out. Just go and enjoy yourself without goals or commitments. Hey, would you like some company?"

Evelyn warmed to the idea. "Of course. With you, I could weather Mom's expectations and we could both have a good time. Perhaps it might work. Dammit. Let's do it!"

3

Friday and Saturday were Evelyn's late shift at the Travel Centre. She enjoyed her work as much as she enjoyed travelling, and working as a travel agent gave her access to special offers and low fares. This Saturday, supper hour was quiet. As she checked her filing drawer she heard a familiar voice.

"Hi Evelyn, feeling better?"

She looked up and fell back. *Why is it every time I see this guy he's looking down on me?* "How did you find me?"

"Computers are my work. Research is easy. You weren't hard to find."

Evelyn resented the lack of control she felt when this huckster was around. *Why can't he just do his good deed and disappear?*

Her response was curt, her fists curled on the desk. "What do you want?"

"Oh! I was thinking of going somewhere. I thought you could help."

"Where do you want to go?"

"Can you suggest somewhere?"

"Perhaps. You have to give me some idea."

"Can you suggest a good restaurant?"

Evelyn grimaced. "You don't need a travel agent for that."

"No, but I'd like that travel agent to come with me."

Time for me to take control. "Look, Mr. Whatever-your-name-is—"

"Logan, Clark Logan."

He smiled, exposing those dimples. Evelyn felt her face colouring, but was determined to keep the conversation professional.

"Mr. Logan. This is a professional office, and I don't have time for personal conversations or—"

"Doesn't look too busy." Clark's gaze swept the empty office.

Evelyn doggedly continued. "*Or*, Mr. Logan, am I interested in a date with you."

"Oh! Call me Clark, please. After our experience together, we should be more friendly."

That does it. If I ignore him, perhaps he'll go away. Evelyn pulled a file out of the drawer and dialled a number. She spoke to a non-existent client. Clark watched her for a minute, then picked up a scratch pad from her desk and wrote on it. Evelyn pursued her fake phone call until he disappeared. She waited a few minutes in case he returned and then picked up the pad. She tore the top sheet off, and without reading it, screwed it up and dropped in the trash. The phone rang, and the office became busy.

She finished her shift at ten and took her trash can to empty. The crumpled note fell out last. Curiosity trumped her better judgment and she dropped it in her purse. She would read it later at home. But by then, tired, she crawled into bed forgetting it.

Evelyn had no shift on Sundays. Phyllis went to the local United Church. The youngish female minister didn't seem to have much to say that Evelyn couldn't read in the newspaper, so she dropped out to her mother's dismay. She rose later. Phyllis had left for church and Evelyn went to the kitchen for coffee and a muffin, then went back to her room to dress. She was only one step short of beautiful. She knew instinctively what outfits suited her, and spent hours looking for the right clothing and accessories. Her model figure and long straight blond hair—curled for special occasions—garnered constant admiring glances. She spent time dressing and redressing hobby-like, until she was satisfied.

Her cell phone rang. It was Barbara, who usually went to church with her family. Evelyn glanced at the time; it was past one o' clock.

"Wondered how you're feeling today, Ev?"

"Okay. A bit flat." Evelyn twisted a long blond lock around her forefinger as she talked. "Have you had lunch yet? I haven't and I'm hungry."

"Yes. But I could join you for some dessert."

They drove to the Robson Street coffee shop. It was still early spring, in the last year of the second millennium, and the mild temperatures and warm sun tempted them onto a sidewalk table. Evelyn bought a sub for herself and slice of Barbara's favourite cake to the table. They ate slowly, talking between mouthfuls.

"I've been thinking about the talk we had at the river where you fell in," Barbara began. "Perhaps you should see someone about your bouts of depression, or whatever it is."

"Well, right now it's past, and I feel pretty good—especially with some food inside me. And I'm usually okay when I dress up a bit."

"You look fabulous," agreed Barbara, "but what about when you don't?

"Aw! It's probably a passing phase. Let's leave it there." When Evelyn felt good, it was better out of mind.

"Okay." Barbara stood up. "I'm getting a coffee. Want one?

"Sure."

Barbara disappeared inside the coffee shop. Evelyn leaned back and surveyed the bustling scene: the incessant slow traffic along the narrow street, the variety of people and dress passing by, others around her chatting amiably, or quietly sipping their coffee. Everything seemed so normal and comfortable. Yet . . . she felt dissatisfied, and still couldn't pin down why.

A fresh cup of coffee appeared before her, relegating her thoughts to the background. Evelyn looked at her friend sitting across the table and the familiarity brought comfort. Barbara looked happy, her face shining, bright auburn waved hair to her shoulders, and a casual tank top expressing her smooth skin and ample figure. *My God, she really is lovely,* Evelyn thought. *I hadn't really noticed it before.* Evelyn's absorption with herself had given way to her appreciation of Barbara's sensible approach to life. She saw her with fresh eyes.

Barbara seemed unconscious of Evelyn's gaze. "Ev. Have you thought any more about a trip to England?"

Evelyn was suddenly her old self; there was always something to fill the void.

"I smoothed things over with Mom and said I would consider it. She seemed overjoyed. Haven't seen her that animated since Dad died."

"What are the brothers like? Any idea?" Barbara was curious.

"Sophia sent a photo to Mom with the letter. I hadn't seen it until yesterday. Take a look."

She handed a picture to Barbara. The picture showed two unkempt guys in baggy pants and heavy sweaters. The corners of Barbara's mouth drooped.

"I hope they don't turn out to be the wild backwoods men they look like," she exclaimed.

"Oh! I thought you could do with some wildness," Evelyn giggled. "The taller guy on the left is Nigel. He's a couple of years older than David who's twenty two. Are you ready to book fares?"

"Sure. But can you really leave your friend Clark for that long?" teased Barbara.

Evelyn's tight lips met that comment. "Do you know he had the nerve to come into the office yesterday—just to ask me out?"

"You accepted, of course." Barbara giggled

"I ignored him till he left. Even then he left a—Oh! I forgot! I have the note he left in my purse."

Evelyn rummaged around in an overloaded purse until she found the crumpled paper.

Barbara was impatient. "Well what does it say?"

"I don't know, I didn't read it, I was so mad."

Evelyn laid the paper on the table and smoothed it out for them both to read.

> Hey Evelyn. I'd just like to be friends, no expectations. I really like you. Pls call.

His telephone number was at the bottom. Evelyn wilted. Her jaw dropped. She looked searchingly at Barbara.

"Have I been too hard on him, Barb? He almost certainly saved me from drowning! Why would I respond like that? I guess men make me nervous and irritable, and he was just too close for comfort." Evelyn paused, cupped her chin in her hands and looked away. "Although as I think about it, it's probably the sex thing, rather than the men themselves."

Barbara reached across the table and rubbed Evelyn's arm.

"Maybe he's the guy to help you beat this, Ev. What do you think? Worth a try?"

Evelyn looked back at Barbara with a long, wistful look. "If it's just friends, I'll think about it. Perhaps give him a call."

Evelyn thought about it a great deal. She enjoyed mixed company and was attracted to some men, but now, at the age of twenty, she had not held a steady boyfriend. Friendships she tried faltered as the men grew close or demanding. Clark Logan surfaced in her thoughts continually. He wasn't what she'd call handsome, but definitely attractive, especially those dimples. But was his tone superior, or fatherly? Her independent streak wasn't comfortable with either. But since the fall in the river she was increasingly conscious of her emptiness and fearful of the fate to which it might drive her. Such thoughts became her constant companions.

Her independence also kicked against the idea of therapy. But a trip abroad, or even a male friendship, both seemed a lesser evil that might lower her distress. The more she considered the two options, the more comfortable she felt about them—at least the thought, acting on them was a higher hurdle. However, the trip to England was about three months away in the summer. Evelyn determined not to wait that long. Clark was available right now. His note suggested she could keep a healthy distance within a friendship. She would call him this coming Saturday morning.

She called twice, but got an answering machine. She left no message, and decided to call Sunday afternoon. Again, a recorded message. But arriving at work on Monday morning, he'd left a message on her machine.

"Just in case you call me—still hoping—I've been called away on an assignment for a major company's computers. Won't be back until the end of April. I'd love to see you then. I called your office because I thought a call to your home might embarrass you."

Evelyn's heart sank. She'd been building up to this moment, now snatched away so abruptly. She began to spiral down, left work early complaining of sickness, and drove to the river where she'd fallen in. She stared at the passing, murky current. So simple to end it all; the futility, the fear, the striving.

The tide was out revealing a short muddy foreshore. She took a few slow, uncertain steps toward the river. Then she saw it in the mud, glinting in the sunlight.

That Monday Barbara had a late shift at the hospital. A chance for a sleep-in. She heard her father and younger brother, Roger, in some discussion during breakfast, and her mother's occasional interruption to bring balance. Barbara tried to block it all out. By the time she arose, her mother was alone in the kitchen sipping a second coffee.

"What was all that discussion about, Mom?"

"Dad is concerned about the millennium bug. Doesn't know if the world's computers will be fixed by the end of the year. Of course, Roger needled him by making out it'll be a major disaster worldwide. Frankly, I think it's a storm in a teacup."

Patti's faint accent and her use of English expressions betrayed her origin. British reserve made her the steadying influence in her family, and Barbara took after her.

"I know Mom. I hear all those dire warnings about computers not able to roll over to the year 2000. I'll just buy a new one if necessary. I don't know what all the fuss is about either."

"Well, to be fair, it's the major computers that control so much of our lives that are the problem. They say millions of lines of programming need adjustment, and if not done in time, chaos could erupt. Dad can fix his or buy new, but since his computers are linked into so many others, he feels he doesn't have control over his business."

Barbara shook her head and shrugged. "Is there another cup of coffee left?"

The coffee was a bit stale, but warm and comforting. Don, her father, was in the investment business. Barbara didn't know too much about it, but it provided a good income and security for the family. She worried some about the millennium, but decided she couldn't do anything about it, so left it on the back burner. Right now, Evelyn was her concern.

If Evelyn envied Barbara's serenity, Evelyn's normally effervescent spirit attracted Barbara. Their complementary personalities meshed and they grew together like sisters. But Evelyn had recently become morose and the events of the last week disturbed Barbara. Discussions about England and Clark had given some relief, but for Barbara, Evelyn's risky thoughts remained a major concern. She hadn't spoken to Evelyn all week as their work shifts had not coincided. The phone rang and interrupted her thoughts.

"It's for you Barb. It's Phyllis, Ev's mom."

A frown crossed Barbara's face. *Bad news?*

"Hello Mrs. Summers. Is everything okay?"

"Of course, dear, why not? Quite the reverse. I think you and Ev have discussed a trip to England, is that right?"

Barbara's face relaxed into a smile. "Yes. It sounds like a great idea."

"Good. I want to ask you a favour. I would like you both to correspond with my cousin Sophia's nephews in England. They manage the hotel of her brother who passed away. But Ev's so erratic these days I wondered if you would do that?"

"I guess so, but I don't know—"

"I'll have one of the boys email you and introduce himself. Would that make it easier for you?"

Barbara wasn't sure, but she had nothing to lose.

"Okay. I look forward to hearing from them. And I think Evelyn would enjoy the break."

"I do too, Barb. Thanks. I'll write Sophia today to ask the boys to email you. Bye."

Patti had heard Barbara's end of the conversation.

"Everything okay?"

"Sure."

Barbara explained about the visit to England, to which Patti offered a, "great," as she left on an errand. Barbara was alone with her thoughts. *Even Phyllis has noted Evelyn's change in behaviour.* Barbara had some sympathy with Evelyn's dilemma. *Like her, I sometimes wonder what life is all about, why we're here and if there's anything beyond this life. The daily routine, even goals for life, seem insufficient reason for the existence of everything. The simple cycle of birth, life, and death—if that's all there is— is meaningless.* Eventually, she came down on the default position: *I can only do my best. God—if He exists—can't expect more.*

Barbara wondered if others had the same questions. Most seemed to be sufficiently involved in life's pursuits to be satisfied with that or at least distracted from further thought, and few would even talk about it. "Politics and religion are not discussed in polite company." She'd heard that too many times. The danger Evelyn posed to herself required more than polite conversation, but Barbara had too many questions and too few answers herself.

It was in the middle of Barbara's shift at the hospital that evening that the admin desk called her to come and take a phone call.

"Your mother's on the phone. Sounds concerned."

Barbara took the receiver. "Mom?"

"Phyllis called. She hasn't heard from Evelyn. Thought she might be with us. She's not here. Have you heard from her?"

"No, I haven't. Is Phyllis worried?"

"I don't think so, but Ev's usually home for supper."

Barbara checked her watch, it was past eight. Her brows knit in concern.

"She's a big girl Mom. Probably at a friend's house. But call me if you hear anything."

"Will do. Enjoy your evening."

Thanks Mom, but I probably won't. Barbara went about her duties mechanically, Evelyn foremost in her mind. At her break, she wandered down to emergency— just in case. Some broken bones, but no reports of accidents or . . . Barbara didn't wait for the rest.

Barbara's mother suddenly called her cell phone.

"Hey Mom. Heard anything about Evelyn yet?"

"Phyllis called. Ev's home. Apparently went to a friend's house to do some photography or something. Forgot to call her mother. Gee, you girls!"

"Thank God. Glad to hear she's safe."

The rest of Barbara's shift was uneventful, but she carried a sense she had just missed a bullet.

Barbara didn't have a shift Tuesday evening, so determined to talk with Evelyn. They agreed on a walk together through the British Properties. The evening was cool and called for coats and scarves.

"I was worried about you last night Ev, when you were late home."

Evelyn was non-committal. "I just forgot to call Mom that I'd be late. No big deal."

"But after the river episode and what you told—"

"I'm fine now. Just drop it, okay?"

Barbara backed off. Evelyn was firmly on the defensive.

"I found the camera," said Evelyn, "and I was anxious to check the pictures I took."

Barbara's curiosity took over. "You went to the river?

Why?"

"The tide was out. I thought I'd check again," Evelyn lied, "and there it was in the mud, glinting in the sunlight."

Barbara thought the story sounded improbable. Surely the water had spoiled the film, and the camera useless. And what was so special about the pictures? *I doubt Evelyn will come clean about yesterday. Typical Evelyn: on a high, ignore the problem.*

"Well, I'm so glad you're feeling better about yourself. How did the pictures turn out? Can I see them?"

"Nah. The water spoiled them. You remember my friend Betty? She has a dark room in her basement. But we had a good time anyway. Take a look at this." Evelyn pulled the camera from her pocket. "The water got in. It's ruined."

At least that much was true. But Barbara remembered Betty, the party girl. She and Evelyn would attend raves together, something that didn't appeal to Barbara. She never liked Betty and now had doubts about Evelyn's story.

"Oh! Too bad." Barbara changed the subject. "Did you contact lover-boy Clark yet?"

"Nah." Evelyn screwed up her nose and waved him away. "Who needs him? Who needs anyone? I shouldn't still be living at home either, except Mom would be alone."

Barbara glimpsed Evelyn's sense of desperation, but ignored it.

"Okay. Forget him. What about our trip to England? Still ready to go?"

"You bet. Anything to get me through this dreary life. Need something to look forward to. Shall I book fares?"

"Sure. Sometime in July?"

The girls walked home arm-in-arm. But Barbara retained a sense of unease. *What really happened yesterday?*

THE SILENT REMAINDER

4

David walked up a flight of stairs, unlocked the door of his two-roomed office in Brighton, walked past his desk and looked out the window. He liked his office space overlooking Grand Parade, a major thoroughfare lined with Victorian four story terraces. The original elegance suffered from the ignominy of conversion to offices and apartments. Poor upkeep of some left vertical scars between brightly whitewashed neighbours. A wide landscaped median separated the reverse lanes of double deck buses, trucks, and cars jostling the roads. A cosmopolitan populace salt and peppered the sidewalks.

A few blocks away, his father's hotel, the Belvedere, faced the English Channel. Demetrius Hektor, David's father, had come to England from Greece as a young man and parlayed his property acumen into the hotel on the Brighton seafront until his death two years before. At twenty-two, David had completed his accountancy training, and accumulated sufficient work to start his own business. At this stage, much of it was book-keeping drudgery for which he hoped soon to employ a book-keeper/secretary. But for now, it was sufficient.

Nigel, David's brother, was two years older. After taking some business management courses, Nigel joined his father in running the hotel and took over at his death. Nigel enjoyed the work as it was seasonal and left time for other pursuits.

THE SILENT REMAINDER

The boys' mother had died from cancer when they were young, and David had only vague memories of her. So he had grown up in an all male household which gave him a disadvantage in dealing with the female sex. He never really understood women and felt awkward in their presence. He recalled his father talking a couple of times about his cousin in Canada, with whom he kept infrequent contact. But distance and personal affairs denied that connection from flourishing. He knew of their existence; that was all.

David sat down at his desk shuffling papers for about half an hour when Nigel walked in.

"What no coffee? What have you been doing all morning?" Nigel proceeded to brew some.

"More work for me?" queried David. That was the usual reason for Nigel's visits.

"No, not this time. Something different."

"Oh! Another discussion on religion?" David asked. He was committed to the Christian faith but Nigel claimed to be an atheist. The brothers were close and enjoyed each other's company, but this difference made for some lively discussions.

Nigel watched the coffee brew. "Nope! You're going to have to continue converting me some other time. This time it's about girls!"

"Girls? Are you going soft in the head?"

Both men had little time for girls; work and personal interests absorbed them. They liked the free lifestyle, and avoided the interference of female relationships. They both agreed on that. Nigel poured the coffees and sat down facing David at his desk.

"You remember Dad's cousin in Canada, Dave?" David nodded. "Well, he has a daughter, and she and a friend are coming to visit us next summer. Sophia's asked if we would give them a room and show them around."

"How long are they coming for?" David could see his summer wrecked already.

"Don't know for sure. Three or four weeks perhaps."

"What are they like? It might help if they're decent looking. If our summer is to be disrupted, the entertainment factor might alleviate things."

"Got something for you. Here." Nigel reached across the desk and handed David a photo of the two girls.

David looked at it intently. "Hey, not bad," he responded. "May be we can put up with them for a short while."

"One more thing, Sophia wants you to correspond with the friend, Barbara, to arrange details."

"Why me?"

"You've got the time."

"You've got just as much time as me."

"But it's your Christian duty to be hospitable."

"Oh! So your atheism means you don't have to be?"

"As far as these two girls are concerned, yes, I shall stand aloof! I don't want to get involved. Besides, you said they're not bad. Now's your chance!"

"Okay. Okay. I'll look after it."

"Good. I'll send you Barbara's contact info." Nigel pushed his chair back and made for the door. "Thanks for the coffee I brewed for you."

David picked up the photos of the girls again. He was becoming mildly interested. He looked at Evelyn, his relative. She looked the model type, perfect figure, with long blond straight hair, parted in the middle. Her friend, Barbara had a fuller figure and captivating smile and wavy auburn hair to her shoulders. The picture evoked old feelings of despair he'd long since buried, but also a sense of longing he was unfamiliar with.

Avoiding girls this far in life had prevented desire for any girl in particular. Now he faced two girls to whom he was connected in some way. But this sudden desire for the company of someone of the opposite sex came as a depressing shock. He was sure that attaining a relationship of that sort was beyond his capability; his ineptness with women would deter any girl.

He thought of talking his fears through with his brother Nigel. He, despite his desire to avoid female entrapment, always seemed more at ease with women than David did. But on second thoughts, he was more likely to make fun of David's predicament than help. Nothing else for it. *Must keep a professional relationship,* he thought, *that way I can keep a respectful distance.* They *were* good looking girls. But he'd need to be on his guard, you never knew with women. His first correspondence with them proved how hard that would be. He started his first letter to her.

Should it be "Hi Barbara" or should he use her family name to keep it formal? "Hi Miss Williams." But she was a family friend, however distant. However, he would use her full name; "Barb" was much too familiar. Then, he should probably use "Aunt Sophia" rather than the impertinent "Sophia," and then the first sentence came easily. So far so good. But he didn't want to appear "happy" or "glad to put them up," but rather "would provide accommodation to suit their needs." He thought it better to "escort them to places of interest," than "show them around a bit."

Most of his letter received this careful consideration to maintain correct propriety and keep the relationship at a formal distance. He spent some time puzzling over how to sign off. "Yours respectfully," was too business like, but "Yours sincerely" seemed too personal. He finally decided "Kindest regards" showed sufficient formal concern for their welfare.

He looked over the finished letter with some satisfaction.

Hi Barbara:

My Aunt Sophia asked me to contact you regarding details of your projected visit here with your friend this coming summer.

Please let me know your itinerary, so we can meet you at the airport.

If you would kindly let me know what sleeping arrangements you prefer we will provide accommodation to suit your needs.

We will also venture to escort you to some places of interest during your stay.

Kindest regards,

David Hektor

Numbers 6:24–26

Putting his full name maintained what he considered suitable formality. He wasn't sure about the Bible reference—would she even know what it was? But his faith wanted to express his desire for her wellbeing as for anyone else; it wasn't meant to be particularly personal.

He read it a second and third time, and eventually satisfied it reflected the friendly formality he wanted to project, hit the "send" button. He switched his computer off and left the office for the day.

Whatever Barbara's concerns for Evelyn—she still had no more information about that lost evening—they were put aside on receiving David's email. She wasn't sure what to make of its tone. Was he really that pompous? She called Evelyn.

"Got a few minutes before work to drop in? I've got an email from your cousin David. I'd like you to read it."

She arrived and they read it together. Evelyn burst out laughing.

"Is this guy for real. Who the hell does he think he is? And does he really think we are a couple of escorts? Let's get together this evening and compose a suitable reply."

Evelyn gave that mischievous grin so familiar to Barbara. She was glad to see it, but wondered how David would receive Evelyn's playful, often sarcastic, wit. They both left for work, but that evening they sat in front of Barbara's computer again. Patti stopped by and looked over their shoulders.

"What a smart letter. Sounds like a nice guy, don't you think?"

Evelyn rolled her eyes, and Barbara pushed her mother out the door. Patti grinned as she left. The girls took as much time as David had done to craft a reply—but for different reasons.

"Let's make him feel at home with us," suggested Evelyn, really meaning something flirtatious. "Let's try, 'Our dear David.' That'll fill his sails a bit!"

Barbara shook her head and grinned. "Okay, I'll try it. How about this as an opener? Our Dear David: What a pleasant surprise to receive your email. I asked Evelyn to read it and help me with my reply. Actually it's from both of us."

Barbara didn't want any repercussions to fall on her alone. She should make it clear that the reply was from them both. Then she thought she should comment on his toffee-nosed English. Even Evelyn caught the whiff of English humour in that and nodded enthusiastically.

"I like that Barb. And we need to comment on his 'escort' bit," she said. "Something about escorts having a dubious character in North America!"

Barbara added, "And something about the accommodation that suits us. But we need to appear friendly as well," said Barbara. "Let's close with a response to his offer to pick us up."

Evelyn added, "I'd like to comment on their photos as well."

The letter was finally finished:

Our Dear David:

What a pleasant surprise to receive your email. I asked Evelyn to read it and help me with my reply. It's from both of us.

We enjoyed your careful command of the English language to express yourself.

The idea of being escorted around England tickles us immensely. Of course, you know that escorts have a dubious character in North America!

Regarding accommodation, a room with beds would serve us well.

We are delighted that you will meet us at the airport. We haven't booked our flights yet but will send details when we do.

We liked the photo of you and Nigel your aunt sent us. Very earthy!

We really look forward to meeting you both.

Fondest greetings from your long lost cousin (a couple of times removed?), and friend,

Evelyn and Barbara.

The girls giggled as Barbara hit the "send" key.

David read this first response from the girls with dismay and irritation. He was aware of the informal character of most North American non-business correspondence. But even so, it appeared the girls were poking fun at his formality. David's letter clearly amused them. For both David and the girls, something was lost in the translation!

David passed his letter and the girls' reply to Nigel. Nigel guffawed.

"For Pete's sake, David, these are North American girls. They would use this language with anyone. What did you expect? Middle class English Anglican prims? You Christians make me laugh. Join the almost twenty-first century."

David was nettled. His plans for a respectable few weeks with distant cousins were in shambles, and Nigel thought it was a huge joke.

"I just hope you don't fall for one of them and have to eat your words," David replied. "Then *I'll* be laughing." He grinned at his brother.

"Don't worry. I can be obnoxious if necessary, I can put them off. It's one advantage of having no god. I'm able to adjust my morals to fit the situation."

David thought Nigel's morals sounded more like immorals, but he was more concerned at that moment with their reply than pursuing another debate with Nigel. He decided he needed to write the girls an apology, or at least an explanation. This time, it was less pedantic if just as thoughtful.

> Hi Barbara and Evelyn—can I call you Barb and Ev?
> I think you might have thought my email to you rife with English superiority. If you did, I profoundly apologize—I'm sorry! If you really thought that, your response was understandable.
> My intention was to be respectful, especially to ladies—what do I call the fairer sex over there?
> But in rereading your reply, I recognize your humour—it's almost English in its dryness!
> Anyway, I'll try to be more cousin-like to you in future communications.
> Fondest greetings to you both,
> David.

That letter wasn't easy for David. He was still unsure how the girls would receive it—he would have been unsettled to receive one similar. But it went anyway. David received a reply almost immediately. This time, it was only from Barbara.

Hey David:

So you're human after all! Please call me Barb—everyone else does!

Actually, now I understand your motives, our sarcasm was uncalled for. To be honest, daredevil Evelyn helped me a lot with our reply. I won't show her this letter.

I look forward to visiting England and getting to know you all.

David. You and Nigel may *certainly* escort us, and I'm sure your intentions are honourable.

My mother showed me where to find the Scripture you referred to. I was touched to receive such a blessing:

> The Lord bless you and keep you;
> The Lord make his face shine upon you and be gracious to you;
> The Lord turn his face toward you and give you peace.

I need to get this to you right away, but I hope we'll correspond with more information about each other soon.

Your excited friend,

Barb.

David looked forward to that next letter from Barbara. He wanted to know about life in Vancouver, but especially about Barbara herself. So began correspondence between David and Barbara as they exchanged information about themselves, their families, dreams for the future, and, of course, details of the travel and time in England as they were confirmed. David, for his part, began telling her stories of England providing an environment for places Nigel and he could take them.

In a significant development, David and Barbara began two streams of correspondence: those that contained information about their visit she would share with Evelyn, and another that contained personal information about themselves. Photos regularly accompanied those emails, each one a "better" picture that the previous. Those letters, David copied and placed in a box concealed in his apartment.

As time of the girl's visit approached, David's attitude towards the free life he enjoyed began to change. He looked forward to the disruption of his summer and spending time with Barbara—and Evelyn, of course. He had the occasional picture of Evelyn, but wasn't sure if he could cope with the sort of antics Barbara related about her. It seemed Nigel didn't notice subtle changes in David's attitude to the visit. Their conversations indicated Nigel still planned to be obnoxious to the girls. David guessed the varied temperaments, attitudes, and beliefs would make for an interesting time. He had no idea how interesting.

5

Evelyn awoke to a dull Sunday, the first day of May. But the weather didn't bother her. She had forced David's letter to keep her amused for a week. She had been disappointed—more than she had anticipated—at Clark being away. She felt guilty in not coming clean to Barbara about that lost evening and also the idea of drowning having taken hold of her again that day. Disappointment and surprise over Clark's absence had affected her so much she'd been driven into a sudden fit of despair.

Evelyn thought back to the previous Sunday. She recalled driving to the river that day. Seeing the camera in the mud had distracted her morbid thoughts. Evelyn considered finding the camera somehow closed the watery episode and the reason for suicidal thoughts. Everything was going to be alright again. That the camera was ruined didn't figure into her thinking. Her depression lifted and a shallow cheerfulness replaced it. She walked down to the water's edge and washed the mud off the camera. She opened the back; the film was useless. She threw the film away, wiped the camera, and put it in her pocket.

Then she had climbed in her car and looked in the vanity mirror. The face she saw didn't match the relief she felt, and she started applying make-up. Her favourite lipstick was empty. She drove to K-Mart and wandered the make-up aisle. Lip gloss, new colour nail polish and other items took her fancy and she dropped them into the basket. She strolled towards the checkouts and stopped at the jewellery display. A rack of inexpensive watches caught her eye, and after fingering a few, dropped one she liked into her purse.

She maintained a nonchalant air as she paid for the make-up items and walked through the exit. An intermittent buzzer screamed. She looked around. A uniformed security officer approached her.

"Ma'am, wait up. Can I see your bill please?"

Evelyn stopped, nonplussed, and fumbled in the K-Mart bag. She handed the cash register bill to the man. He scanned it and went through the bag.

"Ma'am, may I check your purse?"

Evelyn was about to indignantly deny his request, but noticed two or three people watching.

"Sorry sir, I'm in a rush to—"

"I must insist Ma'am. We have you of video, and if you refuse, I will have to call the police." Seeing a crowd gathering, he added, "Would you like to come inside and discuss this?"

She looked around and nodded, and followed him to an office in the store. He motioned her to a seat and she sat, clutching her purse tightly. He sat opposite across a desk.

"Ma'am, do you have anything in your purse you haven't paid for?"

Evelyn looked at him defiantly for a moment, but a poker face continued to ask the question. It seemed he held all the cards, especially the video—if there was one. Slowly she looked down at her purse, retrieved the watch, and placed it on the table between them.

"Would you give me your name, Ma'am?" his request was polite, almost sympathetic.

Evelyn frowned, hesitated, uncertain. "Do I have to?"

"Yes. But at this stage, it's purely for our records. If

this is your first offence I doubt it'll go any further, and co-operation will be in your favour."

Evelyn had heard this numerous times on TV shows, and it never turned out that way. He seemed to read her thoughts.

"Don't be put off by what you see on television," he said, now with a disarming smile. "We take our job very seriously and want to retain good relationships with our customers."

Evelyn curled a long blond strand of hair around her forefinger and returned a hesitant smile.

"Evelyn Summers."

She fumbled in her purse again and produced her driver's licence as proof in an attempt to gain additional favour. The security officer made a few notes.

"Well, Ms. Summers—Evelyn, you have a choice. You can pay for the watch or return it. What's your pleasure?"

"I'll leave it, I didn't really want it."

"Then what made you take it?"

I felt I was someone, different, noticeable. "I really don't know. It was a spur of the moment thing." *It made me feel good.* "I won't do it again." *I hope*.

His smile returned, but Evelyn couldn't tell if he believed her. *Oh well! Whether or not he does, I'm free this time.*

"Goodbye Evelyn," and he waved her out.

The encounter at K-Mart had actually raised her spirits. She had status, even if it was as a thief. But it was her secret, her private source of esteem. But guilt still played on her mind. Reluctant to go home, she had driven aimlessly until late that evening.

Hearing her mother in the bathroom getting ready for church, brought Evelyn back to the present. She recalled ending the interview with the security officer by feigning a gracious "thank you." *But May will be different. Clark will be back about this time.* But that didn't seem important any more. *I'll wait and see if he calls me. If not, that's his bad luck.*

It was about lunchtime Wednesday when Clark called Evelyn at the Travel Centre. She wasn't surprised to hear from him, and in her elevated state of mind felt in command of the situation, able to be off-hand again, even playful.

"I'm so glad you called, Clark. I've felt badly about the way I treated you before you went away. I'm really sorry."

"Oh! Er, perhaps I was a little forward. I'm sorry too."

Sounds as though I caught him off guard, Evelyn surmised happily. "You know I was pretty shook up over the incident?"

"Of course, and I was too ignorant to notice. You must think me thoughtless."

"Not at all. You're a man. Men don't easily think that way. And how could I think you thoughtless, you saved my life. I need to thank you better than I did."

He took the bait. "You could come out to dinner with me. That would be a sufficient 'thank you.' Saturday Evening?"

"Sorry, I work late Saturday."

"Sunday then?"

"Let me check and call you. I don't have your number," she lied, "I threw away your note."

They exchanged home numbers.

"Ev. How are you feeling now? Are you over the dip in the river?" She noted Clark's voice carried concern.

"Pretty much. It haunts me once in a while, but remembering your heroism makes it bearable."

"I'm no hero. Any man would have stopped by to rescue a pretty girl like you."

Evelyn was satisfied with the compliment and her

apparent success in boosting his ego.

"I'll call you—one way or the other. Gotta go. Bye," and she hung up.

Control meant worth, and the last three weeks or so since the river incident had provided opportunities for that. She leaned back in her chair, a sense of contentment washing over her. She relished the control she felt over her budding relationship with Clark. Perhaps this is a relationship I can handle, provided I manage it. Yet . . .

She pulled out the note from Clark and smoothed it out slowly several times. She recalled first reading it with Barbara and felt again regret at her response. Where did this sadistic streak towards men arise? Why did she feel it necessary to be in charge? Tears slowly ran down her cheeks, both at her attitude and her frustration with it. Clark seemed a nice enough guy, but her mind continually played up his faults. There must be a better way. Why keep the poor guy waiting?

She picked up the phone. She dialled his home number and heard the outgoing message. He must have called from work.

"Hi Clark, this is Evelyn. I'm free Sunday night." *I always was.* "Call me for arrangements. I look forward to our date."

It wasn't an earth-shattering announcement, but Evelyn felt she had jumped from a plane, with little knowledge about guiding a parachute. But having made the effort, she felt an inner peace she hadn't known for a long time. She wondered how long it would last.

Evelyn considered the dinner date with Clark a success. The cocky demeanour she recalled was absent and his conversation respectful as befitted a first date. This enabled her to maintain comfortable control of the encounter. She hung on his words of that evening.

"Evelyn, I think we got off on the wrong foot, and I hope this evening will put that behind us. I'm not really the smart-ass you seem to think. In fact, that comes out to play when I'm nervous, and I was when I saw how attractive you were—are."

Evelyn recalled the hospital encounter. "Attractive? In that state? You must've been dreaming."

"Believe me, Evelyn, I could see through the state of the moment. And seeing you this evening, I was right."

Following a satisfactory evening, Evelyn's question was whether he would follow through on his other promise—and she still had the note to prove it: he just wanted to be friends, no expectations. Thus began a tenuous relationship in which she would pull back if she felt threatened, yet flirted easily to keep him on the hook. She considered that, by and large, he kept his word, mostly as a result of her careful manipulation of the friendship. Eventually, Evelyn felt secure enough to introduce Clark to her mother, and Phyllis invited Clark to spend an evening with them.

It was still several months to the new millennium, but the fears that when it occurred it would unleash a computerized chaos was prevalent on many minds. Clark's work suggested no such calamity, but many weren't sure.

"I hope your new year's resolution is to fix the world's computers," said Phyllis, "so we can all breathe easy for the next year. There's some talk out there it's going to lead to Armageddon."

"Oh, Mother!" Responded Evelyn. "That's all superstitious nonsense. You don't believe all that religious stuff do you?

"Well, at least it makes people think about their future," replied Phyllis. "Too many don't consider it at all. What do you think Clark?"

Clark put his hands up and backed up in his chair.

"Don't get me involved in that one. There are no winners." He leaned forward again. "But, I'll tell you, there is frenzied activity in the computer world to ensure a safe transition into the new millennium. There's a lot of work needed. Without it, there could be some major disruption. Just too much is at stake for companies not to fix it."

Phyllis pulled a tight grin. "I just don't trust anyone when it comes to technology, although I'm sure you're sincere Clark. Just hope you are right."

After Clark left, Evelyn wondered how her mother felt about him. Evelyn felt secure enough to consider calling him a "boy friend." Phyllis' reaction was less than helpful.

"Do you really think you are ready for a steady relationship? You know how past friendships turned out."

"Perhaps Mom, because you always pour cold water on the idea when I've tried it before. Don't you want this to work for me?"

"I just don't think you're ready, that's all. I wouldn't lead him on if I were you."

Phyllis's reaction mystified Evelyn; it was always the same. *If I rely on Mom's approval it's never going to happen.* Evelyn decided it was time to make her own decisions about guys. *I'll let Mom in on as little as possible.*

"Okay Mom, I'll take it easy with Clark if that's what you feel."

Phyllis nodded and withdrew into herself and her bedroom. "Time for bed, see you in the morning my dear."

Why is this talk of boyfriends always so difficult with her? Slowly it dawned on Evelyn that her mother must be afraid of being alone. *Yes, that must be it. Why hadn't I thought of that before? I need to try and convince her I wouldn't leave her alone. Next time I must assure her she will always be part of the family.*

Evelyn retired to her bedroom feeling better about

herself than she had for a long time. She'd found the camera, surely a good omen. Her relationship with Clark was going well; in fact she'd not had a depressed spell for some time. Now, it seemed she had an answer to the distant relationship with her mother. All these added up to an improving self-image. She was only subconsciously aware that she could be wrong about her mother's reticence or that the friendship with Clark depended on her own fragile management of it. The chance of something going wrong briefly presented itself, but appeared so unlikely she dismissed it. She became drowsy. Restful sleep engulfed her.

Through the spring, the relationship between Evelyn and Clark developed. Clark was as good as his word, although occasionally suggesting he'd like it to "develop" some day. But he was gregarious, always good humoured, and matched her spontaneity. *Plenty else besides sex to keep the relationship alive.* Although she met Barbara less frequently, they still met regularly. The topics of conversation were usually much the same: Evelyn's relationship with Clark, and the summer trip to England.

But the very success that Evelyn desired and achieved, slowly, almost unnoticed, became a source of concern for her. She met Barbara at the Robson Street coffee shop in early June. The weather was cool and drizzly. Barbara noted Evelyn was especially withdrawn.

"Ev. It's been so good to see you enjoying life over the last months, a huge improvement over your earlier escapade. Do you remember?"

"How could I forget?"

"But you seem more distant for the last few times we met, and today is no improvement. I'm worried about you. What's going on?

"Clark."

"What about him?

Evelyn paused, unsure how to approach the issue.

"I'm getting another coffee. Want one?"

"No! I want to know what is bothering you."

"Well, Clark doesn't seem . . ." her voice trailed off.

"Doesn't seem what? Spit it out, Ev."

"He doesn't seem interested . . . in . . . ?

"For God's sake Ev! Not interested in what?"

"In sex." Evelyn finally yelled, and then sheepishly looked around as heads turned toward her. She lowered her voice as she leaned across the table toward Evelyn. Quietly, "He doesn't seem interested in sex."

"How do you know?"

"He hardly ever mentions it."

"Well, haven't you told him to avoid it, you know, no expectations?"

"Yea, but it still seems un-guy-like not to pursue it sometimes. That seems unusual to me. What do you think?"

Hardly a subject Barbara was an expert in, but she hazarded a guess. "You think he's gay?"

"Good God no—at least I hope not. Why would he be interested in me if he was?"

"For appearances?"

"I doubt it. He mixes generally with guys, but doesn't have a particular *boy* friend."

"Even if he did, it wouldn't mean he was gay, would it? We're not gay are we?"

Evelyn shivered. "God, I hope not!"

"Then perhaps he's impotent," Barbara offered.

Evelyn wound a blond lock around her finger. "You don't really think that do you?"

"Of course not! From the times I've met him he seems perfectly normal. Perhaps he's a perfect gentleman as well."

"How can I be sure? I need to know."

"Well there's only one way, but I don't think you're ready for that yet."

Evelyn shivered again. Her shoulders drooped. Her hesitancy, even fear, of sex, pricked her composure and deflated her spirit. Encouragement and assurance from Barbara made little difference.

"I'll have that coffee now, Ev. How about you?"

Evelyn made her way slowly to the counter, staring into space as she waited. Barbara joined her at the counter.

"Hey Ev. We're off to England in a month. You ready for it?"

Evelyn's face broke into a characteristic smile.

"You bet. Perhaps I can forget about Mother and Clark—"

"Forget about Clark?"

"Yea, I'm not sure about him. I'm confused. He's nice enough and I enjoy being with him, but is that enough for a permanent relationship? I mean, I'm not even sure about being in love, if that's what it is. What is love anyway? Is it just good sex or what?"

The coffee interrupted her philosophizing. They carried it back to the table and sipped quietly for a few moments.

Barbara put her mug down and leaned back.

"I think it's more than sex," she said. "It has to be. I couldn't settle for sex alone, however good it was. What happens if sex fades? Ev, I think you're on the right track by building a friendship first, even if it's a bit rocky to start. Don't give up. And a spell away from him should help to sort out your thinking."

Evelyn's smile returned. "Yep. I think you're right. Have you sent David our flights?"

"Of course."

"You correspond with him regularly?"

"Enough to keep him informed."

"And . . . ?"

"And what?"

"And what else?"

"That's sufficient."

"Sufficient for him or sufficient for me?"

"Both."

Whatever more there was, Barbara was not opening up. Evelyn gave her a coy, knowing look, which Barbara ignored.

"Time to go. Work calls," was all she said.

THE SILENT REMAINDER

6

The build up to the Millennium—although a few months away—meant increasing work hours for Clark. Clark's employers took on an associate, Joe Garner, to assist in Clark's work.

Clark and Joe became good friends. A few years older than Clark, Joe and his younger sister Adele had lost their parents in a car crash several years before. They lived together in a condominium, purchased with the subsequent inheritance, overlooking False Creek. This gave them a special connection, Clark had lost his parents, so to speak, through divorce. Of the two, Adele was closer to his age, quietly reserved, still mourning the loss of her parents. Joe, more gregarious than his sister, had a small yacht tied up nearby—another attraction for Clark.

A week before Evelyn's flight to England, Clark met her at the Robson Street cafe, and confided something of his job and growing friendship with Joe.

"That must be a real help fighting the 'Millennium bug,'" said Evelyn.

"Absolutely. I really like the work, and don't have a lot of friends here. I've been too busy with my work and this is good experience for us both."

"But I'll be gone in a week's time. So let's make the most of this week."

"Perhaps Joe will let us take his boat out for a day. I'll see. You know, if it wasn't for my current job, I never would have met him. I'd like you to meet him and his sister."

"I'd like to. Let me know. And a day sailing would be exciting. I'm so glad *I* met *you*." He felt her squeeze his hands.

"Just because I can take you sailing?"

"Of course. What else would I need you for?"

"More than that I hope," Clark replied, and reached across the table kissing her slowly. "Something more like that?"

Evelyn gave a half smile. "What did you have in mind?"

Clark floundered for a moment. What was the point of her question if she only wanted a simple friendship? Was she asking for a deeper experience? His heart quickened.

"Something more than a kiss."

He couldn't keep the desire from his eyes. He'd spent to much time with this dazzling girl for his senses not to be blurred on occasion—like now.

"Oh Clark! You really do want me, don't you?"

Clark felt a surge through his body and an erection began to throb. *With her looks and so much time together, how can she ask such a question?*

"I don't know how I've lasted this long without making love to you. Sometimes, like now, you make me desperate. Why do you lead me on sometimes and then say no? Is that what you're doing again? I don't know if I can last much longer."

Clark noticed a satisfied gleam in her eye

"I'm so sorry if I led you on like that. I just need to know that you want me. I'm sorry if I seem so difficult, but the day will come, I promise."

Frustration boiled over. "That's no longer good enough. When? When's it going to be Ev?"

Clark got up, glared at Evelyn, and walked out the door. Evelyn followed, running.

"Clark. Clark, wait." She grabbed his arm on the sidewalk. "Clark! Please. I'm sorry. Please! How can I put this right? Please. Don't go."

Clark stopped and held her shoulders firmly in his hands.

"Give me a straight 'yes' or 'no.' I can't have my emotions kicked around like a football any longer. What's it to be Evelyn?"

"Oh Clark! Just give me time—"

Clark dropped his hands and opened them beating the air emphasizing his question. "How much time. You've had all the time you need. When, Evelyn?" His fists clenched.

"Give me until we go sailing. We'll come to some arrangement then. Will you wait till then for an answer?"

"All right. Till then. Pick me up Friday when we go to Joe's," said Clark and he left for his car.

Evelyn looked forward to the weekend with mixed feelings. Clark revealed his attitude to sex with an unexpected demand. Her answer would make or break their relationship The following Wednesday she would be flying with Barbara overnight to London, and she had wanted make up for the time away on the sailing trip. Now that was weakened by uncertainty.

She picked up Clark from his apartment Friday evening.

"We'll not be sailing alone," Clark said as they drove. "They like to use the boat weekends, so we've been invited as a foursome. Not sure about time to ourselves. I'm holding you to an answer."

"I just want to be with you. We'll make the time somehow."

Joe answered the door. "Hey! Come on in. Good to see you again Clark. And this is your friend Evelyn. Wow! You sure know how to pick 'em don't you!" And he gave Evelyn a hug.

Evelyn answered with a broad smile, liking Joe right away. They discussed the next day over coffee, Joe outlining his plans.

"I'm thinking of a two day trip. Up Georgia Strait Saturday and return back here Sunday. What do you think?"

Clark agreed it was a great way to spend their weekend together before Evelyn's flight.

Evelyn called her mother, telling her that she would be going out with her friend Betty on Saturday evening, they'd be late, and she'd stay over at Betty's house that night.

The weather forecast for the weekend was clear with light breezes, perfect for sailing. Evelyn and Clark sat in the rear of the boat as Joe and Adele did the sailing.

"We want this to be a special weekend," said Joe. "You just relax and enjoy it. Make the meals if you wish."

In the evening, Clark and Evelyn prepared a light supper, working close together in the small galley. The four had the benefit of a glass or two of wine and the conversation flowed easily on the rear deck.

"How about some fishing?" Joe suggested after supper and handed Clark a rod. The two flung their lines over the stern while the girls took the dishes and leftovers down to the galley. Evelyn looked about her at the cramped cabin space and suddenly wondered about sleeping arrangements. She had assumed a motel or something on shore. She asked Adele.

"Goodness no," she replied. "We sleep on the boat. There are a couple of narrow bunks that pull down either side of this cabin. Joe and I sleep on those. Through the galley is a small cabin with a double bed. You can both use that."

"Oops. We didn't think far enough ahead. Clark and I aren't sleeping together."

"Oh! We assumed you were. Doesn't everybody?"

"Everybody except us, I guess." Evelyn wondered about the sheltered existence her parents tried to force on her. Perhaps they weren't so bad after all. Or were they keeping her from a fuller life? Was that the reason for the emptiness she often felt inside?

"One night wouldn't hurt, would it?" Adele's question brought her back to the immediate.

"Adele. I'm not prepared to risk a pregnancy." It was a good cover for her fear of sex.

"But that's no big deal. That's what abortion's for, isn't it?"

Evelyn shivered. "Perhaps for others. I'm not sure I could deal with that."

"That's probably what most girls feel at first, but they have it anyway. Better that than the alternative."

"What? Having a child?"

"Yes. And all the responsibilities that go with it."

There seemed to be some rough logic to Adele's argument, but this wasn't solving Evelyn's immediate problem.

"Let me talk to Clark, Adele, and see what we can work out."

Adele went up on deck, presumably to discuss the dilemma with Joe, and sent Clark down. Evelyn explained the situation.

"I guess that brings our situation to a head, doesn't it, Ev. So what are you going to do? Yes or no?"

Evelyn began to shake. "Hold me Clark I'm really scared. I lose both ways."

She began to weep quietly.

Clark softened. "We both lose if you say no. Our time together is over. But how do you lose if we have sex?"

"I can't explain. I'm fearful of sex. I don't know why. Please help me. How can we solve this and stay together?

Clark held her tight. She was torn, either decision was painful for her. She hoped he took comfort from her pain at leaving him.

"Ev. Suppose we just sleep together. We'll keep the sex until later. I'd go for that."

Evelyn looked up, her voice animated. "You really mean that. We could just cuddle. Could you handle that?"

"Yes my darling, If it will keep us together."

Being an only child, sleeping with another was a new experience. They changed into nightclothes separately in the bathroom. Clark was already on the bed when Evelyn walked in. He held out his hands to her, took hers and gently pulled her into the bed with him. They lay locked in a tight embrace, Clark kissing her face and mouth intensely.

"Comfortable?" he asked.

"Yes, very. Just keep holding me."

Shocked surprise swept her as she felt new sensations. Standing kissing was one thing, laying together evoked a longing for a closeness beyond physical touch. But nausea greeted the feeling of his erection against her thighs. She broke the embrace and turned away from him. Still she could feel it on her back.

"Are you okay?" he asked.

"Yes, er, no. not really."

"What's the problem?"

"I'm sorry, It's not you. It's me. Feeling your erection makes me feel sick. But I love the sensation of laying together."

"Oh! I'm sorry too."

Evelyn sensed the disappointment in his voice.

"I don't understand why, Clark. I'm so sorry."

"Would it help if I fix it?"

"Oh Clark! Would you do that for me?"

Without a word, Clark slipped out of bed and went to the bathroom, returned, and slipped in beside her again. Evelyn held him close again, reliving those new feelings, kissing him avidly on his bare chest and face, in gratitude, and sensing an increasing desire for more of him.

"Turn over," Said Clark.

Evelyn settled with her seat in his lap as his arms encircled her again. As she fell asleep, she felt the beginning of a new erection.

The return sail was more subdued. Evelyn and Adele exchanged small talk, Adele's eyes brimming occasionally as she mentioned her parents. Evelyn couldn't identify with her at all but tried to show concern. Evelyn's attention was on Clark who spent most of the day talking and laughing with Joe. She thought of Barbara. *Can I share all this with her?* She decided not to, she didn't want Barbara to criticize what she had done and turn against her as well.

She found comfort in thinking of the trip to England on Wednesday. It was a chance to get away from all this uncertainty and even a growing anxiety about where her relationship with Clark was going. Her goodbye to him that evening was reserved, and her sleep that night was fitful.

But at least, Clark's advances had settled her questions about him.

THE SILENT REMAINDER

7

The plane came to a gentle stop at the gate, unleashing a migration of travellers to overhead bins and under seats to recover hand baggage. The girls fumbled with landing cards and passports, dragging their wheeled carry-ons as they followed signs to "Passport Control" and "Baggage." They negotiated it all without incident. Now to find whoever was going to meet them.

"I've still got the picture of those two ignorant farmer types in my head," Evelyn said. "We may have quite a culture gap to bridge." Evelyn looked every inch the efficient city girl, sure of herself, ready to meet any crisis.

Doors to the public space opened before them, and they looked for David or Nigel, or both. A tall young man in jeans and an unbuttoned golf shirt, stepped forward to greet them.

"Hey, you must be," he looked at a picture and then back at the girls. ". . . Evelyn. And you are Barbara, right? I'm Nigel. Welcome to England!"

He shook their hands, grabbed a couple of bags and with a peremptory, "Follow me," charged into the crowd. They walked for a few minutes before they reached Nigel's SUV.

"Best vehicle for moving visitors," he said. "The front seat's a mess," he pointed to papers, letters, and personal items littering it, "But we try to keep the back seat clean for visitors. Remember I run a hotel." He opened the rear door.

The girls said little; Nigel gave them little opportunity. As he loaded their cases in the back, Evelyn looked at Barbara.

"Well, at least it's not a farmer's truck."

They grinned, and climbed in.

Nigel drove out of the airport onto the M25, the ring road around London. The girls still said little, partly silenced by Nigel's demeanour and they didn't want to interrupt Nigel's driving through the racetrack conditions outside. They talked quietly to each other.

"I hope all the English aren't like this," said Barbara, "or I'll go home tomorrow."

"He seems pretty unfriendly to me," responded Evelyn. "Just pretend he's our chauffeur."

Barbara nodded, grinning. "Actually, from the correspondence I've had with David, I don't think *he's* like this."

"How *much* correspondence have you had with David?"

Barbara was feeling relaxed and generous. "Quite a lot."

"You didn't tell me about that." Evelyn pouted, feeling left out.

"I told you everything that affected you."

"But I want to know what affected *you*."

"Perhaps one day. Right now it's private."

Evelyn looked at Barbara, again with new eyes. *Is she falling for a guy she's never seen?*

"I tell you everything about Clark and me," she said. "Tell me about you and David."

"Nothing to tell, I've never met the guy."

Evelyn pouted again and sat back. Nigel took an off-ramp at a sign reading "M23 Brighton." The traffic on the new highway was lighter, and for the first time Nigel glanced back.

"You girls okay?" They nodded." Sorry about the carousel back there; that road's always crowded and fast." He faced forward, watching the road. "So! How is it back in the colonies?" he asked. *The colonies? Didn't he know Canada was a sovereign country*? "Elizabeth is still your queen, isn't she?" he continued. "So Canada can't be entirely independent."

"Most Canadians are not really interested in your queen," Evelyn retorted. "We can do without her."

"That's not what pictures of the Queen in Canada tell me. People flock to see her."

"She's a very gracious lady," interjected Barbara. "But I don't consider her *my* queen."

"Well, we have a pair of revolutionaries here, don't we?" Nigel laughed.

"Yes. And you'd better mind we don't unseat you." Evelyn didn't laugh, but spoke quietly to Barbara: "He's a stuck up prig. Can't stand his superior British air."

"You sound as if you're interested in him. Be careful!" Barbara grinned.

"Oh! Don't be so stupid."

Nigel continued driving in silence. Had they silenced him, or was he satisfied with his first impression on them? Evelyn watched the passing scenery out the window. The countryside was lush, trees often arching over the road. In the small towns, people seemed to be happily going about their business, life seemed normal. But she hated flying. That, being so far from home, and Nigel's attitude, aroused the old emptiness and made it worse.

He efficiently wound his way through the narrow Brighton streets until they reached the seafront. The car stopped outside the Belvedere and Nigel expertly moved their cases in and up the elevator. He ushered them into a room on the top floor facing the sea with two single beds and a bathroom. Evelyn looked at her watch. It showed seven o'clock; was that a.m. or p.m.? Nigel saw her puzzled look.

"It's three p.m. here," he advised her. "We're having a family meal to welcome you at six. Get settled, then come to our private suite downstairs and join us. Oh! And Aunt Sophia will be here. She's longing to meet you." With that he was gone.

Evelyn looked out of the window at the sea and beaches. Her mood began to lift. "Hey, look at the view from here." She swirled around the bedroom and bathroom. "And this is a great room. Whatever I think of Nigel, the boys are very generous. I'm going to like it here."

Barbara sat on her bed. "Jetlag is catching up to me. I'm going to close my eyes for a few minutes." And she lay down.

Evelyn was too excited to sleep. "I'll unpack our stuff, and then go for a walk around. See you in a while."

That turned out to be a couple of hours later.

"Hey, wake up we've got to be downstairs in half an hour. Only just time to get ready."

Evelyn's words woke Barbara from a deep sleep. Barbara roused herself slowly and Evelyn watched her go through her clothes. Evelyn's closet system left much to be desired, but Barb found what she was looking for: a straight rich green dress that showed off her auburn hair, shoes to match, and a wide dark belt accenting her full figure.

"My God! You look stunning. Anyone would think you were in love!" Evelyn teased.

Evelyn had decided against her signature jeans for herself and opted for a formal straight black skirt and heels, a long sleeved frilly yellow blouse with a large boat neckline. She looked gorgeous as always. They left their room and entered the elevator.

David had a busy day, not able to meet the girls. After his correspondence with Barbara, he was particularly anxious to meet her. From the pictures he had seen, Evelyn was the model type, slim and beautiful. But his attention always stayed on Barbara; her smile, curvy body, and simple attire, made her look, well, comfortable—someone of the opposite sex with whom he could feel easy, something that had eluded him all his life. After the first email altercation, he found it increasingly easier to correspond with her.

He locked his office door and stepped out onto the sidewalk, turning south past the Royal Pavilion with its colonnades and eastern domes. It was really too hot for a business suit, and by the time he reached the seafront, he had removed his jacket, slung it over his shoulder, and loosened his tie. He always felt his smartest when in a suit and tie—which he wore to work each day—and decided to retain it for his meeting with the girls. He turned left along the seafront for a couple of minutes and entered the Belvedere where he joined Nigel in his suite as Aunt Sophia prepared the table.

David had not seen Sophia for a couple of years, but she looked different to what he remembered. Although over fifty, she still looked younger, taking active care of her appearance. She welcomed him with a big hug, which felt suffocating. He was not used to that closeness.

"Don't know how you can wear a suit on days like this," she said. "I think Nigel looks far more comfortable." Sophia was far too motherly for David. *Just as well I don't see her that often.*

Nigel wore a short sleeve shirt and jeans. "Now remember our plan, to keep this formal so the girls don't become dependent on us. Perhaps I should have worn a collar and tie as well! Keep your distance, okay?"

"But, at least, we've got to make the girls feel at home, haven't we? We can still be friendly"

"Not going soft on me, are you David?"

"Of course not. But being friendly is not a proposal of marriage!"

"Okay, you two," chimed in Sophia, "just enjoy these girls. They'll only be here for three weeks, and then whatever fears you have will pass."

David pictured Barbara and doubted Sophia's wisdom. He felt his face flush. Nigel appeared not to notice. David put on his jacket and straightened his tie. He began to sweat from nervousness and warmth as they heard a knock at the door.

"Well, answer it, man," said Nigel. "I'll get the food brought in."

Sophia stepped forward as David backed off. Sophia opened the door. There stood a short man in short shorts and a bulging Hawaiian shirt with a small boy held by the hand.

"We're having a problem with the TV in room 306. Can we get it fixed?"

As the girls stepped from the elevator they saw the short man in short shorts talking to Nigel. They sauntered towards them.

"See you shortly," Nigel said, "Gotta fix this gentleman's TV. Make yourselves at home."

With that, he disappeared into the elevator with the fat man and the little boy. The boy gave Evelyn a crooked smile.

An older, sharp looking lady approached them and introduced herself as Sophia. She led them into Nigel's suite and introduced David. Evelyn thought David looked ridiculous in his suit and tie, especially in that heat of the day, but said nothing.

Once the door closed, Sophia gave the girls the same smothering hug David detested. David ventured a hesitant hand to the girls, but Evelyn grabbed it, drew him to her and gave David a similar smothering hug.

"Hey, David. We're family here aren't we. Don't let's be too formal. And this is my friend Barb. I think you've been in contact with her, right?"

David nodded, and he and Barbara exchanged a short loose hug. David looked distinctly uncomfortable. *But an appropriate greeting, at least for now,* thought Evelyn. *Just glad Nigel is out of the picture for a few moments. Not sure I could handle that one.* Evelyn was still curious about the correspondence between Barbara and David, and hoped to deepen whatever contact they had made. Her skill at manipulating her own love life would be an asset in "helping" them. Besides, she was jealous of Barbara's poise and hoped to dent that a little.

Sophia ushered them all to the dining table. "We won't wait for Nigel; don't know how long he might be."

David sat opposite Barbara, and Evelyn sat opposite Nigel's empty chair with Sophia at the end. Evelyn was glad to have Sophia as a buffer between herself and Nigel. She kept a conversation up with Sophia who entered in easily, in hopes it would shut out Nigel when he appeared. She was conscious of David and Barbara talking easily, but disappointed she couldn't listen in and still keep up her banter with Sophia. She did notice David removing his tie and jacket at one point. However, when Nigel walked in and sat down, he trampled Evelyn's plans and the conversations taking place by addressing them all.

"How's everyone doing? All comfortable? How's the food? Okay?"

The expected chorus of "yes," "fine," "great," satisfactorily greeted his request. But Evelyn resented his intrusion; she felt she was losing control. Nigel was a perfect host, able, it seemed, to stamp his own mark on the atmosphere. She attempted to assert herself.

"Nigel, you and David have made us most welcome. The room is gorgeous and this meal with you all a memory to keep. I hope our continuing stay comes up to the same standard."

"Here's to that," said Nigel

He uncorked the wine and filled each glass. Evelyn raised her glass. *Probably the high point of the visit, unless Nigel descends to our level.*

Nigel continued. "Barbara and Evelyn. This suite is your home for the time you spend here. Choose your meals from the menu and the staff will serve you here. I may not always be here. Or you can check the 'frig and make your own snacks. Just feel this is home."

"There you are girls," added Sophia, "and if he gives you any trouble, just let me know."

Nigel gave a fake shiver and smiled at the girls. Evelyn looked at the ceiling.

Barbara's response was quite different, mainly because she was the only non-member of the family and so she focused her interest on David. She had enjoyed his correspondence, even looking forward to his emails in the latter weeks and was curious to meet him. She was glad to be seated across from him, but thought, like Evelyn, his dress overdone for the climate, even the occasion. They talked haltingly across the table. Words that came easily on paper were much more difficult in person. Reactions, facial expressions, and body language, provided instant response neither was accustomed to.

"Well. It's so good to meet finally," Barbara began.

"Yes."

"You look pretty smart in that suit." She leaned across the table, "but feel free to take your tie and jacket off if you feel uncomfortable."

He did so, feeling a load removed from his mind in the process.

"Thanks. I wasn't sure how formal this was to be."

He placed his jacket on the back of his chair and went on.

"I want to say how much I've enjoyed our correspondence over recent months—once we got over my first clumsy attempts! Never sure of the correct approach in some situations. Thanks for your patience."

"I must admit we had a bit of a laugh over that, but eventually recognized your English reserve. My mother's English, so I understand it. That's you, David. Don't change."

David grinned. "I soon learned to be less formal as we corresponded."

"I'm going to enjoy your company as much as your letters, I think," ventured Barbara.

David showed instant surprise. "You will? I certainly shall—enjoy *your* company, that is."

Barbara noted his uncertain reaction with contentment; a slow beginning is what she desired in any relationship. She saw David put a surreptitious finger over his mouth and nodded slightly toward Nigel. *Is Nigel listening to their conversation*, Barbara wondered? She gave David a brief nod and continued eating.

Dinner over, Sophia suggested "a stroll along the seafront to orient the girls a bit." It seemed an ideal way to complete the day. The evening was still warm and they strolled west past the Palace pier and the West Pier that stretched out into the English Channel. Barbara listened to David showing off his local knowledge and they dropped behind the other three. She noticed that Evelyn ensured Sophia was between her and Nigel. Barbara pointed it out to David.

"Nigel is afraid of being tied down with one of you, so he said he would be as obnoxious as possible to put you both off."

"So that's what's going on. He's succeeding very well."

"It's all an act. He can act that way easily when he wants to, but he's not really that bad."

"Well, tell him from us he's done his job, so he can relax and be a bit friendlier. After all, we've got to put up with him for a whole three weeks, haven't we?"

David nodded. "I'll see if I can get him to come down from his perch! But I must admit we were both concerned that your visit might upset our female-free lifestyle."

"You were?"

"*Were*, yes. But I changed my feelings after corresponding with you."

"With me? How so?"

"I began to like you, and looked forward to meeting you."

"Well, David, you are more engaging than I expected."

"Sounded pretty stuffy in my letters, did I?"

"A bit," she agreed, "but always interesting." *Perhaps interesting because it came from David. Would it have been with another writer?* The thought was disconcerting.

I want to, to say," David began, "I want to—I'm sorry, I'm a bit tongue tied, you, you look so, so diff—actually, so much more, er, attractive . . ."

Barbara sensed his awkwardness. "Go for it, David, don't be bashful,"

"More attractive than your pictures. Sorry if I'm too personal," he added hastily.

"What girl wouldn't like that sort of compliment?" She tried to be non-committal, but flushed a little, more perturbed that she enjoyed it.

Despite that, Barbara strolled along the seafront feeling content. She was feeling more comfortable with

David than she had expected. She was amused and flattered by his faltering beginning and his hesitant compliments of her. His compliments wouldn't have felt the same from someone else, even downright forward from some. In fact, she welcomed his hesitancy; it showed a measured approach to her, and gave her a sense of security.

They turned back, and after about twenty minutes were close to the hotel.

"Can you girls amuse yourselves tomorrow?" Nigel asked. "We're busy tomorrow, Friday, but we'll have some free time on Saturday and we'll meet up then. The weather's supposed to be fine, so spend some beach time, or just get over jetlag."

"Shopping would be nice," suggested Evelyn.

"Great idea. It's all within walking distance, and you don't need us for that!" Nigel sounded relieved.

Sophia, Nigel and the girls started up the steps to the Belvedere.

"Barb," David called. She turned back. He put out his hand and she responded, expecting a handshake, *A tame ending to the evening,* she thought. But he took her hand in both of his. "I have to return to my apartment, and I'm working tomorrow. But meeting you made this a special day."

"For me too, David."

"Sorry I have to work tomorrow . . . but . . ."

"Yes?"

"I'm free in the evening. Would you come out with me?"

"Yes, I'd like to."

David gave a broad smile. "I'll call you—there's a phone in your room, or I'll leave a message at the desk."

"Okay, see you then."

She turned and walked up the steps. She felt him

watching her and she turned and waved before she entered the hotel.

Evelyn was waiting for her in their room.

"You are positively glowing. Now tell me there's nothing going on!"

"Well, I admit, I enjoyed meeting David. And he's asked me out tomorrow evening."

"Oh, great—for you! You know I'm missing Clark already and it's only been two days."

"Maybe Nigel will take . . ."

"Forget that! I'm not that hard up!" Evelyn began to undress. Jetlag was finally taking its toll.

"You know it's an act."

"What is?"

"Nigel's obnoxious behaviour—he's afraid of us! David told me. He's going to tell Nigel he's safe with us, and to be a bit more pleasant."

"I doubt that will change my mind." Evelyn said as she slipped under the bedclothes.

"You sound too sure of yourself."

A muffled "Huh!" was all the response.

"Let's give it a day or two, and see how you feel." Barbara spoke more to herself, Evelyn was asleep.

8

The next morning, Friday, Evelyn woke first, although both girls slept late—home time was eight hours behind. Jet lag affected her less than Barbara. She went down to Nigel's suite; it was empty. She made herself some coffee and scanned a newspaper laying on the table. Nigel came in after a few minutes.

"I've made coffee if you're interested," Evelyn offered.

"Thanks." He poured one and sat at the table. Evelyn continued reading the paper. She wasn't going to give Nigel any excuse for abuse.

"Sleep well?" Nigel offered some simple conversation. "Where's Barb?"

"Still sleeping."

"Oh!"

"You interested in her?" Evelyn teased.

"Certainly not. I think David's got that covered. Not interested in any girls right now, thanks." He picked up his coffee and left without another word. Clearly, the morning was not Nigel's best time.

He's frightened of us alright, Evelyn mused. *Seems particularly afraid of me!* Evelyn had no doubt most men were attracted to her. She had recognized the apparent brush-off by other guys as protection against that attraction. It appeared Nigel was no different, but she still considered him an obnoxious, stuck-up bore.

She returned to their room and related this to Barbara,

who was dressing.

"I hope he softens up. Otherwise we've got three more weeks of this," said Evelyn.

"You really think he likes you?"

"I see all the signs; sneak glances when he thinks I'm not looking. Particularly while talking to Sophia over dinner last night."

Barbara laughed. "I thought you were studiously avoiding Nigel Aren't you trying to protect yourself?"

Evelyn looked annoyed at Barb. "I'm very happy with Clark—remember him? Don't try to palm me off with some snooty stuffed shirt! Let's get out of here."

"Okay." Barbara was still laughing.

The weather was inviting. They decided on some shopping for the morning and donned tank tops and shorts for walking and stuffed bikinis in shoulder bags for some beach time that afternoon. They found a cute coffee shop and paid about twice what they expected for a cup of coffee; very milky in a soup bowl of a cup. That was sufficient for breakfast. Jet lag was churning Barbara's stomach, and neither felt hungry. They walked through a shopping mall.

"Hey, look at these prices," Evelyn exclaimed. "The price tags are about the same as back home!"

"Don't be fooled by them. Those prices are in pounds, and we pay two dollars for each pound! That's why the coffee seemed so expensive."

"So the prices are actually twice what we'd pay?"

"Right. So keep that in mind!"

That knowledge moderated their natural shopping instinct. They decided to simply window shop for the morning—unless, of course, something completely irresistible turned up.

After lunch, they wandered down to the beach, laid out and worked on suntans.

"I'm going for a swim. Coming?" asked Evelyn.

"Not right now, but go ahead. I'm fine just dozing. The sun's delightful—not too hot."

Evelyn stepped cautiously across the beach—the shingle beach was hard to walk on—and then ran into the waves. After a few minutes, she sat on the edge of the beach, knees up and arms around them. Two bronzed guys, walking the beach stopped to chat with her, and eventually sat either side of her. Evelyn chatted gaily, shaking her drying blond hair side to side as she spoke with one and then the other, enjoying the attention. She pointed back at Barbara a couple of times. After a few minutes, the guys stood up and pulled Evelyn to her feet. They walked together up the beach towards Barbara.

"Hey, Barb. These guys have been telling me that there is great night club activity here in Brighton and wondered if we wanted to join them one night. What do you think?"

Barbara nodded a brief greeting to the men. "Let's get settled here first Ev. Nice to meet you guys. See you." And she turned away.

Evelyn shrugged at the guys, and they walked off.

"You messed that up easily, didn't you?" said Evelyn. "You can be a real killjoy."

"I'm not against a fun night out," replied Barbara, "But I'd want to do some research before I jump into a scene like that. You know yourself what most guys are after. We could at least talk to David or Nigel for advice."

Evelyn plonked herself down beside Barbara. "I guess you're right. And I think Nigel would have some experience. Not sure about your religious friend David."

Barbara grinned. "Wouldn't you feel safer with David than with Nigel?"

"I wouldn't want to feel anything with Nigel, thanks Barb."

The girls both laughed.

Evelyn considered the day had passed pleasantly enough, although the shingle beach was hard to lay on, and they returned to the hotel about four thirty for a shower and to dress for the evening. David had left a message for Barbara he would come for her at six for dinner and to be prepared to walk some.

"What are you going to do while I'm gone?" asked Barbara

"Are you worried about me? I'll be fine."

"Yes, I am a bit. Of course, I'm forgetting, you've always got Nigel, haven't you?"

Evelyn snorted "Believe me; if I see him over dinner, I'm ready for him. I'll give him as good as I get. But don't worry about me. I picked up a novel at the shops this morning. I'll sink myself into some torrid love story."

The girls dressed. Evelyn wore jeans and a tank top. Barbara decided to go with the outfit from last night. "Don't want to expose my wardrobe to David too soon," she said. They went down the elevator together. David was waiting, and he and Barbara disappeared out the front door. Evelyn, wondering what she'd find on the other side of the door, placed her hand on the doorknob. She opened the door to Nigel's suite and saw more than she expected. Nigel was seated at the table opposite an attractive dark skinned girl, clearly of Indian descent.

"Hey, Ev. Come on in. I'd like you to meet Mahita. She's visiting from India. I asked her to join us for dinner this evening." Nigel stood up and grabbed Evelyn's hand in a warm handshake, holding onto her hand and gently guiding her with his arm round her waist, to the seat beside him. "Mahita, this is Evelyn, a cousin from Canada," and turning to Evelyn again: "The waitress will bring us dinner in a minute. Can I get you anything Ev? Water? Coffee?"

"Er, No. I'm fine." In fact, she wasn't fine. Stunned by this sudden change of attitude, obviously a display for Nigel's visitor, she was speechless. *This guy can certainly put on a show if he wants to.* As she recovered, she could only respond in kind in deference to his guest. "Mahita. How nice to meet you. We have found Nigel to be a very kind and gracious host, who's been treating my friend and me so hospitably." She turned to Nigel. "Thanks so much Nigel. I'm sure Mahita will find the same."

Nigel smiled. He was taking it all in stride. When it came to duplicity, Evelyn felt she and Nigel could be pretty evenly matched. Amicable chatter accompanied a pleasant meal. At least the food was real. Nigel carried on a perfectly chivalrous conversation with Mahita, and was hardly less to Evelyn to ensure she was included. Evelyn bristled under this paternalistic behaviour, but could see no way out of the threesome.

Dinner over, Evelyn excused herself and went for a fast paced walk along the seafront, hot and humiliated by the whole charade. If she disliked Nigel before, now she positively hated him for his two-faced performance. She wondered how Nigel could get under her skin like this, and was shocked and frightened at the answer.

She had always suspected that love and hate were two sides of the same coin. *Oh God! I can't be attracted to that snob.* She rebelled at the thought. *I'm not interested in him. I'm not. I'm not,* she repeated to assure herself. She summoned the earlier hatred she had felt, but it was ebbing. Slowly, she began to appreciate Nigel's old English chivalry, even if he put it on. Or was it? Perhaps that was really him. Was it the obnoxious behaviour that he contrived? Barbara had suggested that.

She arrived back at the hotel and went straight to her room. Now she was totally confused. She picked up her book, determined to forget the whole evening; a good love story usually held her attention. But she found it hard to concentrate. How should she handle this new Nigel? Which one was real? She decided to play it safe, and assume the condescending prig was the real one.

Only two days and this trip was turning out badly. Could she survive three weeks in Nigel's company? Perhaps she could excuse herself some of the time, she especially didn't want to be alone with Nigel. *Barb,* she thought, *I wonder how she's getting on. She's enjoying this trip more than I am. She'd better tell me all about her evening when she gets back.*

She tried to get into her book again. Her mind refused to focus, her eyes felt heavy. The excitement and challenge of the day was beginning to fade. Her spirit plummeted. She lay down, and instantly fell asleep.

Barbara was enjoying *all* her new experiences; mostly a deepening friendship with David begun by their emails. As she left the elevator she saw David, again smartly dressed in a dark suit and colourful tie. She smiled broadly. He smiled back. He opened the hotel door for her, took her hand, and held her arm as they descended the hotel steps.

"You know, I'm quite capable of walking down steps myself," she teased as they reached the bottom. He dropped her hand and arm. "But I really like to feel protected," she added, laughing. She couldn't believe he had taken her seriously, but liked his sensitive spirit; it touched a motherly chord. They walked along the seafront for a while, then he turned into town and dived into a narrow alleyway.

"Where are we going?" She hesitated.

"This is known as 'The Lanes,' a series of narrow alleys with specialty shops and my favourite restaurant."

Barbara felt reassured. He led her to a cozy restaurant, where he'd reserved a table for two in a secluded corner.

The staff all seemed to know him. He obviously came here often.

"Being single, I eat out a lot," he explained.

"I love it," she said, looking round at the old world charm with its heavy beamed ceilings and rough stuccoed walls. "I can see I'm going to enjoy this trip to merry old England."

"And I'm enjoying having you here. I'm so glad you came."

"Me too."

"Will you let me order for you? I want to share my favourite meal with you—nothing exotic, but real tasty British food."

"Of course. After looking at the menu, I'm not sure what to order anyway."

They talked little during the meal, enjoying each other's company as much as any conversation. But over a cup of coffee, Barbara mentioned the beach incident and asked David about night clubs.

"If you want my advice, stay away from them. They are notorious for sexual hook-ups, often with unwilling participants. If you don't know the precautions necessary—for instance, never put your drink down; it will get spiked—you're likely to get into trouble very quickly. The problem with disoriented youth—especially girls—coming out of night clubs has prompted local churches to provide patrols called Street Pastors to find and help them. They work closely with the police who provide back-up. Does that answer your question?"

"Wow. That's an eye opener. I'm glad I was cautious with those two guys. They might have been legit—"

"But it's not worth the risk. You did the right thing."

"Thanks David. I'll pass that on to Ev. She was mad at me for pushing the guys away. I know she wants a night out somewhere, but some action—I doubt this type of evening would suit her."

"I'll check with Nigel. He takes a girl out to the Metro Restaurant on occasion. I haven't been there, but they have dancing. Perhaps she might like that. A foursome perhaps?"

"Perhaps not. Ev seems dead set against Nigel. But let's see what we can work out."

"Sure," David said. "Now, it's a warm night, fancy a walk on the seafront?"

They walked back to the seafront and wandered among the milling holidaymakers. It was a warm still evening. David took her hand in his, and she didn't resist; the evening was too perfect. As the sun set, they stopped for a fancy coffee in a seafront café, saying little, just enjoying being together.

"David," Barbara said, as they walked back to the hotel. "This has been a great start to our vacation here in England. And this evening has made it special."

David beamed. "Thank you for coming out with me. I didn't think I would enjoy a night out and feel as comfortable with a girl as I did tonight. You made it easy for me.

They stopped at the steps up to the Belvedere. Barbara gave him a hug, more friendly than the previous one, and a brief kiss on the cheek that surprised even Barbara. She noted David's flush.

"See you tomorrow?" she asked as she freed him.

"Sure. I do have some errands to run in the morning, but we could all meet up for lunch somewhere. Check with Ev and I'll warn Nigel."

"Okay! It's another date," she said as she climbed the steps and after a wave, disappeared into the hotel.

When Barbara arrived in their room, Evelyn was dozing on the bed, her book on the floor,. As Barbara closed the door

Evelyn dreamily asked how the evening went.

"Okay," said Barbara. "David's a nice guy, and really quite shy. I find that comforting and even a bit amusing—it's so easy to tease him. But mostly, I feel safe with him."

"Safe?" teased Evelyn. "That's the last thing I'd want to feel. Where's your sense of adventure?"

"Safely stowed, thank you. Oh! By the way," Barbara said. "I spoke to David about night clubs."

"I doubt he was very complimentary."

"You're right," Barbara replied, "but with good reason." After repeating most of David's comments, she added, "I think we'd be well advised to avoid them."

"That probably puts a nix on any entertainment. Any other ideas?"

"Sure. David suggested a foursome—if you can handle Nigel for an evening—to a restaurant he knows. They have some dancing there and you might enjoy it." Barbara suddenly felt concern for Evelyn. She had been on her own all evening. "We'll come up with something. We want you to have fun. What do you think?"

"Hmm. Maybe."

"Did you enjoy your book?" Barbara asked

"Didn't read much of it. As it happens. I had quite an eventful evening myself."

"You *did*? Tell me about it."

Evelyn expressed her frustration over Nigel. She recounted his underhand ways, as she thought, of getting to her, her subsequent mixed feelings about the whole episode, and her decision to maintain a guarded approach to him.

"You know," Evelyn continued, "Nigel is afraid of me—afraid of being attracted to me. I think he and Mahita cooked this evening up deliberately to push me away."

"But I thought you said Nigel and Mahita were very pleasant to you." Barbara was puzzled.

"Yes, but only to humiliate me. And believe me, they succeeded. I think they resent my attitude and want me to go away. Perhaps I should fly back tomorrow."

"That's ridiculous! Certainly not! We've spent a lot of money to be here, and we need to make the most of it. I think your imagination is running away with you. You'll feel different when we meet up with them tomorrow."

"Okay, maybe. But it's really more complicated than you think." Evelyn seemed resigned.

Barbara wondered if they *would* find greater complications in the week ahead. The phone rang. Barbara took the call. It was Nigel.

"Hello Barb! Sorry to say that I have a problem visitor who will require my attention for a couple of days. Can I leave you in David's capable hands for a day or two? I'll let you know when I can meet up with the two of you again in person."

"I guess so, Nigel. We will miss you." She hung up.

She winked at Evelyn who scowled.

"I told you! Nigel wants nothing to do with me," Evelyn yelled. "And I've a pretty good idea who that 'problem visitor' is—it's that Mahita girl."

"Listen Ev. We are going to enjoy ourselves—without Nigel. I thought that's what you wanted. And he's avoiding me too. It's not just about you!"

Evelyn snorted.

Barbara ignored it. "Let's get a good night's sleep. We're not meeting David till noon, so we can have a late sleep in. We'll work out plans for the weekend tomorrow. I'm sure David will have some ideas as well. Okay?"

Clearly, Evelyn was not in good spirits, and Barbara retired that night with questions on her mind. She was becoming more concerned with Evelyn's inability to handle risky situations that might arise.

9

Evelyn awoke first the next morning feeling lonely. It was Saturday, rarely a good day for her. She felt estranged from her family after the episode with Nigel, and abandoned by Barbara's friendship with David. She looked at her watch; past ten. She put on slacks and a long sleeved top—the weather looked cool—scribbled a note for Barbara and left the hotel. She had no plan, just to wander. The shops often cheered her up, and she explored some and then wandered in and out of the cheesy souvenir outlets on the beach front. She tried the renowned British fish and chips for lunch, but it was greasy and unappetizing. The gloomy weather matched her mood. She rented a deck chair and dozed on the beach for a while. She opened her eyes upon hearing her name.

"Well, Ev. This is a coincidence, or is it fate at work," said one of the guys she recalled from the day before.

They were standing in front of her, and a weak sun behind them obscured their features. Evelyn sat up.

"Remember, you were with a friend who didn't seem delighted to see us," added the second guy.

Evelyn stood up. She wanted to be on a level with these guys and see into their eyes. Barbara's warning still rang in her head, but they *were* good looking.

"Oh, yes. I remember. It was Marty, wasn't it," she said to the dark, tousle-headed one—he reminded her somewhat of Clark. "And you," nodding to the blond one with a couple of day's beard, "are . . . ?"

"Matt," he filled in for her.

"Right."

"Where's your friend?" asked Marty.

"Ha! I left her sleeping off jetlag. Probably still asleep."

Matt asked, "Can we buy you a beer? There's a bar just over the road."

"I'd love one."

They sat at a window overlooking the holiday traffic and people jostling the streets and sidewalks. It all seemed so normal, Evelyn relaxed.

"So! Are you ready for a night out?" Marty asked.

"Maybe. We need to take some time to decide on our plans, so I can't commit right now. I think we are planning a dinner evening tomorrow at the Metro—do you know that restaurant?" They nodded.

"What accent is that? American?" queried Marty.

"Certainly not. I'm Canadian."

"Really. I've always wanted to go to Canada, maybe emigrate for a while some day. We should get together and talk about it."

"Perhaps, but right now, I think I should check on my friend. Thanks for the beer."

Evelyn left as her old fears began to arise. *Better play it safe, not sure about these guys.* She didn't check on Barbara, but wandered aimlessly until she was unsure where she was. She noticed a small general store a block away, went to it and entered. She found a map of Brighton, bought it and the server showed her where she was on it. She took it outside and laid the map against a red cylindrical mailbox adjacent to the curb. She noted the direction to the seafront. *Once there, turn left and I should easily find the hotel.*

The day was becoming warmer, and she found a park with shade trees and laid down for a rest. She dozed.

Barbara awoke late. She looked at her watch, almost eleven. She wandered sleepily into the washroom, finished her toiletries, and then noticed Evelyn was missing. *Probably gone for a walk.* Then she saw the note taped to the door.

> Gone for a walk to think. Don't wait for me,
> have a good day with David. Ev, xoxox.

Barbara felt uneasy, but little she could do about it. She fumbled through her purse and phoned David's number.

"Hey Barb. Just coming to get you guys. Ready for some lunch. Weather's not so—?"

"David, Ev's not here, says she's gone for a walk to think things out. And Nigel begged off. Seems he's got a problem visitor to take care of."

"I know. I got Nigel's message on my answering machine. And maybe Ev needs time to herself. But that leaves the two of us. Can I take you to lunch?"

"Love to, David."

"Be there in fifteen minutes. Really look forward to seeing you again." He hung up.

Barb felt a warm satisfaction, yet . . . She liked the guy enough, but it was only two days, in a distant country, and a totally uncertain outcome. Barbara was normally too well organized not to also feel some apprehension. But like most holiday makers, she figured this was a time to relax, travel around, and ease back on some inhibitions. She would probably spend more than she expected, have her routine broken, and now even explore her feelings some.

She waited in the lobby until an MG TD sports car pulled up and, as he held the door open, she saw it would only seat two in cramped comfort.

"Perhaps I should have warned you I wouldn't be

driving a limousine. But this little beauty is my pride and joy. I've put the hood up as the weather is cool, but I usually drive it down when It's nice. But are you comfortable?"

"Hey, David, this is fun. Vacation is a time for new experiences and I think I'll enjoy this one."

"Me too!—and having you ride with me."

Barbara noted the protection of the handbrake and gear shift between them, in the unlikely event of unwanted advance.

"This must be a few years old?" Barbara queried. "Don't see many of them around."

"Nearly fifty years. Hope I look as good at that age. I . . . I'm sure you will."

Barbara glanced at David. He was looking ahead, driving, but coloured a little. She would normally have brushed off that sort of compliment, but David seemed hesitant. She felt warmed again, rather than irritated.

"Perhaps, David, both of us will if babied like this little treasure."

"It takes time and money, but gives me a great deal of pleasure."

David was quiet as he negotiated overcrowded narrow streets, but finally emerged into the country.

"Thought I'd take you to a favourite country place of mine. You know, old world charm and some good food."

The place looked a hundred years old, maybe more; worn half timbering, heavy stucco and brick infill, with mortar oozing out of the joints. Inside, low heavy wood beams and worn wood floors greeted them.

"Don't be fooled. This isn't that old, but made to look like it. But it gives the atmosphere, doesn't it?"

"Oh! David. I love it. I hope the food is as good."

"What do you think of steak and kidney pie?"

"Ooh!" Barbara screwed up her face. "Kidney doesn't

appeal to me."

"Okay! I'll order steak pie—no kidneys. Would you enjoy that?"

They both agreed on steak pie, which came with a generous helping of chips and peas.

"Coffee to finish? Black or white?" asked David.

They sipped coffee slowly. David fumbled with his napkin.

"Barb. I want to be up front with you. I'm not comfortable with girls; you may have noticed." David went on, hesitantly to explain to Barbara his upbringing and awkwardness with girls. "So if I appear clumsy at times, I hope you'll understand," he finished up. "I enjoy your company so much, I don't want to upset it. I hope this confession hasn't done that already."

Barbara felt embarrassed. This was a novel approach, if that's what it was, but David seemed genuine enough.

"Thanks for sharing that David. I'll keep it in mind." She saw the consternation on his face. She hurriedly added, "but I enjoy your company too."

She changed the subject. "I'm really concerned about Ev. Could we check back at the hotel and see if she's there?"

They drove back to the hotel, mostly in silence. Barbara sensed David's discomfort with his admission and offered the occasional comment to break the silence, to which he would simply nod or shake his head. As they drove toward the hotel, they saw Nigel and Mahita walking along the seafront. It was a welcome distraction.

"Ev said Mahita was probably the 'problem' visitor," exclaimed Barbara.

"I suspected the same. That brother of mine can be devious at times."

"I don't think you're like that, David. You're far too open," Barbara affirmed.

David grinned. "I guess you've seen through me. I can't have secrets from you."

They checked the girls' room, but no Evelyn. David checked with some of the staff, but no-one had seen her. David suggested a walk along the front, perhaps they might meet up with her. As they walked, Barbara felt it was her turn for some confession. She shared Evelyn's recent troubled history to explain her concern. David listened intently. The weather was warming. And they sat on a bench overlooking the sea.

"I don't have any answers," said David, "but we can pray about it."

"What here?" Barbara was alarmed.

"No, of course not, if that makes you uncomfortable. But I'll make it a point of praying about it myself."

"Do you think that will make any difference?" Barbara was mildly curious about his Christian faith.

"That depends on whether you believe in God, and that he's interested in our welfare."

"I believe in God," said Barbara, "But I'm not sure he's interested in us."

"Well. That's a good start. We both believe in God." David smiled at her, a relaxed smile Barbara noticed.

"More than Nigel does, I understand," said Barbara. "His atheism seems pretty illogical to me. Some intelligence must have put all this together." She gestured at the scenery around them.

"Well, Nigel would say it all happened by accident, you know, a totally natural process, but there must have been an origin at some point to get things going, big bang or not."

"But all that talk of demons and angels and that sort of thing goes a bit far I think," Barbara ventured.

"But if you believe in God, you have already ventured into the unseen world. After all God is unseen. In fact,

Nigel suggests that's proof he doesn't exist and we can't prove he does. But absence of proof is not proof of absence. Whether we believe he exists or not, both positions require faith."

Barbara suddenly grabbed David's arm; something had caught her attention. She pointed to two guys sauntering along the beach below them.

"I'm sure those two were the ones that spoke to us yesterday inviting us to a night club. You remember I asked you about it. Are they familiar to you?"

David squinted in the sun. "Nope. No idea who they are. But they look harmless enough. Probably a couple of holiday makers looking for some fun."

"Probably. But I'm still worried about Ev. Can we check the hotel again please?"

David called. Still no Evelyn.

Evelyn awoke to a voice. "You okay miss?" A policeman was looking down at her.

"Yes. Just having a little nap, thanks. Is that a problem?"

"No, miss. But we like to be sure. The parks are often a haven for druggies to sleep off their addictions. Sure you're okay?"

"Yes. Thanks for checking on me."

The cop put out his hand and helped her up. *Probably checking me for steadiness*. But he let her go with, "Have a good day miss." She opened the map, checking her route for the seafront again, and suddenly felt hungry. She checked her watch. Past four. *No breakfast or lunch, just a beer*, she recalled. Reaching the seafront she entered the first bistro she found and ordered a steak and chips. Her stomach became full, but she felt numb and empty. *Wonder how Barb and David are getting on?* She was glad to leave them together, but envious. *How come Barb has all the luck and I'm left wandering the streets?*

As she walked she recounted the meeting with Marty and his friend Matt. Strange co-incidence—or was it? She couldn't think of a reason it wouldn't be. But their invitations were attractive, something to fill the emptiness she felt. Instinctively, she thought it wise not to tell Barbara about the meeting, although she couldn't figure out why; everything seemed above board. But with a tinge of guilt, she decided to keep it secret.

Lassitude led to tiredness, despite her naps, and she returned to the hotel. She met the receptionist who told her David and Barbara had been looking for her. They'd had a light supper at the hotel, and left for the evening. The receptionist promised to call David's cell phone that Evelyn was back and okay. She nodded and went to her room. *Another chance to read my book,* but she dozed on and off.

Barbara and David decided on an evening walk, and were relieved to hear that Evelyn had returned.

"That makes this evening more enjoyable," remarked Barbara. "I couldn't relax not knowing where she was."

"Me too, Barb, because I know how concerned you are for her. But she's a big girl. She makes her own decisions. Don't make yourself responsible for her."

"I don't think you understand, David. We are like sisters. I can't be happy if she is in trouble of some kind."

"Okay! But there is a limit to what you can do. But we'll work on it together."

"Thanks David. I'm so glad to have your support. I've no-one else here to turn to."

Did she see his chest puff out a little? It felt good to affirm him, he seemed fragile at times. But did this mean she would end up supporting him as well as Evelyn? Probably not, but she'd be on guard. They stopped at a

86

coffee shop and had a long fancy coffee. They faced the sea and felt the cool evening breeze brush their cheeks. Barbara felt good, and as she sensed David's gaze on her, felt she looked good too. She felt his compliment coming.

"Barb, if you don't mind my saying so, you look really good this evening."

"You mean I didn't look good before?" she teased.

"Of course not. You just look special tonight."

"David, you can compliment me all you like. I can take it."

They finished their coffee in silence, David with a permanent grin on his face. They walked outside.

"Barb! Anything special you'd like to do this evening."

Barbara though for a moment. "Yes I'd like a ride on a double-deck bus."

He looked surprised for a moment. "You've never been on one, have you? Okay. We'll wait at this bus stop."

Within a few minutes they boarded a bus, climbed the stairs, and walked to the front seat. They sat together, instinctively leaning into each other. Barbara couldn't remember feeling the contentment she enjoyed now. They watched the scenery pass from their elevated position, David commenting and answering her questions.

David began standing up. "Time to change buses," he said, "And find one that will take us back to the hotel."

It was getting late. Buses were infrequent. David found a taxi. He held a rear door open for her, closed it behind her. To Barbara this gallantry felt like a soft cushion she could lean back on. She wasn't used to it. *I could live with this. This guy's sensitive, attentive nature is so different to many North American guys.* David joined her from the other side, gave instructions to the driver and they drove off.

David turned to her. He took her hand slowly in both of his.

87

"Barb! You've no idea how happy you've made me by coming out with me. Thank you."

Barbara listened to this culturally correct announcement, with private amusement, smiling at him.

"David, so thoughtful . . ." she began.

Then a sense of longing overwhelmed her. She passed her free arm around his neck, pulled him toward her and kissed him slowly, gently on the mouth. She pulled back for a moment, stared into his surprised eyes, herself surprised at the sudden excitement she felt.

She let him go. "Oh! Sorry David, I didn't mean to—"

She stopped as she saw the disappointment cross his face.

"Don't say that Barb. I would have paid a ransom for that kiss."

He pulled her toward him, resting her head on his shoulder.

"Please don't say that Barb. We won't kiss again if it makes you uncomfortable. Please, just enjoy being together."

"Of course, David. I *am* enjoying our time together. Don't get me wrong, that kiss is so out of character, it frightened me."

But she felt comforted by David's soothing comments and his closeness. They finished the journey in each others' arms. The taxi stopped at the Belvedere. David opened her door, took her hand, and helped her out of the car. He put his other arm around her waist and they walked up the steps together.

"Hey you lovebirds. What about payment?" yelled the taxi driver.

David stopped suddenly, released Barbara and ran down the steps. Having satisfied the cabbie, he returned to Barbara, still halfway up the steps.

"So sorry," he said. "You had me carried away!" He

put his arm around her shoulders and they climbed to the front door together. They faced each other. Barbara felt unfair to him.

"David, I'd like to try that kiss again, this time deliberately."

It was a gentle kiss, but with all the sweetness of a warm rug on a cold day. Then she felt David's arms, stronger than she expected hold her close. It felt so good. After a short eternity they parted.

"Come in for a coffee?" she asked.

"No. I don't think so. Not this evening. I want to enjoy these last few minutes while they are fresh."

He kissed her again, this time slowly on the lips, holding her hands in his.

"I'll see you tomorrow," he whispered, and abruptly turned and left.

He climbed into his MG as Barbara waved and entered the hotel. Evelyn was waiting for her as she reached their room. Opening the door, she saw Evelyn, apparently relaxed on her bed reading her book. Barbara leaned back against the door, feeling weak and disconcerted by the events of the evening, and wiped her hand across her forehead. Evelyn leaned forward, looking concerned.

"Are you okay?" she asked.

"Oh! Yes. In fact, more than okay."

"Oh! So things went well?"

"We kissed," was all Barbara could say.

Evelyn grinned excitedly. She sat up straight and patted the bed beside her. "Come and tell me all about it."

Barbara shared much of the day's events, but kept some details secret. Evelyn listened intently, sometimes hugging her friend in pleasure for her. But she saw the downside.

"Are you prepared for a long, very long distance relationship?"

"Haven't really had time to think about that. I'm not sure."

"Perhaps we should discuss that soon. And, you know, that's pretty soon for a kiss. We only arrived two days ago. Isn't that a bit quick? You'd reprimand me for that!"

"You forget I've been corresponding with him for months. I think I've been attracted to him ever since that first stupid email—do you remember?"

They giggled at the thought of it.

10

It was gone nine the next morning, Sunday, when Barbara stirred. Her mind was full of the previous day's experience, and left her a little unsettled. Events that moved easily on a warm starlit evening seemed hasty in the light of day. In unfamiliar territory and out of routine, her impulsive actions disturbed her usual planned, orderly life. She didn't necessarily regret what had happened, just felt unnerved by its swiftness.

She opened her eyes abruptly. *Is Evelyn still here?* She looked over to Evelyn's bed. She was there with a satisfied smile on her face. Barbara relaxed. Evelyn opened her eyes. Barbara crossed to her bed.

"Why the satisfied smirk on your face, Ev?"

"Just thinking of you and David." The smile stayed put. "Nice to see you in over your head for once."

"I know, and it worries me a little. I'm not used to things moving that fast."

"That's what I told you last night, what changed since then?

"Daylight, not moonlight, I guess," responded Barbara with a sigh. "Not that I regret it. Just that things feel out of control."

"That's what love does, Barb. It's something you can't control in your predictable, orderly life. Join the real world!" Evelyn sat up, looking gloriously dishevelled. "So what's on the menu for today?"

"Well, David's at church this morning. Said he'd call when he was free."

"And Nigel's off with his 'troublesome' Mahita," added Evelyn grinning, "so I guess we're on our own—for this morning at least. I assume we're still on for a dinner and dance this evening?"

The phone rang. Barbara dashed for it, to Evelyn's clear amusement. It was David as they had both surmised.

"Hey Barb," David was in good spirits. "How are you this morning? No regrets I hope?"

Barbara wasn't going to have a detailed discussion with David in Evelyn's hearing.

"I'm fine David. I really enjoyed our evening yesterday. But we were just discussing plans for today. Are we still going out this evening as planned?"

"Absolutely. I do want Ev to feel included. And I want you to enjoy it too. Look, I'm booked up till after lunch, but can we meet at the Palace Pier coffee shop about two?"

"Yes."

"Good. We'll finalize arrangements then. Can't wait to see you again."

"Me too, David. See you then."

Barbara replaced the receiver. "We meet him at two to make final arrangements for tonight. Does that suit you."

"Absolutely, Barb, and it gives us time to finish our conversation about you and David."

Barbara rolled her eyes. But she felt warmth from her encounter she wanted to express, and Evelyn was clearly experiencing vicarious joy at her expense. They both wanted to discuss it.

A clear sky allowed the sun to bathe the sea with sparkling ripples, and the beach with holiday makers. The girls puton their summer attire and found a small restaurant for brunch and lingered over several, now familiar, bowl-like cups of coffee. Barbara couldn't get David out of her mind, especially the events of the past evening.

"So tell me about David," said Evelyn.

"You know, I've been attracted to David by his emails, but he's not what I expected."

"Better or worse?" Evelyn asked.

"Oh! Better definitely. But he's not at all like someone I expected to fall in love with."

"You mean Prince Charming?"

"I guess so. We all have fantasies and lists about who Mr. Right might be, but it hasn't turned out that way."

"He's not a prince or—?"

"But he is charming," Barbara interjected. "Gallant—if that's not too strong a word—he opens doors, and is continually concerned for my comfort. That, with his shyness and hesitancy, made me feel both pampered and secure. And I find him so interesting; even stuff I'm not interested in. Perhaps that's just me; simply because I'm attracted to him."

"Do you think you're in love?"

Barbara shook her head uncertainly. "How can you fall in love with a bunch of emails?"

"Tell me about those emails." Evelyn had been pressuring Barbara about them for some time, but until now, Barbara had been reluctant to share them. "Barb. I'm curious of course, but I want to see you happy. If some guy treated you badly, they'd have to answer to me."

Barbara shivered. She knew what a tigress Evelyn could be, but basked in the unusual role reversal between them.

"So glad you're my friend," Barbara said. "With you and David looking out for me, how can I go wrong?"

"The emails," said Evelyn curtly.

"Oh, yes! Well, once we understood some cultural

differences, I began to enjoy his letters. After a while, I looked forward to receiving them and eventually, couldn't wait for the next one. They were every day or two towards the end."

"And some you never told me about, right?"

"They were, and still are, private between us. But yes, they do exist. That's all you're going to know about them."

"Barb. I'm just happy for you. But keep me informed. I want to know all—well some—of the details. I suppose we should pay for our brunch and move on."

"I think we've spent more on coffee than lunch," added Barbara with a chuckle.

By this time it was noon. No point in going back to the hotel, as they were meeting David at two. They pulled bikinis out of their beach bags and changed in the washroom. The sun welcomed them onto the beach and they smothered themselves with suntan lotion. As the sun heated up, they sought refuge in the souvenir shops that lined the beach below the promenade. Finally they found the Palace Pier coffee shop.

David was already there, munching a muffin. They were close to his table before he noticed them. He looked up, stood up, and dropped his jaw.

"What's the matter David? Haven't you seen girls in bikinis before?" teased Evelyn.

"Er, yes, but . . . not any girl I might be close to. Others have always been a distant dream. Sorry, you took me by surprise."

"Was it our presence or our beachwear that surprised you?" asked Evelyn.

"Hey Ev," cut in Barbara, "David's embarrassed enough. Leave him alone."

As they sat down at the table, Barbara turned to David.

"We take your surprise as a compliment, David, and

we are delighted to be with such an attractive man."

Evelyn nodded. "Okay, okay. Enough with the flirting, you two. Let's get down to business. Arrangements for tonight?"

David appreciated the question. He took cover with something he could control.

"As you know Barb, my car won't take all three of us, so Nigel has offered use of the 'paddy wagon,' as he calls it, for the evening. He has is own car to ferry Mahita around. But he needs it back by ten to pick up guests when the pubs close. So if I pick you both up at six-thirty, would that be okay?"

"Sure." Barbara spoke for both of them. "What about dress?"

"Very informal. Whatever makes you comfortable. Dress, pants, even shorts. It's a fairly young hangout. But," he risked looking the girls over, and gestured toward them, "probably not bikinis."

"Hey David," said Evelyn. "Not only attractive, but a sense of humour as well. What more could a girl ask for? Now I'm going to walk a little and then spend a couple of happy hours dressing for tonight. See you both later."

David and Barbara watched all the heads turn as Evelyn walked off. The promenade was her fashion runway. She was clearly used to it. Barbara looked concerned.

"Why the frown?" David asked.

"Evelyn is fully aware of her attractiveness as you must have noticed, but seems oblivious to the dangers that it might invite. Especially here, where we don't know anyone. At home, we have a circle of friends that we trust. But here, for Evelyn, every male is a potential predator."

"Well, let's not sit in here and discuss this. It's a glorious day outside, let's take advantage of it—especially as you are well dressed for it."

Barbara smiled at him. "Flatterer!"

David paid the bill and they found a seat on the promenade outside. Barbara breathed in the salt air heavily and smiled contentedly at the sun.

"Why is it David, that when we try to enjoy the good things of life, bad things always interfere. It just doesn't seem right. This could be perfect, just you and I, but I'm continually worried about Ev. It shouldn't be this way."

"Yea. It's what I call, 'somewhere, over the rainbow' syndrome. We're always searching for the perfection that should be. Do you know why?"

"'Somewhere, over the rainbow!' I like that description; I'm so often aware of it, but don't know why."

"Simply put, we all have that instinctive longing for a perfection beyond us—you know, we're all conscious that the world just isn't right; there must be something better."

Barbara mused, "I suppose that's why most people believe in Heaven."

"Probably, but not just Heaven. The Bible declares that what is seen is temporary, but what is unseen is eternal. The eternal is the place we all aspire to, that place of perfection we can only glimpse here. That's what we all experience. But we can experience the joy of that place here on earth. Perhaps we are sensing that now."

Barbara didn't know what to make of this sudden revelation. She thought it all too ethereal and impractical for the day to day physical existence necessary. But she couldn't deny both the longing she often felt, and the contentment and happiness of the moment. She thought again of Evelyn, also seeking similar answers to the emptiness in her life. She felt David's gaze on her.

David said, "You look stunning with that puzzled expression. You look . . . "

"Yes, David? Go on." He needed encouragement.

"You look . . . "

She turned full face to him. "What are you trying to tell me David? I want to hear it."

"You are . . . gorgeous. There, I've said it. But you must have heard that before."

"If I did, I've forgotten. But David, it means more coming from you. And I meant it when I said you were attractive. Has no-one ever told you that—or do you never look in the mirror?" she added with a cheeky smile.

"Actually, no—that is no-one ever told me," David responded. "I've rarely been out with a girl—certainly never long enough to receive that sort of compliment. Never thought about it really—being attractive to women. But I do look in the mirror sometimes," he grinned and relaxed again. "I'll check to see if you're right next time I do."

"We're like a couple of kids, David, trying to outdo each other. But it feels good."

David nodded. For a while, it seemed like the place of perfection they both sought.

Evelyn was still fussing over what to wear when Barbara returned.

"Barb," Evelyn said, "you look fabulous in that bikini. No wonder David lost his breath when he saw you."

"Probably, but he got past it eventually," replied Barbara, "but I'm more concerned about tonight. I particularly want you to enjoy yourself, and put some of your morbid thoughts to rest."

Evelyn laughed. "Don't worry, I won't do anything drastic before I've had time to enjoy myself tonight."

Barbara gave a wry grin.

The time to six-thirty passed quickly, mostly engaged in dressing, redressing, laughing, advising, trying, retrying jewellery, and generally in happy anticipation. Eventually they looked at the finished products. Evelyn favoured the low boat-neck yellow blouse of their first evening at the Belvedere, but with tight jeans and a gold choker. Barbara chose a silk white tank top—showing off her newly acquired tan—and black pants. Some colour? She chose a rust red long bead necklace that hung over her full breast.

David met them in the lobby. Evelyn looked him over. Despite her own problems, she felt protective toward Barbara. *Barb's right, he is a good looking guy. Not handsome, but certainly attractive in his black pants, shirt, and colourful tie. Definitely seems right for her.* David drove them to the Metro, and chatted as they walked to the entrance.

"Really hope you girls have a good time tonight. I thought this place would be fun, but a little more orderly than the average night club, and a lot less risky. I think the food is at least acceptable, and lots of modern dancing you'll be used to. Ready to go?"

The receptionist seated them at a table a short distance from the dance floor. Even before looking at the menu, Evelyn stood up.

"Come and dance with me David. Please."

"Sorry to disappoint you girls, but I don't dance. I've two left feet!"

Evelyn placed her hands on her hips. "You mean you've brought us here and you're not going to dance?" She feigned indignation. "Come on, just rock gently to the music, I'll show you how."

"David. Go!" chimed in Barbara. "I'll look over the menu and have some suggestions when you come back."

Evelyn was a good teacher, showing greater patience for David than she would for others. She liked David, straightforward and clean, but his hesitancy would try her patience. *Not for me*, she mused.

"Hey that's good, enjoy yourself, be freer, that's it, doing good." *He seems to be enjoying himself.* It was a start. *Must loosen him up for Barb.*

They walked back to the table. The food, as David had said, was acceptable if not special. A bottle of wine helped. David refrained as self-appointed "designated driver."

Evelyn suddenly stiffened. She noticed Marty and his friend Matt across the room. She remembered she had mentioned coming here this evening to them over the beer yesterday. She doodled with her food, wondering how to handle his approach which seemed inevitable. *Tell Barbara I forgot to tell her of the meeting? Or pretend it was a co-incidence?* She decided to "play it by ear," if and when they met. She heard Barbara's voice.

"Hey, Ev, don't like the food? You okay?"

Evelyn looked up, smiled. "Sure, I'm fine," and finished what she wanted of the meal.

A young man approached Evelyn. "I'm John, and wondered if you would care to dance with me."

Evelyn brightened right up. "Sure," and joined him on the floor. He was a good dancer, Evelyn style, and the concentration was on dancing, not talking. That suited Evelyn. She noticed David and Barbara walk onto the floor, and lost track of them.

"Mind if I cut in?" a voice asked.

Evelyn turned and saw Marty. "Well Ev, fancy meeting you here, Do you mind if I dance with you?"

"Er, of course not." Evelyn felt trapped as she began dancing with Marty. "I'm here with some friends."

"Great, I'd like to meet them. I take it one is your friend we met on the beach recently."

"Yes, and my cousin who lives here in Brighton. We're visiting with him and his brother."

"Staying with them?"

"Yes, they have a hotel and kindly gave us a room."

"Oh! Maybe I know it. Which hotel?"

Too many questions. "I doubt it. Small and

insignificant"

"Try me."

"Let me introduce you." She led Marty to their table noting David and Barbara's return.

"Hey Barb. Look who turned up here, the guy we met on the beach. His name is Marty. He's here with his friend Matt." She turned to Marty. "This is my friend Barb who you've met and my cousin David."

They all shook hands, Marty seating himself. The conversation was perfunctory, but Evelyn noted Barbara seemed to warm up to Marty, or was it the wine? Eventually, Evelyn and Marty moved back to the dance floor. Barbara and David remained at the table, talking, and Evelyn could see the enjoyment they had in each other. Perhaps Marty would provide some male company for herself while she was here.

"Hey," said Marty, "I'd like to chat more with you about Canada. How about a drink later?"

It seemed like the ideal opening, but Evelyn wanted Barbara on her side.

"I'd like to switch partners and dance with David for a while. Do you mind?"

"Not at all. Perhaps I can get to know your friend a little better. Perhaps she'll dance with me."

Evelyn persuaded David back on the floor for a while, but Barbara was content to sit and agreed to Marty joining her. She chatted with Marty; clearly trying to size him up. Evelyn and David returned to the table.

"I'm thinking of immigrating to Canada," Marty said, "and I asked Evelyn to come and have a drink with me and tell me more. There's a cute pub just up the street,"

"You're welcome to have that discussion here," said Barbara.

"But it's so noisy here, and I like the pub atmosphere," Evelyn explained.

Marty went to get his jacket. And David went to pull the car up to the entrance.

"Besides," Evelyn went on, "I like Marty. He's easier to get along with than Nigel, despite Nigel's best efforts. And, as you know, I enjoy men's company."

"You don't have to remind me of that, Ev. But I'm not sure you should go—"

Evelyn interrupted. "I've got to know him, he's okay, Barb. He even talks about his mother. You always put a damper on things."

"Ev. This is a strange country, and you really *don't* know him. He may be okay, but there is always a risk."

"Of course there's always a risk, but I see little risk here. We're going to be among people. I wouldn't want it any other way. I can look after myself. I'll be fine. Stop being a mother hen."

"Not listening to the 'mother hen' could be your downfall some day." Barbara smiled. "Okay. I should come with you, but we need to get the car back to Nigel, and I want to spend the rest of the evening with David. It's early yet, only about nine. Sure you'll be okay?"

"You don't need to come. Marty said he would get me back to the hotel,"

"Well, have a good time," said Barbara.

Evelyn smiled as Marty opened the car door for her. This chivalry was still something new, and Evelyn was beginning to enjoy it. With that sort of gallantry, a guy should be trusted. They drove for about ten minutes.

"Hey, Marty, I thought you said it was just up the road?" queried Evelyn. She had no idea where they were.

"Well driving distance is relative," Marty replied. "But we're here now."

She saw the pub built into the corner of a two story terrace of shops and apartments, with a sign that said

"The Pink Dragon."

"Strange name for a pub," said Evelyn.

"All English pubs have strange names: Elephant and Castle, Pig and Whistle, and so on. You name it!"

He opened Evelyn's door and escorted her into the pub. It was full and noisy, mostly working class. Men with pint glasses of beer in front of them sat at small round tables, two or three were standing up at the bar, and a few were playing darts at the far end. Marty led her as they squeezed their way to the bar. She was conscious of the looks she got; she was accustomed to them, but felt distinctly uncomfortable at some bawdy leers.

"What'll you have, Evelyn? I'm paying as I'm hoping to gain lots of information about Canada. That's only fair."

"Okay. I'll have a beer." Evelyn usually drank out of a bottle, but she wanted to try an English stein; it was a new experience. They sat at a half empty table. She enjoyed the first beer; wasn't sure she wanted a second. But they were drinking slowly and Marty had lots of questions. She drank about half the second beer, and began feeling dizzy.

"Probably had one too much," she heard Marty explain, as he placed his arm around her and helped her to the car. "I'll help you back home."

"Thanks," she mumbled. "Just get me to the hotel . . . "

11

Barbara and David drove in to the back of the Belvedere and parked the paddy wagon. There was sufficient parking for visitors' cars, including David's. David wanted to ensure Nigel had the keys for the evening, and suggested they finish the evening with a coffee in Nigel's suite. Nigel was watching TV when they entered. He switched the TV off, and seemed eager to talk.

"Good to see you guys. It's been a hectic weekend. How have you been getting along? Coffee?"

They sat around the table sipping coffee.

"We've had a really good weekend, thanks Nigel," offered Barbara. "Had some good weather and managed a bit of a tan so far. Finally, I think, got over jetlag."

"Yea," Nigel responded. "That jetlag can interrupt your day for a while. How was the Metro? And where's my favourite cousin Evelyn?"

David explained, "She met a guy there and went off to have a drink with him. He was interested in Canada and wanted to ask her about it."

"Do you know the guy?" countered Nigel.

"No. But he seemed nice enough."

"We chatted a bit with him," added Barbara, "and tried to get a sense of his character. As David said, he seemed fine, although we warned Evelyn that there was a level of risk, but she was determined to go."

"Ah! She'll probably be okay," said Nigel. "Seems the

sort of girl that can look after herself."

Barbara smiled. "You've got that right. But how was your weekend Nigel? Managed to handle your problem visitor okay?"

"Ah! Yea. Do you remember that fat man who wanted his TV fixed. Well his wife is in a wheelchair—that's why the TV was important—so I offered to help them out; you know, show them around a bit."

Barbara wondered how he could be so blatant.

"Actually, David and I saw you out with Mahita on Saturday."

"Oh! Yes. She's a great girl, offered to help me while she was here. She left this afternoon. Must say I enjoyed her company."

I'll bet you did, thought Barbara, *and you slipped out of that one easily enough. I think you and Ev would be a match for each other.*

The phone rang and Nigel answered it briefly.

"Well, gotta go and pick up some inebriated folk who have decided not to drive. Those civic-minded people sure help my bottom line!"

David handed him the keys for the SUV and Nigel left. Barbara left the table and poured more coffee.

"Some for me?" asked David.

"No, I finished it up. Shall I make some more?"

"Sure, I'll come and show you where everything is."

Barbara opened an upper cupboard, and David came and put one arm around her waist; with his other hand, took her right arm and guided her hand to the package of coffee.

"There, did that help?"

"I could have found it on my own," she replied, spinning around and placing her arms around his neck.

They kissed slowly and softly, their bodies nestled comfortably together. They lingered in that position for minutes it seemed. Neither had that experience before.

"Been wanting to do that all evening," said David as they released, "you look so good. But priorities! Need the coffee."

Barbara grinned and they shared the exhausting work of brewing coffee together. David turned some soft music on, and offered Barbara a dance.

"Don't usually do this, but this isn't a usual time. If you can put up with my clumsy feet I'd love to dance some more."

"So we are at last livening up your dull life are we?" Barbara said as they slipped into each others arms and began to dance.

"Life will never be same again since you girls invaded this country, and you," he kissed her gently, "invaded my life."

The coffee gurgled its ready message.

"I think Nigel's got some biscuits—er, cookies to you—here somewhere," said David opening cupboard doors.

"You seem quite at home here, rifling through your brother's cupboards."

David brought the trophies from his search and fresh coffee for them both. He placed them on the coffee table and they settled on the couch close together.

"This is like a second home. There's an extra bedroom, and when Nigel's busy and needs some extra help from me, I often sleep there. I have my own flat—apartment to you—of course, but I can bed down here whenever. So we can be quite at home here."

"Home, eh! I'm not sure about bringing this up now, but my home is on the other side of the Atlantic. I wonder what sort of future we could have. Is this just a holiday fling—it feels like more than that—or do we have some future?"

"I've tried to put this idea on the back burner, because the way I increasingly feel about you is raising the same questions for me. Barb, honestly, I don't know. Perhaps it's too early to try to plan. Besides, a lot can happen in over two weeks that could change the whole situation. Let's just enjoy the time we have now, and see how things unfold over the next few days."

"We'll have to discuss it sometime, David, but I just want to enjoy our time as well." Barbara turned to David and took his hands. "Right now, I'm just happy to be here with you."

David put his arm around her shoulders and held her face in his other hand. He kissed her gently on the lips, cheeks and eyes—a kiss of comfort, and she hoped, signaling future happiness. They sat back savouring the moment, and feeling some emotional exhaustion. They continued sipping coffee and munching biscuits silently.

Barbara spoke first. "You know, there's something that bothers me about Evelyn, and Nigel for that matter. They are both inclined to lie, or at least, hide the truth they don't want to come out; really a form of deception."

"Not uncommon, Barb. I guess we all do it to some degree."

"True, but with critical issues it can be dangerous. In fact, I have a theory that deception has two parts: the spoken lies to cover it up, and the unspoken truth. What is hidden will always threaten to derail the deception. That silent remainder is a constant snare."

"Interesting. That makes so much sense. But you know, as I think about it, it can relate to life as a whole as well."

"It can? How?"

"If what we believe is not the truth, there must be a hidden remainder that will show the falseness of our belief. After all, believing something does not make it true, however passionately we believe it. At some point, that silent remainder will upset our beliefs."

"I think you've lost me. What belief are you talking about?"

"The truth that God will be our judge if we reject him, but he has made provision for freedom from our guilt if we are willing to receive it. There will be a heaven and hell when good is separated from evil. That is the truth about life, whether we believe it or not. Believing something different is a lie that will eventually come back to bite us."

"Oh! David. I didn't think my little theory would have such huge implications. I really want to know more about what you believe. But not tonight, I guess, it's getting too late. And I want to be in our room when Evelyn comes in. I want to know all that happened to her—get my own back!"

"Okay, Barb. I'll slip out the back way as my car is there. Let's say goodnight till tomorrow. I'll pick you both up for lunch."

It was a long, promise filled, kiss goodbye. The future would tell if those promises would hold.

THE SILENT REMAINDER

12

Evelyn woke slowly. She had difficulty focusing. She felt cold. The surroundings were unfamiliar. As through a fog, she saw a bare bulb hanging from open wood joists and dimly made out concrete walls. The fog closed in. Where was she? She thought back, recalled a flight from Canada, a hotel, the Belvedere, Nigel, David, and Barbara, the Metro, Marty, the pub: then nothing.

"Good. She's coming around," said a man's voice.

As her eyes focused slowly once more, she saw she was lying naked on a mattress on the floor. Several men surrounded her in various stages of undress, some naked. She screamed, and tried to get up, but two of the men pushed her back down and pinned her arms to the mattress.

"Stan. You go first and give 'er a test drive. Let's see how she runs."

Evelyn let out a scream, and one of the men instantly taped her mouth shut.

"Don't want all that noise interruptin' our work, do we?" said a voice.

She felt the first stabs of pain as Stan tried to penetrate her. Somebody handed Stan a jar of Vaseline.

"Need to grease 'er up a bit," said someone.

Again, hard thrusts made her writhe and moan in pain.

"Good to feel 'er move. Makes it more enjoyable," said Stan. "

Her pain together with nausea began to build with the entry of other men. She passed out from the pain, then passing in and out of consciousness and, always awakened with a bucket of water. Slowly her conscious state disengaged from the pain and humiliation and watched dispassionately, as if from above.

The men left one by one, until Marty arrived. He looked at her spent, motionless body.

"Ready for me, beautiful? Saved the best for last."

With that he entered her numb vagina until he satisfied himself. Then he jabbed her arm with a syringe, and she passed out again.

Evelyn shook her head, trying to clear her vision. She was still naked, laying on a dirty, wet mattress on the floor. Her top and jeans were beside it, but her underwear was missing. She scrambled into the available clothes, and fell back dizzy with the effort. Again, she tried to clear her head.

"Hey," she called out. "Help, anyone. Anyone there?"

A door opened, and a half naked man appeared.

"Oh! You're awake. You can go."

He grabbed a fistful of blond hair and half dragged her up concrete steps and pushed her out through a door onto the street. She stumbled on stone steps, landed on the sidewalk, and passed out. Streetlights came into focus. She looked around at an unfamiliar street. Where was she? Slowly, automatically, she stood up, unsteady and with blurred vision, began to walk, weaving from side to side. She had not walked far when déjà vu took hold of her. This experience—or was it place?—seemed eerily familiar. Apparently her confused mind was playing tricks and she walked on. She lost track of time and distance.

A car pulled up beside her. She backed up against a high garden wall. A car window rolled down; an eldery woman leaned out. Exhausted, Evelyn slid to the sidewalk. The lady opened her door; she and an elderly male driver came and helped her up.

"We're street pastors," the woman said, and showed Evelyn her identifying tag. "We were on our way home after our shift, and saw you. You really look the worse for wear. We'd be glad to take you home. Where do you live?"

Evelyn looked at them suspiciously, and remained silent.

"We're only here to help, my dear," the man said. "We'll take you home if you tell us your address."

"I . . . " Evelyn struggled to remember the hotel. "The Bel . . . the Bel something."

"That's not an address—"

"Hotel . . . not my home."

"You're staying at a hotel?

Evelyn nodded, "the Bel . . . Belv—"

"The Belvedere? On the sea front?" the man responded. "We'll take you there."

Evelyn nodded. he hadn't strength to resist, but pushed away help from the woman into the backseat of the car. She felt tired and sullen, still wasn't sure she could trust this couple, but had little option. True to their word she saw the Belvedere come into view, and her spirit revived. The car pulled up in front.

"Let us help you in. We want to make sure you're all right," the woman offered.

But Evelyn's independent streak was returning. "I'll be fine. Thank you so much for the ride."

"Wait," the man said. "Here's my card. If you need anything, please call us. We're here to help."

Evelyn slid the card into her back jean pocket. As a she opened the car door, the woman said they'd wait until Evelyn was safely in the hotel. Once inside, she made for the elevator, glad no receptionist was behind the desk, only a bell to summon one.

The opening door woke Barbara.

"Thank goodness you're back. I was wondering . . ." She broke off, Evelyn was disheveled and crying. It was three in the morning. "Oh my God, what happened to you?"

Barbara rushed across the room and helped Evelyn onto her bed, Evelyn sobbed incessantly. Barbara held her for a full minute.

"I, I do-don't know where, where I've been," Evelyn gasped out. "I w-woke up on a m-mattress on the floor s-somewhere. I found some of my c-clothes and some guy t-turned me out. I walked till I was p-picked up by s-strangers; my p-purse, watch, and underclothes are all m-missing. Th-that's all I know."

Evelyn started crying again for several minutes, and Barbara just held her.

"Ev. You're safe now, you're with me. Are you hurt anywhere?"

"My b-body aches, and my vagina's r-really sore."

Barbara feared the worst. "Let me check."

There was, in fact, some dried blood around her vagina, and Barbara noted bruising on her thighs and arms. Clearly, Evelyn had been badly abused. She told Evelyn.

"I think I was gang raped, I-I can't remember much," she said, tears welling up again.

"Clearly. Tell me what happened when you got to the pub with Marty, or whoever he is?"

"He ordered me a drink, then I remember no more, Perhaps I drank too much, or someone put something in my drink."

"You don't know where you woke up?"

"No. I don't know the city at all."

Evelyn began crying again. Barbara bathed Evelyn's sore feet

Barbara walked over to the phone. "I'm going to call the police, we can't—"

Evelyn sat up. "*No!* No please don't, I couldn't bear the humiliation, please don't—"

"It's okay; I won't as long as you say not to. We'll discuss it later."

"Please, no, please don't," Evelyn repeated and sank back on her pillow exhausted.

"Okay, okay!" said Barbara softly.

Barbara pulled the bedclothes over her. Evelyn renewed her sobbing. Barbara stroked her hair, calming her. And with Barbara's soothing presence close to her, Evelyn fell into a troubled sleep.

Barbara sat back on her own bed. *How could this happen? It happens to others, not to us. Perhaps we shouldn't have come to England. I should have stopped her. Why didn't I go with her? I should have listened to my gut; I didn't feel comfortable with that Marty guy.* These thoughts and questions began to harass Barbara as she tried to make sense of the inconceivable. Looking at Evelyn in her disturbed sleep, the time and place seemed unreal; a bad dream that tormented her with its reality. *What to do now? Who to talk to? Where to go for help?* Evelyn was emphatic: no police. Perhaps she'd consent later. Then Barbara's anger began to build. *Who are these guys who could prey on a woman with impunity?* She couldn't bear to visualize Evelyn used like a rag doll and tossed out like trash. *And they are going to get away with it.* It seemed there was nothing she could do about it.

Evelyn stirred. "Oh no!" escaped her lips as she awoke to her reality. Barbara went and sat beside her.

"How are you feeling, Ev?"

"Terrible! As if I'd been dragged under a bus. Please,

Barb, don't tell anyone. I couldn't stand the boys to know, especially my mother back home. I'm already ashamed and humiliated enough. Don't tell anybody. Please."

Barbara saw the desperation in Evelyn's eyes, and didn't want to distress her further. She dropped the subject.

"Can I get you anything? A cup of tea, something to eat?"

Evelyn sat up in bed. "Just a glass of water, thanks Barb."

Barbara stayed with Evelyn as she dozed on and off, periodically sobbing and shedding angry tears. At about seven-thirty, Barbara began to think ahead. If she went down for breakfast in an hour or so, Nigel would probably ask after Evelyn. How to cover Evelyn's absence? There was no way she would be able to join them with her current unstable condition; it would last for a while yet. However, for the moment Evelyn had recovered some of her poise.

"So how do we cover your absence at breakfast?" queried Barbara, "in case somebody asks."

"Easy. Tell them I had a good time, and I'm nursing a bit of a hangover. That'll give me time to recover."

"Do you feel ready to tell *me* as much as you remember?" Barbara asked.

"I don't remember anything beyond what I told you."

"What do you remember about the pub? Could you remember it if you saw it again?"

"Probably. I don't know. I think the name was Pink something."

"Well, that's something to work on, try and remember Pink what? What about the house you woke in?"

"Just one in a long terrace."

"How many floors?"

"Two, maybe three."

"Would you recognize that?"

"I doubt it. There are so many streets like it."

"What about the people who drove you here? Would they know the area where you were?"

"Unlikely. I must have walked for an hour or more before they saw me. I was disoriented or drunk. My memory is a blur. The only thing I do recall is a strong feeling at one point that the place, or the experience, was something from the past. I think my drugged mind was playing games."

Barbara thought that too vague to be of use. Even if they went to the police, there was little information they could give them, although she still considered it important to report the incident. But Evelyn was adamant. She began to weep again.

"I keep having flashbacks," she said, covering her eyes in a futile attempt to block them out.

Barbara held her close for a few moments. Evelyn wasn't in a shape to meet anyone. She recovered for a moment and pushed Barbara gently away.

"Go and get some breakfast, Barb. I need to be alone for a while. I can cry if I need to, and I want to think."

"Okay. Can I bring you something to eat?"

"Coffee would be good, but I don't think I could hold any food down."

Barbara went down to breakfast but couldn't eat much herself. As it happened, Nigel didn't appear which made excuses unnecessary. She made some toast, poured a cup of coffee, and sat quietly wondering what the next move should be. Evelyn was determined no police or anyone else should know, although Barbara wasn't sure she could handle this by herself. But there was one idea that Evelyn might agree to.

THE SILENT REMAINDER

13

On returning to their room, Barbara found Evelyn in the shower. *Probably been there for a while*, thought Barbara, *trying to feel clean again*. There were some loose slacks and a light long-sleeved top on the bed. Evelyn came out wrapped in towel and gulped down the coffee Barbara had brought. Barbara sat on the bed beside her.

"You know, I shouldn't have gone with that Marty last night. I should have known better. But he seemed okay."

"Listen, I have an idea I hope you will agree to. Please hear me out without interrupting—even if you disagree."

"Okay." Evelyn gave a hesitant nod.

"Ev, I understand your reluctance to speak to the police or your family. But I don't think I can handle this on my own, I need some support and help making any new arrangements we require. If David will agree to keep this in strictest confidence . . ."

Evelyn began shaking her head.

Barbara continued. "Ev, we'll not be able to handle this on our own. We need someone to cover for us if you go back to Canada. I trust David, and he has given us some wise guidance since we've been here. If you agree to this, I'll agree not to go to the police."

"You mean you'll go to the police if I don't agree?"

"No, not necessarily, I know how important it is to you not to. But I *do* need to have someone on our side."

Evelyn was hesitant. "Barb, I desperately need your

support, but I see that you need some support too. But it must be kept to us three. Agreed?"

"Of course."

"I'm still not comfortable with this idea," responded Evelyn, "but you're right. We will need his help. I'll leave you to make the arrangements."

Barbara gave a sigh of relief. "I'll take care of it. We're going to get through this Evelyn."

A specific plan will give Evelyn hope and strength, thought Barbara, *something we both desperately need*. She called David.

David put down the handset. He was mystified and worried by the call. Barbara said they wanted to see him urgently, but would give no details over the phone—above all, not to tell anyone they were coming. He invited them to his office; they could walk there from the hotel. He drove to his office, pulled a chair to the couch, and put the kettle on. *Tea is what they need, sweet and warm if they had some bad experience*, although he could only guess what the real trouble was. He heard the girls coming up the stairs and went to the door to greet them.

He ushered the girls to the couch.

"I've made some tea. Want some?"

Barbara nodded. They both looked harassed. Although Evelyn was looking her beautiful self, he noticed her makeup seemed garish on an unusually white face. He poured the tea, handed it to the girls and sat opposite them.

"So what's the big news?"

"David, I'm so glad you've agreed to see us. We do need your help. But before we say anything there are two critical conditions you must agree to." Barbara looked at Evelyn who nodded in David's direction.

David looked bewildered and responded with a

cautious "Okay?"

"First, you may consider this a police matter, but you must promise you will say nothing to the police."

"If that's the case, I'm not sure—"

"If not, we're finished here." Evelyn rose to go. Barbara caught her hand to restrain her.

"David, this is not an option. You must agree. Please. For me as well as Evelyn."

"Let me hear it first," David suggested.

"Not good enough." Evelyn pulled on Barbara's hand. "I didn't think this would work."

David interjected. "Evelyn. Please sit down. I want to help." Evelyn's demeanour and pasty face were suddenly beginning to make sense. "Ev, have you been assaulted?" Evelyn wilted under the realization her rape was no longer a secret. She sat down again.

Evelyn's jaw set. "I'm not admitting to anything unless you agree not to go to the police."

"Okay. Now I know what it is, and you wish not to make a complaint, I'll keep it to myself. I was concerned it might be something of a public matter I might not be able to stay silent about. But assault is a criminal matter, and at some time the police may be interested. So let me say this. I'll say nothing unless there is a change in circumstances, but if they do change, I'll not do anything without discussing it with you, and then we will only do whatever is necessary together."

"Ev. David's right," said Barbara. "For instance, if the assault surfaced from some other source, it could change the whole situation."

Evelyn was not convinced. "Where else could it come from? Only us three know about it."

David intervened. "Not true, Ev. The perpetrators know about it; maybe others. But Evelyn, for now it's our secret."

Evelyn wouldn't be silenced. "I only agreed to come and talk to you because we will need your help; Barb especially needs some support. But I can't face the pity or accusations that may come if everybody knows." At this, Evelyn began to tear up, but continued defiant. "Barb trusts you, and I want to—we do need your help."

Barbara put her arm around Evelyn. "David, the second condition is that it must remain just between us three. You will help us, won't you?"

David was not used to acting without full information. He was hesitant in agreeing to silence until he knew what the problem was. Now, he wasn't sure what he could do without knowing what the girls needed.

"Evelyn. I can see that you are hurt, angry, and frightened. My hesitancy is not that I don't want to help you, but I want to be sure I have all the details you can give me before promising anything. As my cousin, you are important to me, just as Barb is also becoming increasingly important to me—"

And as if to confirm her impulsive nature, Evelyn suddenly reached across to David and gave him a tight hug.

"Well, I guess we are now all on the same page." David grinned. "Now, tell me all about it."

David remembered Marty and between the three of them they could identify him if it ever became necessary. The pub name beginning with Pink could be helpful. David would look that up in the telephone directory later. Despite his knowledge of Brighton, David could shed no light on the house Evelyn went to. It could be any one of a hundred streets. Finally, David finished asking questions.

"Ev, if this is any comfort at all, you came back. Many with your experience don't. They are sold into the sex slave trade—and many girls, less attractive than you, sell for large sums. It's my guess that the guys who took you are not related to organized crime—yet!"

"Well, that's something to thank God for," Barbara ventured. "But Ev might want to go back to Canada early. That's where we particularly need your help, to provide a ruse for her to go."

"I can help you re-arrange flights, but my first thought is homesickness. But that seems rather thin to me, Ev, you're not the type to get homesick easily! Do you have a sick relative or friend back home you need to return for?"

"I could make one up,"

Barbara was hesitant. "That could easily collapse if our parents started corresponding."

"This needs some more thought," said David. "What do you two think?"

"I need some rest to clear my thinking," suggested Evelyn. "I'm still feeling a little drugged, But Barb, stay close to me, please."

"I wish I could never let you out of my sight again," replied Barbara. "But you'll be quite safe at the Belvedere."

"Okay," said David. "Barb. Go back to the hotel with Ev. Once she's settled, come back here and we can talk this over."

With no other options, and wanting to avail themselves of David's help it seemed a short term solution at least. Barbara wondered aloud if Evelyn might be hungry. She hadn't eaten that day. David kept a fridge in his office with snacks that Ev delved into. But the day was not finished, and a further surprise awaited them later that day.

Having made arrangements to meet with David for lunch, Barbara walked Evelyn back to the hotel. Evelyn still felt weak, and wanted to rest. Even the new familiarity of the hotel room seemed to relax Evelyn. But she wanted to talk first. They sat ready to chat.

"Something is bothering me," said Evelyn.

"Yes?"

"You recall last Sunday David mentioned Nigel went to the Metro sometimes."

"Yes."

"I'm wondering if Nigel knows Marty and set this whole thing up."

Barbara was taken aback by the suggestion. "Oh, Ev! I agree Nigel has his problems, but I can't think of him involved in anything like that. The idea is absurd. What on earth made you think that?"

"It's funny that Marty met me on the seafront Saturday morning—"

"You met him Saturday morning? You didn't tell me."

Evelyn flushed. "I didn't think you'd approve. Anyway, it wasn't really your business."

"After what has happened, it would have been good if you had. But it begins to sound suspicious. Too convenient for a co-incidence. I wish I had known."

"Right. I wish I had confided in you. In fact, I think somebody had tipped him off to my location and he followed me. Otherwise how would Marty be able find me on the seafront? O-oh! I think I mentioned the Metro to Marty. But Nigel knew we'd be there."

Barbara was shocked at the plausibility of the idea. Some-one may well have been feeding Marty information about Evelyn's movements.

"Evelyn, anyone could have been trailing you and passing information back to Marty," suggested Barbara. "Marty himself may have been stalking you. I really cannot believe that of Nigel."

Evelyn was too weak and confused to argue with Barbara. "Okay. Perhaps you're right." It was a half hearted denial of her suspicions.

"Ev, I shouldn't have let you go with Marty—or

whoever he is. I didn't feel comfortable with him; I should have been firmer or come with you," added Barbara. "We both feel we have some blame for what happened, and that's quite natural. We could have avoided what happened to you, but not stopped those guys assaulting someone else, if not you. They are the ones who are totally responsible for what happened. *We* are not responsible for what *they* did."

"But the feeling is still there, even if I know it's not true," responded Evelyn.

"And the feeling may persist for some time, but it's the truth you need to hold onto."

"I know that really." Evelyn squeezed into Barbara's chair and hugged her. "Thanks for being here for me, and for being my friend."

Barbara returned her hug. "Of course." They wept together.

Evelyn got up and began pacing. "Barb, you were right. I can't stay here any longer. I have to go home. It may be an emotional reaction but that's who I am. This place gives me the creeps. I'm almost afraid to go outside in case it happens again. I will feel safe, or at least safer, at home. It'll be no loss to never set foot in England again. Do you understand?" Evelyn flopped back in her chair again.

Barbara nodded. "I suppose you're going to feel every male is a potential predator, but less so in familiar surroundings. But that may take a day or two to arrange. I'll talk to David over lunch and see what we can do about that. Right now, try to rest and sleep if you can. It will help."

Barbara met David at his office again. He'd picked up some sandwiches, and it was a private place to talk without interruption. Barbara let David know of Evelyn's suspicions, but didn't mention Nigel.

"She also wants to return to Canada right away. Can't say I blame her. We need to come up with a story to cover her return from England, don't we?"

"I know. That's a tough one. We must try to come up with something by tomorrow. I'm going to try booking a flight for mid-week. But do you think Ev's okay to fly back on her own? Do you think—I really hope not—you need to return with her?"

"We'll drop her off at the airport and someone will meet her at the other end. She may be emotional, but she is strong. Her biggest problem is keeping all this from her family and friends—especially Clark, her boyfriend back home. That may be her greatest challenge. Anyway, I couldn't be with her all the time. She has to face much of it on her own even if I were there. And I'll be back there in a couple of weeks."

David seemed relieved. He walked Barbara back to the Belvedere where she could to spend time with Evelyn. They kissed and clung to each other for a few moments before Barbara watched David walk back. She walked into the hotel.

Evelyn burst out of the elevator. "Barb, there's a message from my mom. Please come and read it."

Barbara read the scribbled message from the receptionist as the elevator ascended. It read:

> The bank called to say it appears someone is using your credit card. Call them as soon as possible to check on it. Their number: 800-555-7430. Mom.

"Barb! My purse! I forgot all about it. It has my credit card and my driver's licence with my signature. Someone is using my card."

Barbara looked at Evelyn with shock. "Let's go to our room and make the call. This is urgent."

Evelyn made the call, and confirmed that her purse had been stolen. The bank cancelled the card and offered to send a new one to her home address. Then she called her mother. No answer. She left a message saying her purse was stolen, but she had contacted the bank and would return home as soon as possible to straighten things out. She made no mention of the assault.

"I guess we have our cover story, Ev," remarked Barbara, uncomfortably aware this was cementing Evelyn's denial. She called David. He had just walked into his office. She explained about Evelyn's stolen credit card.

"Thanks for letting me know," David responded. "See you tomorrow. I love you."

That was the first time he had used those words, and she felt a brief thrill flow though her.

"I love you too, David. Will I see you tomorrow?"

"I'll pick you up at nine-thirty."

They both hung on the phone in silence, neither wanting to end the call.

"Nine-thirty then, it's a date. Bye my love." Barbara finally replaced the handset.

Evelyn began weeping. "Barb, I'm so happy for you, I really am. But my life seems to be going in the opposite direction. I'm frightened for the future. Is life worth living?"

Barbara held her. "None of us know what the future holds; it could yet be good for you and bad for me. Who knows? Don't anticipate something that may not happen."

But the future depended on choices as well as chance, and Evelyn's choices would determine what lay ahead for her.

THE SILENT REMAINDER

14

Barbara had a restless night. Evelyn woke up a couple of times with nightmares. But on arising, they both attempted to prepare themselves for a new day.

"We made it through the first twenty four hours," Barbara remarked. "Now for today. Are you ready for breakfast?"

"You mean meeting Nigel? I'm not sure; but we have to. Let's do it."

Nigel was in the suite kitchen. He greeted them as they came in.

"Hey, you two. Haven't seen much of you these last few days. David's been hogging you to himself; I thought this was a partnership. What about some change today?"

Barbara went to the kitchen counter and poured coffee for them both. Evelyn sat at the table.

She said, "We're meeting with David again this morning—"

"Be careful. He'll try to convert you," Nigel chipped in. "He doesn't waste any time."

"Maybe, Nigel," Evelyn shot back. "Not that it's any of your damn business. While I'm more inclined to think like you about all this God stuff, I'm sick and tired of your paternalistic, superior behaviour ever since we got here. I'd rather have David's company than yours any day, God or not!" with that she left, slamming the door behind her.

For once, Nigel was dumbfounded. He stood up and

looked at Barbara wide-eyed.

"Where the heck did that come from?"

"Grab a coffee and sit down for a minute. I'll explain," Barbara replied.

"Something happened?" he asked as he poured his coffee and sat down facing Barbara across the table.

"Yes. She lost her purse and someone's been using her credit card."

"Well, she should inform the police."

"Not necessary. She spoke to the bank and they've stopped the card. But more to the point, she's going back to Canada, probably tomorrow, to sort it out. So she's not in the best of moods, and you aren't helping."

"Oh! I see. I'm sorry to hear that. But leaving us just as I was beginning to like her? I like a spirited girl, and she has certainly shown that! Is there anything I can do?"

"I think right now, just stay out of her way! David is helping re-arrange her flight. If there is anything, I'll let you know. Now, I'd better see how she's doing."

Evelyn wasn't doing well. Her anger had turned to tears, and she was trying to clean up her face.

"You know you can stay here if you wish. I can meet with David and sort arrangements with him."

"No. I'll come. I'm not staying in this place alone, where I'm likely to meet up with that pompous Nigel. Thanks anyway, Barb. You're a good friend."

Barbara still sensed Evelyn was attracted to Nigel, despite her well-founded protestations, but now was not the time for banter on that subject. Evelyn was not in a position to know her feelings about anything at that moment. That would take time.

David called that he was a couple of minutes away. The girls collected their things and took the elevator down. David was waiting with the car door open. He apologized for only one seat for the two of them and they squeezed in. Evelyn looked morose, and Barbara filled the car with chatter to lighten the atmosphere. She explained the confrontation with Nigel, even taking some satisfaction in Nigel's temporary embarrassment.

"Evelyn. I'm sorry it's been difficult for you and Nigel," David said. "But right now we need to concentrate on getting you home. I've done some research, and we'll get together over lunch and book your flight."

Over a light lunch at David's office, they confirmed Evelyn's flight next day, Wednesday, and then David drove them back to the hotel to pack Evelyn's belongings. There was a vase of fresh flowers in their room with a note from Sophia, inviting them all to a family meal at six downstairs. Barbara asked Evelyn how she felt about that.

"I'm not sure I want to go, but the guys have both been good to me, so I'll just put up with Nigel this one last time."

Barbara started placing Evelyn's clothes on her bed.

"Barb. Thanks for helping, but I can pack my own clothes. It's a couple of hours before dinner and I want to be on my own for a while. Why don't you and David go for a walk or something, and meet me back here before six."

"You're sure?" Barbara was still concerned about her emotional state.

"Yes Barb. I can take my time packing and prepare myself for meeting the others at dinner." She sounded steady, so Barbara reluctantly let her continue packing and went to the car with David.

"Let's take a drive," David suggested. "There's some beautiful country driving east of here. It will help take your mind off things for a while."

David drove, and Barbara circled his arm with hers. "David. I'm sorry that Evelyn is taking so much of my time. Once she has returned to England, we'll have more time together."

"Of course, I understand. And you're worth waiting for!"

Barbara melted. "It *will* be worth it, I promise," she said with twinkling eyes.

They drove along the white cliffs overlooking the English Channel, and they stopped at Beachy Head. They looked across the English Channel and could dimly see the French coast. They walked to the edge of the cliffs, and looking over, saw the famous red and white lighthouse guarding the cliffs.

"This," said David, "is not only a favourite tourist spot, but a popular, literal, jumping off point for suicides, with a sheer six hundred feet drop to the rocks below." David smiled as he told Barb of its notoriety. "There is a chaplaincy here to counsel would-be suicides. They have deterred several, although not all, who decided to jump."

"Would that be a Christian organization?"

"Yes it is."

"Like the Street Pastors of Brighton?" Barbara queried the significance of Christians initiating that type of work.

"It is a ministry to reflect God's care for people, especially for those going through difficulty. Everyone has worth and dignity."

Barbara nodded pensively. They walked together as close to the edge as they dared and peered over.

"If this were in North America, there'd be high barriers and notices everywhere," said Barbara, astonished there were no barriers.

Holding hands, they walked slowly back to the car, viewing the spectacular scenery.

Barbara spoke as they walked. "I'm glad Evelyn suggested we go out for a while, I think she may have said it for our benefit as well as hers. She has been with me, or both of us, for most of the last two days."

"I'm certainly glad to have you to myself for a while," David responded, squeezing her hand. "But I've been thinking of the suicide leap at Beachy Head. I certainly don't want Evelyn thinking along that line."

"I doubt she will, David, she's far too strong willed for that."

"I hope you're right. But, you know, there are many other ways we can destroy ourselves. I'm concerned that Evelyn's determination to keep this incident to herself is going to come back and haunt her. It's really a form of denial; she's deceiving herself, as well as others."

"But right now admitting it would be humiliating, and she feels she has no options."

"I understand Barb, and she has my sympathy. But I'm thinking when it comes out, as it almost certainly will, it will be worse than the humiliation she is feeling now. More people could be hurt by then."

Barbara furrowed her brow. "David. We need to give her time. She isn't ready for that yet. But I agree with you; I hope she comes to terms with it soon."

"I hope so too Barb. I recall your theory, 'Deception has two parts: the spoken lies to hide it, and the silent truth. That silent remainder always threatens to expose the deception.'"

"I know. But let's keep it the way it is for now."

"Of course."

They drove back to the hotel, mostly in silence, each pondering the possible outcomes of the situation ahead of them.

"So," David said, as they joined Evelyn in their room. "Are you ready for dinner?"

"Yes." she said. "How do I look?"

She had regained her colour, and she had dressed for the occasion. Clearly, appearance was an important part of coping.

"Ev, you look fantastic," said Barbara. "I need a few minutes to change and try to match you Evelyn—and that's not so easy. David, why don't you join Sophia and Nigel downstairs? We'll be down in a while." She disappeared into the bathroom.

David smiled at Evelyn, who guided him to the door. "I'll make sure the wait is worth it," she promised, and gave him a friendly push and shut the door behind him.

The girls entered Nigel's suite shortly after. David wondered how Barbara could look more beautiful each time she appeared. To his eyes, she outrivaled Evelyn. Sophia welcomed them both warmly, seating Evelyn at the head of the table. She seated Barbara and David on one side, with herself and Nigel on the other side, seating herself adjacent to Evelyn.

For this occasion, Sophia ventured herself, being the oldest, as head of the family. "Evelyn, my dear, we're so sorry that you are leaving us, when we've had so short a time to get to know you. We hope this won't be our last time together. It's been great to have you with us, and I hope you've enjoyed our hometown of Brighton—"

On the verge of tears, Evelyn could take it no longer. She took hold of Sophia's arm with both hands and stopped her mid-speech.

"Sophia, I've enjoyed the company of you all, and David has become a close friend. I know Nigel and I have had our differences, but I'm probably to blame as much as he is."

She let go of Sophia and looked beyond her directly at Nigel.

"Nigel. I'd like you to drive me to the airport tomorrow—even if it is the 'paddy wagon'—but you'd better clean off the front seat first. Maybe this is my last chance to get to know you better."

Barbara was speechless and David astounded. *You can just never tell with Evelyn!* But Nigel was up to it.

"You mean I have to deal with another 'problem visitor' tomorrow?"

"Who do you mean?" Evelyn's eyebrows furrowed.

"You, you my dear cousin, Evelyn."

Evelyn shot up from her chair, ran round the table and gave Nigel a not-so-playful punch from behind. "You brute," she cried, and then flung her arms around his neck in a tight hug.

"Hey! Don't choke me, I have one more day to live yet," Nigel yelled.

"And you'd better make it a day worth living," Evelyn shot back. "Or I'll finish the job." And she let him go.

"I will clear the front seat for a real lady." Nigel stood up and bowed towards her. "Your chauffeur, milady."

Evelyn laughed, gave him another, more playful, punch, and returned to her chair; perhaps laughing for the first time since her ordeal. Barbara breathed an inward sigh of relief and David felt her squeeze his hand. The tension eased. Both the meal and the small talk were delightful.

THE SILENT REMAINDER

15

Nigel was as surprised as anyone by Evelyn's request. He was sure she would have nothing to do with him after the morning's altercation. She was stunning, and if for that reason alone, he looked forward to Wednesday morning. The family met at the Belvedere front door to see Evelyn off. Nigel noticed the two girls having a private conversation, hugging each other and shedding a few tears while he heaved her luggage into the van. After hugs all round, lots of waving, and a few more tears, Nigel began their drive out of Brighton.

"Let me get out of this tangle of streets and then we can talk. Okay?"

Evelyn nodded. Nigel drove deftly through the narrow streets and crazy traffic, until they reached the highway.

"Are you quite comfortable madam?" asked Nigel. "And is the seat clean enough for you?" He looked at Evelyn with that charming impudent smile she tried to detest but couldn't help liking.

Evelyn squirmed in her seat, flicked a couple of imaginary bits of dust off the seat. Nigel watched as much as he could without going off the road. Her movements were magnetic.

"Just be a little more careful next time," she warned.

"Sorry, I'll use my binoculars next time." *But not on the seat, on you*.

"I bet you're glad to send me back to the colonies, aren't you?" she asked impishly.

"The colonies are too good for you. A female penal colony would be more fitting, where you can't fog a man's senses."

"I'll take that as a compliment."

"No. Actually, you're too good for the colonies. You should stay here at the centre of the empire and reign as queen."

"Believe me, I'm no queen, or saint. Right now, just remember you're my driver, and act accordingly."

"Yes Ma'am."

Nigel reached into his door pocket and put on his chauffeur's cap. Evelyn doubled up with laughter.

"Oh you're incorrigible . . ."

"Do you know what that means?"

"What, incorrigible?"

"Yes, incorrigible."

"No, but that's what you are."

"So you don't really know what I am?"

"I can figure most men out pretty quickly, but I'm never sure about you."

"So I'm a dark horse, an incorrigible dark horse?"

There was that impudent smile again. She laughed again.

Nigel went on. "And if I am, you're a dark mare. I really don't know too much about you either."

"What would you like to know?"

"How do you keep the boys at bay?"

"That's my secret. Ask me something else."

"You have a boyfriend, don't you?"

"Very definitely, yes."

"Serious?"

"Yes."

"He's a lucky man. Let me know if he throws you over, he'll have me to answer to."

"You'll have to stand in line."

"I believe it. But seriously, tell me something about yourself—family, interests, hopes and so on. If you do, maybe I'll take *my* dark horse out of the stable."

The remainder of the journey went as swiftly as the conversation ran smoothly. Nigel liked his time with this girl; certainly for her looks, but enjoyed her company; she gave back as good as he gave. He parked and walked her through check-in, and up to security.

"Glad to see you smiling," he said. "You've looked so forlorn up to now."

"I really enjoyed my time on the drive with you. It was a real tonic."

"So now I'm a doctor as well as chauffeur." That smile again.

"Just give me a goodbye hug," she said. It was a lingering hug. *It feels like more than a hug*. He shook the thought off, waved goodbye to her as she disappeared and he returned to the van. He felt lonely, something he'd never really felt before. When he tried to dismiss it, he thought of Evelyn. He was sure you could never feel lonely when she was around.

Evelyn sat back in seat 22B, an aisle seat away from the window. Her drive with Nigel had been like an oasis in the desert; he had briefly lifted her from her distress. As she recalled him and the drive to the airport, she was comforted. But now she felt the anger building again: for allowing herself to be abused, at guilt for her inability to speak out, but above all, furious at those who had abused her so violently, and were going to get away with it. Now the fear of flying added to her misery.

A young man in the aisle smiled at her and pointed to the window seat beside her. That didn't help.

"Sorry to inconvenience you," he said, "but I guess we're going to be neighbours for this flight."

Evelyn felt both fear and revulsion at this intrusion and moved out temporarily without answering or looking at him. The last thing she needed was some Casanova hitting on her. He sat down, making himself comfortable, when a portly, imperious woman stopped at Evelyn's side, looked at her neighbour and barked: "That's my seat." She showed him her boarding pass: 22A. He looked at his: 23A. He'd tried it on and it didn't work. Evelyn breathed a sigh of relief as she moved out again to let the exchange take place. Mrs. Portly read or slept for the journey, ignoring Evelyn. That was fine with her.

This was the first time Evelyn had been alone for any length of time since her rape, and she had time to think. Her first thoughts were of Clark. If there was anyone she didn't want to know about her experience it was him— more for the humiliation she felt than uncertainty of his reaction. As far as he was concerned, she would just bury it. *The less he knows, the better for our relationship.* She avoided the idea that this deception, intended to preserve the relationship, was likely to lead to the opposite if it deepened.

But first she had to face her mother who would meet her at Vancouver Airport. Phyllis Summers was the epitome of correctness, and ventured to display it to all. She attended church to highlight her uprightness, and expected children to conform to her example before the world. For Phyllis, this meant an enforced, if anaemic, politeness in all family affairs and maintaining a brittle peace at all times. Appearance trumped reality.

As the plane descended, Evelyn could anticipate her mother's greeting almost word for word. *"Hello dear, glad you made it back safely. So sorry you had leave early. But it was irresponsible for you to lose your credit card. You've no idea the trouble it caused me. Perhaps it would have been better if you hadn't gone. But it's all over now, and we're glad you're back where you belong, my dear."*

The idea that *she* had taken care of a difficulty of *hers*, and Phyllis's refusal to call Evelyn by name always went together. Phyllis reserved the use of Evelyn's full name for any sharp rebuke to bring Evelyn into line; she still employed it, even though Evelyn was over twenty. When he was alive, her father, Mark, approved the household strategy in consenting silence. After all, that was a mother's job, and she did it well, while he had his responsibility to provide for the family. Of course, in this atmosphere there were the occasional flare-ups, but what family didn't have occasional disagreements? Venting cleared the air and enabled the family to return to its preordained status. The ability to maintain the ideal family and to overcome any obstacle was their hallmark.

These memories confirmed Evelyn's decision to hide her experience. She wasn't sure the two of them could survive such dishonour, although Evelyn was less worried about their honour than she was about the additional trauma she would have to endure if Phyllis discovered it. Disapproval over her loss of a credit card would be far easier to handle.

Her thoughts returned to Clark. He wouldn't be at the airport to meet her, because she hadn't informed him of her return. Her mother would object to him being there anyway, unless they were engaged or married—that would upset family protocol. But Evelyn also wanted it to be a surprise; she would call him once she was home.

Mercifully for Evelyn, the flight ended without mishap, and she negotiated her way through customs and luggage retrieval. She stopped for a minute to take deep breaths before pushing her luggage cart into the public space. True to form, her mother was waiting for her, and they hugged.

"So glad you're back safely," said Phyllis. "Was the flight okay?"

"Yes Mom, and it's nice to be home," although Evelyn didn't elaborate on what "nice" meant. But it kept the peace.

"Too bad you had to cut short your trip. Were you having a good time?"

"Yes, Mom, the guys over there were very good to us."

"And the weather was good?"

"Most of the time, yes, Mom."

"The car's waiting, and I'll bet you are tired. Let's get you home."

They found the car, and stacked the luggage in the trunk, and negotiated their way out of the parking lot, over the flyovers leading to the long drive down Granville Street in silence. Being on home ground again, gave some comfort to Evelyn. Even being with her mother was a relief, despite waiting for the inevitable disapproval. Clearly, Phyllis had been holding that for a respectable time.

"You know, you really should take better care of your personal things. Your loss of the credit card took much of my time to resolve." Phyllis wanted to make it clear *she* had resolved it, and it was an inconvenience to *her*.

"It was an accident, Mom."

"An accident is a brick falling on your head. Losing your purse is carelessness," rejoined Phyllis.

Evelyn decided a row over this was not worth it and she was too tired anyway. "Yes, Mom, I'm sorry for the bother it's caused you. I'll take care of it from now on."

"Well, never mind, it's all over now anyway." Phyllis was satisfied and family life was back on track.

Phyllis took the rest of the drive home to reprise Evelyn on family and neighbourhood life while Evelyn had been gone. Arriving home, Phyllis offered Evelyn some supper, but she'd had enough to eat on the plane.

"Thanks, Mom, but I need to unpack and sleep. See

you in the morning."

She went to her room, found her cell phone, and called Clark.

"Evelyn? Where are you? Are you calling from England?" was his immediate response on hearing her voice.

"No, I'm back home. I had to cut short my visit there."

"Why, what happened?"

"Lost my credit card. No big deal, but my mother thought the end of the world had come! But I'm longing to see you. Can we meet at our favourite Robson Street cafe tomorrow?"

"I've missed you terribly too. How about this evening?"

"I've already had an extra eight hours added to today, I need to sleep."

"Alright. See you there at ten tomorrow."

She started unpacking, then decided it could wait and went to bed.

Evelyn woke up about three in the morning. She was wide awake. It would take a day or two before her internal clock would adjust to Vancouver time. Finishing her unpacking, she went downstairs, made coffee, and sat in the kitchen sipping it. The emotional upheaval of the trauma was beginning to subside, and a steady hard edge of resentment at the experience began to replace it. It was directed towards men in general, and anything that reminded her of her ordeal. A growing fear added to her deteriorating disposition: might she be HIV positive? How could she check that without revealing her secret? She chose to put that on the backburner for now. It was one further issue she'd rather not address.

She calculated that it was about noon in England and decided to call Barbara. She would still have about two weeks before returning. The receptionist called her room, but there was no answer. *Probably out with David,* she thought, and was surprised how bitter she felt about that. Her thoughts went back to Nigel and how warm his final hug felt. That was one more thing that was now distant from her, and she became angry. A walk through the Properties might alleviate it, but it was still dark. She walked outside, and saw a youth on his bike delivering the morning papers. Frightened, she hid in some bushes until he passed, and then berated herself for her foolishness.

Returning home, she began preparing breakfast. Not her usual habit, but something to do to keep her dark thoughts at bay.

"Wow. This is nice." Her mother said coming into the kitchen. "Are we turning over a new leaf? The English trip must have done some good after all."

The backhanded compliment angered Evelyn even more. She plonked a coffee in front of her mother, and walked out of the kitchen. Phyllis stared after her, unaware of her turmoil inside. Evelyn drove to the cafe where she was to meet Clark, and sat drinking coffee until ten. That didn't help her attitude, although she softened somewhat when she saw Clark's familiar strong form walking towards her. She ran to him, flung her arms around him, and kissed him passionately, regardless of the looks of those around them.

"Wow. I must admit I've been waiting for that," he gasped. "But can we find somewhere a little more private?"

"Sure. Skip the coffee. Let's drive into Stanley Park and find a quiet spot. Take my car and you drive."

As they drove, Clark asked Evelyn about her return.

"Mom was more concerned with my lost credit card than about me," replied Evelyn

"Why, what happened to you?"

Evelyn was startled by the form the question took. He couldn't know, could he? "Why, nothing happened," she retorted. "I simply lost my credit card. It was just difficult for me to lose it, you know, being so far from home and all."

"Of course, I hadn't thought of that." He pulled into a parking stall in an empty lot

"It seems no-one thinks of me," she blurted out, and immediately burst into tears. She didn't really mean it that way, her outburst was just the culmination of mounting anxiety and anger.

"I'm sorry. I didn't think it would be that big of a deal." He held her tight.

She just wanted to be held, she sobbed for a few minutes longer, while he rubbed her back soothingly. She pulled apart and dried her face, checking her makeup in the visor mirror.

"No. *I'm* sorry. It's just the build-up of leaving Barbara, a flight that frightens me and jetlag. And then the relief at seeing you. Right now, you are the only one I can rely on." She kissed him again and held him tight. "You won't ever leave me, will you?"

"Why would I? You are everything I could want: love, beauty, and passion. I'm passionate too. Why are you so reticent about sex? I don't know how much longer I can wait."

She pulled apart, looking him in the eyes.

"Believe me; it's hard for me too. But here's what I think. If any marriage is to work, it depends on discipline before marriage. Without that, it would be harder to restrain our instincts after marriage. Engaging in sex any time we want now, we may be inclined to do that outside of marriage later. I don't want that for my marriage. I want to settle for the cuddle we had on the boat. That was incredible. I can handle something like that again. But perhaps not too often, it could go all the way."

In fact, she was repeating what she'd heard from Barbara's philosophy of life. It seemed a great defence against Clark's pitch and the nausea it aroused. But as she said it, it began to make sense. For a moment, she partly understood love reaching beyond sex; a love she didn't yet quite understand.

"So if I want to go all the way, it has to wait until marriage, does it?"

Evelyn wondered if she'd gone too far. Would he back off without sex? This additional fear prompted her to push harder.

Evelyn grabbed his hands. "You said you'd never leave me. Is that conditional on sex?"

"Ev. I want you more than anything in the world. You're not making it easy for me. But if that's what you want I guess I have no choice."

Was that an underhand way of saying he'll marry me? She wondered. It was worth an extra push. "Are you asking me to marry you?"

Clark pulled his hands away. "Well, I hadn't thought of it that way. I would give the same respect for any girl I took out. Sex before or after marriage would have to be her decision."

"But I'm not any girl. Are you putting me off?" Her anger was beginning to assert itself again. She thought a measure of threat might make him decide. "Let me know when you're ready, but don't leave it too long." *Am I pushing him to a decision for which he's not ready?* But having gone this far, there was no turning back.

"Evelyn, I want to marry you. But . . ." He suddenly seemed to realize a decision was necessary. "Will you marry me? I can't think of any reason not to!"

"That's a pretty half hearted proposal. The answer to that is no!"

144

He seemed baffled. "I thought that's what you wanted."

"You obviously have no understanding of women. Like any other woman, I want a proposal from a man who is so madly in love with me, he's *driven* to ask me to marry him. Anything short of that is not a proposal. It's just a suggestion!" she looked at him. Was he weeping?

He pulled a handkerchief from his pocket and wiped one eye. From inside the handkerchief he produced a ring.

"Evelyn. I've known for some time I couldn't live without you. After you left, I knew life without you would be empty. I desperately want you to share life with me. Please. Will you marry me?"

Evelyn's disdain for his previous comments slowly turned to incredulity and then astonished joy.

"You bastard. You've been stringing me along all this time." She started pummelling his solid chest. "I should say no, but like you, I have no choice." She flung her arms around his neck. "I desperately want to marry you too. Yes. Yes, I'll marry you," she whispered softly in his ear and felt his arms encircle her.

Eventually, he sat back and placed the ring on her finger. *At last life is going my way,* she thought. *Great news to give Barbara when I contact her.*

THE SILENT REMAINDER

16

Barbara was perplexed after Evelyn returned home. She was sorry to lose Evelyn for the rest of the vacation, especially under the violent conditions that led to it. Would Evelyn be alright alone on the plane? She wasn't sure about Evelyn's request for Nigel to drive her to the airport. If it was not a good trip, it would only add to the burden she already carried. And if it was a good experience . . . ? Her reasoning failed her at that question.

Now two weeks of the vacation lay before her, and she thought of David. The rest of the time was theirs. But her joy at this opportunity was tinged with guilt that Evelyn's loss was her gain. The Wednesday Evelyn left for Vancouver, Barbara spent with David. The weather was fine, and that morning they walked the seafront together, finally sitting contentedly looking out to sea. She felt comforted and safe with his arm around her.

She confided her concerns to David. "I will worry about her until she calls or emails me."

"She will, and I'm sure she'll be okay; she's a strong resourceful girl. You know, we can leave her in God's hands. That is my ultimate comfort. Her future, our future too, is in his hands, and we can trust him with it."

"David!" Anger etched Barbara's voice. She twisted out of David's embrace and faced him. "I'm not likely to trust a God who can allow that to happen to someone I love. And I can't believe you would either. How would you feel if it was me?"

David's jaw dropped. "Oh! Barb. You have every right to be angry, And I would be just as angry."

"So how can you still believe in a good God, David? Where was God when Ev needed him during her ordeal? Why did he let it happen?"

"You think he should have stopped those guys for assaulting her?"

"Of course, don't you?"

"I certainly wish he had. I don't want anyone to go though that trauma, Barb. I may believe and trust God, but I don't have all the answers. What I do know is, God has provided a friend in you and those street pastors who found her. Her abductors let her go—it could have been much worse."

"You think that makes up for it?" Barbara's anger was not mollified easily.

"Of course not. It was a horrific ordeal. But you know that we all, at sometime in our lives, go through difficult experiences—some, like Evelyn, worse than others."

"That still doesn't answer why God lets these things happen."

"Barb, we all have our free will. Others can harm us and we may harm others. God doesn't interfere with our choices and make us into robots. What I do believe is that God will go through the bleak times with us—even the 'valley of the shadow of death.'"

"David, I envy you your trust in God and the sense of security it gives you. I'm just not convinced. I need to think this through. It's so far removed from my gut approach to life."

"I understand Barb. You have a legitimate concern. I have to look at the big picture. God won't violate the free will he's given. One day he will call us all—including Ev's attackers—into judgment for how we use it."

"I just hope those guys get what they deserve—here, not necessarily in some unseen future."

"Barb," said David. "I'm really as angry over the situation. But I direct my anger at Satan who seduces people's free will to oppose God and create chaos. Let's direct our anger at the one really responsible."

"The devil is a stretch for me, David, and I'm not angry at you. Perhaps, I just don't understand what makes you tick in this part of your life."

Barbara couldn't shake the sense of betrayal and resentment she felt, but was unsure where to direct it. She allowed the warm sun and calm sea flood her mind, even as they underlined the total contradiction life seemed to be.

"Oh, David! I don't want to spoil a glorious afternoon. Let's give this whole thing a rest for now."

"Of course, my darling." David let out a sigh of relief "Hey, let's go to my place for lunch. I have something for you."

They drove to David's apartment.

"It's pretty cramped, but it's all I need," David explained as he showed her in. "I'm a lousy cook, and decided I couldn't inflict that on you. I'll order in Chinese. I hope that's okay with you?"

It was. While David was on the phone, Barbara wandered around the limited space. The place could do with a woman's touch; it was pretty spartan and devoid of any decorative attempt. Perhaps she could do something to improve that. The food arrived, and they sat around David's small table, poking their tall packages with chopsticks.

"I'll put some coffee on, and then I have something for you," David said.

David took a Bible down from his bookcase, gave it to Barbara, and sat down beside her.

"I think this will give you a glimpse into my faith," he said. "Read the first chapter of John here," he pointed to it as he opened the book. "When we next get together, I'll try to explain anything you can't understand." He placed a book mark in the page and gave it to her. "On second thoughts, let me have it back for a moment." He opened the fly leaf and wrote in it.

She took the Bible back to see what he had written:

> To my dearest Barbara, with all my love,
> David.

"It's the best gift I could ever give you," he added. "It tells of the greatest gift God ever gave us. But I have something else I want to show you."

As the coffee gurgled, Barbara went to the kitchen counter to pour it. David went straight to a shelf and took down a box. Barbara was curious to see what was so treasured. David opened the box and pulled out the sheaf of emails he'd received from Barbara. He placed it on the table and joined Barbara at the kitchen counter.

"I think I fell in love with you before you came here. I had to keep these emails because I didn't have you to hold."

"You do now," she said, and turning around, wound her arms around his neck. "I can't believe you loved me through my letters—but when I think of it, I was drawn to you by yours; I couldn't wait to meet you. And I'm so glad I did," she murmured as she drew him into a tight embrace.

His arms went around her and he kissed her passionately. They stood for a long moment. Abruptly she grabbed his hands from behind her, and went to the counter.

"Okay," she said, "I'm ready for coffee. You sit and I'll pour some."

They sat and happily enjoyed their coffee together.

Barbara heard from Evelyn late Friday morning. She packed her laptop and walked to David's office. He was at his desk.

"David. Am I interrupting you?"

He looked up with a huge smile. "No. No, of course not, Barb. You can never be an interruption. Seeing you brightens my day. Besides it's almost lunch time, and we can have something together."

Barbara sat down opposite him. "I heard from Evelyn today, and she has some good news. I want to share it with you."

"I want to hear it. Let me clear up what I'm doing here first, and then my time is yours. Grab a coffee for a few minutes."

Barbara poured herself some coffee and sat down on the couch. She sat quietly, not wanting to distract him from his detailed work. She watched David work through the papers left on his desk. She admired the steady systematic way he organized and progressed. She wouldn't label him an exciting personality, although she found him stimulating. But that methodical dependability gave her a settled comfort.

"Okay," he said at last, "open your laptop on the coffee table there. I'll join you on the couch and we'll read Evelyn's letter together."

They sat close together as Barbara read Evelyn's email out loud.

> Hi Barb:
>
> Sorry it's been a couple of days before I finally confirmed my arrival in Vancouver. But it's been eventful. I had a good trip to Heathrow with Nigel. Still not sure if he's putting it on, but I actually enjoyed his company!
>
> My mother met me at the airport and was her usual stodgy self, but I have great news about

Clark. We're engaged! He strung me along as though he wasn't interested in marrying me, and then produced a ring.

I'm so happy about this since I returned home. It has helped me get over what happened in Brighton. Without Clark, I would feel so much alone.

So be happy for me. Enjoy the rest of the time you have with David. You don't need to worry about me.

Give David and Nigel my love.

Love you,

Ev.

"David, you've no idea how happy and free that makes me feel. It would've spoiled my time with you, thinking of Evelyn unhappy at home."

"For me too. That's really good news. I know how concerned you've been for her; you really are a good friend. Now how about some lunch?"

"Do you have your sandwiches?"

"Yes, but they'll keep. This is a time to celebrate. Let's go out for lunch."

They walked to The Lanes and had a simple lunch in David's favourite restaurant. David explained he needed to spend time in the office most mornings to keep his work up to date, but would keep afternoons and evenings free for Barbara.

For her part Barbara found wandering through Brighton fascinating, her memory of The Lanes making it a favourite place to wander. She sauntered through the remarkable Royal Pavilion with its eastern theme, and buried herself in the shopping and souvenir outlets, or, if the weather was good, took time to enjoy the beach. Occasional bus tours out of the city, gave her a glimpse of the winding British lanes with their thatched roofs, thousand year old churches, and occasional castle with its intriguing history. Life in this country was so multi-layered, different from the classless North American society she was used to.

She would rather have enjoyed these experiences with David, but didn't want to disturb his work. But the absence made their times together all the more precious.

The next Sunday, about halfway through Barbara's time in England, David invited Barbara to church. Barbara looked at the old church building. *It must be a hundred years old,* she thought. It reminded her of the dreary perfunctory services she recalled attending with her parents. They went inside. She looked around in amazement. There were no pews, only loose chairs in informal rows. In the platform area, a small band—some guitars, a drummer, and a keyboard—was practising. *Are we coming to a rock concert?* she wondered. *And where's the minister?*

"You can see that we're quite informal here," explained David. "That's our pastor, over there." He pointed to—in Barbara's eyes—an insignificant character in a short-sleeved shirt and jeans. "I'll introduce you if you like."

"I don't think I'm quite ready for that yet," responded Barbara. "Thanks anyway."

"Of course, let me show you to a seat. I have to take part, but will join you later in the service."

David joined a small group of singers on the platform: *a motley crew,* Barbara thought, looking at a group comprising young and old, black and white, male and female. *But at least there's no discrimination!* Once the service started, they must have sung for twenty minutes or more. What struck Barbara was the joy with which they sung, prompted by their belief in God's greatness and his care for them. Then David joined her.

The pastor spoke briefly from Psalm twenty-three,

which Barbara recalled dimly from her childhood.

> Even though I walk through the valley of the
> shadow of death,
> I will fear no evil for you are with me;
> Your rod and your staff, they comfort me.

The words Barbara retained from the pastor's message that morning were: "No-one needs to go through life alone." She wondered how she would cope with an experience like Evelyn's. *I certainly wouldn't want to go through that alone.* But it confirmed to her that, whatever she felt about Christianity, suffering and death were a part of life. How we faced and dealt with them was just as important.

Barbara felt more relaxed during the coffee time after the service. David introduced her to some of his friends there.

"This is my good friend, Kevin," he said. "But don't believe everything he says about me!"

"Barbara. It's so good to meet you," Kevin responded. He was a little shorter than David, with short red hair and goatee to match.

"Kevin believes God made all women beautiful, but I told him God made you extra lovely for me. I told him I discovered that even before I met you."

That compliment and Kevin's affability helped Barbara feel at ease.

"That's right Kevin," she said. "I think I fell for this guy before I met him too."

"Pen Pals Fall in Love." Kevin said, making a banner with his hands as he spoke. "I'm really happy for you both. Dave deserves a great girl like you. I appreciate his faithfulness, to his friends, but especially to God. Do you know what I mean?"

"I can certainly believe that from the time I've known him," Barbara responded, although unsure what "faithfulness to God" meant. She would ask David later. But the conversation moved to more immediate affairs. Kevin wanted to know more about Vancouver, and she discovered Kevin was a probation officer, although he certainly didn't look like one to Barbara. She'd always thought of probation officers as big heavy set men with a stubbly face, a bit unkempt to match their clients.

Barbara had a thought. "Tell me about some of your disreputable clients," she said. "Of course, without divulging privileged information."

Kevin spent a few minutes describing the antics of some of those he worked with, without giving names or details. "I'm surprised you'd be interested," he finished up.

"Ever hear of a guy called Marty?" she asked. "A friend told me about him and some stuff she'd heard about him." David looked askance at her.

Kevin stroked his beard. "Can't say I recall the name, but what sort of stuff?"

"Soliciting girls for the sex trade."

"Hmm. Really bad stuff, eh? Well, I'll keep it in mind. But it's a bit out of my area. There's a police detachment that looks after sex crimes." He turned to David. "Looks like this girl of yours is keeping some dubious company. Better look after this lovely lady."

"I'll have to give her a curfew," David replied.

"And what will you do if I don't keep it? Ground me?"

"I'd find something," David replied, smiling. "But I'd make sure you enjoyed it!"

Barbara smiled back, and grabbed his arm. "I'm hungry, and I'm excited to know what delightful punishment that might be."

As they drove to David's apartment, David questioned Barbara's exchange about Marty. "Do you think that was wise, considering Ev's plea to keep it secret?"

"There's no reason to believe Kevin will connect Marty

to someone who's never made a complaint," she answered. "And you never know what help it might be if Ev decided to speak up. I'm still hoping she will one day."

"I think it would have been better if we'd kept that question to a time when she did open up."

"But that might be too late if Kevin discovers something now we could use later. If it's left till sometime in the future, information may be lost, or memories forgotten."

"I still think it's a risk. Ev will feel betrayed if she ever found out."

"Who's going to tell her? You?"

"No of course not, and you won't will you?"

"Certainly, I won't. So where's the problem?"

"There are always unknown future events, or a slip in a conversation or email, that could let the cat out of the bag."

Barbara sighed, and looked out of the car window for a few moments, then looked back at David. "Hey, this is the second argument we've had," she said. But her eyes twinkled. "We're sounding like an old married couple!"

"Hey that's a sign that we're feeling really comfortable with each other."

"Not that comfortable, I hope," Barbara rejoined, not wanting to lose the newness of their relationship.

David stopped the car outside his apartment and turned to her. "I don't think I could ever see you as old, or less desirable than you are now, however long we're together." he answered. "But as for our discussion about Marty, let's leave him to God—he knows more than us anyway."

"You're not mad at me?"

"No, of course not. We've had a disagreement, but who knows who's right? Let's leave Ev's future in God's hands as well."

"Then I'm not mad at you," she replied smiling, wanting to confirm her equality with David. "But you're right, we don't know the future, and whether my questions to Kevin are going to help or not."

She kissed him on the cheek before stepping out of the car. They climbed the stairs to David's apartment.

Barbara quipped. "And what am I going to find in your fridge, David?" She'd previously noticed his sparse supplies. "Anything worth eating?"

"Not sure. For me, yes. But probably not enough variety for a 'proper' meal for you. But there's always McDonalds." He smiled as he unlocked his door.

"Trust a man to consider McDonalds a 'proper' meal. But we'll make do with whatever you have." She went to the fridge and opened it and surveyed its meagre contents. "Yes, I guess we'll make do. Do you think being with you will make up for it?"

"Certainly, if I have anything to do with it," David replied.

Barbara hummed as she prepared a simple meal, content to be in his company. They spoke infrequently as they ate, David checking items in the Sunday paper. She watched him frown at one column, and then a grin replace it as he read another. It may be a dinghy apartment, and a peasant's meal, but she felt content. *I could live like this with him, if necessary*, and realized how few material wants she needed to be happy. David folded his newspaper and saw Barbara looking at him. She smiled, and he beamed.

"Sorry if you felt ignored during lunch."

"Not at all. I enjoyed watching your facial expressions as you read."

"What did they tell you about me?"

"Little I didn't know already and nothing for you to worry about. Now, do you have any plans for this afternoon?" she asked as they finished their meal."

"No. What do you have in mind?"

"Ev mentioned the name of the pub: Pink something. Perhaps we can locate it."

David reached for the telephone directory and they thumbed through the Ps together: Pink Boutique, Pink Cat Nightclub, Pink Dragon—

"That must be it, I know where that is," cried David. "We could drive past. What d'you think?"

"Oh! Yes! Let's go."

David picked up his keys and they drove to the pub.

"Ev recalled it was on a corner. That must be it," Barbara pointed. "Now what?"

"I'm still cautious about doing anything that might tip someone off to Evelyn's story," replied David. "If Ev decides to make a complaint, at least we've identified the place where it all started."

Barbara wanted to check the place out. "Oh! We can be discreet, David. Besides, I could use a beer. How about you?"

"I could use a coke."

They entered the pub, quiet on a Sunday afternoon, and sat down at a table.

"Are you always this quiet?" Barbara asked the waitress.

"Goodness, no!" The waitress replied." This is a working men's pub, and it'll be crowded this evening like every evening."

"Do you get many drunks?" Barbara grinned as she said it.

"Oh! We call the police in maybe once a month, but they're not usually a problem."

"Any recently?"

"About a week ago, a guy had to help his girl out because she'd drunk too much. I noticed it because I was serving them, and she'd only had two beers—hardly enough to get that drunk on. I assumed she'd been drinking before she arrived here."

"Was the man a regular?" Barbara pursued her questions, while David raised his eyebrows at her.

"No. Never seen him before. Why?"

"I assume if you knew him, you might have reacted differently."

"Probably, but I've never seen either of them since. We don't need that type here, thanks." With that she smiled and left to prepare their drinks.

"Well," said David, "your questions have confirmed this is the place, despite my misgivings. But I think that's enough for now."

"Trust me, David, I won't risk Ev's confidence. I want her to enjoy this time with Clark. And knowing she's in good spirits makes it easier for *us* to enjoy our limited time together."

"You're right," David conceded.

They finished their drinks and drove to the seafront. It was a glorious day.

"David. If we're going to the beach, I need to change into some beach clothes. Can we go back to the hotel first."

"Of course."

David waited outside the Belvedere while she changed. She came out wearing a simple tank top and shorts, but David did a double take. It seemed the more he got to know her, the more beautiful she looked. Any man would be proud to be with her. He locked the car and they walked down the esplanade together.

But their peace of mind would have been sorely disturbed had they known the plans Evelyn, now back in Vancouver, was making for the following Sunday.

THE SILENT REMAINDER

17

Evelyn's ecstatic mood following Clark's proposal of marriage cooled overnight. The knot in her stomach she had experienced before reappeared. This time she had to acknowledge it; she had to deal with the HIV possibility. Barbara would be back in Vancouver in two weeks, but she couldn't wait that long. She made some enquiries among the girls she knew and located a clinic that would do a confidential test. On Friday, a week later, she received a letter with the result. Her eyes fixed on a critical sentence.

> We are pleased to inform you that your recent tests indicate you are negative for HIV. However, your urine indicates a probable pregnancy.

A pregnancy? No. It couldn't be. Her fear of HIV had obscured the thought of pregnancy, but now the idea staggered her mind. She sat, reading and rereading the letter, as if to find a loophole in the words; a clue that might deny their message. She checked the time of the month. Again, she'd lost track of her period during the events of the past days; she was well over a week late. The pregnancy was now more than a probability in her mind.

Of course, the simple answer would be an abortion, but the idea upset her: not so much the loss of the baby, but the trauma she herself would have to face. She pondered the problem for the day. An alternative formed in her mind, but would require immediate action. She guessed Barbara would sharply disapprove and for once she was glad Barbara was not around. She didn't want to hear her advice.

Clark had offered to take her out for dinner on Sunday evening. She called him.

"Clark, about our dinner date Sunday evening. I really don't feel like going out. How about a quiet evening in your apartment?"

"Sure, if that's what you want. I'm not much of a cook, so come at five and help me prepare something."

- - - - - - -

Clark noted that evening would be the first time Evelyn had spent any time in Clark's apartment beyond the occasional drop in to pick Clark up. Evelyn said it was too convenient a place to be drawn into sex. Clark thought she might have had a change of heart, but probably not. Too many discussions on that already. He spent most of the day cleaning and arranging his place for a woman's eyes—even planting a couple of candles on the table—and buying a variety of food to ensure enough ingredients for a decent meal. He also bought a packet of Trojans, just in case.

Evelyn arrived at five, also carrying groceries.

"I had no idea what you might have on hand, so I brought some stuff to be sure," she said, setting her bags on his kitchen counter.

"In that case, I think we should have enough." He opened his fridge door and grinned. He knew Ev adored his dimples.

She looked in and nodded. "I think we'll have enough,"

As he closed the fridge door and turned to her, she circled her arms around his neck and held herself close to him. "Yes. I think we have all we need," she said, then let him go and turned to the kitchen. "Let's get this meal on its way, shall we? What's it going to be?"

Clark was happy with whatever; his primary focus was on Evelyn. He was always stirred by her presence which seemed even more magnetic this evening. Neither of them were especially good cooks, but between them they produced a passably tasty meal. The wine Evelyn had brought improved the meal, set the mood, and relaxed their spirits.

"I enjoyed that—it wasn't too bad a meal," said Evelyn, "and your candles made it special. Are we ready for dessert, or shall we keep it for later?"

"What do you have in mind for the meantime?" Clark wasn't sure how to handle the evening.

"I'd just like to sit and talk," replied Ev. "We should think about the future. We are engaged, aren't we?"

"Of course." Clark didn't care what they talked about; just sitting close to Evelyn made any subject worthwhile. "Okay, let's get married tomorrow, as soon as possible would suit me."

"Hey, a girl needs time to prepare," protested Evelyn. "Sometime in the New Year would be about right."

"That's an awful long time to wait—for *me* to wait."

"Maybe we don't need to wait that long."

"You mean before we're married?"

"Well, we are engaged. Isn't that almost as good?"

Clark felt the excitement welling up within his belly. What was she suggesting? Now? Sometime soon? He feared a let down, and pushed Evelyn away.

"Are you changing your mind about sex Ev? Don't play with me on this. It's not fair and I can't take it any longer."

Evelyn looked surprised. "That's not the response I expected," she snapped. "But if you're so fired up you can't discuss it, then perhaps we should forget I even mentioned it."

"Give me an answer. Yes or no." Clark's voice was rising with uncertainty.

"Don't badger me with questions. I came here for a great evening together, and all you can do is get angry."

Silence. He looked bewildered. She burst into tears.

The conversation was not going the way Evelyn had planned, she had felt sure Clark would happily and easily fall into a sexual relationship the moment she opened the door. But it seemed Clark was more confused by her abrupt change of heart. Would his rising anger dampen his passion? She needed to repair the damage. Perhaps the tears would do it.

She felt Clark's arms come around her and he held her close. Not an ardent embrace, but one of compassion.

"Ev. I'm sorry. I hate to see you cry. Please forgive me."

She stifled some sobs. "Clark. I've been trying to tell you I can't wait any longer either. I'm sorry it came out all wrong."

She felt Clark relax. "Where does that leave us now?" he whispered, kissing her gently.

"It means I'm ready," she said quietly, trembling at the knot that was tightening in her stomach. But there was no going back now.

Suddenly, Clark stood up, gathered her in his arms and carried her to the bedroom and laid her on the bed.

"Are you sure?" he said.

"I'm sure."

He pulled the Trojans from his pocket. Evelyn sat up. She stared at the package in unbelief.

"Where did those come from?"

"I bought them this morning—just in case."

"You mean you planned to have sex with me this evening?" Evelyn looked dismayed. At Clark, because he presumed upon her, but really because she had not anticipated protection. Then, she couldn't be sure he'd really bought them today. Did he have them for other hook-ups he hid from her? Some of the distrust she'd felt for him earlier arose again.

"I bet you keep them around the apartment for the other girls you date," she questioned with a half smile.

"Of course not. You're the only one. You always have been since we first met."

"Then you had others before you met me?" Her distrust was beginning to sideline her plans.

"If I'm honest, yes. It's common practice. But finally I fall in love with you and it changes everything."

At that, Evelyn began to soften. "But you still assumed we'd have sex this evening?"

"As I said, just in case. And it looks as though I was right."

As it turned out, he *was* right. She'd assumed she would catch him off guard with no precautions at hand, and nature would take care of the rest. Now her plan was in jeopardy. If she made a later suggestion her pregnancy was the result of a failed condom—which was most unlikely—that could make him suspicious. After all her protestations, would it be difficult now to persuade him a safeguard was not necessary? She needed time to think.

Evelyn rolled off the bed. "Clark, Let's have our dessert and coffee now. I need time to get over our arguing. I'll make it up to you."

Clark was flushed; from arguing or desire, Ev didn't know, but he needed time to recover also. Besides, he had no choice; Evelyn was on her way to the kitchen.

"But you're not reneging on your decision?" He was still on edge.

"No. I'm not. Just give me a little time. What do we have for dessert?"

Evelyn dished some ice cream into two bowls, and found some blueberry sauce to top it. Clark came up behind her.

"I want you to know I'm still ready," he said.

"I know. I can feel it," and she swung around and kissed him, squeezing him to her to be sure. "But ice cream first—forget the coffee. It takes too long."

They sat together on the couch once more as they ate the ice cream.

"Clark. I really appreciate you thinking of me and buying those condoms. But as our first time, perhaps we can take a chance."

Clark reared back momentarily. "That's a bombshell. Are you sure? Aren't you—?"

"It's not my time of the month, and I want you to get the most enjoyment this first time. Are you going to say no to that?"

Clark was still dumfounded. "Of course not. No guy would say no to that invitation. But, are you *sure?*"

"Just carry me in as you did before."

Clark picked her up gently. She clung tightly to his neck. Wasting no time, he strode into the bedroom, kicking the door shut behind him.

18

A further week passed since the Sunday afternoon Barbara and David began looking for clues to Evelyn's attacker. They had no further communication from Evelyn and Barbara assumed things were continuing to improve for her. It didn't occur to her that by now Evelyn had something more to hide and so avoided writing to her.

Their last Sunday afternoon together repeated much of the sunny weather Barbara and David had enjoyed, and reflected a steady deepening of their relationship. As they walked the Brighton esplanade, thoughts of Evelyn had mostly ebbed from their minds.

Barbara wondered about David's faith. He certainly wasn't reticent about it, but neither did he make it an issue. If he had, she doubted whether their relationship would have lasted, or even begun in the first place. His emails to her had hinted at it, but with no sense of pressure. She enjoyed the church services as much as she understood them, and felt comfortable interacting with the friendly crowd after church. They certainly weren't the kooks and firebrands she associated with TV evangelists.

But having religious faith as part of their relationship was something she needed to explore. She had heard somewhere that religious sentiment went to the core of the soul. It wasn't important to her, she wasn't that particular about religion anyway. She recalled her sharp retorts to David. Perhaps disagreement on this issue could ruin their relationship quicker than the usual cause—disputes over money. They only had a few more days together. How would this affect their future?

They strolled hand in hand along the seafront. She gave David an uncertain glance.

"David. I've been thinking about your faith and I want to know more about it—especially if it's going to be important to our relationship. It's all new to me. I've always thought of religion as far above and away from life. Now, it seems it's facing me in a way I've never encountered before. I need time to think about what you've told me."

"I'm thinking about the time we have left," David said. "This evening is a family supper at the hotel. Tomorrow I have commitments for the morning. That leaves the afternoon and two full days Tuesday and Wednesday. How about I pick you up at noon tomorrow," he suggested, "then we can buy some food to take back to my place, and discuss it over an extended lunch. What do you think?"

"Good idea. And I can make sure your fridge has something appetizing in it," Barbara responded, chuckling.

"And talking of food, it's soon time for the family supper this evening. Sophia will be there. I think since you girls came, she feels she needs to keep a motherly eye on what's going on."

Barbara looked forward to supper with the men that evening. She thought the relationship had improved and she wasn't disappointed. Supper that evening with Sophia and the brothers was upbeat and friendly.

"So what have you two lovebirds been up to today?" asked Nigel.

"We went to church this morning, and spent some time on the beach this afternoon," replied Barbara. "It was a good day."

"So, David's got you converted already, has he?" Nigel

had to push the religious issue.

David responded. "No. But at least she's thinking about it, which is more than you do."

"Nonsense. I think very seriously about my atheism."

Anxious to prevent a heated discussion at a family meal, Barbara turned to Sophia. "What do you think about religion?" she asked.

"I'm a firm believer that religion and politics should not be discussed in congenial company. I know both the boys disagree with me, but I think we should obey that rule for this time together. Don't you think so, Barb?"

"Well, I know those subjects are both volatile, so for us to enjoy this meal together"—Barbara turned to Nigel and David, "I think that would be a good idea."

Barbara's presence as a guest, backing up Sophia's request, left the brothers no option. They all sensed the influence in Barbara's words. Her measured ways instilled confidence in her opinion.

"Okay. Truce for now, but the discussion isn't over, of course." Nigel grinned at David as he spoke.

The talk turned to how Barbara could enjoy her last few days with them. Today was Sunday and she would fly back to Vancouver on Thursday.

"Any special plans?" Sophia asked David.

"We haven't discussed it yet," David replied. "But I'm going to take Tuesday to Thursday off. I have a temp who can fill in for those days. But I have some commitments tomorrow morning."

"Well, maybe tomorrow morning is an opportunity for me to get to know my cousin's friend better," said Nigel. "What do you think, Barb?"

"Are you offering to be my escort for a morning, kind sir?" Barbara replied mimicking Nigel's accent.

"Yes, milady. The paddy wagon is waiting."

"As long as it's somewhere other than the local jail, I'd

be delighted. Is that okay with you, David?"

"Hey, David doesn't own you yet," interjected Nigel.

"Maybe Nigel, but you'd better have her back here by twelve," David warned.

"I might want to take her for lunch," Nigel argued.

Barbara grinned as she watched the exchange. "Oh! Are we going to have a duel—over *me*?"

"Nigel's a hopeless shot, so you're safe with me, Barb," David assured her.

Sophia interrupted. "Okay! Sparring is over. I want to be sure both our British and Canadian branches of the family stay in touch in future. It has been a delight to have you, Barb, and of course, Ev, with us. I hope we see more of you. But I want to suggest a going away banquet here Wednesday evening. All agreed?"

Nods and "yes" murmurs signalled all round agreement.

Nigel stopped Barbara and David as they were leaving.

"Hey, Barb. Join me for coffee about 8.30 tomorrow morning and then I'll take you for a late breakfast at my favourite cafe out of town. What do you say?"

"Sounds good, see you then," Barbara replied, as she and David went to the door for an evening walk.

They had a short brisk walk along the seafront. The evening felt cooler and they soon turned back toward the hotel. They walked quietly, each in thought. Barbara spoke first as they approached the hotel.

"Are you sure you don't mind me going out with Nigel tomorrow morning?"

"Of course not," David replied. "It will be a chance for you to know him better."

"He's not my type anyway," Barbara added, "too changeable and not too reliable. You're the opposite; that's what I love about you." She held him closer against the sea breeze.

"I hope that's not all you love about me. I have other qualities too, you know."

"Oh? I'm looking forward to finding out what *they* are," she said with a mischievous grin.

"I'm saving those for the right girl, and I'm hoping that's you."

"Me too," she answered simply, and they kissed goodnight.

Barbara's main concern on Monday was a morning with Nigel, he was so changeable. But as he seemed at home one on one, she hoped for a pleasant morning.

"Let me get you a coffee," Nigel said as she entered the suite. He brought it over to her ready to discuss the day. "My favourite cafe is about half hour from here up some of the country lanes you apparently enjoy. Drink up and we're ready to go."

If he'd grabbed her by the hair, she couldn't have felt more rushed. She gulped down her coffee, really too hot to drink, and followed him out the back of the hotel to the SUV.

"Is the whole morning going to be a rush like this?" she asked, climbing in the car. "Is this a forced tour?"

"Oh! Sorry. I'm used to setting my own pace. I'll try to slow down a bit."

She wasn't sure how far "slow down" went. It certainly didn't apply to his driving, as he weaved his way through the busy Brighton traffic. But he took a more leisurely pace along the country roads. Barbara relaxed some.

"How was your drive with Evelyn to the airport last Monday?" she asked. "She said it went well."

"More than went well. Very enjoyable. I like her spirit. I'm glad she was here, if only for a few days."

"You didn't have any more arguments?"

"No. I was a perfect gentleman and she was the perfect lady. Couldn't have been better."

"So you parted friends?"

"More than friends. I really think we had a bit of a connection."

Barbara wasn't sure what that meant. *Is this just his typical bravado?* But she was thrilled they had parted friends; Evelyn had enough on her plate without her visit finishing on a sour note.

"I'm so glad," Barbara said. "She was pretty upset at what happened and then having to cut her time here short."

"Glad I could be of assistance. Although I thought losing a credit card was not that big a deal."

"I guess it was for her; you know she's pretty excitable." Barbara wanted to ensure Nigel saw anxiety over a lost credit card was fitting for Evelyn.

Nigel nodded agreeably, and turned the car into a gateway that Barbara recognized.

"You boys have some similar tastes," she noted. "David took me here for a cream tea. It's a most delightful place. And can we make this a leisurely breakfast?—more time than I had for coffee this morning!"

This breakfast was not to be rushed at any time. A full plate from the grill—eggs, bacon, sausage, tomato, and potatoes, followed by fruit waffles and clotted cream. It seemed the British had cream on everything. This breakfast was not for everyday.

"Would you like coffee or tea to finish?" Nigel asked. "Both if you like." He grinned.

"Tea while I'm here. I have all the coffee I need back home."

The waitress brought a tray with a huge teapot, another pot with hot water to extend the tea, and sugar and cream.

"So." Nigel sat back relaxed and took a long sip of his tea. "You asked me about Evelyn. Now tell me how you and David are getting on? I've a pretty good idea already."

"What's that idea?"

"That you are lovers."

"No, *not* lovers. But we are falling in love." That distinction was crucial to Barbara. She wanted it quite clear they weren't sleeping together.

"I'm glad Dave found you. He's been such a klutz with girls."

"He's no klutz with me," Barbara responded sharply. "He's a perfect gentleman—even more than you. He's not only chivalrous, he's also sensitive!"

"You're right. I can be insensitive. David accuses me of being selfish. Perhaps he's right. But I'm used to having my own way, and I doubt marriage is for me. I am concerned though for my little brother, and I couldn't pick a nicer girl for him. But let's talk about you. I'm concerned that David is drawing you into his Christian beliefs. You know it's a pack of mumbo jumbo, don't you? There really isn't any God, or real evidence of *anything* beyond this life."

Barbara felt challenged, not just to defend David, but to defend what she believed at that moment.

"As it happens, I've not accepted David's beliefs, although from the little I know about them, I'm sympathetic. But in regard to belief in God, I'm closer to David than you. Whatever process got us where we are today, to consider it all happened by chance is just nonsense. From what I've learned, there's no such thing as spontaneous generation of life. Life can only come from life—and life comes from God."

"Hey! A real philosopher," exclaimed Nigel. "Just don't say I didn't warn you!"

"Good. Now can we change the subject? I don't want

to finish my time here at war with you. I don't think faith is a game; it's too important."

"Okay. Lesson's over for today! We have an hour or so. I'll drive the long way home for a little more of the country side you enjoy. I promise you'll be home before David goes on the rampage looking for you." He gave that impish grin Evelyn had tripped over.

Barbara smiled back. "You really are fun to be with, less intense than David, but somewhat unpredictable. I can see what Evelyn liked about you. Thanks for a great breakfast and, I assume, a well intentioned warning."

19

David couldn't shake the uncertain feelings he had since his exchanges with Barbara about his faith. He felt a soft barrier erected between them, porous enough to continue enjoying their relationship, but blocking possibilities about the future. It left David with a sense of panic; wanting to see Barbara embrace his faith, but not wanting to pressure her. He was elated to be with this lovely girl, but knew that the faith issue was critical if they were to have a future together. Barbara's look of uncertainty might well be about their relationship as much as her understanding of the faith. After all, it was clear that they must settle this issue one way or another to determine their future.

So he was more nervous about the planned discussion than he'd felt meeting Barbara for the first time. Then, a relationship was only a possibility. Now the relationship had deepened sufficiently a break-up would be traumatic for both of them. His hope for her acceptance or even some form of accommodation was pinned on Barbara's open interest. He found it difficult to concentrate on his work, watching the clock for noon to finally arrive. Not only was he nervous about the outcome of their afternoon's talk, he just couldn't wait to be with her again. Fortunately, the weather was warm and clear, perhaps a sign of things to come.

Then, of course, he wondered how Barbara's morning

with Nigel was going. He wasn't really worried, he had confidence in Barbara. But Nigel could be devious at times—an advantage he claimed from being an atheist; he didn't have to live by any preordained rules. And would he try to convince Barbara to become an atheist too? David was convinced he would. This made him more nervous about the afternoon, although the more he thought about his conversations with Barbara, he didn't think she'd fall for Nigel's pitch. His mood swung between hope and uncertainty, sapping his energy.

At last he completed his work. At twelve, he drove to the hotel, and saw Barbara watching for him from the hotel lobby. Her broad smile at seeing him, her animated scamper down the steps, and her loose summer tank and shorts lifted his spirits. She stopped to give David a hug and kiss as he opened the door of the MG for her. Her shapely legs drew David's gaze as she settled into the seat. *There's a reward for chivalry*, he thought as he closed her door. His joy at her presence revived his strength and humour. Whatever the outcome, he just loved being with her.

"Well, how was your morning with my brother?" asked David, as they began the drive to his apartment. He hoped his insecurity didn't show.

"We had a good time, David, and a breakfast to beat all breakfasts. He has definitely softened since that first drive from Heathrow—almost enjoyable to be with him."

"Not too enjoyable, I hope."

"I said, *almost* enjoyable. But he still has that slightly superior air, although he tried hard not to show it."

"I was pretty sure he would try to convince you of his atheism. Did he?"

"Oh! He tried, but I told him it doesn't make sense. He gave up after that."

David was heartened by this news. *If she was put off*

by his atheism, it bodes well for our discussion. Also, she is less likely to find Nigel attractive. Of course, I can trust Barbara, he told himself again. But Nigel was always better with the girls that he was.

"Well, I'm glad you had a good time with Nigel. It's important to me that you have a friendly rapport with my family."

"I asked him about his ride with Ev to the airport. That apparently went very well too. So I don't think we need to worry about the family or Evelyn."

David grabbed her hand and squeezed it. "Thanks Barb. You would definitely fit well into our family." His hand dropped to her bare thigh, stroked the smooth skin and stayed there.

She looked at him and leaned over. "That feels good," she murmured in his ear, softly kissing him on the cheek.

Barbara had less anxiety about the afternoon than David, mostly because she didn't see their religious views as so critical; something that they could eventually work out like most differences of opinion. Still, if David considered his faith critical to their relationship, she wondered how far she might have to bend if she wanted the relationship to continue—and she wanted that intensely. But where was the balance between being committed to David and faithful to her own views?

This dilemma came to the heart of being a woman. Where was the balance between being faithful to a husband, yet not falling into subservience? Perhaps the heart of the discussion would be between equality in the marriage against what she understood as the Bible's stand for the man to be the head of the house. Then there was . . . but as her head began to swirl, she decided not to cross all those bridges too soon. Things rarely turned out as expected.

She watched David drive, concentrated and alert, negotiating the busy traffic through narrow streets. Despite—perhaps because of—his passion for the Christian faith, he was someone she could respect as a man and enjoy as a friend. Surely, that must be the basis of a secure marriage; marriage was for life. She wanted that as much as she wanted her relationship with David to work.

They stopped at Sainsbury's for groceries. They wandered through the store holding hands the whole time in a subconscious desire to remain together in spite of the life values that could drive them apart. This was an absorbing exercise for Barbara; checking the food offerings and prices compared with back home, but watching what David bought.

"As I suspected," she said, "you go after the starch, protein, and fat, at the expense of the fruit and vegetables."

"Do I?" He looked surprised. "I do buy apples and cabbage occasionally, but I much prefer meat and potatoes."

"And biscuits!"

She pointed to a long aisle with the largest assortment of cookies she'd ever seen.

"Yes," he admitted. "That and the chocolate aisle for me is a bit like a pub to an alcoholic." He grinned. "Don't you eat biscuits and sweets, er, candy, in Canada?"

"Yes but in moderation. We girls need to keep our figure! But more than that, it's important to our health."

"Hmm. Moderation in all things," David mused out loud. "Doesn't that moderation include fruit and vegetables?"

"To some extent. But natural and real food over processed food—your biscuits, for instance."

"I can see we need to discuss a lot of things as well as

Christianity. For instance, how many children do you want?" He grinned again.

"We're not there yet. Let's get the food sorted out first. Start with the easy things."

"Like money and politics?"

"Don't be flippant. We've still got one major hurdle if we want to make this work. And I want to." She held his arm tightly.

"Me too. I'm not really being flippant; just trying to lighten our time together. And you're right. We must be serious about the values important to us." He gave her back a comforting rub; Barbara returned a grateful smile.

At the checkout, she was glad to see a reasonable compromise on their food shopping. *Perhaps our other discussion will be as rewarding*, she thought wistfully.

On returning to David's apartment, Barbara started putting the shopping away. She learned where David kept everything by trial and error. She felt David watching her.

"Hey this is your place, come and help clear up," she demanded.

He came up behind her and placed his arms around her. "I had to stop and watch you; you looked so right working in my kitchen."

"Oh! So now I'm your kitchen maid, am I? If so, I'd better be well paid."

"I'll pay you right now," and he spun her around, took her into his arms, hugging her tightly, and gave her a long, slow kiss. "I've been longing to do this since I picked you up, you looked so good. I hope this is payment enough?"

"No, It's not." She wriggled free and gave him a serious grin. "Come and help put these things away." She pointed to the remaining food items on the counter.

"Okay," he said with mock resignation. "But I need payment too."

"We'll see how well you do," she replied, and then opened all the cupboard doors to check his handiwork. "Hmm. Not bad for a man, I suppose," and gave him a peck on the cheek.

"You call that payment?" he asked.

"That's just a deposit. I'm keeping the rest for later, depending."

"Depending on what?"

"Not sure yet. I'll let you know when I decide." *Important for a woman to maintain the air of mystery that men rarely understand.* David's puzzled look confirmed her view. "Now! What are we going to have for lunch?"

Barbara enjoyed the closeness of the activity as the two of them worked together preparing lunch. She felt David's hand brushing her every time he passed behind her. By the time they had finished peeling, chopping, dicing and everything was in the oven or pan, David considered the result.

"This isn't lunch, this is dinner!" he observed. "By the time it's cooked it'll be two o'clock at least, so we'll consider it dinner, shall we?"

Barbara nodded. "And there's some time for the meal to cook, so let's sit and relax for a bit."

They sat together on the couch, David half turned towards Barbara, with his legs bent up beside him. *How do I start the conversation?* David opted to jump right in.

"You know, Barb, there are a couple of things you should know about the sort of response that Christians receive. Paul letters in the Bible predicted two thousand years ago that Christianity would be an offence and foolishness to those who disagree with it. This has been confirmed throughout the succeeding history by the ongoing persecution of Christians."

"But that's not true now, is it? We all have freedom to

worship in the west, don't we?"

"True, but that is an exception rather than the rule. In other parts of the world Christians are imprisoned, oppressed, and killed for their faith. In fact, it is calculated that more Christians were martyred for their faith in the twentieth century than in all of the nineteen hundred years before."

Barbara pulled a questioning face. "That's news to me. I rarely hear of Christians being persecuted."

"That's because the subject isn't newsworthy to most people. But inside Christian circles a constant parade of incidents comes to us, especially from China and Islamic countries."

"I must admit," Barbara said, "I hear a stream of anti-Christian rhetoric even in Canada, usually against some bigoted statements by Christians. And that criticism isn't hard to agree with."

"Of course, the only news you hear is the bad news, and it all builds up to animosity against Christianity that can lead to persecution of Christians. But my concern is that you, or anyone else who embraces Christianity, will not be popular with everybody. You need to know that."

Barbara raised the question. "Then why would anyone want to be a Christian?"

"That's a valid question. At first glance there are too many arguments against Christianity. Suffering, the reliability of the Bible, other religions, a divine Christ, absence of proof, and so on."

"Exactly, I've thought of all those at various times." So how do you answer them?"

"By an encounter with Jesus Christ. Those questions don't go away, but the relationship with him becomes more important. It becomes intensely personal."

Barbara shook her head. "I don't understand that."

"Well, let me give you an example from life. Have you

ever put together a list of features you require in a husband?"

"Every girl does. For me, he should be intelligent, have a well established income, be well built for my protection, sensitive, romantic, and have a sense of humour."

"And I'm sure you could add a few more to that! You said you love me. I doubt I've fulfilled all those ideals?"

"Okay. some, not all. But it's you I love. Really, you are more important than the ideals I was looking for. Now, you're my ideal."

David melted under this revelation. "Is that really true, my darling?" asked David. "You are certainly the answer to all my desires. And what's true of us is also true of those who meet Jesus Christ personally. All their questions—legitimate though they are—become secondary to the relationship with God they suddenly discover."

"Okay. I see your point. And are all the questions answered?"

"Some maybe, others perhaps never. God desires us to come to him on his terms, not ours. His question to us is: are we willing to trust him for what we don't understand? It's up to us to decide which way we—"

Suddenly, Barbara shot up and rushed into the kitchen. "We forgot the oven," she yelled back. "I hope our dinner isn't burnt!"

David followed her, and they pulled the meat from the oven. "Looks good to me," David said. "I think it's time we ate. The smell is making me hungry."

"All that discussion is making me hungry too," Barbara added. "You're right, it *is* time to eat."

David laid the table while Barbara set the plates and brought them to the table.

"Are you thankful for this good meal?" David asked

"Absolutely, I can't wait."

"Then let's give thanks," suggested David, and they

both bowed their heads.

Dinner over, David went to the kitchen, took the dirty dishes, and loaded the dishwasher. Barbara made coffee, pulled mugs off the shelf, and retrieved cream from the fridge.

"I love doing things with you—even pottering in the kitchen like this," she said. "It confirms my idea that love is not just making out, but involves the whole of life together."

He nodded.

As he closed the dishwasher, David wondered how Barbara was reacting to their discussion. He greatly wanted to share his faith with her, but only as she was ready for it. *Let her ask the questions when she is ready*, he had decided. But he knew how important common ground on faith was; to be able to share in the deepest beliefs of life could only deepen marriage. *Not that we're anywhere near marriage yet*, he hastily reminded himself.

"Agreed," he said, "Go and make yourself comfortable on the couch and I'll pour the coffee." He brought a tray with coffee and cookies, and placed them on the coffee table.

"Look!" he went on. "It's a beautiful day out there, too nice to stay in any longer. Let's finish our coffee and continue our conversation on the seafront."

She smiled and nuzzled against him. They sat back and enjoyed the coffee quietly, each absorbed in their thoughts. She linked her arm through his, grabbed his hand and leaned into him. He felt the warmth of her body, and relished the peace he felt from her presence.

David drove to the seafront and parked between the Palace and West piers. They dropped to the lower promenade at the top of the beach, watched the swimmers and sunbathers, and drifted in and out of the novelty stalls against the seawall. They climbed back up to street level to a seat opposite the coffee shop. The calm of the late afternoon and the peace they felt with each other made further conversation less important than savouring the moments.

David held her tightly. "I can hardly think of life without you, even your flight back on Thursday—"

"Don't remind me," she replied with a shiver, and responded to his tight embrace.

"I think we should skip supper at the hotel tonight," suggested David. "I don't need it after that meal."

"Agreed, with that meal *and* the breakfast Nigel gave me this morning. In fact, I have a further suggestion. I fancy one of those English cream teas, but perhaps we can share the cream."

David took Barbara's hand in his and led her to the coffee shop. He sensed some of his anxiety draining away—at least for that moment. They enjoyed a "moderate" cream tea and a large coffee in a soup bowl cup.

"So what do you have planned for me for our last two days together?" Barbara asked.

"Well, tomorrow, I thought we'd do a final ride into the country side. There are several more places to see yet. And Wednesday, would you like to do some final shopping before you return? And remember we have a final meal with Sophia and Nigel that evening—a banquet, Sophia called it!"

"David, that sounds delightful. I love having you look after me. But there's one thing more. I'd love a ride on a double deck bus again. It has such delightful memories."

"And a taxi ride back?"

"If necessary."

"Well the evening's young yet, how about now?"

They stepped outside the coffee shop. David looked at

Barbara, her full figure and shapely legs even more appealing in the soft evening light. *I still can't believe she's interested in me,* he thought. He put a possessive arm around her waist as they walked to the nearby bus stop. They stepped upstairs on the first bus that arrived.

"Do you know where we're going?" Barbara asked.

"No. I never use the buses, so we'll just see where it takes us," said David. *I'm not sure where our friendship is heading either.*

They sat in silence, watching the world from their private booth, David aware of her softness pressing against him. But sadness tinged his enjoyment on this bus trip; she would be leaving in a few days. What then? The bus reached its terminus. They could have taken the bus back, but opted for the taxi ride instead: "to relive past memories," David said.

They sat in the rear, wrapped in each others' arms for most of the journey. David felt the softness of her face with his hand, combing his fingers through her bright auburn hair, running his thumb over her rich olive eyes and full lips, then kissing her cheeks, and placing a soft lingering kiss to her lips. She stayed still in his arms, absorbing every movement, then responded, pulling him closer to her, passionately returning his kisses.

Suddenly, she sat back. She was weeping. "David, I'm so happy being with you, and I can't bear the thought of leaving in a few days. What is going to happen to us?"

David pulled a handkerchief from his pocket and tenderly wiped the tears from her cheeks. "I don't know what the future holds; only God knows the future," David replied. "I'm sure it will work out for us, but right now I don't know how." David took both her hands in his. "You know, I believe we really fell in love while we were apart— you in Vancouver and me here. If it's real, it will stay strong when we are apart again. Besides, Vancouver and

Brighton are really not that far apart with the ease of today's travel."

Barbara laughed through tear filled eyes. David marvelled afresh at the beauty he saw.

"David! Always the accountant, calculating the options! You are right. It may seem like the end, but it doesn't have to be. It's given me an idea. You must come and stay with us in return for your family's hospitality; maybe later in the fall, or certainly for Christmas. What do you think?"

"Great idea. Let's work towards something like that." The taxi pulled up at the hotel. "I'll see you for the day tomorrow. How about breakfast together in the suite, about eight?"

"David, you're such a darling. I've had such a good time while I've been here." She pulled him to her for a last lingering kiss. "And don't forget to pay the driver," she reminded him, grinning. "See you tomorrow."

She skipped merrily up the steps and, with a final wave, disappeared into the hotel lobby.

David didn't sleep well that Monday night. Despite his optimistic forecast for the future, he was beginning to dread that ride to Heathrow on Thursday. Correspondence had worked for them before they met, but now it would be laced with longing more than delight.

Tuesday morning he drove to the hotel for breakfast with mixed feelings. Fortunately, the forecast for the rest of the week was for warm sunny weather. That cheered his spirits. When he walked into the suite, Barbara and Nigel were engaged in some cheerful banter, but Barbara's face lit up as David walked in. To David, she looked more beautiful than ever. Certainly, for those in love, beauty is very much in the eyes of the beholder, but it was clear that her love for David also added sparkle to her eyes, and joy seemed to throb through her whole form. That was not lost on Nigel.

"Barbara, you look so gorgeous today, if it wasn't for David, I'd grab you for myself."

"Thanks for that, Nigel. But it's just as well David got to me first. I wouldn't like to be grabbed by anyone, not even you."

Nigel sighed in mock resignation. "Always the bridesmaid," he said, pulling a defeated face.

David gave him a friendly punch. "Hang in there, brother, you may yet find someone who's willing to put up with you."

"And that may take a while, Nigel," added Barbara. "But I assure you it'll be worth it."

"Well Barb, if your radiance is anything to go by, it's something I'll look forward to."

David and Barbara ate a light breakfast, anxious to start their day. They walked out of the suite together.

"David. I've something important to tell you," Barbara said as they walked to the car. "It's about our discussion yesterday. Once we are on our way, I'll share it with you."

Does she mean our discussion about my faith? That was David's first reaction. As they started to drive, David anxiously asked her what was so special.

"I made some phone calls to Vancouver last night. Remember Vancouver is eight hours behind us here?"

"Yes?" David was impatient.

Barbara went on, "My parents would be delighted for you to visit us when I'm back home," she explained. "Timing is up to us."

David gave an inward sigh of relief. *So that was the important thing she wanted to share.* "That's great Barbara. Perhaps that will soften our parting a little."

"Very little, David, but at least we'll have something to look forward to."

"How much have you told your parents about us?"

"So far, just that we are attracted to each other. I don't want them getting ideas about us too soon."

"Okay. So any idea when I should visit?"

"I'd like you to come at Christmas certainly, but do you think you could make a visit before then? Christmas is so far away."

"Perhaps I could get away mid-October, halfway between now and Christmas. What do you think?"

They began discussing plans excitedly, taking the edge off Barbara's soon departure. That day and the next passed all too quickly, spending every minute together.

20

Evelyn awoke that Monday fresh from success in seducing Clark. But now the triumph began to sour. The emotional upheaval of her deception left her flat, and possible consequences of her ploy began to flood her mind. First the danger she had discounted too easily, that Clark would discover her subterfuge, loomed large. Then, how would Barbara react? She was aware of the real cause of the pregnancy; it would be impossible to keep this deception from her. That would include David as well.

Evelyn's mood darkened. Would Barb, David and Clark get together to derail her plan and expose her rape and subsequent actions? Perhaps they had already. Was Clark actually in on her secret and simply going along for the sex she had conceded to? Flights of fantasy occupied her mind setting off conspiracy networks that spiralled out of control or reason. She felt nauseous, remaining in bed till late trying to banish the disturbing visions.

On arising, she wanted to call Clark, but doubts about his honesty deterred her. Her cell phone rang. It was Clark.

"Good morning beautiful. Sleep well?"

"Yes." Evelyn was still suspicious.

"You should have done after last night," he said. "I did. Thanks for a special evening. We must do it again sometime."

Clark's even voice calmed her fears somewhat, but she

was still non-committal. "Yes, I guess so. But I'm not feeling so good today. Perhaps we can get together later in the week?"

"Hey we're engaged, I want to see you as much as possible. If you're not so well today, how about tomorrow?"

Evelyn had something else on her mind that discouraged her from meeting Clark. "I hope you don't think we're going to have sex every time we meet, do you?" Suspicion gave a hard edge to her voice.

"Well. I thought after last night—"

"Well, you thought wrong," Evelyn interrupted. His apparent desire for continued sex began to confirm her fears. "I need time to think. I'll call you later in the week." She rang off, without even a "goodbye."

Clark was surprised by Ev's cool reception. After a fantastic evening, he expected a hot reception. Why had she suddenly changed? Did she regret having sex? Perhaps she regretted suggesting unprotected sex. He'd wondered about that briefly at the time, but was too fired up to care.

The more he thought about it, her decision for sex seemed too sudden. Up to last evening, she adamantly refused sex. Now she quickly wanted sex and without any protection. Did she want to get pregnant for some reason? Clark was getting close to Evelyn's dilemma, but fortunately for her, Clark failed to explore that far. The possibility of her subterfuge never entered his mind. After all, if she was so against sex with him previously, she was unlikely to have sex with anyone else. He convinced himself her reticence on the phone was a momentary distraction. Perhaps she was emotionally disturbed after their sexual encounter, and would come around in a day or two. He would wait for her call.

As it happened, fate intervened.

Phyllis called Clark. "Hi Clark. This is Ev's mom. I'm having trouble with my computer, and wondered if you could take a look at it?"

"Sure. When would be convenient?"

"Come to supper on Wednesday evening and you can try to fix it then. Would that work for you?"

It was arranged.

Evelyn desperately wanted to talk with Barbara before she saw Clark again. She had a good idea what Barbara's response would be to her deception of Clark, but had no-one else to confide in. Evelyn suggested to Barbara's parents, Don and Patti Williams, she would meet Barbara from the plane on Thursday.

When Phyllis told her Clark was coming to supper Wednesday evening, her first thought was how to get out of it. But her mother was insistent.

"I need him to fix my computer, and I see so little of him, it seemed a good way to get to know him better."

Evelyn said nothing, just nodded. *She doesn't know how well* I've *already got to know him.* She grimly resigned herself to facing the evening somehow. Thus the following couple of days were as difficult for Evelyn as they were for Barbara and David pondering their final days together. She needed to find something to alleviate her mood.

Evelyn thought of Adele. The sister of Joe, Clark's friend. At least she wouldn't consider her sexual encounter with Clark anything unusual, might even have something positive to say about it. She knew that Adele's work in a bakery was an early shift, normally finishing about three. She called her and they agreed to meet that afternoon at the condo.

Adele was very positive. "Good for you. What took you so long?" she asked when Evelyn arrived.

"I'm not sure that sex whenever you want it with

whoever is a good thing," Evelyn responded.

"Glad you got over that. At least with this one guy." Adele said. "I agree. Sex with any guy who comes along is probably not a good thing. But why hold off with a guy you like?"

Evelyn plopped down in a chair, chin in her hands, staring at the floor.

"It was horrible," she said. "At least the sex part was. It was a strange mixture of pain and pleasure. I really like the closeness, but the penetration always makes me feel sick."

Adele was dumbfounded. "What . . . why . . . why did you do it then? And what made it so horrible?"

"Sex is so frightening, I couldn't enjoy it."

Adele repeated. "Then why do it?"

"I felt I owed him somehow." Evelyn lied.

"You don't owe any man anything," Adele countered with pursed lips. "If it frightens you, then avoid it. He can wait till you feel differently. I don't understand, though, why you find it frightening."

"Neither do I. He needed me to feed his fat hairy weapon into me; he couldn't find my opening, I felt sick handling it. It was repulsive and painful. I avoided looking at it or him. I was dry and it wouldn't go in. He had no cream—he finished up using wet toothpaste as a lubricant—is this the way it's supposed to be?" She looked up; misery etched Evelyn's face.

"Absolutely not." Adele banged the coffee table with her fist. "It's meant to be enjoyable. I've had some experience with men, and usually found it enjoyable. You have to be turned on or you *will* be dry. I had that problem with the odd guy who was just using me to masturbate. That I didn't enjoy. But was Clark considerate, or was he forceful and rough?"

"Frustrated is a better description. I made it clear I

enjoyed him close to me, kissing and fondling me but he could see I was just enduring the penetration and glad when it was over. I felt sorry for him, but I couldn't help it. I can't believe he's still interested in me—he even suggested we should try it again sometime. Some hope of that!"

"But Evelyn, something else bothers me. It sounds like he went bareback. Back on the boat you said you were afraid of pregnancy. Didn't you demand he wear protection?"

"It was spur of the moment," Evelyn lied again. "And I thought it was a safe time of the month."

"Well, as I told you, pregnancy is not really a problem. Abortion is easy."

"No. That's not an option. I would spend the rest of my life feeling guilty. I couldn't simply dispense with a child's life like that."

"It's not a child till it's born." Adele was scornful.

"I could never be sure of that," replied Evelyn. "I couldn't take that risk."

"Well. You can't be pregnant, it's only been overnight. What's the problem?"

"It's just that we didn't use anything."

"Oh! Then we'll just have to wait and see, won't we?"

That was a waste of time, Evelyn thought as she left Adele's condo. *Adele was positive alright, but was no help in dealing with a pregnancy or with Clark on Wednesday.* She was no further ahead. But Evelyn had not given all the facts to Adele, who dismissed those she heard as irrelevant.

Wednesday arrived. Evelyn worked during the day, but returned for supper. She stayed as close to her mother as possible, keeping her conversation with Clark perfunctory. Chat over supper was mostly over computers and Clark's prospects. Phyllis finally exploded the evening.

She leaned forward to Clark. "So. Are you two thinking of getting married?"

Evelyn cringed. *Does she know about my pregnancy? How much has Clark told her*? In a flash it seemed her subterfuge may be discovered.

She broke in. "Why? What makes you say that?"

"I think you've been together for some time. I'm interested in Clark's plans for my only daughter."

Evelyn breathed an inward sigh of relief. "Mom. We became engaged a few days ago, and plan to marry early next year." Evelyn considered she had no choice despite her misgivings earlier in the week. "We should have told you sooner, but were waiting for a suitable time."

Clark gave her a relieved smile, and then turned to Phyllis. "Mrs. Summers. I really love your daughter and promise I will make a good husband."

"Promises are cheap, But if you are her choice, you have my blessing." Phyllis was beaming.

Clark left his seat to extend his hand to Phyllis. Unexpectedly, and to Evelyn's surprise, Phyllis stood and gave Clark a hug. She seemed human after all.

"You two go and fix my computer," said Phyllis. "I will clear up."

The computer was working fine.

"Perhaps it just needed rebooting," said Clark. "Your mother probably never turns it off."

But Evelyn felt used. She was sure her mother had engineered this supper and interrogation. The computer fixed, Evelyn grabbed Clark's hand, and with a brief, "See you later, Mom," led him quickly out of the house to her car.

"This calls for a celebration—even if it's only coffee," she said as they drove off. Now her mother was aware of their engagement, it made life easier—perhaps an indication of the future. She had hit another high point in her roller coaster life. But would this be one she could maintain? She relegated the warning of the constant threat, Barbara's silent remainder, to the back of her mind.

Wednesday evening was the send off dinner for Barbara. She wore a white sleeveless shirt, open at the neck, white knee length tights, and wedge sandals. The white clothing set of her newly acquired tan and, she hoped, provided a casual but elegant attire for this last supper.

Sophia set a formal table, placing Barbara at the head. Sophia sat to one side adjacent to Barbara, David opposite and Nigel next to him. The kitchen staff catered and served the meal: a typical roast beef dinner with all the trimmings including yorkshire pudding. Dessert was English trifle: a concoction of ladyfingers and fruit in jelly, topped with a thick layer of custard and, of course, cream. The conversation was somewhat muted, although Nigel was his usual jovial self.

"I guess you two are going to burn the wires between here and Vancouver, eh?"

"I'm sure we'll build up a stack of emails between us," said David. "But I'm hoping for a visit to Vancouver myself."

"Can we all come," asked Nigel, half jokingly. "I should make sure the colonies are being run properly."

Barbara chimed in. "You'd better clean up your act on your own bit of the planet. Then we might allow you into Canada."

"Guess I'll never make it then," sighed Nigel.

"Seriously though, I think my family would love to meet up with you all—maybe Christmas?" Barbara said. "Let's make it a tentative date."

Sophia wondered if that would work over the busy Christmas season.

"Oh! I'm sure we can have someone in to run it for once." Nigel was impatient.

"Well. Give me some time here and I might be able to fill in for you," said Sophia. "But this is a time to celebrate. Barbara, you have brightened our lives considerably during your time here, and I think stolen all our hearts—of course, none more than David's! If it ever came to it, we would wholeheartedly welcome you into our family. A toast to Barbara."

The brothers rose with "hear, hear," as they clinked their glasses.

Barbara blushed. "You have all been so hospitable and kind to us. I've enjoyed myself so much here, I'll be really sorry to leave. Thank you."

"No more sorry than Dave, I'll bet," added Nigel. "But, Barb, I agree heartily. I'll miss you."

"Thanks, Nigel. Believe it or not, I'll miss you too!"

David and Barbara slipped out to be on their own after the meal. It was a warm summer evening and they found their favourite coffee shop. They discussed plans for the next day. Barbara's plane left about ten in the morning, so David would pick her up early, about six thirty. They wandered across the street to the waterfront seat they had used before—it was almost theirs.

They sat quietly for a while, watching and listening as the waves crashed on the shore, and the bustle of holiday makers behind them, engulfed in their own thoughts. What was there to say? It seemed a big gulf was opening up between them. Was their love strong enough to bridge that divide? Was their friendship merely a getaway seduction? David thought not. But he realized more distinctly a common faith would bind them together. Without it, distance and faltering communication could cause them to drift apart.

He decided he needed to be clear with Barbara on this.

"Barb! I'm not sure how to say this. But as you think about the Christian faith, I want to be sure it's your own decision, not something to embrace simply to ensure our future together. That would probably be as bad, or worse, than a life together with conflicting views. Although it would tear me apart, I am prepared to accept your decision to break up if you felt you couldn't accept my faith as your own." David could hardly believe what he was saying.

Barbara gripped his arm tightly. "David. As much as I love you, I am not sure of our future together either. What you say, and the distance between us will be the test, I suppose. But I promise you, whatever decision I come to in regard to your faith, it will be *mine*. And I want to say again, I feel very positive towards it, but I still have questions."

"It's going to be essential to keep our correspondence alive," David replied. "But keep something in mind. From my experience, answers to our questions become clearer *after* we come to faith in Christ. To quote an old master of the faith: 'I believe, therefore I understand.'"

"Strange! I would have thought it's the other way around."

"I agree with you. It is strange. It's just one of the mysteries of our faith. It tends to turn much of what we naturally believe on its head."

She suddenly turned to face him. "But this is our last evening together. What do you suggest?"

"On our own, or with people?"

"On our own. And remember I have to pack for an early morning tomorrow."

"Okay then. Let's just walk west along the beach—the tide's out; lots of space down there—and watch the setting sun."

They walked slowly with their arms around each

other, each conscious of making memories as they kicked pebbles, scattered seagulls, and stopped for lingering kisses as dusk enveloped them. They turned back and walked leisurely hand in hand along the promenade to the Belvedere. The thought of separation played havoc with David's desire for her; it grew by the minute.

They stopped in the shadow of the entry. David was transfixed by Barbara's alluring tan glowing against her white attire and the way auburn curls framed her face. They clung together for a last lingering kiss, neither willing to let go. David felt the exhilaration of her body pressed against his, sure there was no other feeling like it. He took her face in his hands and tenderly kissed her eyes, cheeks, and her lips. He slid his hands down her soft arms, kissing her neck, chest, and exposed cleavage. Barbara wound her fingers around the back of his neck and fondled his hair pressing his head against her breasts. He took her in his arms pressing his pelvis against her, as much in desperation as desire, and felt her tremble.

"Barb, I want you so badly. I don't know how I can last this separation."

"I know, David. I know. Me too."

David felt an answering press as she pulled her body tightly against him, kissing him slowly on the lips. He saw tears forming in her eyes, even a flush emerging through her tanned face. Suddenly, she pulled away,

"See you tomorrow," she said softly, and disappeared into the hotel.

Barbara almost ran to her room, her heart pounding from the closeness of their bodies. She could still feel the warmth of his kiss and the hardness of his arousal. Her quick disengagement masked the sweat that slowly engulfed her; the surprise at her body's response to his embrace and wandering kisses. She sat on the bed for minutes, savouring the euphoria that engulfed her, the sense of perfection promised in that brief encounter, and the intense longing for consummation the closeness evoked. Her increasing love for this man in three short weeks intensified her desire; she wouldn't feel the same fervour for any man.

Sadness at next day's separation began gnawing away at her pleasure, and she started packing mechanically. Final things could wait until the morning. She opened her laptop. There was an email from Evelyn. It was upbeat.

> Hi Barb.
>
> Just wanted to let you know I'll be at the airport to meet you in Vancouver tomorrow.
>
> Looking forward so much to meeting you and catching up. Long to hear how you and David have been doing.
>
> My dear mother has approved of my engagement to Clark. Makes me feel so much better. Things are going good.
>
> But have something to discuss with you when you arrive.
>
> Love, Ev.

Barb wondered if there was a shift in tone in the last sentence. But there was nothing for it but to wait until they met. She put it out of her mind. *If Ev doesn't want to put it in the email, then there's no point in asking her about it before we meet.* She responded with a quick "see you tomorrow" email and slept fitfully thinking of the morrow's parting..

21

David arrived early at the Belvedere Thursday morning. Barbara, Nigel and Sophia gathered in the foyer awaiting him. David hated formal goodbyes and waited impatiently while Sophia and Nigel said theirs.

"This isn't going to be the last time we get together, Barb," said Nigel. "I'm going to install my Aunt Sophia as chief cook and bottle washer if necessary so I can visit you at Christmas. Hey, I might meet up with that delightful upstart cousin of mine"—he pulled a mock frown—"What was her name . . .?"

"Don't get your hopes up, Nigel. She became engaged to her boyfriend Clark when she arrived home. Perhaps she'll be married when you see her next and clear of your clutches." She grinned at Nigel and gave him a long hug. "I'll miss you Nigel."

"Less than you'll miss David I'm sure. I envy you both." Nigel let her go.

Sophia held Barb's hands. "We'll work on a Christmas visit by the boys if I have anything to do with it. You being here brought us closer together." And she gave Barbara the ususal suffocating hug.

"Okay guys," called David. "Enough with the love-making, we've a plane to catch. See you later." Nigel loaded the luggage and David opened the MG door to Barbara for the last time.

Barbara's heart sank as she saw Sophia and Nigel waving until they were out of sight. She felt the tears stinging behind her eyes. She was suddenly aware how much the Belvedere and both Sophia and Nigel had come to mean to her. Certainly, her love for David had a lot to do with it, nonetheless, she'd felt so much at home there.

They drove in silence for a while, each absorbed with their own thoughts. Barbara began mentally preparing for the return home, and thought of Evelyn. Initially, her thoughts were positive. She was thankful Evelyn's relationship with Clark was working out. But she had a niggling feeling that things could easily go awry. In particular, she was fearful of the rape surfacing unexpectedly as long as Evelyn insisted on keeping silent about it and not revealing it in an orderly fashion. She hoped that wasn't what Evelyn wanted to share with her.

She considered sharing her concerns with David, but thought better of it. This was their time and there was no room in the car for Evelyn, or Sophia and Nigel, or anyone else. The little MG was heading up the M23 taking them to a long parting. She snuggled close to David, as much as the bucket seats would allow. Just being together seemed enough for a while. There would be fond farewells later. David took her hand and squeezed it.

David eased the car onto the M25 and took the Heathrow exit, parked the car and trundled her luggage into the terminal. They stood in line at the check-out, arms around each other. Having dispensed with luggage and obtained her boarding pass, they had an hour to spare. They bought some breakfast and sat facing each other across the table.

Barbara looked at David despairingly. "There's so much I want to convey to you, but the words I have are too light to carry it. I just can't express my feelings as I want to."

"Barb, you express your feelings well without words. I hope I do the same. The depth of what we feel is inexpressible in words. I think that's why we have non-verbal ways of communicating love. Even being together in silence we can feel it, can't we?"

Barbara nodded. "You're right. I just love being with you. Even our quiet ride up here gave me great pleasure in spite of the sadness of leaving."

"I have to say Barb that my faith in God is like that. I see his care for me—for all of us—not only in his eternal sacrifice to redeem us, but also all around me, especially bringing you into my life! And my response is one of love I can feel toward him, same as I feel love for you."

"Are you saying emotions play a part in your faith, David?"

"Of course. We are made up of intellect, emotions, and will, and they are all involved in a relationship with him as with anyone else."

"David. Every time you talk about your faith, I see something new. It seems it can be an exciting life. As we correspond, keep telling me more. I want to know."

David reached across the table and grasped Barb's hands. "There's nothing better I want to do. And I hope it will also convey my love for you."

They sat, looking into each others eyes. For an onlooker, clearly no-one else existed in the busy airport. After a few moments, Barbara looked at her boarding pass. "David, time to go I'm afraid." They picked up their belongings and walked to security.

"Everybody kisses in an airport," David said. But Barbara needed no encouragement. They held each other close for a last kiss.

Barbara's eyes fill with tears, a mixture of happiness and sadness. "We'll be together in October. In the meantime I'll look for your emails. Perhaps I'll keep them in a box like you have. Let's talk on the telephone Saturday mornings as well."

He nodded. "My computer and telephone will be my best friends until then. I love you Barbara. Never forget that."

"I love you too. Go quickly, David. I hate long goodbyes." She picked up her hand baggage and moved briskly to security, turning to wave as she disappeared inside.

Evelyn had not communicated much with Barbara after emailing about her engagement to Clark, other than the note saying she would be at the Vancouver airport to meet her. She didn't want Barbara to worry about her during the remaining time with David. At least, that's what she told herself, but really she was fearful of telling Barbara what she had been up to since arriving home. Barbara knew nothing of her pregnancy or her plan to deceive Clark into thinking he was the father of the child. There was no turning back and Barbara had to be told.

Barbara's plane was due about four o'clock. So Evelyn had most of Thursday to decide how to approach her. There seemed to be no easy way. She'd just have to spit it all out at some convenient moment. She waited for Barb to exit from customs. Barbara's face lit up as she saw her, running to her and holding her in a long embrace. They walked to Evelyn's car, Evelyn pushing Barbara's luggage buggy.

"Glad to be home Barb? I'm certainly glad to see you."

"Home? I'm not sure where home is any more, I felt so much at home in Brighton with David," Barbara replied. "I don't know how I'm going to last for the next three months until I see him again."

"That bad eh?"

"Ev. I've never felt so happy as I was in Brighton. But

hey! How about you? I've been so glad things have turned out well for you."

"Got news for you," said Evelyn. "But let's get out of the airport and I'll tell you." *No good putting it off, it will only make it harder.* But Evelyn felt bad for upsetting the happiness she saw on Barbara's face as they drove out of the airport.

"So what's the news," Barbara asked beaming, evidently expecting good news.

"Not such good news, Barb, sorry to say."

Evelyn recounted the events of the previous week, keeping her eyes on the road, only occasionally glancing at Barbara. She noticed Barb's joyful look turn to dismay as she talked. Barbara remained quiet for several minutes, biting her lip after Evelyn had finished,.

"Evelyn. I wish you'd held back on all this until we had a chance to talk," she said. "Or at least talked to someone else before going this far. I know you think this will all work out for you, but if it doesn't, the effects of this to yourself and others, especially Clark, could be severe."

"Barb. I thought you would understand. I had to do this for myself. How else am I going to keep the assault in England secret?" Evelyn couldn't bring herself to use the work rape.

"I understand how you feel, honestly I do. But acknowledging the assault would have been the less risky path in the long run, however hard that would be. I fear you may be substituting that pain for greater pain later on if this all comes out. A lifetime is a long time to keep a secret, Ev."

"Well, we're getting married early in the New Year. I will announce the pregnancy sometime before that and tell Clark he's the father. That will only cement our relationship and make sure the marriage takes place. Clark never needs to know he's not the father—and you mustn't tell him."

"Ev. I'm sure Clark can count. He'll get suspicious when the baby turns up early."

"I'll just say it's a premature birth."

Barbara shook her head as she often did at Evelyn's escapades. But of all her crazy plans this was the most precarious.

"You've got it all figured out haven't you Ev? I won't say anything to anybody. But if it comes out, I *will* speak the truth. The truth is always the simplest, if not the easiest path. Lies build on one another and compound the problem."

Evelyn said little more on the drive to the British Properties, giving Barbara a grudging thank you for her silence, and remained sullen for the rest of the journey.

"Thanks for the ride, Ev," Barbara said as they deposited the cases at Barb's front door. "Perhaps we can meet for coffee tomorrow?"

"Maybe," said Evelyn and drove away.

Barbara saw life returning to what passed for normal for the Vancouver families as the fall approached. Evelyn spent time with Clark and Barbara spent time with her computer. Emails flowed profusely between Brighton and Vancouver, neither David nor Barbara losing any of their passion for the other. Absence doesn't always make the heart grow fonder, sometimes it just creates emotional as well as physical distance, but the old adage held true for those two. David arranged to visit Vancouver for ten days early in October, while he and Nigel were seriously considering Vancouver for Christmas and the New Year.

But Barbara's relationship with Evelyn became strained. Clark was Evelyn's excuse to spend less time with Barbara. It seemed that Barbara's presence became an increasing threat to her relationship with Clark. By

September, the pregnancy would be two months and beginning to show soon, but Barbara didn't know if Evelyn had informed Clark. About mid-September, Barbara finally persuaded Evelyn to meet her for coffee. The Robson Street coffee shop seemed the obvious location, the scene of happier times.

"Ev, I've really missed you." Barbara began the conversation. "How is it going with Clark?"

Evelyn was not very forthcoming. "Okay. No problems yet."

"Does he know about the baby?"

"No not yet."

"You'll show very shortly. Are you going to tell him soon?"

Evelyn was becoming irritated. "Barb, it's under control. As far as he's concerned it's only just over a month. Too soon to be sure."

"You know that David will be here in a couple of weeks, don't you?"

"Yes. What has that got to do with it?"

"I don't want him to guess what's going on, or risk him asking a silly question at the wrong time. I'll have to tell him."

"He doesn't have to know more than anyone else," Evelyn protested. "I'll take a chance on it."

"But I'm not prepared to. If David spills the beans by accident, it'll be my responsibility. He knows too much already. I'm not taking that chance."

"You and David are ganging up on me," Ev cried. "I thought I could trust you."

"Evelyn. I told you. Your secret is safe with me, and even safer if David knows ahead of time what's going on."

Evelyn appeared not to hear. "You and David told my mother about Clark and me being engaged, didn't you?"

"What are you talking about? Absolutely not."

"Then Nigel was in on it as well with you. It must have been them. How else would my mother have known?"

"Evelyn. What's the matter with you? None of us would do that. You're paranoid."

Evelyn shot up and grabbed her purse. "Don't lie to me," she shouted, arousing startled looks from other tables. With that outburst, she strode out of the cafe.

Barbara looked sheepishly around at the customers, found a fiver in her purse, and left it under a mug. She rushed out to see Evelyn's car disappearing up the street. *Great, now I'm without transport. Guess I'll need to find a bus home*. Suddenly she felt alone. David was so far away, and she had no-one else she could talk to. *What a mess. I'm not sure I can cope with this, let alone Evelyn*.

Other drivers were well advised to avoid Evelyn's car when she was angry. She drove to Clark's apartment. *He'd better be there*, she vowed as she screeched to a halt outside his building. On second thoughts, she sat quietly, trying to compose herself before she saw him. This needed to be a calm meeting. *I'd better tell him about the baby now*, she decided, *before Barbara or her family take it into their heads to inform him*. She felt isolated. Clark was her only friend. He would understand.

She rang his doorbell.

"It's Evelyn," she said when he answered.

"Oh! Okay. Wasn't expecting you, But come on up."

She went to the elevator. The doors opened and Adele walked out.

"Oh! Hi Evelyn. Here to see Clark?"

"Yes. What are you doing here?"

"Joe lent Clark some tools, and I dropped by to pick them up." She opened a plastic bag with tools in. "He's a really nice guy, Ev. Look after him."

"Yes, he is," was all Evelyn could say.

"Bye," Adele shouted back happily as Evelyn escaped into the elevator.

Clark's door was open and she walked in. "Saw Adele downstairs. What's she doing here?"

"She picked up some tools Joe left me."

"That's what *Adele* said. I'm asking *you*."

"To pick up some tools," Clark repeated. "What did you think she was doing?"

"You said you weren't expecting me."

Clark sat down. "Evelyn. Joe and Adele are just good friends. There's nothing going on. Come and sit down with me." Clark's even, compassionate voice eased Evelyn's suspicions, and she joined him on the couch. "Now what are *you* doing here," he asked.

Evelyn realized her suspicions were once again interfering with her reason for coming. "Sorry," she said. "Just had a bust-up with a friend, and I was feeling irritable. I was missing you," At least some was true. She snuggled up to him, and he put a comforting arm around her. "But I need to tell you something else."

"Good news?"

"Depends."

"Depends on what?"

"On how you take it," she replied.

"Oh?"

"I'm pregnant."

Silence. Clark looked at her quizzically. "You're serious?"

"Yes."

Silence again.

"How far along?

"More than a month."

"When did it happen?"

"I, I think our, our first time." She was hesitant. She had told him it was safe.

"But you said—"

"I know what I said. I thought I was safe. I guess I was wrong."

Clark rose from the couch, facing away from Evelyn. He spun around.

"You said it was safe," he repeated wildly. "You should have insisted I wear a condom. Why did you even suggest I shouldn't?"

"I, I wanted it nice for you . . ." she realized in the present situation that sounded lame.

"Now this is the result . . ." His voice trailed off, his anger obscuring where to go next.

Evelyn took the initiative. "You had a choice as well. If you were so concerned, you could have worn one."

Clark flung his arms out and began walking in small circles, shaking his hands. Evelyn stayed silent. *Better not to push him,* Evelyn thought. *He needs to work through this.* After a couple of minutes, Clark slumped back on the couch, slowly appearing resigned to the situation.

"Do you want the baby?" Clark asked quietly.

Evelyn was aware he might want to end the pregnancy. "Yes, I do. No abortion. We are getting married in the New Year, aren't we, so it shouldn't be a problem."

"Having the baby is not the problem." He raised his voice again. "How are we going to live?" Then, more measured: "I really need more time to think about this."

"Are you suggesting you won't marry me if I keep the baby?"

"I'm not suggesting anything. I need time to absorb this, particularly the consequences."

Evelyn hadn't thought much beyond the immediate problem the baby posed. She had never been short of money, so was slow to realize making a living absorbed much of Clark's thought and time. Then she wondered if Adele had said anything to Clark about a baby. She had discussed the possibility with her, but not that she was pregnant. Evelyn couldn't make a connection between Adele and the baby, so she dismissed the idea. But it was still strange that Adele was at Clark's apartment when she turned up unexpectedly. Clark's next suggestion raised her suspicions again. Was Adele waiting to return after she left?

"The idea of a baby is a shock. I need some time alone to give it more consideration. Do you mind? I'll call you tomorrow and we'll discuss it further then."

Evelyn felt she had no choice. His reaction was understandable. She gave him a long kiss, but his response didn't seem as passionate. She left, and waited in her car watching the apartment building entrance. It was almost an expected shock to see Adele, carrying a plastic bag enter the building a few minutes later. *I knew it*, she thought, slamming her hands on the steering wheel. Clark would have to explain this tomorrow, baby or no baby. She left immediately, too soon to see Adele leave a minute later without the plastic bag.

Clark sat with his head in his hands. There was a knock at the door. It was Adele.

"Hey, Clark. You said you were out of eggs. I picked some up for you at the store next door."

Clark forced an appreciative smile.

"Happy cooking," she said, "if that's what you are planning."

"Thanks. Maybe. I'll walk you to the elevator." He gave her a hug as the doors opened. She entered the elevator and the doors closed behind her.

THE SILENT REMAINDER

22

David and Barbara's emails to each other provided a growing legacy of feelings for each other that David kept with the previous correspondence from Barbara. While their love began to express itself in ever inspiring ways, Barbara tried to keep him abreast of life in Vancouver. But she avoided Evelyn's pregnancy and her plan to blame Clark for it; there were some issues she didn't want to put on paper. But she felt freer on their Saturday morning call, and would prefer to tell him in person. Particularly, after her fractious encounter with Evelyn in the coffee shop, she needed to bring David up-to-date.

"David," she said, after reminding him again she loved him, "I think Evelyn is in big trouble. Not right now, but likely to be if she continues what she's doing. I haven't told you this before, but she's pregnant from the rape."

"Goodness," responded David, "I was concerned about HIV, but never gave pregnancy a thought. What does she plan to do?"

"Well, she does plan to keep the baby, which I'm thankful for, but she's going to tell Clark it's his."

"Oh!" David was silent for a moment. "That does complicate things. I take it you've not been able to dissuade her?"

"David. You know Evelyn. She thinks she's got it covered and she's sworn me to secrecy. But I had to tell you, and I told her I would, if you noticed her pregnancy you might expose the truth by accident. After all you will be here in a couple of weeks. I can't wait."

"Me neither Barb. But I hope we can meet with Evelyn. It's important to keep in good relationship with her—and Clark, of course. If this thing explodes, she'll need all the friends she can get."

"I'm looking forward to you meeting my family. I've built you up to the perfect man, so don't let me down."

"That's a tall order. You might need to prop me up!"

"You'll do okay. I know you. They'll love you, but not as much as I do." Barbara had no doubts.

"I wish you were here with me now. I miss your touch, your smile and laugh. I want to feel you close to me again."

"Soon, David, soon. Must go now. Talk again Saturday. Love you."

"Love you too."

David's heart was in Vancouver. He counted the days until his flight there. But his work had to be done. Monday, Nigel walked into his office as he usually did, bringing hotel paperwork from the weekend. Autumn weeks were quieter, but people came for weekend getaways. Nigel dumped the papers on David's desk and poured himself a coffee. He slumped down into a chair facing David. He sat, sipping his coffee quietly for a few minutes, totally out of character. David continued working, looking up now and again to see what Nigel was up to.

"You know, David, and I hate to admit it, but I really miss Evelyn."

David laughed. "Ha! I told you, Brother, you might fall for one of the girls."

"I doubt I'm in love," Nigel replied. "I just miss her being around—more than I ever thought I would with any girl."

David thought about the news he'd heard Saturday about Evelyn.

"Nigel. She's pretty unpredictable . . ."

"I think that's part of what I find attractive. I'd hate to live in a rut like you."

"Well, I enjoy my comfortable rut—at least I did until Barbara came long."

"Good Bro! You need some shaking up." Nigel was rapidly becoming his old self, perhaps trying to put Evelyn behind him. "All set for your trip to Vancouver?"

"You bet. Wild horses—not even you could stop me."

"Wouldn't want to. In fact, I'd like to come with you."

So that's what's going on, mused David. *He's angling for an invitation.* "Are you serious?" Nigel was always joshing.

"Wouldn't mind. What d'you think?"

David wasn't sure it would be a good idea knowing what he did. He was just glad Barbara had told him about Evelyn two days before.

"I'll make some enquiries and let you know." David wanted to talk to Barbara before answering Nigel.

"Good enough." Nigel stood up, and went to the door. "Let me know. See you." He appeared nonchalant about the whole idea, but David was sure he was more serious than he let on.

David called Barbara to see what she thought about Nigel going with him to Vancouver. She was on the spot, so would be able to address the idea more knowledgeably. She sounded delighted to get the unexpected call. He outlined his conversation with Nigel.

"What do you think?" he asked.

"I can't see any reason why not. As long as he knows that Evelyn is engaged and pregnant with Clark's baby. That's all he needs to know. You never know, that might put him off, and make it easier for us. But if he comes, it shouldn't be a problem. I'll confirm it with Mom and Dad, and drop you a line. Let me know his decision."

"I'll check with him."

"Whatever he decides, make sure *you* come."

"I'd like it to be permanent," David replied.

"Perhaps one day. Love you."

"Love you."

Those words were becoming their regular sign off.

Sophia was becoming a fixture at the hotel. Her effervescent spirit, motherly tone, and practical bent, made her an excellent host and manager. Nigel mentioned the idea to Sophia. "We can cope," she responded. Nigel sent a note to David.

> Dave:
> I'm ready to go if they'll have me. Let me know, and your itinerary, and I'll try to book on the same flights.
> Nigel.

David replied by return.

> Nigel:
> Yep. They're expecting you. Good to have you with me. Should be fun being together like this, don't do it often enough.
> Something you should remember about Evelyn. She is engaged to Clark. Keep that in mind.
> David.

Nigel began to wonder about his motives for this trip. Was he really interested in Evelyn, as it could appear? He'd had practice at being obnoxious—it seemed to come easily!—so he could fake whatever was necessary. Armed with this strategy, he could go and enjoy the trip. It was only ten days after all. If David was off with Barbara much of the time, he was gregarious enough to enjoy the time on his own.

He checked flights on the web. He could get on the flight out, but would not be able to return for two days after David. He would be on his own for a short while.

Time passed slowly for David. The Saturday prior to their flights, he confirmed the final arrangements with Barbara over the phone. She would meet them at Vancouver, both she and David wanted to meet up at the earliest opportunity. On Wednesday, Nigel dropped by David's office again to confirm final arrangements for the next day's flight to Canada. A friend would take them to Heathrow, picking David up about six thirty; *the same flight Barbara had returned on*, thought David. That made even the flight special. David was excited, his stomach already churning at seeing and touching Barbara again. Good to be leaving very early in the morning. No time to fret while waiting around.

The drive next day to the airport was frustrating. An accident on the M25 created a tailback down the Brighton road. David was sure they would miss the plane.

"Lot's of time yet," said Nigel, slightly amused at David's discomfort. "We've got time in hand. Even if you miss the plane, she'll still be waiting. Remember, anticipation is half the pleasure."

David sat back and said nothing. He was too keyed up to conjure a response.

They arrived with no time to spare. David recalled the walk to security with Barbara. Now she was not leaving him, he was going to her. Only a few more hours.

They found their seats. "Hope this plane stays up there all the way," joked Nigel.

David didn't think it was funny. "If it doesn't, I'll fly all the way on my own," he said, and tried to concentrate on reading a book.

THE SILENT REMAINDER

23

Despite Evelyn's promise to herself to question Clark's relationship with Adele, the next day she decided to let it ride for a few days. *Let him sweat a little*, she decided, *and perhaps I can confirm what is going on by keeping an eye on his apartment*. He called her a couple of times during the week before David's arrival in Vancouver, but she put him off with some excuse. The relationship with Barbara was also frosty and mechanical. But the following morning it changed. She called Barbara.

"Barb. I'd like to come with you to meet David," she suggested. "We can use my car."

"Gosh, Ev. I thought you were still mad at me."

"Oh! I got over that. And I told Clark about the baby. Besides, we are friends, aren't we?" With her suspicions about Clark, Evelyn needed a friend.

"Well, I'm certainly glad to get our friendship back on track, Ev, and I'd love to have you with me to meet David. But be prepared for a surprise. Nigel is coming with him."

"What to Vancouver?" the question was rhetorical. She thought of that last hug at Heathrow. "Hmm. I guess that's okay. Good. I'd like to meet him again."

"You're sure it won't put a dent in your relationship with Clark?"

"It's already dented." Evelyn told Barbara of her suspicions about Clark and Adele.

Barbara didn't know Joe or Adele. "I'm sure you're

wrong, Ev. I don't think Clark would do that."

"He might, if he was mad with me. He wasn't too happy when I told him I was pregnant."

Barbara decided not to remind Evelyn that her crisis with Clark—if there really was one—was largely of her own making. This was not the time for an argument.

"Okay. Meet me at three thirty for an exciting ride to the airport."

Evelyn looked forward to that ride; it was a bright spot in an otherwise dismal future. But she parked outside Clark's apartment a couple of times. She didn't see Adele, but she did follow Clark to Joe and Adele's condo Tuesday evening. She waited for awhile, but Clark didn't appear again, so she headed for home.

The next day, Wednesday, her cell phone rang. It was Adele. Her first thought was to ignore it, but curiosity got the better of her and she opened her phone. Adele, despite an outward placid and reserved appearance didn't "suffer fools gladly," as Joe put it. She was blunt.

"Clark told me you think we're having an affair. We are doing nothing of the sort, so clear your mind of that idea."

"But I saw—"

"What you saw and what you imagined are two different things. I don't have to explain myself to you. *Nothing* is going on." With that, Adele hung up.

Evelyn stared at the phone for a few moments, dumbfounded. Adele's assertion didn't mean one thing or another. *She would say that even if she was seeing Clark.* If anything, her fervent denials reinforced Evelyn's suspicions. *Clark wouldn't be interested in her anyway: a wispy, thin, dull looking girl with rats' tail hair. He is doing it to get back at me about the baby.*

Evelyn discussed Adele's declaration and her own reaction to it with Barbara as they drove to the airport Thursday afternoon. As she spoke, her eyes filled with tears of anger and misery. She really loved Clark, and the imagined affair with Adele left her morose. She pulled over.

"You drive, Barb. I can't see for tears," she muttered. They changed places and Barbara spoke as she drove on.

"Can I make a suggestion?"

"Yes. I always want to hear what you think, even if I don't agree with you sometimes."

"That I know for sure," Barbara answered. "Personally, I still don't think Adele is having an affair with Clark. She would be less likely to phone you if she was. So don't get too cozy with Nigel—"

"Unlikely. You *know* how I feel about Nigel."

"Not sure I do. I get mixed signals from you." Evelyn shook her head. "Anyway," Barbara went on, "don't get too cozy with Nigel, it won't help rebuild a relationship with Clark—even if he is having an affair, which I still don't believe."

Evelyn saw the wisdom in Barbara's words, but began to feel excited at meeting Nigel again. If nothing else, he could distract her from her troubling thoughts. Barbara parked, and they made their way to the waiting area for overseas travellers. Barbara stood as close to the barrier as she could. Evelyn held back a little.

Within fifteen minutes, the brothers burst through the doors, Nigel pushing their luggage. Barbara ran around the barrier and flung her arms around David. They locked in a long embrace. Nigel pushed the buggy farther, until he noticed Evelyn.

"Hey. Didn't expect to see you here. How's it going?"

"Good. Real good," she lied. "All the better for seeing you."

"You really mean that?" There was that impudent smile she found so charming.

"Why not? We parted friends, didn't we?"

"We did. How about a hug?"

Evelyn didn't feel the same connection in that hug from Nigel as the one she remembered when they last parted. *We need another ride like the one to the London airport*, she guessed. *Perhaps there will be a similar opportunity*. Barbara and David caught up with them.

"Oh! I see you two have become reacquainted," David commented. "Evelyn. Good to see you again. Give me a hug too."

"Nigel. Glad you could come too," said Barbara smiling.

"Two people pleased to see me. I've never been so popular!"

Nigel and Barbara exchanged hugs all round.

Clark knew David was due in town that day, but didn't know Nigel was also coming until Ev had mentioned it in passing the day before. Like Barbara, he thought Nigel could be a distraction to getting his relationship on track with Evelyn again. He also had mixed reactions from Evelyn about Nigel. Clark wondered if he could occupy Nigel in some way to get him away from Evelyn. Perhaps Nigel liked sailing; he came from the coast in England. Clark phoned Joe.

"Hey Joe! Evelyn's cousin is in Vancouver and might be at a loose end. Would you be interested in taking him sailing?"

"Sure Clark. Give him my cell number and we'll get together."

Clark breathed easier. "Thanks Joe. You're a good friend. See ya."

Having no-one else to talk with, Clark called Adele about his fears which began a bond that had not existed up to that point. She sympathized with him.

"Clark, I'm not sure how I can help. Anything I say to

Evelyn will probably make things worse. But I can listen to you, if nothing else."

Adele told him about her abrupt conversation with Evelyn, but wasn't sure if Evelyn had believed her.

"Thanks, Adele. You're a good friend to me, like your brother."

Unexpectedly, Barbara's father, Don, called Clark.

"Clark. I'd like you to check our family computers for any millennium bugs. If you could make it on Friday afternoon, you could stay for supper. The Canadian boys will be here."

Clark checked his schedule. "That would be fine. Would you mind if I brought Evelyn?" *An opportunity to smooth things with her.*

"By all means. Glad to see you two together."

Friday noon, Clark called Evelyn. She made no attempt to end the call; she seemed more receptive to him.

"Ev. I know you've been avoiding me, but I dearly want to get our relationship back to where we were. I've been invited to Barb's house for dinner this evening, and I'd dearly love to go with you. Don said to bring you."

"Barb's already invited me, so I'll be there anyway."

"Okay, I'm going to be there during the afternoon, but I need to go home to change. I'll drive up there and see you there then, shall I?"

"Clark, I'll pick you up from your apartment. It's important to me that our relationship looks right to my parents. They don't know of the friction between us."

"Perhaps we can mend that at the same time. Thanks Ev. You know I love you, don't you?"

"I know. And I do really love you," she replied. "I look forward to this evening. Pick you up at five?"

THE SILENT REMAINDER

24

Nigel surveyed the assembled people with a detached air. He was not that comfortable being in a strange crowd, unless he could single someone out to converse with, but a glass of wine helped him indulge in some limited banter for a while. Clark and Evelyn seemed to be happy together, and no-one could miss David and Barbara's attraction to each other. Don, Phyllis, and Patti were engaged in animated conversation.

After supper, Barbara went to the kitchen to help Patti clean up. Don took David to the living room, where they made themselves comfortable on the couch. Clark and Evelyn disappeared, and Phyllis approached Nigel.

"Get yourself another drink, Nigel and join me in the den," she said. "I want to thank you for your hospitality to the girls while in England. It was comforting to know they had someone over there."

"It was very enjoyable to have them with us," Nigel replied, as they sat facing each other. "I'm just sorry Ev had to cut short her time with us."

"Yes. Strange thing that. At the time I didn't think losing her credit card required her to come home. The card was cancelled, and I would have provided some cash to tide her over."

"I know she's an excitable girl—fun to be with. But she did seem more distressed than I thought the loss really warranted. Just couldn't seem to get home quickly enough."

"Well, Women aren't the easiest to understand, are they," Phyllis said with a smile. "Do you have anyone special over there?"

"No. Not really in a rush to settle down to a shared life. I have a good life in the hotel, and it gives me sufficient free time to do the things I like."

"Such as?"

"I like to travel. I spend a fair amount of time on the continent, partly for fun and also promoting the hotel."

"Maybe I should come and visit you sometime—as a paying guest, of course. I've never spent any time across the Atlantic. Must do it soon."

"Look forward to having you," said Nigel, as Phyllis went to fill her glass.

Nigel had previously wondered about Ev's sudden departure from England. Phyllis' mention of it increased Nigel's suspicions something else was going on.

Don poured another glass of wine for himself and David. "Come and join me on the couch for a few minutes. I'd really like to chat with you."

David wondered if Don's invitation was a prelude to a third degree about his intentions for Barbara. Certainly, for the next few minutes, his questions about his work and qualifications looked relevant. Don seemed to appreciate David's training and liked David's initiative in working for himself, brief though it had been.

"You know David, Barbara's very impressed with you as a person, and I trust her judgment. But I'm interested to know how you plan to use your qualifications in the future. Any ideas?"

"Well, I like having my own business, and that is keeping me busy and providing an income for the present. I think it will grow, but I haven't thought much beyond that."

"You know, I suppose, that my business is investment?" David nodded and Don continued. "So we're both in the money game."

"Barb has told me something about it, and particularly your concern for the millennium bug."

"I think we have that solved now, thanks to Clark. He seems to have a good handle on computers." Then he turned the conversation to Barbara. "Barbara tells me you two became very close during her time in Brighton. Do you think you might be pursuing a permanent relationship soon?"

"I'd very much like to. I've grown to love Barbara deeply. She is a wonderful girl. But we do want to be sure we are agreed on one important issue. She may have mentioned that I'm a Christian, and it's very important we are in agreement about our faith."

"Well, that shouldn't be difficult. We are Christians also; we go to church every Sunday."

David saw that it was important to be very diplomatic at this point. "What do you think it means being a Christian?" David asked.

"Simple really. Follow Christ's teaching and live among others as he did. You know, the golden rule: do as you would be done by."

"Do you think we attain that?" David asked.

"Well, no-one's perfect, but we do our best." Don stared ahead, his elbows on his knees and hands clasped. Clearly, this wasn't his favourite subject.

"I agree with you that far," said David, "but here's my understanding. As you suggested, our best is not good enough, and we all fall short of God's expectation. It's what we won't admit to, that silent remainder, which will call us into judgment. Christ's death on the cross paid the penalty for our failure, and accepting it secures a permanent relationship with God. Then our desire to follow his example is not because we ought to, but is a response of gratitude."

Don did not change his position. David wondered if he had really heard. "Well, David. I admit, I've not thought it through to the degree you obviously have, and I guess Barb is going to have to make up her mind where she stands on this." He leaned back, placed his hands on his knees, and turned to David. "But I hope you both come to an agreement, especially if you think it that important. But let me change the subject." Don sounded more animated. "We are always looking for good, imaginative people like you for our office, and I wondered if you would consider coming here and working for us?"

That came out of the blue. "Well, Mr. Williams. That is unexpected, but very kind of you to think of me in this way."

"Kindness has little to do with it, David. I think you have the ability to assist us and improve our business."

"It sounds very inviting. I'm certainly interested, but I need some time to think about it, if you don't mind."

"Of course. Take your time. It's a major change, and I want to be sure you are committed to it. Let me know."

As if on cue, Barbara walked in and dropped into the space between them. "I hope my two favourite men are having a good conversation." She looked at her father. "What have you been discussing—besides me?"

"I was telling David how impressed we are with him, and suggested he come to work for us."

Barbara looked shocked. "Really, Dad?" and she threw her arms around his neck and kissed him on the cheek. "That would be exciting." Turning to David, she circled his arm with hers. "What do you think, David?"

"It's a great idea. But I need some time to absorb it. And of course, there's the whole immigration process to go through if I decide to come. We should discuss it,

Barbara."

"I can probably help you with immigration. Perhaps a work permit first would help," Don said. "But you two need to think about it together. Have fun. You'd probably like time to yourselves."

Don left them together.

Barbara was as surprised as David by Don's invitation. She clasped David's hand.

"What do you think, David?"

"It sounds very exciting. But new ideas always do. I need a couple of days to reflect on it."

"Always the accountant!" Barbara felt a little disappointed at David's response, Don's suggestion seemed so right for them. "It would greatly help any future we planned together," she added. "You're not having doubts about that, are you?"

"Of course not. I just want to be sure it's really the right thing to do. Any future we plan together would not necessarily depend on my working for your father, as good as it sounds."

"Maybe. But I'd love to have you here in Vancouver with me. It's the best place in the world to live."

"You're not biased, are you?"

"Just look out the window." Barbara knew there was absolutely no view in the world like it.

"You may be right. Vancouver is very appealing, but the view on this couch is far more attractive." David took her in his arms.

"I feel much closer to you here as well," she whispered and they embraced in a long kiss.

After his conversation with Phyllis, Nigel stepped outside for some air. It was still mild enough to be pleasant. He sat slowly drinking a glass of wine. He was not sure he should have joined David for this excursion to Vancouver. He was beginning to feel like a fifth wheel and it was only the second day. They were a pleasant enough crowd, and he was happy for his younger brother. His thoughts turned to Evelyn, and back to the conversation with her mother that evening. He recalled Evelyn's flare up that Sunday morning before he drove her to Heathrow the following day.

As he was thinking about her, Evelyn and Clark came up the garden path. Nigel was captivated again by her looks—she really was beautiful, her classic features and perfect figure accented by the evening light—although she did seem a little thicker around the waist than he remembered. But she wasn't easy to forget.

"Hey Nigel," she called when she saw him. "You look lonely. Perhaps we can keep you company for a while. I want to introduce you to Clark. Did you know we're engaged?"

"Yes Barb mentioned it. Congratulations to you both. You're a lucky guy Clark. She's a great girl."

"And don't I know it," responded Clark.

Evelyn mockingly preened herself.

"I tried to get her for myself in England," teased Nigel, "but unfortunately she was stuck on you."

Clark looked at Evelyn and squeezed her. "Somebody stole her credit card so I could get back her here before you did." He laughed. "Glad it happened."

"However glad it made you, it wasn't that enjoyable for me," said Evelyn. She kept looking at the ground. "Let's change the subject."

"I know it wasn't," added Nigel. "You were pretty upset. If I remember, I got a real earful from you because of it."

"Sorry Nigel," Evelyn still looked at the ground.

"No big deal, Ev. But even your mom seems mystified

why you rushed back home."

Evelyn looked up. "You discussed it with her?" Her eyes narrowed.

"She brought it up. And I had to agree with her, it didn't seem worth all the fuss."

Evelyn looked daggers. "You have no idea how I felt. Don't try and tell me how I should have behaved. You don't know what I went through." Evelyn grimaced at her last sentence.

Clark looked surprised. "What you went through? You lost a credit card didn't you?"

"Okay, so I may have overreacted. You guys will never understand," and she escaped indoors. The men watched her go.

"Clark. I'm sorry about that. I spoke out of turn."

"That's okay Nigel. I thought the same at the time, but Ev is excitable. Give her some latitude. I'll catch up with her and see she's okay. Oh! By the way, I've contacted a friend of mine, Joe Garner. He's willing to take you sailing if you're interested. Here's his number; he's expecting your call"

With that, Clark followed Evelyn into the house.

The exchange, especially a repeat outburst, did nothing to diminish Nigel's suspicions that there was more to Evelyn's hasty departure from England than just losing a credit card—as infuriating as that could be. But, it was none of his business, and he put it to the back of his mind—until, perhaps, he had a chance to discuss it with David, to see how he had felt about it.

Clark caught up with Evelyn slipping on a coat.

"It's getting late," she said. "I'll drive you home." She didn't sound too enthusiastic.

They drove in silence for a few minutes, Clark wondering how to soothe Evelyn. She seemed to grow hot and cold on a whim since her return from England; he had to choose his words carefully.

"Ev. I'm so sorry you were upset at Nigel and me earlier. What exactly did we say that was so upsetting? I really want to avoid that happening again."

"If you want to avoid it, just drop the whole credit card business. It upset me at the time, but it's over and done with. Just don't mention it again."

That seemed simple enough to Clark, but was it really over? It didn't explain her outburst that evening or the day he proposed to her.

"Okay, it's over. I won't mention it again unless you do. Please, can we make up now?"

Evelyn drove a while before pulling over. She turned to him.

"Clark. I have to be honest. I'm still not sure I can trust you, as much as I want to. In fact, I'm not sure who I can trust. Life is very confusing for me right now. That doesn't mean I don't love you and desperately want you, but until I can sort things out in my mind, I might be likeable and not by turns. Please don't hold that against me, just give me some time."

"I still want to go on seeing you, Ev. If it means taking the rough with the smooth, then that's how it will be. But please, don't just cut me off."

Evelyn moved toward him, embracing him. "Oh Clark! I really have been a beast to you, haven't I? I'm sorry. Let me make it up to you. Let's go to your place. But, it'd better not be a repeat of the last time. I want to try and enjoy it."

Clark wondered why sex had been so distasteful to her. He'd try to ensure a more pleasant experience than the last time. He held her tight. She was clearly making an effort to please him.

"Of course, my darling. You lead the way this time," he

whispered, as he felt excitement growing.

They drove on, invigorated by their passion for each other. But Clark wondered how long before she turned against him again.

THE SILENT REMAINDER

25

The guests had left. Barbara and her family, Nigel and David were together.

"I propose a toast," said Don. "To a continuing and growing friendship between our families." They all raised their glasses to that.

"I'm sure Barb and I can assist in that," David added, smiling at Barbara. "Care for a short walk before bed, Barb?"

They walked slowly, their arms around each other. Barbara spoke first.

"David. What did you really think about Dad's offer of a job with him?"

"I'm really interested, Barb. I didn't want to sound too positive until I had thought through the implications. Unless something comes to mind to make it uncertain, I don't know why not. I've been praying about us, since you were in Brighton, and this may be God's answer for us. I just like to be sure."

Barbara leaned her head on David's shoulder as they walked. "The future looks so exciting, David. I hope nothing happens to interfere with it."

"Me too, sweetheart."

They walked in silence, each content with the presence of the other. Barbara knew the one thing that could interfere. For a moment she resented David's commitment to his faith, even though she admired it.

"David," she said. "You didn't say much about your faith in your emails. You said you would. I'm concerned that it's the one thing that could upset our future; you are so committed to your faith."

"I thought about it. But every time I wanted to put something down on paper, I worried that you could misunderstand it. It's easier to discuss it together, so your questions can be answered as we talk. Not so easy when writing. I'd like us to take some time for it while I'm here. What do you think?"

"Tomorrow David, I want to settle this soon, because it hangs like a shadow over our relationship. Tomorrow's Saturday. I'd love to show you around. Mom said we could use her car. We'll find a quiet spot to discuss things."

"Sounds good. Just as long as I'm with you, Barb."

They engaged in a long good night, savouring the sweetness of their lips together, and the closeness of their bodies, before entering the house.

But the evening wasn't over. Barb and Patti retired, and Don invited David and Nigel to join him for a nightcap.

"So glad you two could make it over. And David, I'm delighted that you and Barb are hitting it off."

David gave a thankful smile. "Barb's invited us to join you all for Christmas—if you'll have us. It would be great to greet the New Millennium in together—if everything doesn't collapse on January the first!"

Don laughed. "Thanks to Clark, I think we've got that licked. But here's to a closer bond between us all. Anyway, I'm going to bed. See you both in the morning."

David got up to go, but Nigel stopped him.

"Hey David. I've got a question for you. Sit down for a few minutes longer."

"Sure. Fire away."

Nigel told David of the concerns he had for Evelyn,

and how her behaviour had made him wonder if something other than losing her credit card had happened in Brighton. David became increasingly uncomfortable as Nigel spoke. Although he thought he could trust Nigel if he knew about the rape, David had agreed not to tell anyone else.

"Ah! I think it's your imagination," was all David could conjure up in response to Nigel's concern.

"I don't think so. Even Phyllis felt the same way."

"You discussed it with her?"

"Yes, but only after she had brought it up. She was surprised Ev came home so abruptly."

David needed to kill this line of thought. "Just put it down to overreaction, Nigel. It's all in the past now, anyway."

"Okay, but even Clark was thinking there was more to it. So just be warned. Maybe you need to pray about it." Nigel grinned as he rose from his chair.

David joined him and gave him a friendly punch. "Best advice I've heard from you in a long time. Might just do that."

"Good. See you in the morning."

"Goodnight, Nigel. God bless!" David returned the grin.

David was disturbed that others were questioning Ev's sudden return from England. After breakfast next morning he took Barbara aside and told her of Nigel's comments from the night before.

"I'm wondering if we should try to persuade Evelyn to come clean with the assault before it comes out some other way. What do you think?"

"We have plans for today, David. I've had Evelyn on my mind too much lately. As much as I care about Ev, I don't want her messing up our few days together. She's responsible for her own decisions. I've opposed her decision enough. Certainly, I really hope this doesn't all come out unexpectedly, but she's responsible for it, not us."

For someone so compassionate, especially to her friend Evelyn, David was surprised by Barbara's vehement response, although he was heartened by her determination not to let Evelyn's problems limit their time together.

"There's so much to see in Vancouver," explained Barbara, "and I've taken some vacation while you are here, so we have lots of time. So today, I thought we'd go to Stanley Park."

"You're the tour guide. I'll just follow you."

"Now, or for the rest of your life?"

"Don't push it!"

"Okay. Today's a practice run. We'll see how it works out."

David was entranced with the grandeur of Vancouver's setting surrounded by sea and mountains, the downtown compacted on its peninsula and the size and varied attractions of Stanley Park. They watched the seaplanes taking off from the harbour, the ships cruising under the Lion's Gate Bridge from Prospect Point, and had lunch at the Tea House. The sunny fall day, announced by leaves beginning to turn, created an autumn wonderland they walked through together.

"It's only an hour's walk around the sea wall," Barb suggested, "And the sea view changes constantly as you walk. We can take a leisurely pace and rest occasionally if you like."

"And we can discuss your concerns about my faith," added David.

Barbara replied with a happy nod.

They walked most of the way around the park, and sat on a bench facing English Bay, where several cargo ships rode lazily at anchor. White sails slipped playfully around them, racing and jostling one another. Barbara sat close to David watching the view in silence.

"David. Sitting here watching this peaceful scene, it seems as though nothing could spoil our dreams. Life should always be perfect, just as it appears right now. Yet I know that under this mirage of peace, a world of violence and misery exists. Does your faith explain why this is?"

"It does. But until we recognize that we are part of the problem, we won't understand or accept it."

"You mean you and I are part of the world's problems?" That seemed far-fetched to Barbara.

"If we have ever desired harm to some-one else, in deed, or maybe only in thought, we are experiencing the motivation that makes the world the way it is. Whether we hide or express it, we are complicit in the world's problem."

"I have to admit I've had malicious thoughts at times, but I doubt I would carry them out."

"Even if there were no laws stopping you? Wrecked on a desert island, for instance, with people who made you angry? Frankly, I think we'd soon resort to anarchism or survival of the fittest. You know, the Bible says the heart is deceitful and desperately wicked, but it's not easy to think that may be true of ourselves."

Barbara was trying to grasp the implications. "Are you suggesting we think, 'I'm not the problem, some-one else is.' But we're really all in this together?"

"Right. Here is the underlying problem, and God's answer in one quote. 'We all, like sheep, have gone astray, each of us has turned to his own way; and the Lord has laid on him the iniquity of us all.'"

"The answer? I don't see it."

"God laid on Jesus Christ the punishment that we deserve. When I realize he has paid the price for it on the cross and I accept my need of forgiveness, I am reunited with God for this life and for ever."

Barbara nodded; it struck a chord in her heart. "You know, as I look at my life, there are so many things I wish I could change or even wish I hadn't done. But I can't change them. I wish I could, but that's not possible."

"You're right. That's not possible. But it is possible for us to be forgiven. It's that admission that we need forgiveness, particularly God's forgiveness, which is our initial approach to God, for it is primarily him we have wronged. Then nothing further is required to be reconciled to him. Your church background probably taught you John three sixteen."

Barbara could quote it from memory, burned in her heart from childhood: "'For God so loved the world that He gave His one and only Son, that whoever believes in Him shall not perish but have eternal life.' You mean accepting that makes me a Christian? It's too simple!"

"Of course it's simple. Simple enough for a child to decide and many do. Anything more would be elitist and prohibit the least from coming to him."

"But the Christianity I've heard about seems far more complicated than that." Barbara shook her head, and then looked at David. "Now it seems far too simple."

"Well, there is much more to Christianity, but all Christian living and thinking is built on this one act of belief and response."

"David. What you say is beginning to make sense. In fact, much of the liturgy that I've ignored till now echoes what you've said. I just thought it didn't refer to me. Come to church with me tomorrow. I think it's going to make sense for the first time!" Barbara's face lit up with an excited smile.

David breathed a silent prayer of thanks.

"David. This has been such a wonderful day. I so enjoy being with you. Let's pray—yes pray!—that the rest of our time is just as pleasurable."

They drove home to some unwelcome news about Evelyn.

THE SILENT REMAINDER

26

Saturday morning for Evelyn was rarely good. She returned late from Clark's apartment the night before and woke late. She was going to miss breakfast with Phyllis once again, and would face a frosty day at home as a result. But a niggling sense of discomfort after another sexual encounter with Clark left a familiar knotted stomach. Leaving Clark in a rush, she made no plans to see him today, and the way she felt, she didn't want to. Phyllis was busy in the kitchen.

"Going out for the day," Evelyn called out, and without waiting for an answer drove away.

She had no idea where she was going. Disconsolate, she drove slowly, attracting horns and middle fingers, but was mostly oblivious to them. She drove over the Lions Gate Bridge, down Georgia and turned right onto Burrard. She drove over the Burrard Street Bridge and finished up parking at the Kitsilano beach. She left the engine running. A few people were out walking. The day that David and Barbara were finding so delightful, appeared dark and grim to Evelyn, despite the brilliant sunshine.

Suddenly, without thinking, she dropped into drive, gunned the accelerator, and lurched over the curb, across the grass verge and sidewalk, driving full tilt down the beach. The tide was up and the car slid quickly into deeper water killing the engine. The car was almost submerged. Evelyn plunked her head between her hands on the steering wheel and wept, her mind a blank, unaware of people beginning to wade in around her.

A young man tried to open her door, but the water pressure held it fast. Others were trying the other doors. He banged on the window

"Open your window," he yelled, "let some water in so we can get you out." Evelyn ignored him.

Someone handed the young man a rock, and he smashed the driver's window, and as water flooded in, he was able to open the door. Others helped him ease Evelyn from the car and carried her to a park bench. She looked around. *Where am I? Who are these people, why am I all wet?* The voices around her seemed distant, disconnected. She saw her car in the water, and became aware of some conversation.

"Are you okay?" a woman sitting next to her asked.

Evelyn wasn't sure. "I think so."

"Any injuries?" The woman persisted. Evelyn felt around herself. She had no pain.

"Don't think so."

Evelyn heard sirens. Medics checked her eyes and blood pressure and a police officer arrived.

"She's in shock," she heard a medic say. "We'll take her to the hospital for observation."

The next hour or so remained a blur; fussed around by hospital staff, and questioned by the officer, she couldn't recall his questions or her answers.

Phyllis answered the telephone.

"Mrs. Summers?"

"Yes."

"This is Staff Sergeant Peters of the Vancouver Police. I need to inform you that your daughter is in Vancouver General Hospital. She was involved in an accident. I'm glad to say she's okay, but in shock."

Phyllis' hand flew to her mouth. "Oh! My God. What happened?"

"For some reason we haven't ascertained yet, she drove her car into the sea."

"She did what?"

"Drove her car into the sea, Mrs. Summers. Can't tell you why. You can go to the hospital and see your daughter—and take some dry clothes."

"Thank you, officer."

What the hell did she think she was doing," was Phyllis' first thought. *That girl can be so irresponsible at times.* Phyllis suddenly started shaking. *My God, she could have drowned.* Her anger gave way to terror at the realization she could have lost her. *Something must have really upset her for this to happen; why didn't she talk to me about it*?

Suddenly she ached for her daughter, wanting to embrace her fully in the face of this near tragedy. She reflected on her past treatment of Evelyn, especially the reception Phyllis gave her on her return from England. She softened her attitude.

She drove to the hospital and arrived in Evelyn's room. Evelyn turned away as she entered the room. Phyllis sat on the edge of the bed.

"Evelyn, I'm so glad you are alright, I could have lost you. I was devastated at the thought."

Evelyn turned her head back to see tears on Phyllis' cheeks.

"You're not mad about the car?"

"The car? Ev, dear, you're more important to us than a thousand cars . . ."

Phyllis held her daughter in a tight embrace. Evelyn turned and clung to her mother. "I don't know why I did it. I don't remember anything at all."

"We can sort that out later. But right now, Ev, I love

you and want to take you home. I would have done anything to protect you from this." Phyllis wondered how long it had been since she verbalized, "I love you." *It must be unfamiliar to Evelyn as well*, she thought.

As they drove home, Phyllis said. "Ev, I was pretty curt with you when you returned from England without finding out how you felt. You must have been really upset to cut short your vacation there. I didn't think too much about it. I'm so sorry, Ev. I hope we can find out why you drove into the sea, but that is less important than having you back safely. If you'd like to talk about it, I'm here to listen. But you take whatever time you need. Unless you want to talk, the whole episode is over. We'll work out what to do about the car."

The absence of recriminations amazed Evelyn. *Mom is concerned about me!* Evelyn sat back consoled and reassured. Her strength began to return. She knew the event needed explaining, but her heart was calmer than it had been for a long time.

Barbara was waiting for her at home. Barbara walked her into the house and took her to the bedroom. Evelyn lay down.

"We'll get together once you've had a chance to rest, shall we?" said Barbara. "Important that you rest and get some sleep."

Phyllis came in. "Thanks Barb. You're a good friend. I'll sit with Ev for a while."

"See you," said Evelyn.

Barbara turned to Phyllis. "I'll go back and tell the others Evelyn's okay. I'll call back later."

Phyllis imagined what her husband Mark might have said, were he still alive, mirroring her own thoughts. *"Phyllis, have we spent too much time trying to get things right, at the expense of really loving Evelyn. What do you* *think?"*Phyllis imagined her retort. *"That's fine coming from you. You are probably the whole reason this happened."*

A buried anger at Mark surfaced. Seeing Evelyn so distressed in that hospital bed, Perhaps her own silence was to blame. Guilt added to the anger. The thought of losing Evelyn had really scared her. Phyllis could not recall how long it was since she felt like simply loving her. She was far more important than all the correctness and hiding the past was worth. Her anger at her deceased husband grew.

Phyllis determined it was time to confess the truth about Mark. She would find a suitable opportunity once Evelyn seemed strong enough to face it.

The events of that Saturday were clearly going to overshadow the remainder of the brothers' stay in Vancouver. Barbara began recriminations on herself for failing Evelyn in some way. Barbara and David sat in the local park that evening for privacy, both shaken by the day's events.

"If only I'd taken time to talk to her instead of resenting her interfering with our time together, maybe this wouldn't have happened," she figured.

"Don't get tied down with the 'ifs' and 'maybes,'" David advised her. "No-one knows what difference, if any, your intervention would have made. It could have heightened the tension. It's too easy to take responsibility and flounder in false guilt for something like this."

"I know David. I felt the same when she was raped in Brighton. She felt the same way as well then. Perhaps she still does, making it harder to tell what happened."

She pulled out her cell phone and called Phyllis. "How's Ev doing? Can I come and see her?"

"She's still sleeping. It looks as though she may sleep right through the night. I suggest you come tomorrow sometime."

"I'll be there." Barbara pocketed her phone.

"That sets the day for us tomorrow, I think." Barbara marked off the passages of time with her fingers. "We'll go to church in the morning, visit with Ev in the afternoon, and have the evening to ourselves." She opened her palms with a flourish. "That should satisfy everyone—even God!"

David laughed. "I think you may be right. Sounds like a good plan," and he hugged his girl.

27

The next morning, Sunday, David, Barbara and her parents went to church together. David wondered how Barbara's church service would connect with his understanding of Christianity. He expected it to be far more formal than he was used to, yet identified with much of the liturgy used. Barbara turned to him, pointing out a couple of texts used in that morning's service; she seemed to identify with them.

> I acknowledge my transgressions. And my sin is ever before me. Psalm 51:3.
> The sacrifices of God are a broken spirit: a broken and a contrite heart, O God, you will not despise. Psalm 51:17.

David pointed out a further one to her.

> If we say we have no sin, we deceive ourselves, and the truth is not in us: but, if we confess our sins, he is faithful and just to forgive us our sins, and to cleanse us from all unrighteousness. 1 John 1:8–9.

She nodded to him, smiling.

David joined in lustily with the last hymn of the service, an old hymn that summed up his faith and which Barbara clearly knew well.

> "Man of Sorrows," what a name For the Son of God who came. Ruined sinners to reclaim! Hallelujah! What a Saviour!
> Bearing shame and scoffing rude, In my place

> condemned He stood; Sealed my pardon with
> His blood; Hallelujah! What a Saviour!
> Lifted up was He to die, "It is finished!" was
> His cry; Now in heaven exalted high;
> Hallelujah! What a Saviour!
> When He comes, our glorious King, All His
> ransomed home to bring, Then anew this
> song we'll sing Hallelujah! What a Saviour!

David and Barbara looked at each other; tears filled Barbara's eyes. She looked away, head bowed, squeezing his hand. David's heart soared.

They decided to walk home together.

"We'll get some lunch prepared; it'll be ready when you get home," Patti promised as she and Don drove off.

"David," Barbara began. "I feel such a peace I've never felt before. It's as if the burdens of the world were lifted off my shoulders. I don't understand how, but the world suddenly seems a brighter place."

"Barb. The world *is* brighter. Don't you see? We are reconciled with him as we were meant to be. Our sin is no longer a barrier to a continuing relationship with God. Our lives are in his hands; we can trust him whatever comes. We can walk with him through this life, and beyond that, eternity is settled with him. We no longer fear the uncertainty of life or death. This faith in God is a firm foundation for life."

"Suddenly, there is so much I want to know . . ."

"And the best place to find it is in your Bible. Let's take some time this week to explore it a bit."

"Yes. I'd really like that. But right now, Ev is on my mind. I want to see her this afternoon. Perhaps I can persuade her that becoming a Christian can help her."

Lunch proved interesting. Barbara was so enthused about her new understanding of her faith, she wanted to share it with her parents. The day continued sunny and warm. Patti had prepared a cold lunch and they sat on the terrace together taking pleasure in the warmth and the view across English Bay. David expressed his admiration for the scenery; like yesterday, peaceful and romantic.

"But what happened to Evelyn reminds us it's not so perfect." David's comment went without saying. Don nodded agreement.

Don finished his coffee, and sat back with his hands clasped behind his head. "How did you feel about the service this morning, David. Different to what you're used to, wasn't it?"

"Yes. Much more formal. But I really enjoyed it. Much of it confirmed my understanding of the faith—our need of reconciliation with God."

Barb joined in. "Dad, I have come to an understanding of the Christian faith I never knew before, despite of all my years going to church. David explained much yesterday, but the service today confirmed it. Our relationship with God depends on our acceptance of Christ's death as the penalty for our sin. Is that what you understand?"

"Sounds a bit like what David was saying to me on Friday." Don was non-committal. "But have you and David come to an agreement on the subject? Does this mean some plans for the future?" He couldn't miss the excitement in Barbara's eyes.

"Don!" Patti interjected. "I think they will tell us that when they're ready. More coffee, anyone?"

Barbara called Evelyn. "How are you feeling today, my sister? Can David and I come and visit?"

"Feeling so much better. In fact, I'd like to go for a ride. Can you pick me up?"

When they arrived, Barbara was uncertain of Evelyn's request. "Please drive me to the Kitsilano beach where I drove my car in the sea."

"Are you sure?"

"Yes. I need to try to relive those few minutes. It might help me sort out why I did it."

"Okay," said David. "I doubt it can hurt."

They drove the route Evelyn had taken the day before, reached the Kitsilano beach parking area, and stopped and viewed the scene. The car tracks across the grass were clearly visible, but the car had gone.

"I remember setting out from home. I don't remember coming to this beach. I can't recall anything until I found myself soaking wet on that bench over there."

"You've been under a lot of stress lately," suggested Barbara. "I think you must have snapped and acted without thinking."

"Or you wanted to commit suicide, and your mind has blanked it out," added David. "What to you think, Ev?"

Evelyn sat quietly for a while. It was good to see her composed, but Barbara wondered how long that would last.

"I don't know what to think. Let me tell you how I feel. I don't know who I can trust; I'm not even sure about Clark. He called a couple of times, but Mom told him I was sick. I'll have to call him later to explain and tell him I'm okay. He's going to hear all about this anyway. One thing though. I expected to get balled out, but Mom acted completely the opposite; she was kind to me. She suggested I see a doctor, and get a check up. Maybe I will. But she doesn't know all the truth, and I feel guilty for not telling her."

"And keeping secrets is stressful," Barbara reminded her, "and you have too many!"

Evelyn stiffened. "Don't tell me to come clean. I've gone too far to go back now. I can handle it."

"You think dumping your car into the sea is handling it?"

Evelyn bristled. "That, or anything like it won't happen again. Now drop it."

"Okay Ev." Barbara eased back. "We're your friends, whatever happens. And it seems your mother is as well, from what you say. Let's keep it that way, shall we?"

"Thanks Barb." Evelyn leaned forward from the back seat and wound her arms around Barb and hugged her. "You too, David," and winding one arm around him, kissed them both gently. "You two are the closest friends I have, and you've been with me all along."

Barbara wasn't relieved much. Another crisis was past with, it seemed, little human damage. But she couldn't be sure it was the last.

That evening, Evelyn spent at home, providing a convenient window for Phyllis to have a long delayed talk about her childhood. Evelyn was tentatively enjoying a renewed relationship with her mother, but didn't know if it would last.

"Glad you're home this evening Ev," Phyllis began, "because I need to talk with you about something. Can you spare me a few minutes."

As Phyllis rarely showed interest in talking, Evelyn nodded expectantly.

"Tell me what you remember of your childhood," Phyllis asked.

"I guess the most I remember is feeling I was an inconvenient addition to the family. I rarely remember a time to talk like this."

"How much do you remember of your father?"

"Mostly somewhat distant, although he always showered me with gifts."

"You don't recall him as a loving father, Ev? You never sensed him close to you?"

"Not really. Although I get shivers whenever I think of

being close to him. I don't know why."

Phyllis pursed her lips. "I think I can explain," she said slowly. "Prepare yourself for a shock."

Evelyn stared at her mother, a slow comprehension forming in her mind. "Did he . . . molest me in some way?"

Phyllis's eyes began brimming over. She was silent, only a slow nod providing an answer. They were both silent for at least a minute. Then Evelyn spoke.

"Why don't I remember it? Are you sure it happened?"

Phyllis nodded again, "You've blocked it out, Ev. I thought it best not to tell you, but after yesterday, I realize it's still upsetting you, despite your memory loss. Ev, I'm so sorry."

"Did you know about it?"

"Yes, but I tried to pretend it wasn't happening. I couldn't face the truth. But it caused me nightmares. In the end, I was relieved when your father died."

Questions filled Evelyn's mind, but the enormity of what she'd just heard crowded them out.

"Mom. I'm not sure what I feel just now, but I really need to be alone for a while. I'm going out to try and think this through. But please don't worry, I won't do anything stupid. I just need some time."

With that, she left, walking aimlessly, seeking some sense or meaning to this new revelation. Try as she may, she couldn't recall any instances of her father abusing her. But it made sense of the distance she felt from him. *If it's there in my subconscious, I should be able to retrieve the memory,* she thought. Suddenly, she thought of Clark, and the revulsion she fought at the idea of sex. It all made sense. And her mother's coldness: probably fear that closeness to her daughter might expose the truth somehow. And no wonder there was a huge hole in her heart—dug deeper during her father's repeated molestation.

But as she pondered her lost memory, another thought struck her. She recalled the déjà vu feeling she had after leaving the rape house. Perhaps that might be the key to retrieving her lost memory. For that moment she had possibly touched subconscious memories of her father's abuse.

Then she recalled the place where she had that experience. The place had seemed familiar. *How could it,* she questioned, *when I'd never been to Brighton before.* But the feeling persisted, and she saw the corner store where she'd bought the map and saw the circular mailbox at the curb side. That could be a way to find her perpetrators.

But the weight of the discovery of her father's abuse flooded her afresh. Whatever those memories meant, they would have to wait until later. What now? She felt a deepening anger and pity for her mother. She should have stopped it; she hadn't, and that resulted in Phyllis carrying the pain of it most of her married life. But how should Evelyn herself respond to this? Would it affect her relationship with Clark and with others for that matter? Whom should she tell, or should she keep it secret like her mother had? Now, they had this new secret bond of guilt and pain between them.

She walked home. Her mother was sitting alone in obvious distress. Evelyn, although emotionally exhausted felt she needed to confide in her. She sat in a chair opposite her mother.

"Mom, I've something to confess as well." Evelyn paused, her mother looked up surprised. "Mom . . . I'm having Clark's baby."

Phyllis just looked at Evelyn for a few moments. Evelyn couldn't tell what her mother was thinking.

Eventually Phyllis responded "Oh! My dear. I'm not sure whether to be sorry or glad. How do you feel about it?

How far along are you?"

"Fine Mom. I'd rather you felt glad for me. This will be your grandchild, and I'm early yet, a month or so." Evelyn needed to keep the timing of the pregnancy vague.

"Have you seen a doctor?"

"Not yet."

"I'll arrange for our family doctor to ensure you're okay. If you're happy about it then so am I."

Phyllis went over to Evelyn and gave her a long hug.

"I guess this means a wedding soon, eh?"

"We haven't sorted that out yet Mom. Right now, this has been exhausting I have to go bed. I want to sleep on this. See you in the morning."

Nigel didn't know how to sail despite living on the English coast. He had too many other interests to that point. This time on the ocean with Joe was a new experience for him, and he took advantage of a lesson. *Got to get one of these when I get home*, he decided, and then sat back to the lilting motion of the small yacht. He liked Joe; he was a bit like himself. They were both outgoing. But Joe had firm ideas about Evelyn.

"That girl's a pack of trouble. You'd be well advised to keep your distance," he warned. "I don't know why Barb's so stuck on her."

"Probably the same reason I like her," replied Nigel. "She's exciting and fun to be with, even if it does create a mess occasionally."

"I can do without the 'mess' as you put it. But you're reasonably safe. Clark has to deal with her."

Nigel thought he should take this opportunity to do some evangelism for his non-beliefs, but the weather and sea were so delightful, he was lured into an emptiness of mind that drifted serenely with the wind.

28

The days before the brothers returned to England, passed uneventfully; at least, there were no more crises. For Barbara and David it was their most exciting time yet. David agreed to work for Don, depending on getting immigrant status established, and shared his decision with Nigel.

Nigel thought it was a great idea. "Now I can have family on both sides of the Atlantic and live in both places."

Barbara was beside herself with excitement. Her newfound faith, coupled with the probability of David coming to Vancouver meant there was nothing barring them making their relationship permanent.

They sat one morning facing the sea discussing David's work opportunity.

"Barb. I really feel God has been working things out for us. I often had doubts that we'd be able to work things out—with distance and our beliefs—but there is little else now separating us."

Barbara guessed what might be coming and could hardly wait to say "yes," but wanted David to finish his speech.

"Barb, you stepped into my world and changed it completely. I never thought I could attract a girl, let alone a girl as beautiful and wonderful as you. The fact that you love me and want to be with me is a miracle from God himself. I can't live without you now, and if you'll have me, I want you to . . ." David hesitated, taking a deep breath.

"Yes?"

"Is that a question or an answer?"

"Answer to what?"

"Will you . . . ?" Breathing in again.

"David, spit it out." Barb was laughing, almost delirious.

"Please, Barb. Will you . . . ?" Deep breath. "Will you marry me?"

"I never thought you'd get there," she said, encircling him in a tight embrace.

"But will you?"

"Will I what?"

"Marry me?"

"Oh! My goodness. Didn't I answer you?" said Barb with mock seriousness.

"You didn't."

"Of course I'll marry you. Did you expect me to say no?"

David relaxed with a long exhale. "Of course I didn't. But I wanted to hear you say yes."

"Didn't I say that?"

"Not yet."

"Yes, yes, *yes*, David. I couldn't live without you either. I'll marry you right now if you'll have me."

The long embrace that followed caught the attention of passers-by, but neither noticed. That afternoon, they searched the jewellers for a ring that, according to custom, Barbara proudly displayed to whoever would show the mildest interest, and joyfully showed it to her parents that evening.

After supper, Patti looked at the ring again. "Both Dad and I are delighted to have you, David, as a son-in-law. If you two stay as happy as you both look now, you're in for a long and exciting marriage. Here's to a joyful relationship."

"I second that," added Nigel. "Never thought my little brother would make it, but you've beaten me to it. And Barbara, I'm delighted to call you my sister. You've stolen my heart too."

"As long as you don't steal *her*," David advised, "I'll drink to that!"

"Nobody's going to steal me away, David. I'm too stuck on you." Barbara grabbed his arm and planted a passionate kiss on his cheek.

Evelyn thought long and hard about her father's abuse of her. It caused the same sense of shame the assault in Brighton had produced. For that reason alone she decided to keep it secret, especially while Nigel and David were in Vancouver. She could decide on perhaps talking to Barbara later, and others . . . ? She couldn't think that far. Phyllis happily agreed with Evelyn. It was as embarrassing for her mother, having kept the secret for so long, as it was for Evelyn.

Evelyn heard from Barbara of her engagement to David. Despite her suspicions of them on occasion, the news warmed her once again to the close bond she'd always had with Barbara. She adored her as much for occasional unwanted advice, as their frequent fun times together. She knew deep down what Barbara said about her deception was true, even though she couldn't bring herself to be honest about it. But the engagement called for a celebration, and that Friday evening, before David's return flight on Sunday, the two engaged couples settled for a Chinese dinner together.

Evelyn couldn't keep her happiness at David and Barbara's engagement to herself, in turn hugging both

David and Barbara every time occasion permitted. She was the happiest and most composed she had felt for some time, thanks to thinking that discovering her source of emptiness was equivalent to its cure. If she was trying to convince herself that her wild thoughts were behind her, she was succeeding.

"So when's the wedding going to be? What about a double wedding?" Evelyn was well ahead of the rest of the company. The idea of all marrying together had the illusion that she and Clark would share David and Barbara's stability.

"Have you a date for yours yet?" Barbara asked.

"No specific date," replied Evelyn, "but early in the New Year because of the baby."

"Ev, we haven't fixed a date yet. A lot depends on David getting papers to come here. But neither of us wants to wait too long. But a wedding together is a possibility."

David interjected. "You may know Ev, Barb has recently come to accept Christian beliefs similar to mine. That may colour the sort of wedding we'd like. We wouldn't want to involve you and Clark in a ceremony you might be uncomfortable with. You'd need to keep that in mind."

"That's a good thought, David," responded Clark. "I think Ev and I should talk about that. I know Ev's sceptical about religion, and I'm quite ambivalent. But like Ev, I'm glad of your friendship, and certainly respect your views."

"How's Nigel doing?" asked Evelyn. "He must be on his own a lot."

"Joe, although he has to work, has taken Nigel under his wing," replied David. "I've been sight seeing with him, and he's okay with his own company much of the time. But he'll have a couple of days after I've returned. We weren't able to get the same flight back."

Evelyn made a mental note of Nigel's later departure,

but said nothing in front of Clark. She dearly wanted to spend some time with Nigel again. She loved Clark, but found Nigel stimulating in a way that Clark wasn't.

It was a delightful evening. Although they had their differences, and the car sinking episode and knowledge of her father's abuse were still raw, it was a comfortable and constructive evening that lessened rifts they were all aware of.

Barbara had doubts those rifts would all eventually heal. Her thoughts were taken up with David's soon departure. That Sunday morning, they stayed together, visiting the places around Vancouver where they'd made memories over the past days. After goodbyes to the family, they rode together to the airport. This ride held more promise for the future than the last, and lessened the sorrow of parting. But the sense of being torn apart was still there, and had them clinging to each other until the last moment.

"Barb, I'm going feel the warmth of your body against me until I reach England," he whispered, "and I shall carry the memory of it until I'm back at Christmas."

"We're going to be married David! That's the day I'm waiting for. I hope we can set a date soon."

"I'm working on it. As soon as I have some idea when I can get papers for Canada, we'll set a date. Or, if necessary, I'll come for a visit just to get married."

"I love you David." Barbara rested her head on his shoulder. "Keep me in your thoughts and prayers."

"I doubt a minute will pass when I don't," he assured her. "I love you so much." They walked to the security barrier hand in hand, and he disappeared with a last wave to her.

"Call for you Nigel," said Patti. "It's Evelyn."

Nigel was downing his second cup of breakfast coffee

the following morning. Last day to go before his flight home. He picked up the phone.

"Good morning Nigel. How are you doing this morning?"

"I'm doing just fine. Even better hearing your cheery voice Ev."

"Glad to hear it. Wondered if you'd like to join me for coffee before returning home? Three at Tim Horton's down from the house. I'm working until then. Can you fit that into your busy schedule?"

"It'll be a squeeze fitting it into nothing else I have to do today. Look forward to it."

Nigel enjoyed the time he'd spent with Evelyn in England. Attracted to her good looks and feisty spirit, he anticipated the time thoughtfully. He felt safe; she was already engaged.

Don had left for work. Patti was clearing the table.

"Any specific plans for today, Nigel?"

"Not till three," he answered.

"I don't need my car this morning if you'd like to take it for a last run around town."

"Thanks Patti. I think I will."

Nigel drove to his favourite places. Like most newcomers to Vancouver, he was impressed with its grandeur, the bustling tourist spots, and, for him, the beautiful women everywhere. He thought again of Evelyn. *Not really in love with her,* he mused, *just as well; I'm not ready to settle down. But I do enjoy her company.*

He was at the coffee shop at three. As he expected, she was late. *Obviously thinks it's important to maintain independence.* She sat down at his table while he bought her a coffee.

"Ready to go back to Brighton?"

"Yea. Nothing much in this God-forsaken place," he

quipped.

"You mean you have no-one here, don't you? Have you been lonely?"

"No, not really. Joe's spent some time with me and I spent a pleasant morning with David exploring Don's office. You know Dave's been offered a job there?"

"Yes. I'm so pleased for Barbara. Wedding bells are next."

"And how about you and Clark? Still hitting it off okay?"

"Yes, plan to be married early in the New Year."

"Lucky guy. You look gorgeous as ever."

"Thanks. And I hope you find the girl of your dreams."

"You expecting?"

"Expecting what?"

"A baby."

"Who told you?"

"No-one. I guessed looking at you."

"Liar. David and Barbara told you, didn't they?"

"No. You looked a little thicker around the middle than I remember."

Evelyn was on the defensive. "What else did they tell you?"

"You mean about the baby?"

"Yes."

"As I said, they haven't told me anything." Nigel recalled Joe's comment, *"She is a pack of trouble."* "Evelyn, I came here to enjoy some time with you, not to argue. I told you the truth. Look in your mirror again. It's becoming obvious. Does your mom know?"

"You're beginning to sound like Barbara. Always with the advice! Okay, I believe you, but I'm never sure who to believe these days."

"Is that why you went for a swim in your car?"

Evelyn lightened up. "Yes. Maybe. I don't know. All I

can say is: life's confusing right now."

"Evelyn. You must trust those closest to you. As I understand it, Barbara's been a great friend, and I'm sure your mother always gives you good advice." Nigel could hardly believe himself, he sounded like an old parent himself. "Ev, I'm the last one to give advice. I'm independent like you. I say 'I trust no-one,' but it doesn't work like that in practice. What do you think?"

"Sounds reasonable. I'll give it some thought. Nigel, I like you—even if you sound like a Dutch uncle right now. Interesting how two independent people can get along!" She grinned at him. "Sorry I doubted you."

"That's okay." There was that impudent grin of his. "I don't inspire confidence in people generally."

"How about Mahita? Remember her?"

"No. Actually, I'd forgotten her until now. She was just a passing fancy, and I was the same to her, I think."

"How far did it go?"

"Nowhere. High caste I think. I wasn't in her class!"

"Still plan to come visit us at Christmas?"

"Certainly, if Barb's folks will put up with me again."

Nigel thought Evelyn sounded more confident and less troubled. He liked it, she seemed even more attractive. They walked back up the hill together silently. She slipped her arm into his. They reached Evelyn's house and lingered long enough for a good hug before Nigel walked on.

29

Surprisingly, the time until Christmas passed quickly. Don obtained a work permit for David to start in the New Year if he wished; Don had some pull somewhere. David commenced his immigration process for permanent residence. The transatlantic telephone conversations were always animated with potential. Barbara looked for an apartment for David to rent when he arrived.

"I really don't know why we should wait to get married," suggested Barbara during one of their Saturday phone calls. "There's no point in you living alone in an apartment if we're destined to be together."

"I don't want to wait either, Barb. Just need enough time for me to get organized and for us to collect some basic furniture."

"Let's give it a month. How about the last Saturday in January—the twenty-ninth?"

"Sounds good to me," replied David. "Can you arrange for church and reception?"

"Yes, David, and I'll keep you informed."

"You're there, I'm not. I trust you to make the best arrangements."

"And I'll find an apartment, something better than the garret you're in now."

"You said you could live in it with me."

"I know what I said, but I'm still looking for something less like a cave."

David chuckled. "I could live in a cave with you."

"And carry a club and drag me around by the hair, I bet!"

"No. I'd let you walk behind me. Wouldn't want to mess your hair."

"Typical chauvinistic male. I have more civilized ideas. Get used to it!"

"Sounds like I'm marrying a closet feminist."

"Then we're a good match, David. It's going to be fun."

David sensed that intense longing again. "Life will always be good with you," he said. "I just can't wait my darling."

"Me too," she said softly. "Soon."

David spent his time slowly winding down his business, and finding another accountant for the hotel. That, immigration, sorting belongings, and work, kept him busy enough that time passed easily. David booked flights, one way for himself and a return flight after the New Year for Nigel.

Nigel was not looking forward to David leaving permanently for Canada. He was beginning to feel some loneliness already. He would miss their times together, even if David was a religious nut. He found it difficult to forget Evelyn, her face showing at the most unexpected moments. He started dancing more often, sometimes on his own, or with a girl he had dated before, or one he picked up at a bar. The Metro Restaurant became his favourite hangout, although he would go elsewhere occasionally for variety.

As the time approached for both men to leave for Vancouver again, Nigel helped David pack his possessions. David had purchased small trunks to pack his most treasured belongings, and shipped them to Vancouver separately. "Don't want to take more than necessary on the plane," he explained.

Nigel decided to take over David's apartment. It was time for him to have his own place.

A hotel employee was co-opted to drive them to the airport a few days before Christmas. All the luggage was packed and David's trunks were already on their way to Vancouver. Nigel looked forward to some time with Joe again, and thought more often of Evelyn.

Barbara realized that her new-found family was making her more familiar with Vancouver airport. Irregular visits to the airport would be a staple of life for the foreseeable future, with close family on both sides of the Atlantic. This she was glad to do; particularly as this visit welcomed David to Vancouver permanently.

But her time until that day had been busy also. Her church had agreed to celebrate the wedding and the reception was arranged in a hotel banquet room nearby. She found a high rise apartment overlooking English Bay in one direction, Stanley Park in another, a few minutes walk from her dad's office. Her excitement grew with each need settled. She hoped David would be pleased with her arrangements.

Barbara and her parents drove the SUV to the airport; enough seats for all of them and the luggage. The excitement was palpable. They parked the car and waited at the international flights exit. Barbara diligently scanned every passenger emerging until David and Nigel appeared. Don and Patti welcomed Nigel, while Barbara and David locked in a long-awaited, ardent embrace.

"David. I'm so excited to share the arrangements I've made and I'm thrilled with our apartment—that is, *your* apartment until we're married. But I'm going to make it look like mine well before that."

"Barb whatever you've done, I'm happy with it already. I decided that before I came. I trust you to make the right decisions."

Barbara told David that Christmas was to be a strictly family affair, although Phyllis dropped in during the afternoon of Christmas Eve to welcome David and Nigel back. She invited them all to her place for New Year's Eve. They would welcome in, not only a New Year, but a New Millennium. That was agreed, Barbara's younger brother suggesting it might be advisable to be together in case the world came to an end at midnight.

"We'll know before that son," explained Don. "It'll happen twenty-one hours earlier in New Zealand if it's going to happen. We're near the end of the sun's daily cycle."

"David, I think we're in for a glorious time this holiday." Barbara squeezed David's hand.

"And we are going to celebrate it together. It's my dream come true," added David.

Christmas Eve was a candlelight service at the church. Nigel excused himself, but David took the opportunity to explain more of the Christian faith that Christmas introduced.

"It's not just the birth of a baby we celebrate, but this Baby was God himself taking on human flesh. Note part of the Christmas reading this evening":

> The Word became flesh, and made his
> dwelling among us. John 1:14.

Barb nodded. "I remember reading that in the Bible you gave me, but wasn't sure what it meant."

"The 'Word' refers to Jesus Christ. Later Jesus said: 'If you have seen me, you have seen the Father,' indicating he was one with the Father and God himself. This means so much more than the tinsel and jingles in the stores at Christmas—so cheap and shallow by comparison."

"So it matters to us personally that Jesus was born? We're not just celebrating a piece of history?"

"Exactly." David warmed to his subject. "Eventually that baby became the ultimate sacrifice that reconciles us back to God. There is no greater meaning to Christmas."

Christmas day was a late brunch about ten, and dinner at five, although snacks were available during the day. Opening gifts followed brunch, next a brisk walk in the cool afternoon breeze. Barbara and David huddled together arm in arm, talking excitedly about their plans, Nigel was inviting young Roger to visit him in Brighton, while Patti naturally linked arms with Don. After Christmas dinner, they sat around the fire, Nigel regaling the company with stories of the hotel, and Don and Patti telling stories about Barbara, much to her amused embarrassment.

Not to be outdone, Nigel reminded Barbara of David's awkwardness at their first meeting. Barbara had a tale about Nigel which in turn led to a litany of good natured banter about most of the family. David and Barbara slipped out later in the evening for some private time together.

"Think you can put up with my family, now you know all about us?" asked Barbara as they walked.

"I think I could put up with any family as long as I have you," David replied. "But I feel very much at home with them. I was far more intimidated meeting you for the first time; so scared you might not like me."

"David. I found your reaction both amusing and endearing. I felt comfortable at once, and really wanted to put you at ease. I knew immediately I wanted to be with you. Your emails weren't lying; what I felt in them was real."

"I remember how well you succeeded. I had never felt so comfortable with any girl as you made me feel."

"Comfortable eh? Well, the time is coming to make you feel uncomfortable," she said mischievously, "especially on our wedding day."

David was immediately aroused. Barbara spun around and embraced him, feeling evidence of his arousal.

"It'll be worth the wait, I assure you David. I'm longing for you as well. Sometimes just your touch makes me shiver."

They held each other tightly, thrilling at the close physical contact. They sat on the park bench for a few minutes, her head resting on his shoulder

"I think it's wonderful that God created us with this need of each other. I have to thank God for that among other things," Barbara said quietly. "And I thank God for you."

David's mind was fogged by her presence. "Me too," was all he could say.

30

Christmas was one thing; New Year would be another.
Evelyn was nervous, having Clark together with all the families, especially those who knew of her secret. She had confided her nervousness to a work acquaintance earlier who provided something that would calm her. Apart from Evelyn's apprehension, the media frenzy had been building for some time regarding the Millennium bug. Books predicted the collapse of the monetary system and technology generally. Religious books heralded the beginning of the end times, and many personal computers were unable to cope with a new year dated 00.

Barbara's family joined Phyllis and Evelyn about seven New Year's Eve. Clark sat close to Evelyn. Phyllis had the TV going, and the New Year was already old in most of the east.

"No glitches so far," Don observed. "And if the east can handle it I doubt there will be a problem here in the west."

They watched recordings from earlier in the day. Gisborne in New Zealand, closest city in the world to the international dateline—"first to see the light"—had a segment. They saw the fireworks on Sydney Harbour Bridge, displaying a huge sign "Eternity" lit up for all to see. The announcer explained that a homeless man had spent years writing that word around the city. He became something of an icon, and the sign commemorated his life.

They watched the New Millennium celebrated, rolling hourly from east to west

There was a huge sense of relief in the room.

"Looks as though Clark here has saved the world," quipped Roger and spread his hands in mock adulation towards him.

"Just glad I could help," responded Clark and grinned. "Just send money!"

"And if he can save the world, he can save me," Evelyn added. She struggled to understand what she was saying.

"Not from me, I hope," said Nigel.

"No, not you. Those guys who . . ."

"What guys?" Clark was curious. Barbara and David stiffened.

"Oh! Nothing."

"Barbara whispered to David, "Evelyn isn't herself."

He replied, "She looks stoned to me."

Interest returned to the television. Nine o'clock was about to strike midnight in Ottawa, and they watched the countdown and cheering from the capital city as midnight chimed out from the Peace Tower. After a while, a band started "O Canada," and a raucous crowd joined in. Those gathered in the room joined in. Whether it was patriotism aroused by singing the national anthem, or the presence of invading Brits in the room—perhaps both—the images of the Brighton incident were playing on Evelyn's mind.

"Glad to be Canadian," announced Evelyn, "and live here, and not over there where. . ." She checked herself again.

"Over there where?" Clark asked. "are you talking about England?"

"Safer here with you, my darling," Evelyn replied and snuggled to him.

Clark looked mystified, but held Evelyn. Barbara moved next to Evelyn.

"I think Ev's tired and the excitement has her confused." Barbara tried to divert attention away from Evelyn's blundering. "Ev! Maybe you should lie down for a while?"

"Maybe, I think I should lie down . . ."

Phyllis was listening intently. Evelyn left the room and leaned against the wall outside the family room trying to collect her thoughts. She heard the conversation in the background.

"Do you know what she is talking about Barbara?" asked Phyllis.

Barbara hesitated. "Ask Evelyn in the morning when she is thinking clearer. She'll probably have a simple explanation."

Clark sat back, temporarily satisfied. Evelyn returned to the room.

"No. I want to see the New Year in. I can sleep tomorrow."

"Okay, Ev. Let me sit with you," offered Barbara.

She wants to guide my conversation, Evelyn thought. Nigel was a natural skeptic. He turned quietly to David.

"I think Barb's helping Ev hide something. What do you think?"

Now David hesitated. He took his cue from Barbara's answer. "Check with Barb tomorrow. She probably has a simple answer."

Nigel seemed satisfied with the answer, but he watched Evelyn intently. Attention returned to the unfolding Millennium, city after city exploding in riotous colour as the first day of the new Millennium rolled around the earth. London appeared on the screen. The joy of a new century grated on Evelyn's confused and nervous state.

"That damn country. What have they got to celebrate?"

Phyllis walked over to the TV and switched it off.

"Okay Evelyn. What's going on?"

Silence for a few moments. Barbara bit her lip. David clenched his hands. Everyone was looking at Evelyn. She looked nervously around the room, then broke the silence by bursting into tears. Phyllis put her arms around her. Barbara, sitting on the other side took Evelyn's hand. Evelyn looked from one to the other, unsure where to go next: keep her secret or come clean about it. Either seemed equally traumatic. Phyllis backed up. She couldn't bear Evelyn's distress, and she was also concerned her own secret would come out.

"Okay, Ev. You don't have to—"

"It's okay Mom," Evelyn said through sniffles, "I'm tired of hiding it."

"Hiding what?" Phyllis became alarmed.

Barbara broke in. "You know, Mrs. Summers. I think you will want some privacy to hear what Evelyn has to say—"

"What do you know about this, Barbara?" Suspicion lined Phyllis' face, but privacy was necessary. She stood up. "Sorry about this folks, but . . ."

"No problem," said Don. "We quite understand."

"David and I will stay," said Barbara. "We may be able to help. Clark should stay too. It affects him."

"Affects me?" asked Clark. "How?"

"We'll explain," was all Barbara said.

Nigel, Don, and his family departed quietly.

Phyllis spoke first. "So Ev, what's this all about? Remember I'm here to support you, whatever the problem is."

Evelyn's face screwed up. "I don't think I can bear to tell you," and she wept again.

"Let me tell you," said Barbara.

David came and sat beside her, and put his arm around her. Phyllis still looked suspiciously at Barbara, which didn't help Barbara's composure.

"The short answer is, Evelyn was abducted and raped while in Brighton. She insisted we keep it secret, she couldn't face the shame." Barb let that sink in, waiting for the inevitable storm to erupt.

"You didn't call the police?" Phyllis was incensed.

"No."

"No doctor check up?"

"No."

"You did nothing for her?"

"We did what we could to help her—"

Evelyn broke in. "Mom, I insisted they tell no-one. They did everything they could beyond that."

Clark was looking intently at Evelyn with wide eyes, clearly trying to think through this turn of events. She glanced his way and back again, avoiding his gaze.

Phyllis shook her head. "David. You were in on this too, were you?"

"Mrs. Summers. We were 'in on it,' as you put it, to do everything we could within the limits of Ev's request," David replied. "She was distressed enough as it was. Spreading it around would have only worsened that."

"Okay. For now, I have to believe that you two did whatever you could for Evelyn then. We'll have to work with the situation as it is now."

Clark, listening intently to that point, became agitated. By this time he was shaking.

"Evelyn. Is this where the baby came from?"

"Oh! The baby," screamed Phyllis, placing her hand over her mouth.

Evelyn looked at Clark, desperation clouded her eyes.

"Clark. I'm so sorry—"

Clark stood up facing her. "You deliberately fooled me into believing it was mine, didn't you?"

"I didn't know what else—"

"I've heard enough. If you can deceive me over something like this, I can never trust you again. Give me the ring."

"Clark!" remonstrated Phyllis.

David placed a hand on her arm. "Let him go Mrs. Summers."

Evelyn pulled the ring off her finger, and gave it to him. "Clark . . ."

Clark ignored her and walked out of the house and, it seemed everyone could tell, walked out of Evelyn's life.

Evelyn broke down again. Revealing the rape and Clark's rejection were more than she could bear. Barbara's eyes filled with tears.

Phyllis glared at Barbara. "I don't know how much collusion there was in this whole affair, but I assume you acted in what you thought was Ev's best interests at the time. Right now I need to be alone with Evelyn."

Evelyn stood up, hugged Barbara and squeezed David's hand. "Thanks Barb," was all she could say and she collapsed into her chair again.

David rose from his chair in preparation to leave. "Mrs. Summers. There's much more to this story, and I would like to discuss it with you personally."

"I'm sure there is, David. We'll arrange it soon."

Barbara and David began the short walk to Barb's house. Clear of Evelyn's family, Barbara cried freely. She began to question her actions after listening to Phyllis' accusations.

"Perhaps I should have ignored Evelyn's pleas for silence. The silent remainder has certainly turned on us with a vengeance. Have I—have we—been complicit in the deception by remaining silent?"

David tried to calm her fears. "Those questions nag me as well. I guess it's a question of following Ev's wishes as opposed to doing what's best for her. It's easy to have perfect hindsight, but we did what seemed right at the time."

"Now, we have to face my parents. I'm beginning to feel like a naughty child. It's so humiliating. We did nothing wrong, did we?"

They opened the door and walked in. Don and Patti came over to them and ushered them into the living room. Barbara's face was tear-stained. They sat opposite Don and Patti and David leaned forward with his elbows on his knees.

"While Ev and Barb were in Brighton, Ev was abducted and raped. That's the basic fact."

Patti's hands flew to her face. "Oh! My God."

David paused and looked down as the news sank in.

"Go on," urged Don.

"Evelyn swore us to secrecy, despite our pleas for her to go to the police. She wouldn't hear of it, and the thought of doing so at the time only distressed her further. She became pregnant because of the rape, and to keep the rape secret, she seduced Clark and told him the baby was his—that was before Barbara returned from England. Again she wouldn't allow Barbara to say anything, although Barb tried to convince her otherwise. We were both afraid this would happen when the truth came out—as it did tonight. That's the unvarnished story. Looking back, perhaps we should have done differently, but honestly, Ev seemed so unstable, we feared exposing the assault might disturb her further. Perhaps it was that fear that drove her car into the sea."

David sat back. His face registered fear and anguish, and tears rolled down Barbara's cheeks.

"Thanks David for telling us frankly what happened. It was clearly a difficult time for you both. You're right. Perhaps things could have been done differently, but if what you say is true, Evelyn made her choices and has to live with them. Unfortunately we do to. What was Clark's reaction? I'm glad you included him, Barb."

Barbara spoke. "Dad. Clark broke off the engagement there and then. He asked for the ring back and walked out. I think that's over." She went over and sat next to Don. "Dad I'm so sorry this has happened. Can you and Mom forgive me?"

Patti came and sat on the other side of her. "My dear, there's nothing to forgive. I know you. You acted out of kindness to Ev and did what you thought was best. Dad and I will stand behind you, whatever happens. You too, David." she walked across to him and hugged him and that warm act of inclusion caused David's tears to start.

"Let's all get some sleep, and we'll talk some more in the morning." Don thought they'd done enough for one day.

Sleep seemed the best short term recipe. But it would be temporary. A new day, a new year, a new millennium, held secrets from them all.

31

January the first was a Saturday, another Saturday. Evelyn awoke with a headache and a familiar knot in her stomach. But this one hurt too. She slowly pierced the mists lingering in her mind, and reality came into focus. She re-lived waking that fateful morning after the rape, and new tears of anguish and shame flowed freely. The events of the previous evening plagued her mind, and great sobs shook her body. She lay avoiding the sunlight that danced its way through the swaying branches outside. She needed the pain and shadows to atone for her perceived guilt.

Phyllis came into the room with a mug of coffee. "How are you doing, Ev, my dear," she said, and kissed her daughter on the forehead.

Ev clung to her mother, tears flowing unchecked again. "Mom, I've ruined my life. Please love me; I'm sure no-one else can after this."

"Not true Evelyn. But listen," Mom urged. "I've have had time to think things over this morning, and here's what I think. This is important if you are to see clearly and we're going to get through this. First, all the blame for what happened to you is squarely on the ones that assaulted you. In time we want to get to the bottom of that. Second, I've talked to Don and Patti. David and Barb agreeing to keep it secret could have been poor judgment. But they did whatever they could to help you through a terrifying ordeal. I realize they are *not* to blame for what happened to you, and I am so thankful for the support they gave you."

Evelyn sat up in bed, took some sips of coffee, then several big gulps. Warmth of the coffee and words from her mother started to soothe the ache in her stomach. Phyllis plumped up a pillow behind her, and Evelyn relaxed a little.

"Next. We suggest you get some counselling to help you where you are now and to come to terms with the assault. And finally, I take some responsibility for what happened. I haven't given you the care and attention a beloved daughter, so important to me, needs and deserves."

Evelyn put her mug down and flung her arms around Phyllis once more as the tears flowed yet again. Time slowed, Phyllis wept as well. They both finished laughing through the tears.

"What babies we are," exclaimed Phyllis.

"I could have been a better daughter too," Evelyn cried, "I've always been angry with you, Mom. I'm sorry."

"Perhaps I deserved some of that too." Phyllis stood and brightened. "I've prepared a special New Year's breakfast; come and join me."

"Okay Mom. I need to eat. Give me time to dress."

Evelyn dressed slowly. She went to her drawer and pulled out a package containing the remnants of a white powder the acquaintance provided to calm her. It had certainly soothed her mind, but to the point she wasn't clear what she was saying. She finished dressing and flushed the package down the toilet. The knot in her stomach reminded her of the pain denial had caused.

The only secret to hide now was the stupid decision to use the drug. That would be easier, no-one needed to know about that. The knot began to loosen somewhat.

She wanted to call Barbara and talk over the events of last evening. *Not yet,* she decided. *They need some time to process all this as well. Perhaps this afternoon.* Then she wondered about the baby. For now, that was too far in the future to be a present worry. *Time enough for that. I need to get through this day.*

David awoke early, dressed and came downstairs. He made coffee and sat with a cup, idly glancing through the morning paper. His mood was sombre; far from the celebrations on the front page. Barbara was up early too, and he was cheered to see her.

"Barb, pour some coffee and join me."

"I will," she said, "but first . . ."

She came up behind him, put her arms around his neck and tenderly kissed his cheek. Then she poured some coffee.

"At least we have each other. I feel terrible for Ev and Clark. They must be devastated. You know," she added, "while telling the truth seems the right thing to do, just look at the devastation it has left behind. No-one is any the happier for it. In fact, it seems worse than leaving the truth hidden."

"You're right Barb. But it is keeping the truth hidden that leaves us on a powder keg as we've just seen."

"You think telling the truth will heal over time, David?"

"We will be free of the deception that takes so much energy. The scars may remain, but life will improve as we trust in God, who *is* the truth."

But David had something else he wanted to discuss with Barbara.

"Barb, I'm wondering what your dad may think about my working for him after all this. All our plans are in jeopardy."

"Unless he thinks—which I very much doubt—that

you have been deliberately negligent in some way, it shouldn't make any difference. But it's a question we'll have to ask him. Whatever he may think you have done, I have done as well; in fact, I probably instigated it."

The family started to appear, and Don invited David and Barbara into the living room. They sat together on the couch.

"While Patti gets breakfast going, I thought this would be a good time for us to talk things over together, David. Patti and I have had a chance to think about things and I had a long chat with Phyllis this morning on the phone. I knew Mark before he died, and we have retained a close friendship with Phyllis; it will help us weather this difficulty."

David heard much the same from Don as Phyllis shared with Evelyn when she awoke. The ones that assaulted Evelyn were responsible for her distress. Neither David nor Barbara were to blame for what subsequently happened to her. At worst, they may have made a poor judgment call, but they had done all they could do to help Evelyn through her ordeal.

"Dad, I'm so glad to hear that." A relieved Barbara sighed. "I'm so thankful for you and Mom and Phyllis for sorting the priorities in what happened. Especially—and here's our question—how does all this affect David working for you?"

"Neither of you have done anything wrong. You acted in what you considered Evelyn's best interest at the time. Any of us might have done the same. If anything, David, your conduct over the last few hours has increased my respect for you. You've nothing to fear from me. And David, Phyllis said you'd be willing to pass on any more information you have. She'd like that. I guess that should include you too, Barb."

Nigel appeared last—he always enjoyed a sleep-in. He

asked about the previous night's blow-up, and Don and David repeated the sequence of events that led up to it.

Patti called them all to breakfast. Small talk avoided the issue occupying their minds, but Nigel was silent for most of the time. Finally he spoke.

"I've been thinking of Evelyn. I'm really only an observer in this affair, although I was around when this happened back home. I also wondered, as some of you know, that something more than a lost credit card was going on. I'm totally out of my depth when it comes to resolving this, but if Evelyn and her family want to pursue this with the British police, I would be pleased to do whatever I can when I get home."

David laughed. "Nigel, you remind me of Dad. That's the first time I've heard you deliver a formal speech the way he used to."

"Oh! Okay, my mistake. But the offer still stands."

"That's generous of you," replied Don. "I'll put you in touch with Phyllis. She indicated she wants to pursue this."

"And a friend of mine, Kevin, is a probation officer. He should be able to put you in touch with the right people," offered David.

The idea of some positive steps forward lifted their spirits.

Barbara called Ev's mom. "Mrs. Summers—Phyllis. I wanted to apologize for what happened last evening. I know you—"

Phyllis interrupted her. "I should apologize too. But enough of that. I want to invite you and David over this afternoon. I know Ev wants to see you, and it will be a chance to find out as much as we can about Ev's experience. And you've been a good friend to Evelyn for years, and we want that to continue—especially now. Can you both come?"

"Of course. We'd love to come and do as much as we can to help. Can we bring Nigel? He has offered to help in any investigation his end in England."

"Yes, definitely. Bring him along. See you at three."

Evelyn looked forward to Barbara and the brothers' visit. She recalled the value of Barbara's advice throughout the whole time since the assault, even though she fought against it. Barbara had been a trusted friend and the most stable influence in her life, especially during her parents' austere upbringing.

They sat around the coffee table, laden with goodies and a large pot of tea.

Phyllis said. "David and Barb. I was, as you might expect, shocked at what came out last night, and I was short with you. I'm so sorry. I know you did what you could for Ev during her whole ordeal. She also has to take responsibility for some of the decisions she made."

Evelyn gave a weak smile and a resigned nod.

Phyllis explained. "Evelyn's hazy about the events of that evening. Please, tell us as much as you can remember."

Evelyn listened intently, as well as her mother. There were things even she couldn't recall.

Barbara outlined the events of the trip to the Metro and their encounter with Marty. Evelyn cringed at the name. Marty seemed nice enough, but Barbara had her reservations. David mentioned his visit with Barbara to the pub where Marty took Evelyn, The Pink Dragon.

"The Pink Dragon?" exclaimed Nigel. "I know that place. Used to go there when I was younger. Bit seedy, but I got to know the bargirls. I might know the one you spoke to. And I might be able to track this Marty down with some of my contacts at the Metro."

"There's the man of the world talking." David grinned

at Nigel at the half challenge he offered. Nigel didn't bite. It wasn't the time or place.

"I'll get to you later, Dave," he responded. "But perhaps I could be a real help in tracking this incident down. It'll give me something to do."

At that moment, Barbara was more concerned with the human effects of the rape, and asked if they had thought any more yet about the baby. It would be due in about four months.

"I don't want an abortion, but haven't decided whether to keep it or adopt it out," said Evelyn. "There's no immediate rush on that. Right now, Mom wants me under a doctor's care, and we'll work out the rest later."

But Evelyn had other news. "You know, I bottled up the anger at those who treated me this way for too long. I want those bastards caught and punished, and I'm prepared to do whatever it takes to make sure it happens."

"Oh! Ev. Impulsive as ever. So glad to see they can't keep you down for long," commented Barbara. "Any ideas what you can do?"

"I think I might know where the house is—at least the neighbourhood."

"But you said you couldn't remember anything,"

"I know. But I did say something about déjà vu, do you remember? Well, I suddenly realized that the feeling was real. I *had* been there before." Evelyn explained the day she wandered and got lost. "So I bought a map and the serving lady showed me where I was. I still have the map. She retrieved it from the coffee table and showed them the location where she'd bought it."

"Hey!" interjected Nigel. "I know the area. Pretty squalid. But that will be a good start to our investigation."

Evelyn nodded enthusiastically. "Yes. This may seem a bit premature, but I want to go back to Brighton and see this thing through." She turned to Nigel. "Do you think that would help, Nigel?"

Nigel always thought he'd be ready for anything, but he'd been surprised by Evelyn before. He was taken aback at first, but saw the logic of it. "I think it would be most helpful; in fact, the more I think about it, it may be essential for you to be there." He turned to Phyllis. "What do you think of the idea?"

Phyllis shook her head. "As much as I dislike it, maybe she has to go. My main concern is for medical coverage while she's there. Remember, the baby, that's my main concern. Nigel. Could we ask you to look after her while she's there? It's an imposition, I know, but you are the only person we know over there. She might well feel threatened in that environment."

"Well Ev, want to come back to the heart of the empire with me on Tuesday?"

"That soon?"

"Why not. If you're ready, and your mother agrees."

"Okay! I've already started packing."

Nigel turned to Phyllis once again. "We have a spare bedroom in our suite at the hotel. We can keep a close eye on her there; she'll be quite safe. I know my Aunt Sophia enjoyed her company and will be happy to see her once more."

"Let me know what expenses you incur. I'll be happy to pay them," offered Phyllis.

"Unlikely. But if necessary, I'll let you know."

Next day was Sunday. That afternoon, Barbara called Evelyn to see how she was doing. Evelyn sounded bright and cheerful. Clearly a load was off her mind, although her heart might still be sore.

"Hey! Want some help packing?" asked Barbara.

"Sure. Come on over."

They worked quietly for some time, the only

conversation regarding the clothes and other belongings Evelyn needed.

"Mom's out," said Evelyn. "Come and have some coffee with me—payment for your work packing." She grinned.

"So what does the future hold for you Ev? Any ideas?"

"Really I've no idea. Just a day at a time right now, I think. But I'm so glad that my life is back on track, despite the loss of Clark. I think he was really only a prop for me during a difficult time. But I feel terrible about the way I treated him.

"Why not write him a note, Ev. Maybe an apology for deceiving him. What do you think?"

Evelyn looked into her coffee for a moment.

"You're right Barb. I owe him that at least. Would you help me?"

Evelyn opened her laptop. The two girls discussed the letter at length as Evelyn typed and retyped. As she typed, memories flooded back to Evelyn and she wept freely.

"Barb, you'll feel better after we've sent this. Honesty cleanses the soul."

They finally agreed on the letter.

> Dear Clark:
>
> I understand your reaction last evening. My deception of you was dreadful. I have a bagful of excuses, but none is adequate. I was wrong.
>
> You have every reason to act the way you did. I want you to know how very sorry I am for my treatment of you, and if there is anything I can do to lessen the hurt, please let me know.
>
> I hope over time you can forgive me, but I understand if you cannot.
>
> I sincerely hope you find someone who is worthy of you and that you have a good life.
>
> Thank you for loving me though a difficult

time. I'm so sorry I failed you in return.
Love,
Evelyn.

Evelyn read it a couple of times and looked at Barbara for confirmation. Barbara nodded, and Evelyn hit the sent button. She never received a reply.

"Barb, while I'm coming clean I have something else to tell you. Mom told me—and this is confidential—that that I was continually molested by my father while he was alive."

Barbara was shocked. "How come you didn't know?"

"Mom says I blocked it out, although that déjà vu moment after the rape was, I think, a flashback. I'm hoping, yet fearful, of remembering it all at some time. But it accounts for my fear of sex. I hope I can put that to rest now. In fact, perhaps that hole in my heart is mended also."

"I really hope so Ev. But you know, since I've come to understand what it is to be a Christian, I found that hole is something all of us have to some degree. Our Creator placed it there. We try to fill it with all sorts of things, and some work for a while, but eventually, he's the only one who can fill it completely. Don't try to fill it with something new."

"I'm really happy for you, Barb, but I think I've finally got a handle on life. So don't worry about me. I don't think religion is for all of us."

"Well, if you think differently at some point, let me know. It seems to me now, it's the most natural and desirable thing to walk through life with our Creator. Remember, if we don't base our life on the truth about God, that silent remainder is waiting to upset us."

Evelyn hugged Barbara. "You're such a good friend. Thanks for caring—and packing." They both grinned. "And you and David will see us off Tuesday, won't you?"

"We'll be there, and we'll pray for a successful trip to England. Go get him!"

Evelyn knew their talk of prayer was not just small talk.

32

David and Barbara drove back from the Vancouver airport that Tuesday, a little surprised they both felt despondent. They shouldn't have been surprised; those closest to them were leaving for an indefinite period. But the events of the previous days had kept their spirits occupied, up one day and often down the next. Now, life was returning to a more predictable path, and recent events were past—except of course, they had a wedding to plan. That was anything but routine.

David spoke first.

"Barb, it's hard to see them go, but we must be happy this looks like a time of resolution for them, particularly for Evelyn. And now I'm excited that our wedding is so close."

Barbara smiled. "Yes, my darling. But even though it's only a few weeks, it seems like an eternity. Let's make the most of every minute. This won't occur again—at least that's my prayer—it's going to be for life."

David nodded enthusiastically. "But I also need to talk to your father, Barb. I want to know when to start working for him."

Patti prepared a light supper when they returned, and David asked to talk with Don afterwards. Barbara joined them.

"I'm ready to start work with you at any time. Do you have any preferences?"

"I've thought about this, David," replied Don. "Here are my suggestions. I think you will do well in the role I'm preparing. Let me know what you think."

David nodded.

"Mostly our clients come to the office, certainly the business people do, but we have a number of aged retirees who find that more difficult or live some way out of town. I want to develop a part of the business that takes care of this segment. We'd provide a company car for your use as this will involve some travelling, mostly nearby—at least to start with. Does that sound like something you'd enjoy?"

"Most certainly sir. I enjoy working with people, especially helping them to retain and benefit from more of their resources. When would you want me to start?"

"Forget the 'sir' business. Most people call me Don. You can at work as well if you like. And Dad is fine within family—but whatever you feel comfortable with. But right now, give yourself a week to settle in. I'm sure Barb will want to help you set up home in the apartment."

Barbara gave a broad smile, and Don smiled at her.

"I suggest you give us a couple of weeks or so in the office," continued Don. "That way you'll get accustomed to our routine, and then take some time off for your wedding and honeymoon. Any idea where you're going yet?"

David started shaking his head. "We've not really—"

Barbara butted in. "That's easy. I want to go to Paris," she said. "What do you think David?"

"Oh! If that's what you want, then I guess it's decided." David laughed. "I guess I've a lot to learn about women—"

"And I'll be happy to teach you," responded Barbara.

"Well, you two. Mom and I have decided to pay for your honeymoon as a wedding present," said Don. "Would that work for you?"

Barbara hugged her dad and David shook his hand.

"You are very generous, Don," said David, "both with that gift and your working suggestions. We'll be so glad we met."

"I am already," added Barbara.

So the week that Nigel and Evelyn planned to chase Marty down, the Vancouver couple began building a new life for themselves. Barbara arranged for vacation time at the hospital. That gave her sufficient time for wedding preparations, furnishing, and settling in to their apartment following the wedding.

The flight to England gave Evelyn time to think. Her last minute flight had her seat separated from Nigel, so she was alone, sleeping fitfully through the hours of darkness. The plane landed early in the morning. Despite the upset and pain to those closest to her, she was glad the whole affair was out in the open. But she thought of Barbara with joyous envy. She was glad Barbara's acceptance of David's faith and Don's desire for David to work for him in Vancouver had removed the last obstacles to their marriage. She was sad she wouldn't be there, but uncovering Marty's assault was more pressing. Barbara understood that. "Go, get him," she'd said.

Evelyn had been sure she would never visit England again, especially Brighton. But now, anger overcame fear. She settled into the suite with Nigel. It felt like a second home, familiar, although she had spent only a few days there in the summer. She had come to know Nigel well enough, she felt safe and joined him for morning coffee.

"That day you first picked us up from the airport, I was determined I would never like you Nigel, you were so arrogant," Evelyn recalled.

"Yes, you're right. I did a good job of putting you off didn't I?"

"You put on a fine act. Just hope this friendly guy I now consider a good friend is not an act as well."

"Let me know when you find out, I'd like to know."

Evelyn tried to punch him across the table, but her pregnant stomach diverted the action and promptly knocked her coffee over.

"Got to get used to that bump, Ev, It's bigger than you think." Nigel cleaned up. "See Ev. I always clean up after you."

Evelyn wanted to give him another punch, but thought better of it.

"Can we start to clean up this Marty mess right away?" she asked

"I'll make some calls this afternoon, and I suggest some sleuthing in the evening. How about dinner at the Metro? Think you can handle it?"

"If I can handle you, Nigel, I can handle anything. I just want this guy, perhaps others of his gang, in jail. Who knows how many other girls he's taken advantage of."

Evelyn wanted to be useful to pay her way, although at first Nigel wouldn't hear of it.

"But Nigel," she protested, "I can't sit around and do nothing, I'll go mad. Give me something to do."

Evelyn was attractive, radiant as women carrying a baby often are. Her personable nature would make her a fine receptionist, and ensure visitors felt at home.

Nigel left Evelyn in the hotel for the morning. She needed sleep to recover from jetlag. He drove first to the Pink Dragon and banged on the door.

"We're closed," shouted a woman's voice from within.

"That you, Margie? I want to talk to you."

The door opened. Margie recognized Nigel. "Haven't seen you in a while. Found another popsie 'ave yer? Come on in. We can talk while I clean."

Nigel poured a coffee and sat at a table.

"Nobody could replace you, Margie. I just graduated upward."

"Don't blame you. This can be a crass crowd at times."

"Margie. I'm here on behalf of a friend who I believe was abducted from here last summer. She was with a guy called Marty who helped her out of here as she wasn't too stable."

"Not that I recall." She rested on her mop for a moment and screwed up her face in thought. "But yer know, I seem to remember Mabel mentioned somethin' like that to me a while ago. She remembered 'cause a young couple came in about a week later askin' about it."

"Is Mabel in today?"

"She's on at two this af'ernoon when we open. Come in then 'fore it gets busy."

"I'll do that. And I'll bring the girl. Perhaps Mabel will recognize her." He pulled his cell phone from his pocket. "Mind if I sit here for a while and make some calls?" He asked.

"Go ahead, I'll fill your coffee for yer. Should get paid extra for this." She grinned.

"How can I make it up to you?"

"Payment enough if you find out who did that to 'er."

Evelyn's face lit up as she saw Nigel come back late in the morning.

"Any progress?" she asked.

"Come and have some lunch and I'll tell you."

Nigel ordered a cold lunch from the kitchen. He poured coffee for them both.

"Sure that coffee's safe with you?" He pushed the mug across the table toward her.

She poked her tongue out at him. "As safe as I am with you, I hope. Come on, now, what's going on?"

"I found the barmaid at the Pink Dragon who may recognize you. We're going there at two. I called David's friend Kevin, who gave me the name of an Inspector Crawford in the police sex crimes unit. He agreed, a bit grudgingly, to see me at three. Didn't seem particularly interested. But we'll go anyway; have to start somewhere. I drew a blank at the Metro; no-one there recalled a Marty."

Evelyn suddenly looked at him with wide eyes. "This is real, isn't it?" She gasped. "Seemed like a bit of a game till now. Stick close to me, Nigel, especially this evening if we go to the Metro."

"Let's see what the inspector says, but I'm looking forward to it."

"Nothing frightens you, Nigel. You make me sick."

"Oh yes. One thing frightens me."

"Oh?"

"You. You're far too desirable."

"What? Like this?" Evelyn pointed both hands at her stomach.

"Yes you. Oh! you're gorgeous alright. But beyond your looks, *you* are attractive to me."

"Ah, Nigel. I can help you overcome that fear. I can give you the cold shoulder. I can play obnoxious too, you know."

"Playing hard to get, eh?"

"Not playing. Just hard for you to get."

"Careful Ev. You may brush me off just one too many times."

"Good. Then we'd be safe, wouldn't we?"

"Just don't try it. It might backfire."

Evelyn knew enough about her previous ambivalent feelings toward Nigel, he might be right. But banter—if that's what it was—had to give way to reality. They drove to the Pink Dragon and met Mabel.

"I think it was you," she said after looking closely at Evelyn. "But if it was you, you looked a lot different then; really the worse for wear." Evelyn put on her droopiest look. "Yes, that's more like it."

"Would you recognize the man who was with me that night?"

"Doubt it. If I recall, he wasn't a regular. I'd know better if I saw him again."

"Mabel, you've been most helpful." Nigel thanked her. Evelyn thought he sounded more David-like, but said nothing.

Inspector Crawford was polite enough, ushering them to chairs facing him.

"You two married or something?" he asked.

"Not married, nor 'something,'" Evelyn curtly replied.

"Okay. Just needed to know. But *you* need to know, reporting a rape six months after it happened isn't too easy to follow up. I assume you had no medical examination after the event?" Evelyn shook her head. "No other evidence of the actual rape?"

"My friend saw me after," replied Evelyn.

"But she wasn't witness to the rape?"

"No, but she was with me when that Marty guy—"

"Did you say Marty?" Inspector Crawford perked up.

"Yes, Marty."

"Marty McEwen or Mighty Mac, as he likes to call himself."

"You know him then?" Nigel's face lit up.

"We know *of* him. He runs a small gang that likes to assault women, usually those visiting the city who don't know their way about Brighton. We've had a few complaints, even a couple of rape kits proving intercourse, but so far have not been able to track him down. If we could, it might be difficult to tie him to you, Evelyn, but we could probably tie him to some others. Either way, we could put him away."

"Evelyn and her friend met Marty at the Metro," Nigel told the Inspector. "We plan to have a meal there this evening, to see if he might be there."

"Unlikely, but nothing lost. However, if he does happen to be there, you don't want to spook him. If he recognizes Evelyn he'll run and you'll lose him." Crawford stabbed the intercom. "Fred. Bring me a dark curly wig." He looked at Evelyn's smart, if loose attire. "Something more frumpy would help." He smiled. "And dark glasses too."

An officer brought in the wig, and Ev tried it on.

"Big improvement!" That impish smile again. Evelyn punched Nigel this time, but grinned back at him.

"Just be careful he doesn't recognize you or you attract his attention. If you can get a picture, that would help. But not directly, it's too obvious. Take one of Evelyn with him in the background. If it doesn't work, or he runs, we're no worse off. Have fun!"

"One more thing. Evelyn thinks she knows the whereabouts of the house where she was raped. She has a map where she thinks it is."

Evelyn produced the map, and explained why she thought she knew where it was.

The inspector studied it for a moment.

"That is a likely place. We'll keep an eye on that area and ask some of the neighbours if they know anything. The shopkeeper might be aware of something."

"Hey, this is fun," said Evelyn, fingering the wig on the drive to the hotel. "Real cloak and dagger stuff. I'm looking forward to our evening out."

"Probably nothing will happen," cautioned Nigel. "The chances of him being there are pretty slim. That's why Crawford let us go. So don't get too excited."

"Trust you to take the fun out of it," Evelyn griped.

"Hey, I'm supposed to be the fun. Remember me, the T, D, and H, whose taking you out? Not Marty—unless you'd prefer him?"

"Don't." Evelyn shivered. "And what's T, D, and H?"

"Tall, Dark, and Handsome of course. Look here. That must be obvious."

"Bighead. If you're the fun, you'd better make it worthwhile."

"Yes, Ma'am."

Nigel was right. No Marty.

"But I enjoyed myself," admitted Evelyn. "Let's do it again sometime."

33

They tried again Friday evening. This time, to their surprise, Marty was there. They found a table and watched him dancing with a girl that had taken his fancy. *Perhaps he is close to taking her.* What she recalled of the rape flooded Evelyn's mind. She looked away.

"Hey, don't fail me now," urged Nigel. "We could be close to finishing this affair."

They watched Marty sit with the girl two tables behind Evelyn.

"Perfect," said Nigel. "Keep your back to him. He's facing us. I'm going to try a picture."

"No flash Nigel. It'll attract his attention."

"I know that. Just keep still. You make a great picture with that wig." Nigel chuckled as he took a couple of pictures. Evelyn pouted at him. "Trouble is, with no flash, they might be dark and grainy. But it's the best we can do."

They enjoyed a reasonable meal, but anticipation interfered with their appetites. Nigel watched Marty by taking sly glances as he ate.

"He's getting up to dance. It's given me an idea." Nigel rose from the table. "Stay here, I'll be back."

"Where are you going?"

He was gone.

Evelyn took a compact from her purse and followed him in the mirror. He passed Marty's table putting himself between the jigging Marty and his table. Nigel picked up a wine glass and dropped it in his jacket pocket. He went on to the men's room. Evelyn felt alone. She could see Marty out of the edge of her compact mirror, but kept her head down pretending to eat.

Nigel returned and sat opposite her. "I think we can leave anytime. We've got what we came for, but no rush. We want to look casual."

They finished their meal and the waitress came with the bill. Nigel paid with his credit card. He looked up.

"Hey, I can't see Marty or the girl. They must have left."

"Oh! That poor girl, he must have taken her."

"Could be a real girl friend Ev, don't think the worst."

Evelyn shook her head.

They picked up their coats and walked to the car. The car park was dimly lit and deserted. Only small pools of inadequate light surrounded the few lamp standards

"Hello Evelyn. I thought it might be you!"

They wheeled around to see Marty. Two other men looking like gorillas closed in on either side.

"I see you've brought a guardian angel with you this time, but he won't do you much good. I think we can have some fun like we did last time. Remember?"

Evelyn tried to scream, but no sound came. One of the men put his hand over her mouth. Nigel went to tackle him, but Marty pulled a gun and held it on Nigel. Nigel backed off. The other gorilla put a knife to his throat.

"I think you have something of mine," Marty said quietly, going though Nigel's pockets. He found the wine glass and held it up. "Ah! I thought so. Hmm. Stealing glasses from the restaurant. You know that's a crime, don't you? Maybe I should call the police."

"Please do," replied Nigel.

"Take her away," said Marty.

Evelyn couldn't see what happened to Nigel.

The two gorillas bundled Evelyn into the back seat between them. They bound Evelyn's hands behind her and, because she made too much noise, taped her mouth. She continued kicking even though she couldn't scream, so they bound her feet as well. Waves of panic engulfed her as nausea flooded back from her earlier abuse. She and Nigel had planned to wrap up the rape episode. Instead it was likely to be repeated and, this time, with greater violence. The perpetrators should've been in custody, not her. What went wrong?

As they drove, she noticed the corner store and red mailbox. *If Nigel was able to call the police, They have that information,* she reasoned. *But what happened to Nigel? Was he able to escape?* She feared for his life. The car dived into a back alley and stopped at the back of a terrace house a block or so beyond the corner store. One gorilla carried Evelyn like a sack of potatoes into the basement and emptied her onto the mattress she had woken up on previously. The room brought back sickening memories of her previous abduction.

Her head began to spin and fear gripped her as the men left and locked the door behind them. *Had Nigel called the police? What will they do with me?* Thoughts of the sex trade seared her mind. Although she thought little about God, he was suddenly uppermost in her mind. *God. If you're real, help me, help me please.* No answer. *Please God, help me.* No answer. *God! Get me out of here.* Still no answer. She struggled against her bonds in anger. *Thought so. You either don't exist or don't care. I hate you.* Tears welled up and sobs broke unbidden from her throat.

She heard a key in the lock. Fierceness replaced her fear, and she wiped her face on the mattress. She determined to face her attackers with defiance. Marty walked in, smiling. She noticed a rope dangling from his hand.

"Hi beautiful! Glad you could make it."

Evelyn ignored him. He stared down at her. Curious, he rolled her over with jabs of his toe.

"Good God! You're pregnant aren't you? Well, I'll be damned."

He stood astride her as she squirmed in response.

"Got a special place for you," he announced. "Babies fetch a good price."

Marty produced the rope. It had a loop formed with a slip knot. He bent down and looped it tightly around her neck. Angry grunts and moans was all Evelyn could muster. Her eyes blazed defiantly at Marty. He pulled the loop tighter, restricting the carotid artery. Breathing became difficult, and she felt light-headed. He loosened the noose.

"I suggest you keep the rope loose, Ev, my dear. It will tighten but won't loosen if you struggle against it. Now, are you prepared to do as you're told?"

Evelyn nodded. She decided that for now, at least, she'd go along. It appeared that Marty had ventured into human trafficking since the summer. Whatever humiliation she would experience, he would keep her alive for the baby.

Marty cut her feet free and told her to stand up.

"Remember to keep the rope loose," he warned with a sly smile. "Follow me."

Marty led Evelyn out the rear of the house to a black panel van, opened the rear doors and told her to lie on the floor. She kicked fiercely but felt the noose tighten as Marty jerked the rope. She lay still. He bound her feet again and tied them to a structural spar part way up the van wall. Before Marty closed the van doors, Evelyn thought she'd heard a bullhorn. Marty climbed into the driver's seat and slackened the noose slightly as he hurriedly put the van into gear and drove out. Her head was adjacent to the driver's seat. He glared down at her and gave the rope a warning jerk.

The gorilla dragged Nigel to the back seat of a car, the knife at his throat. He sat still as the car was driven off. As his captor talked with the driver, Nigel slowly felt for the door handle and waited. The car turned a corner sharply, briefly upsetting the gorilla's balance. Nigel rammed his elbow into the gorilla's stomach, opened the car door and rolled out.

Nigel finished on his back, partly stunned, as he heard the car screech to a halt. He recovered and ran into a well-lit shop, and glanced out the window. The open car door slammed shut and the car drove on. He felt himself all over, noting some scrapes and scratches, but otherwise seemed okay. He pulled out his cell phone and dialled Crawford.

The inspector listened to Nigel's story.

"Are you okay?" he asked.

"Think so. A few bumps and bruises, but still walking."

"Did you get a good look at the car that took Evelyn."

"I did. It was a black Chevy Impala, It may have been heading to the house where Evelyn was previously held—you know, by the street corner store."

"We'll check that out, CCTV should be able to pick the car up if it passes that corner," said Crawford. "And we'll send a squad car to pick you up."

Within minutes, the squad car arrived. The driver updated Nigel.

"We've a swat team standing by if Marty shows up," said the driver. "Just listen in to the radio, and you'll keep up. We'll drive to the street corner and wait."

Nigel heard Crawford on the radio.

"We spotted Marty's car and traced it to a row of

terraces a couple of minutes beyond the corner. We're working on identifying the house. The swat team will arrive in a few minutes."

It was several minutes later the swat van passed them. *God, what took them so long? Do they think they're going to a bloody funeral?* Nigel wanted to run after them and tell them to get their bloody act together. He held his breath as the swat team knocked on the doors adjacent to the target house, and led the residents to safety.

Nigel heard the bullhorn, but the words were indistinct. he heard a couple more calls, and three men smashed the front door in.

Nigel couldn't sit still, fidgeting with each second, his hands tightly fisted in his pockets. Silence . . . silence . . . He jumped at the radio.

"We just missed the bastards. The house is empty. The car's gone—"

Nigel's phone rang.

Nigel spoke first. "Evelyn? Did you—?"

"Sorry Nigel. They must have taken her with them."

"Where?"

"No idea yet. But one of the officers noticed a black van exiting the lane up the street. Could be them. We'll see if we can pick them up on CCTV, and get a clue which direction they're heading."

Nigel closed his phone. *Damn, damn, damn.*

The phone jarred him again.

"Hi, it's Inspector Crawford again. We've made a clean sweep of the house, and it's clearly held trafficked girls. No sign of Evelyn, or even that she's been here. We've pictures of the black van heading north out of town, and we'll follow them as far as our CCTV cameras allow."

"So you've no fresh news on Evelyn," queried Nigel.

"Not yet, but we'll keep you posted. Nothing more you can do right now. Go home and try to get some rest."

That last phrase is like a mantra, common and useless enough to be meaningless. It should be recorded to save breath. Nigel gave the time honoured reply, "I guess you're right. I'll try."

The squad car drove him to his car at the Metro. He sat in his car for minutes. He pounded the steering wheel in anger and his head in guilt by turn. He sat back. What could he do? He was mortified by lack of control and options for once in his life. *I guess this is where most people would call on God if there was one,* he thought. Suddenly, from nowhere, he wished there was one, and then berated himself for weakness. *There has to be a way to find her and kill those guys.* He surprised himself by his violent anger. Being out of control frightened him. His head spun with inconsequential or useless thoughts, his mind dazed by the escalating reversal of events.

Nigel drove to the Belvedere, sick to his stomach. He wasn't sure if it was guilt—an unusual feeling—for getting Evelyn into this mess, or the loss of her company. He felt the loss more keenly than he expected, and with both frustration at himself and a curious warmth, he recognized a growing attraction for her. He lay on his bed, vainly seeking a way to find her and fell into a troubled sleep.

He was startled awake by his phone. It was three in the morning.

"Yes," he yelled expectantly.

"Is Joey there?" a voice answered.

Nigel smashed the phone down as his hopes plummeted.

34

Evelyn's spirits sunk deeper the longer the van that held her was driven. She had no idea where she was. It was dark, she could see only sky from the limited view she had through the windows. Besides, she was a stranger in a foreign land. *They'll never find me. Where is Marty taking me? What will he—or his gorillas—do to me?* She was convinced her pregnancy wouldn't stop them abusing her. The van stopped, and Marty disappeared. She heard voices, and the back doors opened. A large buxom woman with straight, thin, dark hair, and a wizened face accompanied Marty.

"She's attractive enough," Marty was saying as he untied Evelyn's feet. "But right now the baby is our concern. After that, we'll see."

The buxom woman took the rope and jerked it harshly, pulling Evelyn from the van.

"Hey be careful. They'll want her in good condition," yelled Marty.

The woman ignored him and without a word pulled Evelyn toward a large house, which appeared to be set in its own grounds. The only other building visible was a well-lit shed about a hundred metres beyond the house. Marty followed, and they entered the house. A wide staircase faced them, and Buxom led up the stairs and into a large room with a bed as the only furniture. Buxom grabbed Evelyn's hair and forced her face down on the bed while Marty cut her hands free. He handcuffed one wrist to a sturdy iron bed-head holding her other wrist firm.

"Any nonsense from you and Madam Angela here will handcuff this wrist to the bed also," warned Marty. "No point in screaming. No-one will hear you here. And Madam has no qualms about inflicting pain if necessary."

With a grim smile, he pointed to a whip hanging in the corner of the room. "I'd strongly advise you to be a good girl and do as you're told."

Madam jerked the rope to give emphasis. Then, while Marty held Evelyn's free wrist, Madam removed the rope from Evelyn's neck and hung it with the whip. Switching off the light they both left the room and Evelyn was alone. She ripped the tape from her mouth and let out a long loud scream, as much in frustration as fear. There was no response. She rubbed her neck from the chafing of the rope and lay back on the bed. She was relieved at last to be alone, now she had a chance to think. But the emotional toll of the last few hours left her exhausted and surprisingly she dozed off.

It was light when she awoke. She looked around the room. This would probably be her jail for the foreseeable future. The room had seen better days. Paint was peeling off the wainscotting, corners of the wallpaper drooped, and the ceiling paint was heavily cracked and peeling. Yet the room had a faded elegance. A heavily sculpted picture rail and cornice surrounded the walls. The ceiling was high, and a large rose circled the one centre ceiling light. Evelyn imagined a chandelier had graced the room once; now only a single cord and bare bulb sufficed. To her right a large deep window gave a view of rolling countryside, devoid of life except for a few cattle.

Was there a way of escape? *Not as long as I'm handcuffed to this bed*. She tried sliding the cuff off her wrist, but it was too tight. She rattled the cuff on the bed-frame, but it was secure. She heard a key in the door lock, and idly wondered why they bothered locking the door when she was handcuffed to the bed. A slip of a girl, looking mournfully attractive, perhaps seventeen years of age, come in with a plate and glass of water. With her was a copy of Marty's gorillas—more fat than fit—and with no discernible neck. Evelyn named him Neckless and hoped one day he would have one—a necklace tight around his throat. As if hearing her thoughts, Neckless grabbed her free wrist and twisted her arm behind her. The girl placed the plate and glass on the floor and unlocked the handcuffs.

Neckless marched Evelyn through the hallway into an adjacent bathroom.

"Don't I get some privacy," Evelyn asked curtly.

Neckless said nothing, just dumped her on the toilet, still holding her arm behind her. Without any choice, Evelyn pulled her pants down single-handedly and did what was needed. She struggled to replace her pants as she was dragged back to her room.

"I need to wash up," Evelyn complained. No answer.

Evelyn was dragged back to the bed and handcuffed again, and the girl and her protective gorilla left. Evelyn looked at breakfast: water and jam smeared over dry bread in a plastic glass and plate.

She sipped the water, but the food couldn't tempt her. She flopped back on the bed face down and cried bitterly in misery and fear.

Nigel had a restless night. Not only did he worry about Evelyn, he wondered about calling her family back in Vancouver. He would rather call when he had good news, but knew he couldn't put it off too much longer. He called Inspector Crawford, but he wasn't on duty. Another detective took the call.

"Mr. Hektor—Nigel. I'm fully aware of the case, and here's what we know so far. The van—assuming it's the one Evelyn was travelling in—took off to the north-west of Brighton. We have an APB out for it, and a van of that description was spotted near Guildford in Kent. That's some distance away. We will keep monitoring the situation. If you have anything that might help us, please let us know. Ideally, Evelyn may find a way to contact us or you. Let us know if that happens. Sorry we can't be more positive yet."

Nigel's heart sank as he dropped into his chair. It was mid-morning. Evelyn had been missing for twelve hours. *Nothing for it. I have to call the family*, he decided. *Perhaps I should call David first. It's two in the morning in Vancouver, better wait until they are up. Gives us more time to recover Evelyn.* At three in the afternoon, a call to Crawford indicated no further news on Evelyn. *Time to call the family. This is not going to be easy.* Nigel rang David's number.

"Hi Brother. Good to hear your voice." David was in a good mood. "How are things over there in the Motherland?"

"Not good. In fact, very bad news I'm afraid. Ev and I found Marty, but he turned the tables on us, and has taken Evelyn again." Nigel paused. No response.

Nigel continued. "The police are on the case, and are following some leads, but up till now nothing positive."

Silence at the other end.

"David! Are you there?"

"Yes. It's taking time to sink in. How on earth did it happen?"

Nigel outlined the events of the last twenty hours.

"David, I wanted to call you first as I thought you could talk to the families over there face to face. I didn't want to drop this on them by phone. Can you take care of that?"

"Of course, Nigel. I'll talk directly to Barb's parents and to Phyllis. I'll call you later and let you know their response. But for yourself, you have to handle this alone, I'll support as much as I can from here, and you know of course, I'll be praying for both Ev and you."

All Nigel could muster to that was a gloomy, "Thank you." No mood or time for a cheeky riposte. Nigel hung up as his mind filled with continual thoughts of Evelyn.

35

David replaced the handset thoughtfully. He'd call Barbara first.

"What time do you call this, David? I'm hardly up yet."

"I have some difficult news to tell you, and need to see you and your mom and dad right away. Can you get Phyllis to join you too?

"What's the problem?" asked Barbara, clearly alarmed.

"I'll tell you when I get there. I'll be there in fifteen."

"But David—"

"Sorry Barb, my love, I have to go. See you in a few minutes." He hung up.

On arriving at the Williams' house, David told what he knew about Evelyn's disappearance. Phyllis burst into tears.

"What the hell is Nigel doing? How did he get Ev into this mess again? He said he'd look after her. I shouldn't have let her go."

Patti put her arms around Phyllis. "Phyllis, I'm so sorry this has happened. We're going to be with you in this, you won't be alone. We'll pray for Ev's safe return."

David wasn't sure if Patti's offer to pray was cultural promise of support, or real. But it gave him an opening.

"Mrs. Williams, would you mind if we prayed now? I'm happy to pray for all of us?"

Perhaps Patti had little option: who'd not want to pray in this situation. She nodded, and the others joined her.

Barbara's eyes sparkled at David's practical awareness of his faith. David felt a caring love for Evelyn which impassioned his short, but eloquent, prayer for her.

"Thank you David. We all appreciated that," said Don. "Perhaps we should pray more often for all the issues of life."

Patti offered to stay with Phyllis for the remainder of the day, and Don decided to go to work.

"No point in sitting around. We'll hear if there's any news," suggested Don. "It's good to be occupied at a time like this."

Barbara pulled David into the kitchen, where they embraced fondly.

"Only three weeks to go," David announced excitedly.

"Yes," said Barbara slowly. "I want to talk to you about that."

"You're not wanting to put off our wedding day, are you?" responded David with a playful smile, and ran his fingers though her auburn hair.

"Well, maybe."

David pulled apart. "You're serious, aren't you?"

"I want to go to England for Evelyn."

David sat down. "Barb. How can that help Ev? I don't see the point of going."

"I just want to be there when she is found."

"But Barb that may take time—possibly a long time."

"I know. But she's like a sister. I want to be closer. She may sense I'm there."

David brushed his hand through his hair. He was dumbfounded.

"Barb. You can't be serious. The arrangements are made, invitations sent out, and you're leaving me high and dry. This could put our wedding on hold indefinitely."

Barbara took David's hand in both of hers.

"I know this is hard, David, but I have to go. We *will* be married, but right now Ev's my first concern."

"I think that damned Atlantic has kept us apart long enough. Please, Barb, don't go, please."

Barbara dropped his hand. "David, don't make it harder for me than it already is. I know how much this hurts, but I'm going. I have vacation coming to me from the hospital. I just need to be there."

"Wow. This is not a discussion, it's an ultimatum. Supposing I say I don't want you to go?"

Barb backed up against the kitchen counter and gripped the edge behind her tightly.

"You don't own me. I can make my own decisions," she said softly.

David was silent. Where did this stubborn streak suddenly come from? He hadn't noticed it before. But then they'd had no reason to disagree so strongly. Of course, she had stated that accepting the Christian faith was *her* decision and David was pleased with that. But this issue was a genuine conflict of their interests: David's excitement at the consummation of the relationship that now seemed indefinitely postponed, and she was responsible. Her priorities were elsewhere. Misery gripped David. Perhaps his fears of alienating women were real after all.

David stood up and spoke hesitantly, "I, I think I'd better go. I'll call you later." He still hoped she'd reverse her decision.

She nodded. "Please do, David. We'll talk again later. I'm working late today, so try tomorrow."

Tomorrow seemed like an eternity away, and David left the house confounded. He drove to the apartment and gloomily poured stale coffee and plopped into a chair. It wasn't Barbara's trip to England that upset him. Rather his almost forgotten sense of inadequacy with women had abruptly invaded his being and his misery overshadowed the fact that the relationship wasn't over.

"God, why did you bring her into my life, only to lose her again?" He yelled out loud. *And what the heck am I doing here on this side of the Atlantic?* Question piled upon question, deepening a sense of hopelessness and obliterating the truth. He took a brisk walk in the cold January air to clear his head, but the walk only encouraged a steely obsession that life as he had envisioned it was passing away. He bought a fish and chip lunch in a Denman Street greasy spoon, returned to the apartment, and dozed for an hour.

He awoke to realize he'd not phoned Nigel back as he had promised. He went to the phone and noticed the message light blinking. It was Barbara. She had called while he was out in the morning.

"Hey David. I managed to get a ticket for a flight this afternoon. Please let Nigel know I'll be in London tomorrow, that's Sunday morning. I'll call you when I arrive there."

David began to think more clearly at the sound of Barbara's even voice. *It was just a stupid argument. It's my own insecurity that didn't want Barb to leave. Of course she should go to support Evelyn.* He wanted to feel her and hug her close once more, but she wouldn't even be in phone contact for another twelve hours. His spirits evened out but drooped again, as he realized he was in for another bout of separation. *That stormy Atlantic Ocean has a lot to answer for.*

He called Nigel. There was no more news of Evelyn.

"I've spoken to the family, Nigel, and they are understandably upset but support what you're doing to find Ev. Phyllis felt you had let her down, but I'm sure she'll come around."

"David, I keep kicking myself for not seeing this before

it happened, so I know how Phyllis feels. I'll do my damnedest to get Ev back—frankly for myself as much as anyone else."

David thought that was an unexpected admission from Nigel but said nothing.

David continued. "Barb's already in flight to Heathrow. Can you pick her up tomorrow morning?"

"Of course I can. But why's she coming here? There's nothing she can do."

"I told her that. But she felt it was important for her to be near Evelyn, for whatever time it takes. Women just aren't logical, but I've discovered they may sometimes be right—you know, women's intuition and all that."

"Don't say that in mixed company, you'll get your head chopped off," replied Nigel. "But I'll be glad to look after her for you."

"Better than you looked after Evelyn, brother, or I'll come there and strangle you myself."

"Okay, okay. I get your point. I'll lock her in her room if necessary. But how are you doing? Another separation? Can you handle it?"

"No choice. I have to. Just have to trust a woman's instinct. But keep in touch. Let us know how things are progressing. And please be sure Barb calls me when she arrives."

"Will do. And any news I have, you'll have right away. Talk soon."

David hung up. All he could do now was wait, for Evelyn to be found, but especially for Barbara to come back to him.

36

B arbara sank back into her plane seat with reliefafter a strenuous day: first the news of Evelyn which upset the family, the ensuing argument with David, and then her decision to fly immediately to London. She'd searched the web for a seat, packed quickly for an unknown length of time, and rushed to the airport in time for departure.

She wanted to talk to David before she left. She couldn't understand his adamant refusal to let her go. Had she destroyed their relationship? Hardly. It wasn't an unreasonable request. But it certainly went to the heart of being a woman with her own independence. She had wondered earlier if some outdated religious law might interfere with that. Was David asserting some sort of control? Was it a mistake to accept the Christian faith? Again, she didn't think so. But clearly, accepting the faith didn't answer all the questions. For now, she still wanted to marry him. That's where her heart was, but she had to let it ride for a while.

As the plane took off, she needed to think about what lay ahead in England. Where was Evelyn? How was she faring? Was she even still in England? How was Nigel coping? She knew Nigel was pretty self-contained, but all this was a new experience for him. And how were his feelings for Evelyn? Had they changed when he lost her? It could well be that Nigel was rethinking his life, with this unexpected calamity. Nothing like adversity to force a rethink of priorities.

Barbara slept some of the time, with disturbing dreams of her own abduction. She was glad when the plane landed and, after customs formalities, met Nigel in the arrivals area. They hugged tightly and for a startling length of time. Emotions were running high, even Nigel wiped a tear away. They began the drive to Brighton.

Nigel opened the conversation. "Sorry I've no news about Evelyn beyond what you already know. But it's early days yet. Ev's very resourceful. I'm hoping she'll find a way to contact us."

"Me too. We'll both hang on the phone."

"I didn't think there was any point in you coming," said Nigel, "But now you're here, I'm glad you did—for me, as much as anything. It's been lonely looking for Ev by myself."

Barbara didn't necessarily dislike Nigel's usual brash humour, but this was a new side of him; he was more approachable. She grabbed his arm in both hands.

"Nigel. I'm glad I came too. It seemed the right thing to do, and now I'm sure it is. We'll find Ev together. I'm so afraid for her, not knowing what she's going through."

"Thanks Barb. You're a good friend. David's a lucky guy."

A stab of pain went through Barbara as she recalled the fractious state in which they parted. *I think David's lucky too. I hope he feels the same way.* She tried to put those thoughts behind her as they approached Brighton. For now, she felt comfortable with Nigel, and he clearly welcomed her company.

Sophia was at the Belvedere to greet them, and gave Barbara the smothering hug she'd come to expect.

"Such a trying time for us all, Barb, dear," she said. "But we're going to find Ev, aren't we, Nigel?"

"Of course."

Nigel smiled, perhaps for the first time since Barbara arrived. Barbara felt at home at once, both the familiarity of the place and the joy she'd experienced while staying at the Belvedere calmed her spirit. Nigel showed her to Evelyn's room in his suite

"When we get Evelyn back, we'll put an extra single bed in here," said Nigel. "And as before, this place is yours. Help yourself to anything you need, and yell if you can't find it. I'll leave you to unpack, freshen up and settle in."

Half hour later, Barbara found Nigel in the kitchen, coffee in hand.

"Yes, I've made coffee. Thought you'd like one. Sit and I'll pour you one. And by the way," Nigel turned as he poured the coffee, "David asked if you'd call him."

"Coffee first, and then I will. So do we have any plan for finding Ev?" Barbara didn't expect much. What could they do?

"Really there's not much we can do but wait. The police, particularly Inspector Crawford, have been very helpful, and he has promised to keep me informed. Beyond that, we'll keep positive."

"We can pray," Barbara ventured. "You may know, I've accepted David's faith, and I really believe prayer can help."

"Well, Barb, It can't do any harm."

That was about as positive a response as Barbara could expect. At least Nigel had softened to people, if not their beliefs.

"I should call David now. Can I use the phone here in the kitchen?"

"It's only three a.m. in Vancouver. Leave it for a few hours. Sophia will be supervising guests in the hotel, and I have errands to run, so you two can have some privacy." Nigel gave an impish grin.

Later, Barbara dialled David's number and he answered.

"I'm so glad to hear from you, Barb. Thanks for getting back to me. No problems with the flight I trust, and are you okay?"

"I'm fine, David, but no news on Evelyn yet."

"Oh! Too bad. How's Nigel?"

"Holding up well. David, I'm glad I came. Nigel really needs some support. He has no-one else to help take the load."

"Barb, I'm glad you're there as well. I'm so sorry for arguing with you. I saw it as rejecting me rather than caring for Evelyn. I felt better when I heard your voice on the message you left."

"Where were you when I called?"

"Out walking. I felt so lonely. But it was my own fault. Please forgive me."

"Well, David. I did feel you were being domineering. I wondered where that came from. Was it something I would face in the future when we married? I didn't really think it would be, but I was upset."

"I know Barb. It was my own insecurity taking over. You know all about that, we discussed it in the pub, remember? I've never met anyone like you, and I don't want to lose you."

"I understood that when I had time to think. Of course I forgive you. I was pretty insensitive too, dumping it on you like that. Are we okay now?"

"Yes, yes, Barb. I love you so much. Hurry back to me. Find Ev quickly, please."

"I'll come as soon as I can. I miss you too. Let's hope Ev finds a way to contact us. That's our best chance of finding her. In the meantime, can you take care of postponing the wedding arrangements? Whatever you can do is fine with me.

"I will. See you soon my love."

"Bye," Barb hung up quickly, not wanting an extended goodbye. But she felt they had overcome one hurdle. Now to find Evelyn.

37

E velyn had no idea of time. Someone had taken her watch. All she had for entertainment was a crumbling ceiling above her and moving about on the bed. She kept moving her secured hand around to stop numbness and occasionally sat on the edge of the bed for variety. Nothing changed out of the window, other than cattle moving to fresher grass. *They have more freedom than me,* was her only mental exercise.

The girl returned, this time alone, carrying a repeat of breakfast. Evelyn sat on the bed.

"Is that lunch?" asked Evelyn.

The girl nodded

"Doesn't anyone speak in this hell-hole?" Evelyn glared at the girl.

The girl shook her head, placing her finger over her mouth. But she pushed a piece of paper under Evelyn's thigh and hurried out the door, locking it again behind her. The furtive manner with which the girl acted alerted Evelyn that she was probably being watched, and certainly overheard. She looked around the room carefully and noticed a camera partly hidden in the ornate picture rail. She crumpled the paper in her hand and lay on the bed, her back to the camera. She opened the note hiding it from the camera with her body and read it.

> I am not allowed to talk to the girls. They will
> hurt my family if I disobey. There are many girls

> in the shed waiting to be shipped abroad. You
> are in the house because of the baby. Toilet
> twice a day. Bucket under the bed between
> times. Some better food for supper.

Evelyn crumpled the note again and slipped it in her jean pocket. Despite her hunger, she kicked the breakfast and lunch offerings across the floor. She was determined to show her defiance. No response. She lay on the floor as far as her handcuffed hand would allow and looked under the bed. She could reach the bucket with her free hand. She was ready to use it.

The bed was the last word in discomfort. The wafer-thin mattress was lumpy, creating pressure points in all the wrong places. She peeled back the corner to reveal a simple lattice wire frame as a bed spring. The pillow was small brother to the mattress. *Might be more comfortable on the floor, if I could lay there*. Her feet could reach a blanket, folded over the foot of the bed. She pulled it toward her. Boredom made her tired. She dozed for a while.

A key in the lock woke her, and the girl arrived with Neckless. They performed the same drag to the toilet and back to the bedroom, where she found a cold salad with ham and cheese and a mug of lukewarm coffee. *At least some protein. I guess they are trying to keep me healthy*, and Evelyn took some slight comfort from that.

The days ran together so Evelyn wasn't sure what day it was. Perhaps three days had passed with the same routine. Evelyn broke the monotony by screaming occasionally and yelling obscenities at the camera. Nothing aroused any response. Whoever watched the monitors just ignored her. The girl came at lunch time, alone as usual, placed the food on the floor, and hidden from the camera, pressed a can against Evelyn. Evelyn avoided looking at it. *Gee a can of coke*. She smiled at the girl who twitched a smile in return and retreated out the door.

Evelyn rolled over, back to the camera and looked at the can. Not coke, but black spray paint, with a note around it secured by a rubber band. She had difficulty retrieving the note with one hand, but as she did so a hairpin dropped out. She pushed the hairpin over her waistband, and read the note.

> Use the hairpin to unlock the handcuffs. Spray
> the camera after dark. I'll only pretend to lock
> the door after supper.

She smuggled the can under the mattress—one more lump wouldn't show. The girl was obviously a prisoner like herself but forced to do menial work. Possibly she was a sort of trusty, yet was just as anxious to be free as Evelyn was. It had been a long afternoon. But she half enjoyed the supper, even smiling at Neckless who twisted her arm harder in response.

Darkness came early in winter. Evelyn wondered why they didn't keep the light on to observe the room at night. Perhaps as she was handcuffed, they thought it not necessary. She would still take precautions. She had no idea of time, but waited what seemed a long while after dark. The house was always silent, she never knew who, if anyone, was in the house.

Time to start. With a racing heart, she lay on the bed, and pulled the hairpin from her waistband. She bent a short end at right angles with her teeth and tried twisting it in the handcuff lock. Nothing. She had no idea how the lock worked, but thought it must be a simple mechanism. She bent the other end of the hairpin longer, and tried again. Nothing. In panic she waggled the hairpin furiously, and the lock opened. She rubbed her chafed wrist.

She thought a body in the bed might be an added

advantage, so she plumped the mattress under the blanket like a body. She didn't know if anyone was watching in the darkness but decided to spray the camera anyway. She blackened the whole corner where the camera hid.

She went to the door, it was unlocked. She slowly and silently turned the knob, and opened the door a crack. She could see no-one. She opened it further, put her head out, and looked in the other direction. Again, no-one, but a light showed under the door at the end of the hallway. With the hallway clear, she moved to the door with the light showing. She heard a TV, and decided to wait until the light went off.

She returned to her room, and stood inside the door, leaving it ajar so she could hear the TV. From her experience of the last few nights, she didn't expect any one to come, but she remained vigilant. After a while, she heard a door open and a shaft of light lit the hallway. She closed her door and stood the against the hinge side of the door. The door opened slowly, the light snapped on, and Madam Angela tiptoed across the room toward the body lying in the bed.

Madam was about to pull the blanket back, when Evelyn rushed across the room, pushing Madam Angela hard against the wall. Her head hit the wall, and she dropped to the floor. Evelyn slapped the empty handcuff on Madam's wrist and ran out the door, slamming it behind her. She went into Madam's room. On the bedside table, she saw what she wanted: a cell phone.

She didn't know how long before a bellicose Madam could call an alarm. Evelyn decided she should hide outside somewhere. As she descended the stairs, the house appeared deserted. She found a coat and gum boots by the door, put them on and gingerly opened the door. She noticed a guard to one side, leaning against the wall smoking. She went quietly the other way, aware other guards could be around the building. She was glad of the darkness and made her way to a wooded area not far from the house. She went far enough that she felt sheltered but could still see the house and activity around it.

She opened the phone. It was charged. She punched in Nigel's number. The call was cancelled. *Have I dialled a wrong number? No, I memorized it too well.*

She rang again. The call was cancelled again. Evelyn noticed lights in the house going on and people with flashlights searching around the house. It wouldn't be long before they widened their search. *Who's fooling around with Nigel's phone? Has some kid found it? Nothing for it but to keep trying.*

She made the call again.

38

The days were slow and increasingly worrying. Barbara and Nigel knew that the longer Evelyn remained missing, the harder it would be to find her, but neither voiced that possibility. Barbara had jumped at the chance of receptionist at the hotel at Nigel's suggestion. It gave her something to do, and she enjoyed meeting the guests.

Crawford called a few times, indicating they had narrowed the search to an area around Guildford in Surrey. That assumed the black panel van seen in that area was the one that left the house in Brighton. It might not be. A couple of van drivers were questioned but were not the suspects. The police in that area were searching, but it was a large area.

Evelyn had been missing for three days, although Barbara had only arrived the day before. Barbara, Nigel, and Sophia sat glumly around the dining table after a meal, discussing anything to take their minds off Evelyn. Nigel brought up the Belvedere.

"This hotel has made me a good living—and dad, of course, when he was alive—but I find running this single-handed is more than I can, or want to, handle."

Sophia chipped in. "I always thought you're not cut out for this sort of daily grind, Nigel. Mountain-climbing or deep sea diving is more your style. Thinking of selling?"

"Not exactly, but I would like to take time off for other pursuits and need someone who'd like to take over a portion of the business. For instance, I don't have David's help any more, thanks to Barb seducing him away."

Barbara gave a demure smile.

Nigel went on. "Sophia. How would you like to have a part in the business? I've appreciated your handling of the work here, and enjoyed having you around. Interested?"

"I think I would be," responded Sophia, "if you make it worth it. What did you have in mind?"

It was her turn to smile

"Here's something to think about. We'd pay you a decent salary, and each year worked would earn a tenth of your portion of the business. Your income would increase yearly as your interest in the business increased. That's a general outline. We'd have to nail down the details."

"Sounds attractive." Sophia was animated. "I like the idea of consistent work, and I enjoy my time here with the guests and staff. Let me think about it. I'm sure we could work something out. But time for me to go home and dream of being a business owner. Night all."

Sophia gave her customary hugs and left. Nigel gasped, pretending to get his breath back.

"Fancy some more coffee, Barb?"

"Sure. I like to stay awake later, it helps me sleep."

As he prepared the coffee, Nigel asked.

"I'm curious about you and David. You've not spoken about him much. How are things between you two?"

"Good, Nigel. We have our tiffs now and again, but we're on track to be married when I return."

"Didn't you have your wedding date set for late this month?"

"Yes, but we're postponing it until we find Evelyn."

"That could possibly be a long time. How did David take that. He's gone on you, you know, It'd be hard on him."

"That caused a major argument before I left. But I

think we've resolved it."

Barbara wanted to avoid further discussion on David, she still felt some guilt from her treatment of him. She changed the subject

"Well, Nigel. How were you and Ev getting along?"

"Okay. We're just friends you know, trying to tie up this case and not doing a very good job of it."

It seemed Nigel was carrying some guilt also.

"Nothing more?" Barbara urged with a smile.

"Let's just say I find her very attractive. That's as far as it goes."

"You mean that's as much as you're going to tell me?"

Nigel opened his mouth for a response, when his cell phone rang. He looked at the number and didn't recognize it.

"These damn telemarketers," he muttered and cancelled the call.

"Where were we? O yes, I find Ev—"

The phone rang again. Nigel looked at the number. "Persistent beggar, isn't he," and cancelled the call again. "Next time, I'll give him an earful."

It rang again.

"Listen you damn bastard, I don't want—"

"Nigel?" Nigel's head reared, and his eyes widened.

"Evelyn?" Nigel's face lit up, and he pulled Barbara close to the phone.

"Yes. Listen carefully. I escaped from the house where they were keeping me and stole this cell phone. I don't think they know I've got it yet, but I'll keep it open so the police can track this location. I don't know how long I can keep hidden, but if they find me, I'll hide the phone but leave it open."

"Ev, it's so good to hear your voice. Are you okay?"

"Yes." Her voice was barely above a whisper. "I've got to keep moving, but I'll keep the phone open in my pocket for as long as I can. Don't talk, just listen. I don't want them to hear your voice. By the way, there are many other girls being held here."

Nigel gave Barbara his phone. She could hear rustling sounds as Evelyn moved about. Nigel picked up the house phone and called Inspector Crawford who answered.

"Inspector, Evelyn just called in on a cell phone—"

"What's your cell number?"

Nigel gave Crawford the numbers.

"Good. Keep it open. We can patch in. Is Evelyn still on the phone?"

"She said she'd keep it open as long as she could."

"Okay. We'll move quickly. I'll call back when we have some news."

Nigel replaced the receiver and stared at it for a long moment. He turned to Barbara.

"Keep that phone open. They can patch into it and hopefully track Ev's location."

Barbara nodded. "We can continue listening. At least we'll know if Ev's okay."

They both sat with ears glued to the cell phone.

39

Evelyn looked around her. Apart from the small grove she was sheltering in, she could see mostly open country. The trees were an obvious hiding place, and the searchers would come there soon. The darkness was her friend, but the open country wouldn't hide her for long. Perhaps the last place they would expect to find her was at the house. She decided to get close to the house and find a hiding place in the rambling structure.

The pinpoints of flashlights showed her where the searchers were. There weren't many, perhaps six or eight who appeared to be moving away from the house as she guessed. She made a wide circle to outflank them coming close to the back of the house. The large shed was still brightly lit, and she could make out three men searching within its light fall. She noted some sheds and outbuildings attached to the rear of the house and made for them. Between two sheds, she could make out some lumber stacked loosely against one shed. She moved a couple of pieces and hid inside pulling pieces back to cover her.

She pulled the phone from her pocket and spoke softly into it.

"I've found a place to hide, but not sure how long I'll remain undiscovered. Will the police be able to trace this phone?"

Nigel answered. "Yes. They've patched into my phone

and are listening to you right now. How long it'll take, we don't know, but hang in there."

"Ev, it's Barb here. I've come to join Nigel and find you."

Evelyn burst into tears. The tautness of the past minutes drained away.

"Oh Barb! It's so good to hear you. I'll see you soon. O-oh! Someone's nearby."

She dropped the phone to the ground and covered it. She could hear men's voices and saw flashlight beams passing the sheds. Suddenly one pierced the space of her lumber hideout.

"Here's a likely place," said one voice. "Pull that lumber out of there."

As one of the men reached out and grabbed a piece of wood, sirens pealed out from the front of the house. The men ran. Evelyn stayed still, fearing they might return. She heard some sporadic gunfire, and decided to remain sheltered. She picked up the phone.

"The police have arrived—sounds more like an army. Some shooting, perhaps you can hear it."

"We can," said Nigel. "Stay where you are, it's probably safest. Inspector Crawford can hear you. Tell him where you are, and someone will come and get you. Stay safe. We'll continue to listen in."

Evelyn sounded relieved. "I'm scared and excited all at once. So want to see you both. Love you both."

Back at the Belvedere, the house phone rang. It was Crawford.

"They've found the place where Evelyn was held and, in addition, a score or so of other girls held like cattle in a large shed. We may be on the edge of smashing a large human trafficking ring. We've known about it for some time but couldn't get a handle on it. Thanks to your plucky girl, many girls' lives will be spared. We'll have her back home in a couple of hours."

"Great news. Thank you so much." Nigel replaced the receiver, and Barbara enveloped him with a big, long hug.

"I'll call home right now," she said, and picked up the phone.

It was a long wait for Evelyn to return to the Belvedere. Sophia joined them, anxious to see her great-niece safe again. Nigel took the time to find a roll-away for the girls' room. They drank coffee and talked aimlessly to pass the time. About two in the morning the phone rang.

"Crawford here. I have the distinct pleasure to deliver the delightful Miss Summers to you personally. We are a few blocks away and will be there in about two minutes."

They waited in the foyer for the police car, and all ran down the steps to meet it. Evelyn stepped out of the car, and she and Barbara embraced in a long tearful hug.

"Oh Barb," said Evelyn. "I'm so glad you came to find me. It means so much to me. You're the greatest sister I never had."

"Hey, what about me?" interjected Nigel. "Don't I get a hug in here somewhere?"

Evelyn turned joyfully to Nigel, kissing him so passionately it startled everyone, including herself.

"You're more like a brother than cousin," she said. "But not a brother," she hurriedly added, "closer."

As Evelyn turned to Sophia, Inspector Crawford spoke to Nigel.

"We suggested she might want to go the hospital for a check up, especially to be sure the baby's okay. Everything seems to be okay, no injuries, just some rough treatment. Look after her. Come to the office tomorrow afternoon, and we'll have time for a chat. We should have more information about the traffickers we broke up."

Nigel smiled and nodded. Crawford drove away.

"Anything you need or that we can do for you?" asked Sophia as they mounted the steps to the hotel foyer.

"Nothing. I'm just so glad to be here. All I really need just now is a long sleep—that's if I *can* sleep."

We have a bed ready for you with Barb," said Nigel. "You're safe now, Ev, and you'll be well, er, better looked after."

Evelyn gave a sickly grin. "Anything will be better than what I just experienced. Can we talk in the morning?"

They all settled in for what was left of the night, Sophia taking a vacant room upstairs.

Evelyn and Barbara slept late, and made coffee and toast. Nigel was busy around the hotel. They ate while Evelyn told all she could remember about her ordeal. Her reaction, it seemed to Barbara, was far less traumatic than after her rape during the summer. Evelyn was more in control of herself, almost vibrant with her successful escape and alerting the police. The assertive, self-assured Evelyn was back.

"You know, Barb, I cried out to God when they first took me. I was bound and helpless and needed him. But he didn't answer, I had to work out my escape—and I did—all by myself. I know you have accepted David's Christian faith, but honestly, I can't see where it would have helped me."

"Of course, Ev, I understand how you felt. I've been there myself on occasion. But evil men continue to do what they want with their God-given freewill. And sometimes God has a greater good to accomplish."

"Well, in my case, a greater good was not to be abducted at all."

Barbara smiled. "That's my first reaction. But twenty or so girls would be on their way overseas if you hadn't been there."

Evelyn thought about that. "God could have used someone else."

But even as she said it, she saw the weakness in her answer.

"And God did provide help."

"You mean the mournful miss who gave me the can of black paint."

"Yes, but also that you were pregnant."

Evelyn shook her head at that one. "You mean God wanted me pregnant? And how did that help anyway?"

"I doubt God wanted you pregnant, but he used it."

Evelyn spread her hands out in a futile gesture "How?" It made no sense.

"You were not dumped with the other girls. You were isolated where you could work alone and Miss Mournful, as you call her, could bring you the paint. Remember, she was probably rescued too. And then there are the girls who will not be trafficked in the future because those guys have been put out of business."

"Barb, you are so damned logical. I need to think about this. It all seems so unlikely."

Nigel walked into the suite.

"How are you doing Ev?"

"I'm really doing well, thanks to you and Barb. I couldn't have asked for better therapy."

"Good. I suggest I take you two beautiful ladies for lunch, and then we'll go and see our good friend Inspector Crawford. I'm anxious to find out what Ev's escapade has accomplished."

"We've accomplished a lot, thanks to Evelyn being at the transit centre and her brave attempt to escape," said Crawford.

Barbara smiled at Evelyn.

The inspector went on. "Marty and his gang were only one of several gangs who recently began procuring girls for the traffickers. The traffickers were an organised, international mob that paid Marty and others for the girls, and then kept them in the shed like cattle until shipment. They used modified containers that could be driven into the shed and loaded in private and then shipped to the Middle East and Africa. White girls fetch a high price in coloured or dark skinned cultures."

"Evelyn," the inspector compressed his brows. "You could have been on your way overseas already, together with the other girls held there if you hadn't been pregnant. We owe you a big thank you."

"Better if none of this happened," said Evelyn.

"I wish to God that were true," replied the inspector. "But this is the world we live in, and you've made it a bit better by your actions. How long do you plan to stay in England?"

"Not sure. I have an open ticket, so I can stay for a while, hopefully as long as you need me."

Nigel added, "Inspector. Ev doesn't know this yet, but I'm planning for a few days away, probably for the rest of this week."

"I'm sure we won't need you for a few days," said Crawford. "Plenty of paperwork to do and we have enough to hold the ones we picked up. We'll oppose bail. I'm pretty sure a judge will agree they're too dangerous or likely to run if we let them out."

Barbara was amused by Nigel's announcement, but Evelyn looked stunned.

"Where are you going?"

"You mean, 'Where are *we* going?' Don't know yet, haven't decided."

They drove back to the Belvedere with a great deal of satisfaction. Evelyn's curiosity was unsatisfied. "What's all this about a 'few days away' you suggested?"

"You deserve it, and I'm taking you. Any objections?"

"It seems you've settled it all. But I can't think of any objections. Where are we going?"

"I have an idea. What about a cream tea this evening where we can discuss it?"

"You're not telling me until then?"

"No. We need to keep that unpredictability in our relationship."

"Beast!" She punched him.

Barbara listened silently, intrigued by the growing rapport between the two. There was obviously more going on than they let on. Where was it going?

THE SILENT REMAINDER

40

Evelyn couldn't contain her curiosity, continually prodding Nigel for a hint of what he had in mind.

"Barbara coming too?" Evelyn asked, hoping Nigel would drop a clue.

"I think my time in Brighton is over, I've done what I came for," said Barbara. "You have your own plans to make and lives to lead. You two go and have your cream tea. I want to call David and tell him the wedding is still on for the twenty-ninth—if he hasn't already postponed it. And I'll arrange a flight home."

"So glad you came," said Nigel, and Evelyn nodded. "Sophia will arrange for a ride to the airport. Travel safe."

Nigel escorted Evelyn to the Paddy wagon and drove to his favourite teahouse. The cream tea was delicious as usual. But Evelyn found the conversation startling.

"So where do you want to take me?" asked Evelyn.

"What do you think, Evelyn? Don't we make a good team?"

"Are you suggesting we should take up more detective work? I don't think I want any more, thank you."

"Okay. If not, anything else? Don't you think we'd be good as a team at anything?"

"Hadn't though about it. Never mind that. Where are we going?"

"What about Vegas?"

"Vegas? Why the heck would you want to go to . . ."

Evelyn stopped mid-sentence. Nigel had that impudent half smile playing on his lips. "Are you asking me to marry you?" She was bewildered.

"I think we make a good team. You're adventurous like me, spontaneous, and above all, don't think much about God. Yes. Let's get married. It'll be fun together!"

"Nigel, people don't get married for fun!"

"Most people, you're right. But we're not most people."

Evelyn looked at Nigel. Why had she been guarding herself from him all this time? She had to admit it, she liked him. More than that, she really was attracted to him. She liked to be with him, and despite the previous days' events, she felt safe with him. But was that enough for marriage?

She said the obvious. "Nigel, this is all so sudden." She couldn't think of anything else to say.

"Is it really Ev? You and I have been playing cat and mouse for long enough. Now's the time to stop fooling ourselves and make a decision."

"You're pushing, rushing me."

"How much longer do you want Evelyn?"

"Time to think."

He had a point. Would she feel different towards Nigel tomorrow, or next month? Yes she probably would. That seemed to be the nature of their relationship. But it was a relationship she kept coming back to, and he was serious enough to want to marry her. She knew his ongoing efforts to avoid an entanglement had changed since they first met. She had always desired male company, her flings at college and her hopes with Clark established that. *Perhaps this is the answer to that nagging emptiness I always felt,* she thought, *or is this simply a rebound reaction.*

Only a few days earlier she had been engaged to Clark,

and that briefly bothered her. She thought of Adele. *But I could never be sure I could trust Clark. He's welcome to Adele if he's been after her.* She selectively forgot her own deception. *This must be fate's provision for a better partnership. Nigel is more carefree than the doting Clark, but will I hold Nigel's attraction firmly enough for a lasting bond?* Her experience with him so far suggested she would. So she allayed her doubts.

She recalled crying out to God while lying bound on that mattress. It seemed her prayer was eventually answered, if not in the way she had wanted. Or was it co-incidence? Not even coincidence. *I made use of the resources available to me, and that brought about my release. Life is what we make of it, what's the need of God?* She put those thoughts behind her. But would they stay there?

She noticed Nigel watching her face. *Was he following my thoughts by my expressions?* she wondered.

"You're right. I'm probably as crazy as you, Nigel. And this is the craziest thing I've ever done. I hate to think what Barbara might say—although, knowing you, she might possibly approve!" Evelyn had a troubling thought. "You haven't already booked the flights have you?"

"No, Ev. I haven't. I couldn't take you for granted. Frankly, I wouldn't want to, even if I thought I was sure of your answer. But that I'll never be. It's that unpredictability that keeps me attracted to you."

"Well what are you waiting for? Book the flights man, or are *you* having second thoughts?"

Nigel picked up his cell phone.

They settled back in their seats as the plane took off."

"Nigel. Have you thought about the baby?"

"Of course. I wouldn't have asked you to marry me without giving *that* some serious thought."

"What do you think?"

"It's whatever you want."

"And if I decide to keep it?"

"Then I'll face the challenge of being a father. I might like it!"

"My, you have changed. And what about God, have you changed about that too?"

"We make our own life here. Even if he did exist, we have all the resources we need. But there is no God, so we're on our own anyway. You and I are strong enough. We've managed without him, even through your abduction, thanks to your own initiative and actions. We don't need God."

Evelyn still had doubts about that, but he seemed to have it all together.

"You'd better be right about God. I'd hate for any hidden truth about him—you know, Barb's silent remainder—to come back and bite us. I've had enough of that recently for a lifetime."

"We have that lifetime ahead of us, Evelyn."

She linked her arm in his and pulled him closer. "And that has yet to be written. Let's make it a strident remainder."

Made in the USA
Charleston, SC
11 June 2015